SKELLS

The Midtown Blue Series
The Deuce
The Crossroads
Skells

SKELLS

A NOVEL

MIDTOWN  BLUE

SERIES

F. P. LIONE

Revell

Grand Rapids, Michigan

3 9082 10445 2597

Published by Fleming H. Revell
a division of Baker Publishing Group
P.O. Box 6287, Grand Rapids, MI 49516-6287
www.revellbooks.com

Printed in the United States of America

Library of Congress Cataloging-in-Publication Data
Lione, F. P., 1962–
    Skells / F. P. Lione.
        p. cm. — (Midtown blue series)
    ISBN 10: 0-8007-5962-1 (pbk.)
    ISBN 978-0-8007-5962-9 (pbk.)
    1. Cavalucci, Tony (Fictitious character)—Fiction. 2. Police—New York (State)—New York—Fiction. 3. New York (N.Y.)—Fiction. I. Title.
PS3612.I58S57 2006
813'.6—dc22
                                        2005033662

Times Square and the other New York City landmarks described in this book exist, as do any recognizable public figures. But this is a work of fiction. The events and characters are the product of the author's imagination, and any resemblance to any actual events or people, dead or living, is entirely coincidental.

To our Lord Jesus Christ,
the Light of the World.
Your Word is a lamp to our feet
and a light to our path.

*I*n Times Square, the crossroads of the world, spring doesn't show up like it does in other places. We don't have birds, we have pigeons—flying rats we call them. And they don't migrate. They spend the winter dropping all over the Father Duffy statue in front of the TKTS theater ticket booth and playing chicken with the pedestrians trying to walk by. Sure, the skirts are shorter, the streets are more crowded, and baseball is in the air. But mostly we know it's spring by the distinctive smell of urine and rotting garbage, and by the skells that come out from whatever hole they crawled into over the winter.

My name is Tony Cavalucci, and this is my eleventh year as a New York City cop. Except for the six months I spent at FTU, or Field Training Unit, in Coney Island, I've worked my entire career here in Midtown Manhattan.

Skells is our name for crackheads, homeless, prostitutes, chicken hawks, and other lowlifes that make up the dregs of society. I used to look at them that way. Lately they just look lost and wounded to me, but I still call them skells.

They make up a good portion of the population here in Midtown, at least the population that smokes crack, urinates in public, prostitutes itself for drugs, has open containers of alcohol, and jumps turnstiles. We do a lot of sweeps now, getting them off the street early in the night for the little stuff, so we don't have to come back later when they really get cooking.

It was the last week of April 2001, and the city finally sent a crew to the precinct to fix the heating system. We spent half the winter with the heat blowing cool air, making us put cardboard inside the vents to keep the chill out. Now that spring was here, the vents were finally blowing hot air, making the precinct feel like a sauna.

The city jumped straight from winter to summer. Instead of temperatures in the 60s and 70s like we normally get this time of year, the numbers were up in the high 80s, inching toward the 90 degree mark. I'm sure the papers will have the scientists speculating about global warming and all the other doomsday crap they come up with every time there's a change in the weather.

I was standing in the muster room, waiting for roll call to start. The muster room is a dingy thirty-by-thirty-foot room where roll call takes place. Aside from the podium where the sarge speaks, there's an old metal desk, vending machines, and old wooden benches that run along the walls. The walls are full of crime statistics, bios of perps, and missing persons pictures that nobody looks at.

I was reading a flyer for the second retirement party we've had this month. It was for Brian Gallagher, an old-timer who had done most of his time here at the South. The flyer had a picture of a fat guy on a lounge chair under a palm tree, with a hat over his head and a drink with an umbrella in his hand. Under the caption "Brian Gallagher Is Retiring" someone had written, "Why? The job is so great!" and "This job sucks." They drew a picture of a keg with an IV hooked up to the guy's arm, pretty much summing up Brian Gallagher. The party was at an Irish pub up on 45th Street. It was thirty bucks a head, with food and an open bar.

Originally I wasn't going to go to the party, but my partner, Joe Fiore, and I have court the day of the party and would be working a day tour. I looked around for Terri Marks, a female cop with about eighteen years on, who works behind the desk. She was collecting the money for the party and I spotted her over by the desk, talking to Nick Romano. She was beautiful once, red hair, light blue eyes. But after almost two decades of wear and tear from the job, she looked worn-out as an old boot. No pension is ever gonna give that back.

"Hey, Nick, Terri," I said as I walked over to them and shook Romano's hand.

"You going to Brian Gallagher's party, Tony?" Terri asked.

"Yeah, here's for me and Joe," I said, pulling out three twenties.

"Fiore's going too?" She smiled and raised her eyebrows.

"Forget it, Ter, it's never gonna happen," I told her. She had a thing for Fiore that he politely ignored. She was probably hoping to get a few drinks into him to loosen him up, but that was never gonna happen either.

"Never say never, Tony," she said, writing our names down on her legal pad.

"How's it goin', Nick?" I asked Romano.

He looked like he was hurting from too much drinking. I knew he'd been going to the bar over on 9th Avenue in the mornings, but I haven't said anything to him about it. Last year Joe and I found out Romano's father had been a cop and was killed in the line of duty. He was shot in the face during a domestic dispute. Romano's been a cop for a few years now, and he hates it. He also has a baby with his self-absorbed ex-girlfriend, and they're in court all the time over visitation and any other petty thing she can come up with. It all seems to be wearing on him. A couple of months ago he found out he'd be going over to the fire department. I thought he'd be happier about it, but he's still miserable.

"Pretty good, nineteen more days of this crap and I'm outta here," Romano said with feeling. (He didn't say crap, but I'm editing here.)

"I hear ya," I said. "Pretty soon you'll be one of New York's Noisiest."

Romano smiled. "That's New York's Bravest, Tony."

"If you say so."

"How come you never went over to FD?" he asked.

I shrugged. "I took the test. I got a 96 on the written test, but I was hungover for the physical and I only got an 85. I think I needed a 90 on the physical to have a high enough average to get in."

"I made sure I got 100 on both tests," he said. "I quit smoking for the physical, and I was running five miles a day by the time I took it. I started smoking again after I took the test, but at least I got in."

"The Fire Academy is up on Randall's Island, right?" I asked.

"Yeah, you ever been there?" he asked.

"Yeah, I went to a softball tournament up there for a cop who was killed up in the Bronx," I said. "How long is the Academy?"

"Twelve weeks; I think I graduate like August 7."

"Can't wait to leave us, Nick?" Fiore slapped him on the back when he walked over.

"You know it," Romano said, shaking his hand.

I started working with Joe Fiore last June when my old partner, John Conte, hurt his knee and wound up having surgery. John came back in December on limited duty, but he was out again having a second surgery on the knee. I had been drinking my way out of being dumped by my old girlfriend Kim and dealing with my psychotic family when I wound up with Joe. The summer was just starting, and the last thing I wanted was some do-gooder telling me how Jesus was the answer to all my problems. I didn't think there was anything wrong with me that the beach, the bar, and a willing woman wouldn't cure. When things crashed down around me, Fiore was standing there when the smoke cleared, and he's been there ever since.

It was through Fiore that I met my fiancée, Michele, last July. She's a schoolteacher from Long Island and has a little boy, Stevie, who will be five next month. I'm crazy about the both of them, and in February I got down on one knee with a rock in my hand and a lump in my throat and asked her to marry me. She said yes, and we set the date for November.

"Hey, the guido patrol!" McGovern, one of the cops from our squad, said to Joe, Romano, and me as he came upstairs. "How's the paesanos tonight?"

"Good, just planning our next hit," I said, but he was right, we looked like a bunch of guidos. Joe was taller than Nick and me, closer to six feet, while Romano and I were a couple of inches shorter and stockier. Romano and I had more olive skin than Joe and we both had straight black hair, where Joe's was wavier. They both had brown eyes and mine were hazel, but aside from mixing the features around, all three of us were full-blooded Italians and would never pass for anything else.

Sergeant Hanrahan gave the attention to the roll call order as we filed in. Hanrahan was alone tonight. Usually Sergeant Courtney was here with him, but she had gallbladder surgery and wouldn't be back for another week.

As we mustered up, John Quinn came in with Rice and Beans from the four-to-twelve shift with a collar. It was six collars actually, all drunk and beaten bloody. Four of them were cuffed together hand to hand, chain gang style. The other two were cuffed individually, with their hands behind their back. These two must have been the rabble-rousers, because they were yelling in Spanish, trying to kick the others. They looked like a band of migrant workers and smelled like a brewery.

They were all short, I doubt there was one over five foot six. They were wearing various styles of work boots, filthy jeans, and sweat-stained or bloodstained T-shirts.

Lieutenant Conlan peered at Quinn over his glasses and smirked. "Whaddaya got, John?" he asked.

"Lou, I caught them trying to cross the border," Quinn said, expressionless in his jaded way, pitching the squad into fits of laughter.

Rooney yelled out "*Cerveza!*" to the perps.

They nodded their heads and smiled. "*Si, cerveza.*"

"Well, get your border crossing in the back—they stink," the lou said with a scowl.

"Sure, Boss," Quinn said.

"This way, amigos," he said, taking them toward the cells in the back.

"The color of the day is orange," Hanrahan said once the laughter died down, designating the citywide color code we use to identify undercover and plainclothes cops so nobody gets shot when they reach for their badges.

"O'Brien," the sarge called.

"Here."

"McGovern."

"Here, Sarge."

"Charlie-Frank, 1887, four o'clock meal." That indicated their sector, meal time, and the number of the RMP they'd be driving.

Our command is broken up into eight sectors. Adam-Boy handles Grand Central, Park Avenue, some of the consulates and embassies for the UN, and two active abortion clinics. Charlie-Frank handles Madison Square Garden, Penn Station, the Empire State Building, and the main post office for New York City on 8th Avenue. David-George, which is mine and Fiore's sector, handles the bulk of the garment district and 34th Street. Eddie-Henry handles Times Square, Port Authority, part of the theatre district, and 42nd Street between 7th and 8th avenues. The old-timers call that sector the Deuce.

Hanrahan gave out the sectors, the foot posts, and the return date for C-summons. If we wrote a summons today, that's the date the person would have to go to court. He looked around at us before speaking again, then he looked past us to the doorway of the muster room. We turned and saw the inspector standing there.

"Uh, Inspector O'Connor is here to address the roll call," he said, not looking at us.

Inspector O'Connor came to the precinct a couple of months ago. Most inspectors come in soft. Not O'Connor—he was a big mouth with a big hook somewhere that got him a spot at the largest command in the city. He came in strong with his new oak leaves on his shoulders, picturing himself as a deputy borough chief at his next gig. Whoever his hook was, they had pull.

He walked up to the podium and looked around the room, his usual plastered smile gone and his face set in anger. We were all wary of him. He carried himself like a politician instead of a cop, and he had a "you scratch my back, I'll scratch yours" managerial approach.

"Today was my second COMSTAT as commander of this precinct," he started, his eyes burning into us. "What I would like to know is why four geisha houses were closed in this command and I wasn't notified." He scanned the room again. "Under the padlock law, when a house of prostitution is closed down, it is padlocked and an ID sheet accompanies a request to add the premise to the padlock target list. This list lets COMSTAT know that these were prostitution houses. Imagine my surprise when four of these were closed down in my command and I had no documentation on it and didn't fill out the padlock forms before the meeting." He was seething, saying all of this like he was choking on it. "I will never be made a fool of again for not knowing what's going on in my own command."

Geisha houses or massage parlors are houses of prostitution, or pros as we call them. OCCB or Organized Crime Control Bureau must have closed the houses and didn't give the inspector the heads-up. The inspector was only partially to blame—he's new and didn't know about the geisha houses, but it's his command and he should have bothered to find out.

COMSTAT was initiated by a former chief of police to use statistics to track crime patterns and response times, and to isolate problem areas and then hold the commands responsible for them. The brass hate COMSTAT because they never want to be the ones called on the carpet for a problem in their command. The cops love COMSTAT because it gives the brass the trots.

"OCCB closed them down," Rooney yelled out. "It's their responsibility to notify you when they close a geisha house."

"Now I'm making it *your* responsibility to notify me," the inspector said, smiling like a snake about to bite. "Everyone on patrol has to gather information for me on known geisha houses; I want intel reports from each sector—"

"We don't have time for this," Rooney said. "We're answering jobs all night."

"If a geisha house is operating in one of your sectors and I don't get an intel report on it," the inspector said icily, "you'll walk for a month"—meaning we'd be on a foot post on 8th

Avenue somewhere. He stormed out of the roll call, leaving us stunned for a second.

"Is this guy for real?" Garcia asked.

"Boss, that walking for thirty days," Rooney asked, "will that be in front of the geisha house?"

Hanrahan started to smirk as the comments came up from the ranks.

"Me love you long time."

"Two dollar, two minute."

We all laughed and then heard the inspector's door slam. His office is behind the muster room. If the inspector thought us goofing on him was the end of it, he was kidding himself. We were just warming up. This was war.

The boss ended the roll call with, "By the way, I have some notifications here," then he looked through the slips and read off Cavalucci, Rooney, Connelly, and a couple of other names. When we made our way up to the podium for him to hand out the court notifications, he gave me a letter in a sealed envelope.

"Looks like a letter from the Advocate's Office," Hanrahan said. His usual salt-and-pepper hair had more salt lately, and his blue eyes looked sympathetic.

"The Advocate's Office?" I asked, confused.

"It's probably some skell and his liberal lawyer saying you violated his civil rights," he said.

Hanrahan was a good boss, and in all the years he's been my sergeant, he's done the right thing by me. Last June, when he put me with Fiore and said I could learn a lot from him, was the first time I was angry with him. I had been drinking a lot, even showing up to work still reeking of booze. He told me he was putting me with Fiore and I couldn't talk him out of it. He said I could learn a lot from Fiore; turns out he was right.

"You getting sued, Tony?" Rooney jumped in.

"I don't know, Mike, I didn't open the letter yet," I pointed out.

"Hey Tony, how do you stop a lawyer from drowning?" Rooney asked.

"Shoot him before he hits the water," I said absently, still looking at the envelope.

I opened the envelope as Sergeant Hanrahan went to call the sectors in to Central. Central stands for Central Communications, the faceless voices that transmit our jobs to us from the 911 operators.

The letter stated that I was one of the people being named in a lawsuit for ten million dollars. I was looking at the name, but it wasn't ringing any bells. The date was for almost a year ago, when I was still working with John Conte. I noticed John's name wasn't on the lawsuit. I was hoping it was a mistake and had nothing to do with me.

"Everything alright?" Fiore asked.

"Yeah," I said. "I'm not sure this is for me; I don't remember the collar. Can you pick up my radio? I'm gonna run upstairs and see if one of the detectives knows anything about this."

"No problem," he said. "I'll be out in the car."

I went upstairs to the second floor to see if Jack Sullivan or Eileen Toomey from the detective squad were in. Both of their names were on the suit, but neither was there. They were scheduled to do a day tour in the morning.

I was still shaking my head when I went out to the RMP.

"What was it?" Fiore asked as I got in the car.

"I have no idea," I said.

"Did you talk to the detectives?" he asked.

"No, I'll see them in the morning, then I'll call the Advocate's Office," I said.

"You can't get sued, the city indemnifies you," Romano said from the backseat. I didn't realize he was in the car.

"They only indemnify you if you can prove to them you didn't do anything wrong, otherwise you're screwed," I said, looking at him in the rearview mirror.

"The fire department doesn't get sued," Romano said confidently.

I looked back at him. "Don't kid yourself, Nick. The fire department gets sued."

"But the city indemnifies them," he said.

"You're still dealing with the city of New York. If you get sued for ten million dollars for something during a fire, they'll cover you. But only for the first three million—after that you're on your own."

"I got sued like that once, back in 1998," Fiore said.

"For what?" I asked.

"I was still working out in Queens. I locked this guy up for a robbery, and he was wanted for murder. He wound up doing twenty-five to life for the murder. He filed a lawsuit against me because he said I didn't return his Social Security card. He said that I was trying to steal his identity." Fiore started laughing.

"You gotta laugh," I said. "I never take the originals. I always make photostat copies of their IDs." I'm real careful about that. I copy anything pertinent, like welfare cards, credit cards, licenses. At one point Jersey didn't have photo IDs, so I copied everything. A lot of perps have several IDs, so I copy them all in case I get a hit on one of the other names they carry. I even copy weird stuff that has nothing to do with anything, like business cards and phone numbers.

"You worried about it, Tony?" Fiore asked.

"No, but how many times do you see this crap where a perp gets a million dollars for stuff like this? It's ridiculous," I said, disgusted.

"Remember Isaiah 54:17, Tony—no weapon formed against you shall prosper—"

"Oh here we go," Romano said sarcastically from the back-seat.

I looked back at him, surprised that he said that. "You better watch your mouth, Nick, before I call in a complaint against you and hold up your move to FD," I said toward the back-seat.

"You would do that?" he asked, unconvinced.

"Absolutely," I said.

"You scum," he spat. He waited a beat and said, "So what does that mean?"

"It means that if you don't watch your mouth—" I started to say, facing him while I backed the car out.

"Nooo, the thing that Joe was saying about a weapon," he said.

"What do you care? You act like he's bothering you," I said to Nick.

He shook his head and sighed. "Just tell me what it means in case I ever get sued."

Joe smiled. "It says in the NIV translation, "'No weapon forged against you will prevail, and you will refute every tongue that accuses you. This is the heritage of the servants of the LORD, and this is their vindication from me,' declares the LORD.'"

"Like I said, what does that mean?" Romano asked again.

"It means, Nick, that it is our heritage as Christians for God to protect us from any weapons of force or violence, and also protect us in the courts. People suing people is nothing new—they've been doing it for thousands of years. People think that because they say their lawsuit is in the name of truth and justice, they can falsely accuse someone and make some money. Like the lawsuit against Tony—whoever it was got locked up for doing something wrong, but he's pointing the finger at everyone else instead of taking responsibility for his actions. He should own up to whatever he did and take the hit for it."

"Maybe in Fioreland," Nick said. I stopped the car on the corner of 9th Avenue, and Joe and I turned to look at him.

"What?" he asked.

"You gonna get us coffee?" I asked.

"Why do I always have to get the coffee? Why don't one of you go in and let Geri sexually harass you?"

"Because we have more time on than you," I said, smiling.

"This is ridiculous," he snapped, getting out of the car and going into the deli.

"Get the paper," I yelled after him.

"He needs an attitude adjustment," I said. "What's his problem?"

"I think Geri scares him," Fiore said about the clerk in the deli. She works nights like we do and is always propositioning us. She's cute, about five feet tall, with short brown hair and big blue eyes. She does stupid stuff like drops our change and says "Oops" so we have to bend over and pick it up. It's pretty funny. It bothers Romano more than Joe and me, so we make him go in and get us coffee just to bust his chops.

"He's leaving soon—with all his show about wanting to go to FD, he's probably scared."

"You shoulda been a shrink, Joe," I said, shaking my head. But thinking about it, he was probably right.

"He's drinking a lot. He's been going to the bar in the morning," I said.

"Yeah, I know," Fiore said. "It'll probably be better for him once he's FD. I just hope he doesn't get a house where there's a lot of drinking."

Romano came out of the deli with the *Daily News*, three coffees, and a couple of what looked like blueberry muffins.

He handed us the coffee and muffins through my window.

I handed Fiore the coffee and a muffin and ate mine as I drove us up to 42nd and 8th. I got out of the car to smoke a cigarette with Romano. I had quit for a week in March but started again after Fiore and I grabbed a gun collar one night.

"So, Nick, you been hanging out with Rooney in the mornings?" I asked.

"No, Rooney only talks to me if there's no one else in the bar," he said. "I hang out there alone."

"So why do you go there?" I asked.

"The same reason you went there, Tony—to have a drink. I don't need Rooney to talk to me to do that."

"No, you don't," I said, leaving it at that. When I was drinking and someone tried to talk to me about it, I usually avoided them. If I was gonna say something to him, it wouldn't be in front of Fiore.

I finished my coffee and cigarette and got back in the car.

"Can you pick me up for my meal about a quarter to five?" he asked, leaning in Joe's window.

"Sure, Nick," Joe told him. "No problem."

"South David," Central called.

"South David," Fiore responded.

"I've got a call coming in for an explosion." Central gave a 9th Avenue address between 37th and 38th streets. "Apartment 3 Boy; FD has been notified."

"10-4," Fiore said.

Fiore and I gave each other a "What's this?" look.

"See you later, Nick," I said before pulling away.

I made a left on 43rd Street and took 9th Avenue straight down, wondering what the explosion could be. I narrowed it down to drugs, fireworks, or a bomb. I heard Central giving the job to South Sergeant, and Hanrahan answered, saying he would respond with a delay. He was probably still at the precinct.

There's not many residential apartments in our sector, mostly first-floor storefronts with apartments on the second and third floors of the building. We pulled up in front, and as far as I knew, I'd never answered any jobs here. The address was between a butcher and a pizzeria, both closed. It wasn't a real neighborhood where you'd get a crowd of concerned residents helping us out with information. In fact, there was no one outside.

We pushed on the brown door that screeched and scraped against the floor. It opened into a small foyer with a row of mailboxes. I scanned for 3B and saw the name Healy. The building had a damp, musty smell.

The stairs were straight ahead, the same dull brown as the door, steep and narrow with warped floorboards. They creaked and groaned as Fiore and I started walking up. There was a single yellow light sticking out of the wall with some of its wires showing; otherwise the stairway was dim. The old plasterboard wall next to the stairs was bowed in places. The place had condemned written all over it.

"I don't smell anything," Fiore said. "If they were cooking up chemicals to make drugs and blew themselves up, it would have that bitter almond smell."

"Everybody always says that, 'bitter almonds.' What do bitter almonds smell like? Did you ever smell bitter almonds?" I asked.

He chuckled. "I don't even know what almonds smell like. I know when people blow themselves up making drugs, it never smells like it does around street vendors who roast the nuts."

"Exactly my point," I said.

We reached the first landing. It was long, with a shorter landing going up to the third floor. As we turned to start up the stairs to the third floor, the smell hit us.

"What *is* that?" Fiore said. The smell was a mix of burnt flesh, hair, and something else familiar that I couldn't place.

"Definitely not bitter almonds," I said. Definitely charred flesh. We started jogging now. I grabbed the banister for support in case the stairs gave out, and I heard a loud crack. I let go and jogged a little faster.

At the top of the third-floor landing, 3B was the second door on the left. There was an old man in the hallway. He wore threadbare blue cotton pajamas, a green ragged terry-cloth robe with a yellow stain on the chest, and brown leather slippers. He had longish white hair, a couple of days' worth of white stubble on his face, and he wore thick, Coke bottle glasses.

"Officer, I heard an explosion. Danny, my neighbor, is screaming in there," he said, pointing to the door. He was missing a yellow tooth in the front that matched the stain on his bathrobe.

"Was it a gunshot?" Fiore asked.

"No." He shook his head.

"Are you sure?" Fiore asked again.

"Am I sure? I've lived in this city for seventy-four years. You think I don't know a gunshot when I hear one?" He shook his head like we were idiots. "Gunshots don't explode, and they don't smell like that," he insisted as he aimed his thumb toward the door.

I was already knocking on the door while Fiore tried to get answers from the old man. I could hear yelling from inside, but it was faint.

"Police!" I said, knocking and trying the doorknob.

"I called Eva, his wife," the guy was saying. "She works over at Bellevue. She's a nurse's aide; she's coming home now."

"Do you have a key?" I asked, turning my head toward him.

"If I had a key, would I be out here talking to you or would

I be in there helping my friend?" he said, aggravated. I love when people talk to me like this.

"If he was your friend, you'd have a key," I said.

I took a step back and gave a hard kick to the door under the handle. I heard the crunch of the wood splintering, but it didn't open. I jarred my leg, pain running through my hip. I took a step back, figuring it would take another good shot to open it.

"You okay?" Joe asked. It actually hurt to step on my leg.

I nodded. "Yeah, just finish it," I said.

Fiore kicked it, and it opened with a loud crack. Pieces of wood and sawdust flew from the door frame as it gave, taking the molding off on one side.

"Who's gonna pay for that?" the old man yelled.

"You're his friend, you pay for it," I said, knowing full well the city would pay for it.

We heard the fire engines outside as we entered the apartment.

*O*nce we were inside the apartment, we could hear him louder now, calling, "I'm in here," then moaning.

There was a kitchen to the left, with a half wall into a dining area, a living room straight ahead, and two doors on the right. One of the doors was opened, a bedroom, and the other was closed. The apartment was worn, but surprisingly clean and well kept compared to the rest of the building.

The bathroom door was unlocked, and we opened the door to find a white male lying on the floor, wedged between the wall and the toilet. I could smell burnt hair, flesh, and something else I couldn't place. I took a step in and slipped on the floor. The bathroom was small, with what looked like the original porcelain fixtures, all in white. The floor was small white tile with a colored mosaic design.

The guy's pants were down; apparently he had been on the toilet. There was a saturated copy of the *New York Post* on the floor in front of the toilet. I saw extensive burns on the lower part of his body and a Marine Corps bulldog tattoo on his leg.

24

FD was coming into the apartment now. One of them, I guess the captain, came up behind me.

"Watch your guys with all that equipment on," Joe said. "Those stairs felt like they could give out."

"Yeah, I know," he said. "Whaddaya got?"

"Burns on the lower part of his body. Is EMS here?" I asked about the paramedics.

"Yeah, they just pulled up," he said, coming into the room.

"What happened?" he asked the guy lying on the floor.

"I don't know," he moaned. "I lit a cigarette and the toilet blew up."

"Sewer gas?" the captain mumbled, then asked him, "Was there water in the toilet?"

"I think so," he whimpered.

I heard Fiore calling Central to slow it down so no one else was rushing to the scene.

The water from the toilet was now covering the bathroom floor, so I pulled a pair of latex gloves out of my memo book and put them on. I went over to the side of the toilet next to the tub and shut the valve before we had a flood in there. The toilet was cracked but was still intact.

"How'd the toilet blow up?" the captain asked, looking around the room.

"I don't know," the victim moaned.

"You sure it was the toilet?" The captain was checking the area around the toilet and inside the shower. "We're gonna have to move the toilet," he said. "First we'll let EMS take a look at him."

"Watch the floor, it's wet," I said when EMS came into the bathroom. There wasn't enough room for all of us, so I went to the doorway. Hanrahan was in the living room with Noreen, his driver, six firemen, and the old man. I knew one of the

EMS workers; he was about forty, with balding blond hair and glasses. The second guy was younger, early twenties with the dark hair and olive skin that favors us Italians.

"What is it, a full moon?" he asked as he went past me.

I never put much stock in the theory that a full moon makes people nuts—they're nuts anyway.

"Interesting night?" I asked the older guy.

"Yeah, and this is only our second job," he said, shaking his head. He took the victim's vital signs and started putting sterile wrapping on the burns on his legs. I heard the captain ask if EMS wanted to take him out with the bucket, meaning using the bucket truck up to the window.

"No, we'll wrap him up and use the scoop stretcher," he said.

The victim was quietly moaning now; I guess the burn wrap gave him some relief from the pain. The EMS worker asked the captain and me to move the toilet. I disconnected the coupling, and the toilet cracked into two pieces as we pulled it away from the wax seal.

The charred toilet seat, one of those plastic cushioned types, fell away from the guy's backside, and there was a white ring around his skin where the seat protected him from the blast.

I looked around the bathroom as EMS worked. Aside from the hamper, the only other thing in the room was a small white bookcase-type shelf next to the pedestal sink. Brushes and tubes of creams and stuff were neatly arranged on the shelves.

I heard a rise in the noise level behind me, so I leaned back from the doorway to look into the living room. A hysterical woman with a lot of dark hair came in wearing pink scrubs and a white floral print top.

"Where's Danny?" She looked wildly around the room.

"He's in here," I said, making room for her to walk past me.

"Danny!" she screamed when she saw him on the floor. "What happened?"

"He said the toilet exploded. We're trying to find out what happened," the fire captain said.

"The toilet exploded? How could the toilet explode? Danny!" she yelled again.

The husband was moaning, "It's okay, it's okay."

"Ma'am, were there any chemicals in the toilet? Did you clean the bathroom and leave anything in the bowl?" the captain asked.

She ran her hands over her face and shook her head while thinking. She was staring at the husband, but I saw the minute the lights went on—her hand stalled over her mouth and her eyes got big.

"What was in there?" the captain asked.

She looked over at the bowl. "Hair spray. But how could hair spray blow up the toilet?"

That's what the other smell was, hair spray.

"Why'd you put hair spray in the toilet?" The captain looked confused.

"I was using it and the nozzle stuck. The spray kept coming out, so I put the can in the toilet until it emptied," she explained as she leaned under the sink and pulled a silver aerosol can out of the garbage pail.

"Danny, I'm sorry," she said, and then her face got hard.

"Were you smoking?" she said accusingly to the husband. When he didn't answer, she turned to the captain. "Was he smoking? Because he's not supposed to be smoking."

The husband moaned from the floor, "Just give me a minute with her so I can kill her."

"You'll kill yourself from smoking!" she yelled.

"Ma'am, please step back. We're gonna take him to the hospital—you can fight it out with him later," the captain cut her off.

She stepped back toward the door as the younger EMS worker came in with the fiberglass stretcher that would mold to the guy's body and be secured with straps. It was good for a quick evacuation and had ropes at the end in case you need to drag someone out. The stretcher was narrow enough that they could get him down the stairs instead of lowering him out a window.

The two EMS workers, the fire captain, and another fireman picked the stretcher up by the four ends. EMS had both sides of the front of the stretcher, with FD at the back. The younger EMS worker took two steps and slipped, taking the stretcher with him. The older EMS worker tried to hold up the front, but the weight of the body was toward the front. He lost his balance and the stretcher flew, flipping Danny face-first onto the bathroom floor. You heard the *oomph* of his face connecting with the floor, then he let out a high-pitched moan.

Everyone but the wife was trying not to laugh while they picked him up.

"You think this is funny?" the wife screamed and went over to him. She was crying hard now, calling us everything she could think of. "You're trying to *kill* him!" she screamed. "I'm suing you!"

"Hey lady, we're not trying to kill him," the captain said. "First of all, the floor is soaked and the tile is slippery. Second of all, we're not the ones who blew him off the toilet."

"That was an accident," she spat.

"So was this," he fired back.

Hanrahan and Joe had come up behind me and watched the whole exchange.

"They dropped him?" Hanrahan said, looking amused.

I gave him a quick nod. I didn't want the wife to lose it if we started laughing. Joe looked concerned as he looked at the victim.

When they turned him over, his face was wet with water from the floor mixed with blood from his now-broken nose. He was starting to get that chalky look that comes with shock.

"Let's get him downstairs," EMS said.

The wife went into another tirade when she saw we broke the door. She started screaming about how we wrecked her apartment and anyone could come in and rob it. I figured by the time she finished suing the city, she'd be living uptown somewhere.

I followed EMS downstairs and was standing outside the ambulance when Joe and Sergeant Hanrahan came out. The wife was inside the ambulance, yapping away on her cell phone.

"Ma'am," Hanrahan said, "you need to get the door and the locks fixed. It's up to you whether you want to get your own locksmith or have the police department do it."

"I'll get someone—I don't trust you guys to do it," she spat.

"It's up to you," he said, unaffected. "You have ninety days to file a claim against the city to the Comptroller's Office."

"Don't worry, I will," she said.

"Your neighbor said he would stay in your apartment, or I can have one of my guys stay there," Hanrahan added.

"You've done enough, I don't want any of you in my apartment."

I was beginning to wonder if she didn't blow her husband up on purpose.

"Noreen." Hanrahan turned to his driver. "Go back to the precinct and get the camera. I want pictures of the wet floor, the broken door to show we needed to access the premise, and the dismantled toilet."

"Where are they taking him?" Hanrahan asked me.

"Bellevue," I said.

"Go over there with them, make sure he's okay. Make sure you document everything in case she decides to sue," he said.

"She's definitely gonna sue," I said.

"Yeah, I know," he said. "Get the old man's name from upstairs, see if he'll sign a statement. Do an aided card for the aided's injury with the info from FD and EMS," Hanrahan added, talking about the form we fill out for sick, injured, or dead people. "Do two reports: one for the accident report, one for the city-involved property damage."

The first report would include any city agencies involved, like the police department for Joe and I kicking down the door. The second report was for EMS and FD dropping the guy. The pictures would show that in reality it wasn't our fault, but his wife would still get money.

"Sure, Boss," I said. I had gotten EMS's info upstairs, along with the firemen's names and ladder company, and since the wife was already with the guy, we didn't have to make a notification.

We went back upstairs and talked to the old man who lived next door. His name was Gaetano Mazza. He signed my memo book, saying that the door was locked, he heard the explosion, and the injured man was yelling for help from inside. Gaetano said he would stay in the apartment while the victim's wife was at the hospital. We had given Gaetano the number for a locksmith in case the wife changed her mind and wanted help. The door would have to be fixed before new locks could be installed.

The ambulance had already left the scene, so we drove crosstown on 34th Street and took the service road into the back of Bellevue. When we got into the emergency room, the burn victim was already in with the doctor. The younger of the two EMS guys was talking to a nurse in the hallway when we got there.

"*Meengya*," he said with feeling as we walked up. "What a night already." *Meengya* is a word Italians use to show strong emotion. It's also said when we see something unbelievable, good or bad, but mostly when we see a woman with a great body.

We all turned when we heard the door to the emergency room open, and two cops from the 17th precinct came in with their collar. They looked disgusted. They were somewhere in their thirties and looked like they had some time on. They acknowledged Fiore and me with a cop nod. EMS was with them as they wheeled in a fiftyish white male. He was drunk and cursing, with a gash on his forehead, a busted nose, and a split lip. He had a gray pallor and was sweating profusely. His hands were tied to the gurney with sheets to keep him restrained. The cops looked harassed and tired as their collar yelled, "I know people! I'll get your badge, I'll get your wife—"

"You deserve my wife," the older of the two cops said. "Take my mother-in-law too, I'll give you a package deal."

A nurse came out into the hall to see what the disturbance was. She was a big woman, light skinned, with freckles on her arms. She was wearing blue scrubs with a pin that said "Staffing Is the Issue," and her name tag read Colleen Dewey. You could tell she was a veteran. She had that no-panic, no-emotion, "I don't need to impress anyone" attitude that nurses get when they've seen it all. Contrary to what people think, the nurses don't buddy up to us all that often; they don't have time for it.

Anyway, she started doing her thing when the drunk and disorderly smiled at her and said, "Wanna see my gun?" as he tried to pull his pants down. She gave him a sarcastic look and pulled the sheet up, throwing it over his head.

He struggled his head out from under the sheet, focused his bleary eyes on her, and got this turned-on look on his face, then said, "Kiss me, you pig."

"Not in this life," she said, taking his blood pressure and writing it down on the white sheet that covered the gurney.

Joe and I choked on a laugh, and the two cops from the 17th laughed out loud.

The nurse gave Joe and me a hard look. "Don't you guys have something to do?"

Joe and I looked at each other, shrugged, and shook our heads no.

"What about you two?" she said to the cops from the 17th.

"We're babysitting him," the younger of the two said.

"You could have fooled me," she mumbled as she walked away.

The cops from the 17th were making oinking noises to her back. The drunk laughed and bobbled his head. There was a time that I would have done the same thing, or worse, but now I just tried not to laugh.

Since we had taken most of the information at the scene and the wife was with him, we waited until Danny was stabilized and got the doctor's name for the city involved form.

We walked back out to the car, where Fiore radioed Central "93 Queen 3 times," which means we did three reports.

We took 1st Avenue to 34th Street to get across town. It was now 2:00 as we started to patrol our sector, driving east to west and back again. We handled two alarms that Central gave us. One was on 6th Avenue, the other on 37th Street, and we came up premise secure on both.

"You ready for the big party Sunday?" Fiore asked about the engagement party my grandmother was throwing for Michele and me.

"No—I never wanted an engagement party. Either did Michele," I said.

"Why didn't you just tell your grandmother no?" he asked, shaking his head. "If you keep letting her get away with this stuff, she'll just keep doing it."

"I did tell her no. I feel like she scammed me. She called me up on my way home from work about a month ago telling me to stop there, saying she had something important to tell me. I got to her apartment and she's making gravy, gives me a meatball right out of the frying pan, which she knows I love. Next thing I know I got a plate of sausage, eggs, and potatoes, and she's smiling at me, looking like a sweet old granny in her housedress and curlers."

Joe interrupted me by laughing.

"This isn't funny," I said.

"It's hysterical," he choked. "Scam by meatball, I like it."

I gave him a blank look while he laughed it off.

His face sobered, and he said, "I don't know how you eat the way you do and not get fat."

"She told me about the party after the fact—what was I gonna do?"

"It's simple, Tony, tell her no. Come on, buddy, say it with me, 'No, Grandma.'"

"She already paid for the hall and the food."

"Where'd she get the money? I thought she was on a fixed income."

"That's the best part. She hit the number, for like five grand," I said.

"The daily number, or lotto? Five grand is a lot for the number," Fiore said.

"No, she hit the number. In fact, she hit it twice that month; the second time was for less, but still a couple of grand."

"How'd she do that?" Fiore looked suspicious.

"That's what I said. She's been playing the numbers for as long as I can remember, and she'd hit it at times, but mostly nickel-and-dime stuff—a couple hundred here and there, once in a while a grand. She plays it at the deli near Clove and Victory, where she always played it. So I asked what the deal is that all of a sudden she hits it twice in a month." I shook my head at the memory. "Apparently Grandma and the lotto clerk don't get along. My grandmother swears she saw the woman putting the horns on her, and that's why she never won. It's not funny, Joe," I said when he started laughing again.

"Tony, you gotta laugh. So what did she do, wear a horn?"

The Italians believe the *malokya*, or the evil eye, that someone puts on you can give you bad luck. If you wear the red horn, or *contra malokya*, it will protect you. They also believe someone can "put the horns on you," a hand signal usually given under the table or behind your back. Their hand is upside down, with the middle and ring fingers closed and the thumb, index, and pinky fingers out. I guess it looks like the sign language for "I love you," but upside down.

"She wore the red horn, but she said it wasn't working and the lady must have been very evil to put such a strong one on her. She wore two horns then, a gold one and a red one, and she started winning small amounts. She said the day she won the money for my engagement party, she added a pair of red underwear, and between the underwear and the two horns the woman couldn't touch her and she won five grand." I shook my head, trying not to picture Grandma in red bloomers.

"Do you think there's any truth to that? That someone could put the horns on you like that?" I asked Joe. My family was pretty big on that kind of stuff.

"No," he said with a smile. "Do you?"

"Not really—I mean I have all the medals and pins that my grandmother gives me, but I never put much stock in them.

The family swears my father came home from Vietnam alive because he wore a scapula of the Sacred Heart of Jesus."

"What's a scapula?" Fiore asked, puzzled.

"It's like a necklace, only it's made with silk threading with pictures of saints and stuff on the ends. I don't know how to explain it. You want more coffee?" I nodded as I drove toward the Sunrise Deli on 40th Street.

"Yeah, I could use another cup," he said.

Joe waited in the car while I got coffee and a pack of cigarettes and listened to the clerk complain about a bunch of kids that keep hanging out in front of the deli. He said he thought they were dealing drugs, but they weren't there now, so there was nothing I could do for him anyway.

I drove to 37th Street and parked in an empty parking lot. I looked up to my left, where the Empire State Building loomed above us.

"So what about your brother, did Granny throw him an engagement party behind his back when he got engaged?" Joe asked.

"No, she had a small dinner with my immediate family. Remember it was my first family party without drinking?"

"Yeah, I remember." He smiled. "The one where you pretended to drink and tossed it down the sink."

"That's the one. Anyway, Christie's parents threw them a party at this restaurant down by the marina that the whole family was invited to. Michele and I didn't want an engagement party, and we're trying to keep the wedding low-key."

My brother, Vinny, got engaged last Fourth of July. His wedding is the first week in October, six weeks before mine, which caused even more problems with the family. They said two weddings in one year was too much and I should wait. I think they're just hoping I'll get it out of my system with Michele and decide not to marry her. Things got pretty ugly last

Christmas when my father and grandmother let me know I shouldn't marry a non-Catholic who has a kid and was never married.

"I don't know, Joe, they were never like this before," I said, wondering why I say that every time they do something new.

"Sure they were, you just never saw it."

"Why am I seeing it now?" I asked.

"Because you've gotten to know Jesus, and he's about the truth." Joe smiled. "The truth about him and how good he is, the truth about ourselves and the people around us. The truth doesn't have to change how you love them, just what you do about them. You've never challenged them before," he said with a shrug, "and they don't like it."

"How did I challenge them?"

"You stopped drinking, you go to church—and not their church—and you're marrying someone they don't approve of. You've changed things, and I'm sure they see that as a threat," he said.

I thought about that. Before I met Joe, my family was dysfunctional and explosive, but predictably so. I could always tell just by walking into a room how things were gonna go with them. I drank a lot then and usually boozed my way through family dinners. Now I've changed, and I can see it's affected things—and not in a good way.

I was always my grandmother's favorite. The first grandchild and grandson, the one to carry on the family name. In Italian families, the firstborn son is named after the grandfather. My father's father was also Anthony Joseph Cavalucci. My brother is Vinny because the second son is named for the father. My grandmother came here from Italy as a child and grew up in a traditional Italian home where men are honored and women are secondary. For as long as I can remember, I could do no wrong.

I know Joe thinks that my grandmother is calculating and

manipulative, but he doesn't understand that she just thinks this is the way things should be. Bloodlines are strong in Italian families, and she feels Michele's son, Stevie, isn't my blood. She's even that way with my mother—even though my mother is related to me by blood, it's my father's blood that counts. Italian mothers have a sense of superiority over their daughter-in-laws because they have a blood connection to their sons that the wives don't have.

It's funny that it's so opposite from what the Bible says. Fiore knows how my family is and keeps pointing out that I'm supposed to leave my father and mother, which, trust me, is no hardship, and be one with my wife. My father never did that, and look how things turned out for him.

My sister, Denise, has been raised that way too. I think my mother regrets it now, letting Denise grow up thinking she wasn't as important as me and Vinny. It never seemed to bother Denise before, but lately she's gone the other way, bashing all men.

Denise was always like that blow-up clown I had when I was a kid. You punch it down, and it comes up smiling. She always came back no matter what anyone did to her. But she's different now, like a light's gone out somewhere.

My mother, who up until last summer was a bitter, lonely drunk, is on the wagon. She went to rehab and goes to AA and stuff. It's funny we both stopped drinking around the same time, in fact, after the same weekend. I don't think my mom's changing had anything to do with me, and I guess the changes in her aren't bad. The scariest thought is that lately my mother's the only one who seems normal.

"Did you talk to your father yet about Marie?" Joe asked, interrupting my thoughts.

Marie is my father's wife, the snake he left my mother for. Except for her new surgically enhanced cleavage and the fact that she's almost twenty years younger than my father, I don't get what he sees in her. He was fooling around with her when he was a detective in the 5th precinct, where she worked as a civilian. She had been married to an ironworker who was also a lot older than she was. The ironworker left his wife and kids for Marie. When he picked up the signals that she was cheating on him, he was smart enough to have her followed. He caught her with my father and called my mother to let her in on it. My parents went back and forth for a couple of years, but my father always went back to Marie. They finally divorced, but the family's still a mess.

Last winter my sister, Denise, got wind that Marie was at it again. Denise hired a private investigator, who followed Marie and another detective from the 5th, Bobby Egan. Denise showed up at my apartment with pictures, a PI's report, and a copy of the lease that Marie and Egan signed for an apartment in Bay Ridge. Denise hasn't gone to my father. She wants to wait till Marie screws my father out of money he took from my mother—he sold our family's house out from under her. Then Denise wants to let him know that she knew all along.

"No, I still don't know if I'm gonna tell him. Denise wants to let Marie take his money from him first. She said if I tell him, she'll never speak to me again," I said. "Normally I wouldn't believe her, but she told my father Christmas Eve that she'd never talk to him again, and so far she hasn't."

"I feel sorry for Denise, she's hurting," Fiore said, then added, "Do you think Marie would really take his money?"

"Absolutely," I said. "She's vicious—"

"Central to South David," Central interrupted.

"South David," Fiore countered.

"We have a possible stabbing at the corner of four-o and nine," which is across from the back of Port Authority.

"10-4," Fiore said as I drove to 9th Avenue, going the wrong way on 40th Street.

I pulled up next to the curb where a female was kneeling over the body of a man lying on the sidewalk. Joe and I stepped out of the car and saw the bloodstain on his chest, so we got on the radio to call for an ambulance.

"Central, we have a confirmed stabbing at four-o and nine. We need a bus forthwith."

Lying down, the guy looked about five foot seven. He had on worn-out jeans, no socks, and beat-up sneakers, but the T-shirt looked new, making the bloodstain more prominent. I pulled a pair of latex gloves out of my memo book and threw the memo book on the dashboard.

They had been doing some drinking, the air around us reeked of it. The female was sobbing, "Talk to me, baby, come on, Shorty." They were young, early twenties, and had that crackhead look about them.

"What happened?" I asked, kneeling down next to him.

"Get an ambulance," she sobbed.

"There's one on the way. Tell me what happened," I repeated.

"I can't," she sobbed. "Get an ambulance."

Fiore and I looked at the body. The guy's movements were exaggerated, almost like he was in slow motion. I could see the tear in the front of his shirt where the bloodstain was. Blood wasn't spurting out, more like seeping. I put my hand on his chest and put pressure on the wound to slow the bleeding down.

His breathing was shallow, and I looked at Joe. "Put a rush on that bus—" but Fiore was already on the radio.

"South David to Central, I need a rush on that bus—do you have an ETA?" Fiore said, asking for the estimated time of arrival.

"Two minutes out," Central responded.

"Where's the ambulance?" the girl screamed.

"It's on the way. You need to calm down and tell me what happened," I said firmly enough to get her attention.

"Someone stabbed him!" she sobbed.

"Who stabbed him?" Joe asked her as he looked around. The chances were nil that we'd find the knife with prints on it at the scene, but stranger things have happened.

"He ran down 9th Avenue," she said and went back to begging Shorty to talk to her.

"What does he look like?"

She looked up, trying to compose herself. "Um, six foot, wearing a blue Yankee hat." She paused and stared, then said, "Black shorts, black shirt, sneakers."

"Did you know his name?" Joe asked.

"Easy," she said with a nod.

"Easy?"

"Yeah, I only know him by his street name," she sobbed.

Joe put a description over the air, saying the stabber ran down 9th Avenue four minutes in the past, then the ranks got stupid over the radio.

"Central, did you say cheesy?" It sounded like Rooney to me.

"No," Central answered the moron in her emotionless voice, "that's easy, Eddie-Adam-Sam-Yellow."

"Easy come, easy go," someone chirped.

Someone else started singing "It ain't easy being blue," and I went to lower my radio so the girlfriend wouldn't have to hear the remarks. I heard Hanrahan's voice come over the radio with, "Stay off the air, we got a stabbing in progress." Cops do this stuff to amuse themselves—we didn't say he was likely to die, so they didn't know how serious this was.

A car screeched to a stop behind ours, and I heard Hanrahan tell Central that he was on the scene—"South Sergeant to Central 84."

Shorty was getting that look that people get right before the lights go out. "Look at me, buddy," I said, trying to get him to focus on me. His eyes started to get that vacant look, like a doll's eyes. I shook him a little. "Come on, the ambulance is on the way." He wasn't looking too good, but I've seen it happen a lot with these skells—we figure they're dying, and a week later they're back up on 8th Avenue, smoking crack.

We heard the sirens from the ambulance coming, and the female started to scream again, saying, "Don't leave me!"

Fiore tried to draw her attention away from him by asking, "Why'd the guy stab him?"

"He was making a play for me," she answered Fiore, but she was looking at Shorty.

"This guy?" Fiore asked.

"No, Easy, the one who stabbed him."

"Where'd this happen?"

"Next to the Port, where we been staying." She nodded toward Port Authority.

She meant the cardboard condos, a little neighborhood for

skells halfway up the block from Port Authority. The skells throw up some cardboard boxes, add a shopping cart to hold their stuff, and call it home.

EMS arrived, pulling up in front of our car. Rooney and Connelly showed up next and double-parked next to our RMP.

"Whadda we got?" Hanrahan asked, looking at the victim, then at me.

"We got a likely," meaning likely to die.

"South Sergeant to Central," Hanrahan radioed.

"Go ahead, South Sergeant," Central responded.

"Have South PDU respond to four-o and nine; we got a likely," Hanrahan said, calling the precinct detective unit over to the crime scene. He told Noreen, Rooney, and Connelly to close off 40th Street and wait for the detectives. If the guy died, it would be up to them to call homicide.

"It started over by the cardboard condos and made its way over here," Fiore told the sarge so they'd know to cordon off the area where it started half a block away.

We've worked with these two EMS before. One was a heavy-set guy in his forties, with wire-rimmed glasses and light brown hair. The female was nice, chubby, with short black hair and a lot of silver stud earrings. They gave us a quick nod as they started working on him.

"We're gonna rush him to Bellevue now," the male said, snipping the shirt at the collar with a scissor and ripping it off the rest of the way. For some reason I noticed the writing on the T-shirt; it said "Welcome to New York, Now Go Home." EMS saw my blood-soaked glove pressing on the wound and said, "Let me see it."

I lifted my hand to show it to him.

"Keep your hand on it," he said.

Joe grabbed the victim under the shoulders, and I put my

left hand underneath him. The two EMS grabbed his feet and under his backside, and we heaved him up onto the stretcher and got him into the bus. His girlfriend got in with us and sat on the bench on the right side of the ambulance.

"Tony, stay with the bus and keep me advised of his status," Hanrahan said.

Fiore was behind us as we took 9th Avenue down to 34th Street.

The victim's head and arms were limp, and he must not have had a pulse, 'cause the female EMS yelled "Clear!" so I could move my hand while she gave him a zap with the defibrillator. She put an air bag in his mouth and we started CPR. I tried to remember the sequence of chest compressions to air bag with CPR. I kind of winged it; I did about ten and she gave him a couple of shots with the air bag.

I buckled my knees into the stretcher to keep myself balanced and kept both hands on his chest. The bus was moving with the sirens going, and I could tell when we were getting to the intersection because the driver changed the signal to a fast, continuous whoop. Every time he stopped, I had to plant my feet to keep from moving forward and then backward when he took off.

By the third traffic light on 34th Street, I had my balance and we had gotten into a rhythm with the CPR. The blood was coming out of the wound now, running down either side of his chest. I wondered if I was making it worse by pressing it, but the female EMS worker wasn't telling me to stop. I was starting to feel helpless here, and I was aware of the girlfriend sobbing and trying to hold on with the movement of the ambulance.

I prayed now for his life, and if he was gonna die, I asked God to give him a chance to make things right, to let him meet Jesus. I prayed for the doctor and EMS workers to get him back here so he wouldn't have to die this way. He was just a kid.

When we got to Bellevue there was a doctor and nurse waiting outside for us, and they helped us get the stretcher out and took over the CPR. They had him inside in a couple of seconds and put him in the first trauma room inside the emergency room.

They were announcing a code on the overhead PA system and about thirty people charged into the room, including the nurse who was handling the drunk when we were there earlier.

The girlfriend tried to go in the room with him, but I made her stay in the hall with me. Fiore came in through the emergency room doors, and the three of us stayed out of the way and let them do their thing.

"Busy night, eh?" someone asked.

I looked over and saw the two cops from the 17th. The one who was talking to us was big, with short black hair.

"Yeah, I thought we were done here before," I said.

"Did his wife really blow him off the toilet?" he asked, smirking.

"Indirectly," I said with a shrug, then added, "We'll probably go see how he's doing."

"They transferred him to the burn center at Cornell," he said.

"Really?" That surprised me.

He nodded. "It was pretty serious."

"He seemed okay, but EMS dropped him on his face, so who knows," I said.

The commotion of the code was still going on inside the room. The door opened, and I saw the doctor who met us outside take off a pair of bloody gloves, step on a foot latch, and drop them into a garbage pail with a red bag.

"Is there anyone here with the young man?" he asked Fiore.

"She came in the ambulance," Fiore said as he nodded toward the girlfriend leaning against the wall about ten feet away from us.

She looked up at the doctor, and the three of us walked over to her. The doctor introduced himself and asked if she was the next of kin.

"I'm his girlfriend," she said. I hadn't looked at her before, I was too focused on her boyfriend. She had curly brown hair tucked behind her ears. She was wearing jean shorts, a tattered black tank top, and red rubber flip-flops. Her feet were dirty, and her front tooth was chipped.

The doctor went into his spiel about the internal bleeding being so severe they couldn't control it and he was sorry but the patient expired.

The girlfriend had a blank look and then asked, "Is he dead?"

The doctor blinked, not realizing she was clueless about everything he just said. He cleared his throat and said, "Yes, I'm sorry."

She let out a wail, folding her arms around herself. She collapsed against the wall and slid down to the floor. The doctor looked uncomfortable. Joe leaned down and rubbed her shoulder, talking in a soothing voice to her.

"Can I see him?" she sobbed.

"Sure," the doctor nodded, grateful to be done with the bad news.

I got the doctor's name and the victim's time of death while Joe helped her up and walked her into the room. He waited outside the open door. She was leaning over her boyfriend, kissing his face and telling him she would always love him. I wanted to get out of there, so I told Joe, "I'm gonna go out and raise the sarge."

45

"No problem, I'll stay here and make sure she's okay," Fiore said.

I walked out through the automatic doors and lit a cigarette. "South Sergeant on the air?"

"South Sergeant," Hanrahan responded.

"Can you roll over to 9?" Which is point to point, a private conversation so that the news, Central, and the police group-ies can't hear us.

"South Sergeant on the air."

"Sarge, this is South David. The likely didn't make it," I said. I gave him the pronounced time and the doctor's name. "Anything else you want me to get?" I asked him.

"Do the aided card, the complaint report for the stabbing, and get all the info on the female who was with him. Wait for the detectives to get there, then come back to four-o and nine."

We waited until 4:30, when two detectives from Manhattan homicide showed up. They were old-timers in their fifties, an Italian guy and an Irish guy, both dressed in off-the-rack suits.

The Italian guy talked to the victim's girl, and the Irish guy identified himself as Detective Mahoney and asked Joe and me to walk outside with him.

"Were you the first officers to the scene?" he asked, light-ing a cigarette.

"Yeah, it was our job," I said. Since he was smoking, I kicked one up too as Fiore stepped back from the cloud of smoke.

"You get it as a pickup or from Central?" he asked, taking out a pen and notebook.

"From Central," I said. He looked at our names and the shield numbers on our chests, then checked our collar brass for our command and wrote them down.

We went through the deal, filling him in on the stabbing. He scribbled away in his notebook as we talked.

"This guy Easy, either of you know him?" Mahoney asked, still writing.

"Not by name. Maybe if we saw the face, we'd recognize him," I said.

"His stuff is still at the cardboard condos," Joe said. "Easy doesn't know the victim's dead; he'll probably go back up to the condos to get his stuff."

Mahoney nodded, smoked, and wrote.

The automatic doors opened, and the other detective walked out with the victim's girlfriend. She wasn't crying anymore, just subdued, with a dazed look about her.

"As soon as you point his stuff out, we'll bring you back here," the detective was saying.

"Will they let me see him again?" she asked hopefully.

"I don't know, you can ask them," he said. The truth was, by the time she got back, he'd be in the morgue and they'd be working on someone else in that room.

"We'll take her back to where they're staying, and she'll show us the perp's stuff," the detective said to Mahoney. He turned to Joe and me. "We're gonna need the complaint number and the aided number."

"No problem," Joe said. "We'll get it when we get back to the house."

We left the hospital at 5:00. Joe and I took 34th Street back across town. We stopped at a deli on the corner of Lexington to pick up coffee. We were an hour past our meal, and we were tired now. We'd probably be at the scene for a while and needed to stay awake.

Fortieth Street was cordoned off with crime scene tape when we got there. Sergeant Hanrahan's RMP was parked in the middle of the intersection so no cars could get through. Romano was there redirecting traffic southbound on 9th Avenue. The crime scene tape would keep anyone from walking on the sidewalk and interfering with the evidence gathering.

"How's it goin', Nick?" I asked as we walked over.

"Hey Tony, Joe," he said. "Where's my coffee?"

"If we knew they pulled you off post for this, we would have gotten you some," Fiore said.

"Did the guy die here or at the hospital?"

The rookies are always preoccupied with death.

"In the ambulance; they couldn't get him back."

"Friggin' skells," he said as he shook his head.

While we have a lot of deaths in Midtown, we don't have a lot of murders. I guess murder is relative in New York, but Midtown being a commercial area, the crime is different. In places around the city that are more residential, where drugs and gangs play a part, there's more murder.

In Midtown we get a lot of robbery, burglary, scams, and other fun stuff like that. I've seen death by car accident, suicide, overdose, strokes, and heart attacks, but the ratio of death by murder isn't all that high. In the ten years I've been here, I've seen people die a thousand different ways. The skells stab and beat each other, but usually they're like the Terminator—you just can't kill them. But not tonight.

Hanrahan was talking to one of the detectives, who had on his blue windbreaker with Crime Scene plastered across the back. The other detective, in a matching jacket, was taking measurements and pictures and writing the information down on his clipboard.

The two detectives from Manhattan homicide were there with the victim's girlfriend. She was pointing to the spot where we found him on the curb, and then she pointed up toward the cardboard condos by Port Authority. The Italian detective had his hand on her elbow, and they walked up toward where the whole thing started.

Mahoney was asking Hanrahan, "Did you find the weapon?"

"No." Hanrahan shook his head. "We did a search three blocks down on 9th and up the side streets and came up negative."

The crime scene detective was branching out now, taking pictures of the area surrounding where we found the body. The other one walked up to the cardboard condos and was bagging up stuff and marking it. I was guessing it was Easy's stuff, but I guess it could have been the victim's as well.

"They should be done here within a half hour," Hanrahan said to Joe and me. "Open it up when they finish, take down all the crime scene tape, and take your meal. I'll have Romano take his meal while you guys are here."

"Sure, Boss," I said.

The detective came back with the victim's girlfriend. He put her in the car to take her back over to Bellevue. I guess the hospital was better than the cardboard box she'd be going back to.

"What's she gonna do now?" I asked Fiore.

He shrugged. "I don't know. They were homeless, she had no place to go."

"Where's her family?"

"It didn't sound like she had one," he said.

"What a waste. Stabbed in the chest 'cause of some crack-head." I shook my head. "I hope she was worth it."

Fiore didn't say anything. He knows me well enough now to let me vent.

"What I don't get is how you'd rather live on the street outside Port Authority so you can get high," I said. "Don't they want to do something with their life?"

"It probably doesn't start out that way, Tony," Fiore said. "It's a habit, like smoking or drinking. The drug has a hold on them, and they're in bondage to it."

"Yeah, Joe, all the skells on 8th Avenue are stabbing each other over a pack of Marlboros," I said.

"Okay, maybe not from cigarettes, but people are living on the street from drinking."

"And a lot of people aren't—it's their choice."

"I'm sure nobody who's living on the street from smoking crack or drinking thought that's where they'd end up." He looked at me. "You seem to think it could never happen to you because you're different than they are. And even though you say you wouldn't be in a position to be living on the street, you could have ended up the same way as that guy."

"How?"

"Drunk, in a fight over some girl. Maybe some guy breaks a beer bottle and stabs you in the chest. Didn't you say one of your uncles is doing time upstate for the same thing?" He shrugged and put his hands up in a "it could happen" gesture. "The bottom line is," he continued, "they're caught up in it. If you get down deeper into a person, you'll see there's a reason for things like that. Nobody wants to be a drunk or a crackhead—they're struggling, just like you were struggling."

I always thought it was mind over matter, but the truth is I couldn't have quit drinking without God's help. I just thought I was never that bad. I mean, I wasn't like the skells on the street, so how could I wind up like one?

"That's what happens with a lot of Christians, or so-called Christians," Joe said. "They forget where they were when they start having a relationship with God, or they never lived the way the people they call 'sinners' do, and they look down on them. Smoking crack is a big thing to them, but they forget that judging someone is just as bad, or even worse, when we're supposed to know better."

"Is that what I was doing, judging them?" I asked.

"Were you looking down on them, writing them off because they were crackheads?"

"Yeah, I guess so. But I'm better about the skells than I used to be," I said honestly.

He smiled. "I know."

At 5:30 some knucklehead yuppie tried to pick up the crime scene tape and walk through.

"Sir, you can't go in there," Joe said.

"I have to go to work," he said.

"Where do you work?" Joe asked in case it was one of the buildings within the secured area.

"Forty-first and Broadway."

"Go over to 41st and walk up," Joe said.

"But I walk this way every day," he insisted.

"Not today you don't—today you're gonna take 41st Street," I said.

He sighed loudly and shook his head, mumbling, "This is ridiculous" as he walked toward 41st Street.

"Is it me?" I asked Joe. "He sees it's a crime scene."

Joe chuckled and shook his head. "You threw his whole day off."

Sometimes I wonder how people get through life. How difficult is it to walk a block over when someone gets murdered?

At 6:30 the crime scene guys started packing up their stuff. They called over to Joe and me, "We're done here if you guys want to open this up now."

"Let me get the tape down before we open the street up," I told Joe. I walked east on 40th Street to the cardboard condos and took the tape down. I wrapped it up extension cord style as I walked back over toward Joe. I threw him a wave and he opened up the street. I'd throw the tape in the garbage at the precinct so nobody used it to make their own crime scene somewhere.

The sun was up as we drove back to the precinct, and the streets were filling up with people on their way to work.

When we walked up the steps to the precinct, McGovern was outside alone smoking a cigarette.

"Going back out?" I asked.

"No. O'Brien went home early, so I'm stuck in the cells for the rest of the tour," McGovern said.

"Why'd O'Brien leave?"

"He said he had a lot to do tomorrow, so he took lost time and caught the 1:30," he said, meaning the Long Island Railroad out of Penn Station. After 1:30 the trains get real sporadic, and O'Brien lives out in Suffolk County.

"Who's taking your sector?" I asked.

"They gave it to two rookies from the other squad."

The two detectives from Manhattan homicide were standing by the desk, talking to the lou. They seemed to know each other and were laughing at something. I went into the 124 room where the civilians do paperwork and got the complaint and aided numbers, which is the next successive number from the last complaint report. I wrote it down on a piece of paper and handed it to Mahoney, who said thanks and shook my hand, then went back to talking to the lou.

Terri Marks put us in the book for our meal and gave Fiore a wink and threw me a wave as we went downstairs. We took off our vests, shoes, and gun belts. I asked Joe about that part in the Bible about protection from lawsuits. I sat on one of the benches in the lounge and read it before I went to sleep. I added a prayer to protect me from whatever this lawsuit was about. I reminded God that he said right there in Isaiah that he would. I wasn't worried, but it was on my mind.

In recent years, lawsuits involving police violating the rights of perps have turned into an easy way for perps to get money and press coverage. The careers and lives of police officers, even those not involved, have been destroyed because their names were even mentioned in stuff like this. I knew I didn't do anything wrong, but if something happened to this guy in custody and I was even peripherally involved, it could cause a lot of trouble for me.

I tried to sleep until 9:30, when I changed into my street clothes and went upstairs to talk to the detectives about the letter I got from the Advocate's Office.

Detective Toomey was on the phone when I got there, writing something down on a piece of paper and adding the paper to the pile on her desk. She was Italian looking, with short dark hair, so I guessed Toomey was her married name. I didn't see Jack Sullivan, her partner, so I walked toward her.

"Hey, what's going on?" she asked as I approached.

"Not much, Eileen. I got a letter from the Advocate's Office. I've been named in this lawsuit, but the name isn't ringing any bells," I said.

"What's the name in the case?"

I scanned the paper. "Edwin Sharp, but you and Sullie are also listed on the lawsuit. I don't remember locking anyone up by this name." I didn't add that if the guy had been tuned up during the arrest, I would have remembered it.

"Oh, I got the same letter. You didn't lock him up, Sullie and I did." She rifled through her desk, picked up the file, and handed it to me.

I started reading through the file, but it took me a minute to realize what it was. A little over a year ago, my old partner, John Conte, and I answered a job for a larceny in the past. It was a graphic arts business over on 5th Avenue, with a side entrance on 37th Street. The owner was in at 7:00 in the morning, going over a videotape he had set up because someone was stealing computer equipment from him over the last couple of months.

On the tape he caught one of his newer employees stealing a laptop and other computer components. He said in the past two months over ten thousand dollars' worth of equipment had been stolen in small pieces. He set the camera up for a couple of days and caught the guy. On the day he called us, the employee had stolen about three grand worth of stuff the day before. The boss came in early on a Friday morning to watch the tape.

We waited until the guy came in, but his name wasn't Sharp, it was Alan Houston. I remember because John said, "Houston, we have a problem" to him when he came in and saw us there. He tried to look bewildered and innocent while denying everything until I said, "Let's go to the videotape," and the four of us watched him steal the stuff.

He choked a little then finally came clean. The owner seemed like a decent guy and just wanted his stuff back. Houston said he could get the stuff back. I think he figured if he got the owner his stuff back, he would drop the charges.

John and I took him back to the precinct and started the paperwork on the arrest. We went up to talk to the detectives about getting the stuff back, because they'd need a warrant for whoever he fenced it to.

That was the extent of my connection to the arrest. I processed him, so my name was all over the paperwork. The detectives got a warrant later on and went into this guy Sharp's apartment out in Queens. They used the Queens warrant squad to enforce the order, and apparently when they went in there, Sharp's family was home.

Sharp was suing for the way his family was traumatized by seeing their apartment searched and their husband/father arrested. He claimed he suffered loss of service because his wife won't sleep with him, his kids won't hug him, and apparently the dog cowers every time he's in the room. He felt that a cool ten million would wipe away all the trauma from their lives and they'd all be fine again.

The lawsuit didn't mention the five thousand dollars' worth of stolen equipment that was recovered from the apartment or the fact that the cops could have locked up the wife right along with him and sent her children to child protective services. I'm sure everyone involved didn't want to make this any worse for the kids.

"You believe this?" I said to Toomey. "He's got the stolen merchandise in his apartment and he's suing us."

"Loss of service," she said, laughing. "We enforced a warrant. If he didn't want to get locked up in front of his family, he shouldn't have stolen merchandise in the apartment with his family. Where do these people get off?"

"Why would a lawyer even take a case like this?" I asked. Talk about frivolous lawsuits.

"Because the police department doesn't need any more bad press, and sometimes they'll settle on something like this to keep it out of the papers. Don't worry about this, Tony, you weren't even there. I'll talk to the Advocate's Office. If they need you, they'll give you a call, but I don't think they will," Toomey said.

Sullie was on his way in, so I thanked her, stopped to talk to him for a couple of minutes, and left the precinct by 10:00.

*T*he sun was warm, with a nice spring breeze blowing as I walked out to my truck. It's a black 1999 four-wheel drive Nissan Pathfinder, not that I ever use the four-wheel drive, but it sounded good at the time.

I drove down the West Side toward the Brooklyn Battery Tunnel. Rush hour was over, and I made it through Brooklyn and over the Verrazzano Bridge without a hitch. The usually murky waters along South Beach sparkled in the sunlight, giving them a deceptively clean look.

My otherwise easy commute was ruined by a garbage truck on Lincoln Avenue that stopped to pick up pails every ten feet, backing up traffic for three blocks. I cut down Freeborn Street and across Greely to get home.

I now live in the basement of a white brick ranch, an older home that has a double plot of land. I used to live in an old colonial in Shore Acres, which is on the Narrows of New York Bay. The house was sold last September, the final legal salvo in the war between my parents, Vince and Marilyn Cavalucci. They've been divorced for years, and the house was the last legal tie they had.

A couple of years ago, my brother, Vinny, and I renovated the house for my mother. I think she expected Vinny to buy it, but I was the one with my eye on it. Once the house was finished, my father and Marie took my mother to court and a judge forced her to sell it.

Vinny helped me get the apartment here for seven hundred bucks a month including utilities, which, let me tell you, is a steal.

My landlord, Alfonse, was outside tending to his garden when I pulled up. "What a day, is this beautiful or what?" he said. He put his hands out and looked up at the sky.

I smiled and shook his hand. "Yeah, it's a beauty. What are you planting today?" Every week or so he added something new to his garden as the spring progressed. He had uncovered the fig trees about a week before, and I could see small buds on the figs and the grapevines.

"I put some lettuce and arugula there." He pointed to a section that already had what looked like escarole growing. "I planted the Roma tomatoes." He pointed to the tomato section, where he grew several varieties. There were beets and beans, eggplant, zucchini, peas, string beans, and barlotto beans.

We talked for a couple of minutes about the garden and the grapes.

"You garden, Tony? You seem to know a lot about it," Alfonse said.

"My grandfather always had a garden, down in South Beach," I said.

"Where in South Beach?" he asked.

"Off Olympia Boulevard on Wentworth Avenue." It was actually the house my grandfather grew up in, and then he and my grandmother took it over and raised my father and my aunt and uncle. My great-grandfather came over from

Italy and always raised chickens and rabbits for food at their house in South Beach.

He kept asking me questions about my grandparents. Being from Italy, Alfonse loved hearing about anyone who came from the mother country.

"They raised rabbits?" His face lit up. "My mother made the most delicious rabbit with an orange sauce." He kissed his fingers. "You can't get that anymore. Does your grandmother still make it?"

"She hasn't made it in a long time, but I'm sure she still knows how to do it." I hoped not—the only time I ate it, I threw up after they told me it was rabbit.

"Did he make his own wine?" he asked.

"Yeah, wine and Strega," I said, remembering being little and my father and grandfather laughing as I tried to keep a straight face and pretend I liked it. The Strega was like 90 proof, and the bottle used to have sugarcane in it. I couldn't have been more than seven or eight years old and they were giving me homemade wine and Strega—I guess the alcohol problem later on was a no-brainer.

I said good-bye to Alfonse and went downstairs to my apartment. It was cool and dark; I keep the blinds closed so I can sleep during the day. Now that we turned the clocks ahead, I would open them later to get some light. I had no messages on my answering machine. Michele's a teacher out in Shirley, Long Island, and sometimes I'll hear from her during the day if her class has art or music and they're out of the classroom.

I grabbed half of a meatball parmigiana hero left over from last night, still wrapped in foil on a paper plate from the pizzeria. I was debating whether to eat it cold or waste the energy popping it in the microwave, when the phone rang.

"Hey," Michele said when I answered.

"Hey yourself, where are you?"

"At school. My class is in music, I can talk for a couple of minutes," she said.

"What's up?"

She chuckled. "I wanted to finish our discussion from last night."

I love Michele like crazy, and I find her good manners amusing.

"It was a fight, babe—okay, maybe not a fight, but definitely an argument," I said.

"Things are getting out of hand, Tony. I think we need to back off a little," she said quietly.

"We didn't do anything wrong, Michele," I said, probably a little sharp.

"Yes we did—we're putting ourselves in a position where we could compromise our decision on staying—" she searched for a word, "from being intimate until we get married."

"After that sermon I heard on Sunday, I'm rethinking that decision," I said.

"How could you say that?" She actually raised her voice. "Pastor was saying that anyone you are intimate with, biblically you're married to."

"That's right, so basically I'm married to everyone but you. I figure we could get married now, you know, biblically, and make it legal in November at the wedding," I said, warming up to the idea.

"Tony, that was *not* what he meant," she said dryly.

"Michele, what if we wait till we're legally married and the whole thing's a dud? I think we need a few practice runs, then when we know we're good to go—"

She cut me off. "Tony," she warned, "we've discussed this before—"

I heard a commotion on her end of the phone, her class coming back into the room.

"They're back early," she said. "We'll finish this later."

"I'll call you about eight," I said.

"I love you," she said quietly.

"I love you too."

I've been spending a lot of time out at Michele's house. We had met with an architect and had plans drawn up for an addition on the house. We started the construction, adding a second floor and opening up the downstairs of the house. The upstairs has three bedrooms, one of them a master suite complete with a jacuzzi in the bathroom and a fireplace. It's still a mess from all the work we're doing, but the contractor is good and it should be finished and ready to paint by July.

The way we did it was I paid for the addition with the money I got from my parents when they sold their house. I had been using my own money to renovate my parents' house, figuring I'd either put it toward the house if I bought it from them or they'd pay me back when they sold the house.

Michele transferred the title of her house into both our names. I didn't make her do it, but she wanted the house to belong to the two of us. Now every time I'm at the house, I feel like I'm home, that feeling you can never get from living in an apartment. It only comes from having your name on a deed and having a lawn to mow.

The thing Michele was talking about happened Sunday night. We were getting so caught up in all the excitement of building the house and getting married that things started to get a little heated. We didn't do anything bad, nothing I hadn't done behind the handball courts at the park on Tompkins Avenue, but Michele got upset about it.

Stevie was asleep downstairs and we were up on the second floor, walking through the rooms under construction. Somehow we wound up wrestling and rolling around on the plywood floor of what would soon be our bedroom, and I got a little carried away. She did too but came to her senses before anything could happen.

I was half kidding about getting married in the biblical sense; honestly I'm having trouble seeing that there's anything wrong with it. I'm waiting out of respect for her and for God, but sometimes my heart isn't in it.

I heated up the sandwich and washed it down with a soda. I charged up my cell phone and grabbed my Bible before climbing into bed. I set my alarm clock for 7:00 and picked up the Bible.

The next thing I knew, my alarm was blasting, and I knocked my Bible onto the floor when I hit the snooze button. I hit it three times before dragging myself out of bed at 7:27. I took a shower, shaved, and got dressed before I went out to the kitchen to call Michele.

The light was blinking on my answering machine, and it showed I had two messages. I had my door closed, but I must have been in such a deep sleep that I didn't even hear the phone ring.

"Tony, it's Grandma," a voice said after a couple of seconds. "It's about four o'clock. I want you to come over to go over some stuff for the party. I made chicken florentine and spaghetti marinara tonight, so come for dinner."

I debated whether or not I should go. I'd been avoiding Grandma, but there was nothing in my fridge and I love her marinara sauce. The machine beeped, and Denise's voice came over the line.

"Tony, it's Denise," my sister said. "I'm at Grandma's; she wanted me to come and see the centerpieces she got for your engagement party. Um," she cleared her throat, "they're definitely interesting, but you probably need to see them for yourself. Try to stop by before you leave for work."

I didn't care what the centerpieces looked like. I called Michele, who sounded stressed when she answered on the third ring.

"Hey, everything alright?" I asked.

"Stevie's ear hurts and he's running a fever," she said. "He's been cranky since I got home, and his fever's up over 102."

"Did you give him Tylenol?" Other than giving Tylenol, I was clueless what to do with a sick kid.

"Just now, but he has to see the doctor. I don't want to wait—the last time this happened, he perforated his eardrum."

"When did that happen?" I asked, not remembering it.

"It was when I first met you; I don't know if I told you about it."

"Is that serious?"

"The doctor did an ear test and his hearing is fine, but I'd rather it doesn't happen again. I called the doctor, and I'm waiting for him to call me back. I'm hoping he'll call something in tonight, and then I'll get someone to take Stevie in the morning." She sighed. "I can't take off tomorrow."

"If you want, I'll bang the day and come out in the morning and take him," I said.

"No, my mother can take him. Save that for when we really need it. I just hate for him to be sick when I'm not here," Michele said, and to be honest, I hated for him to be sick when I wasn't there either.

"Can I talk to him?" I asked.

She put him on the phone but he sounded miserable, so I only stayed on for a minute.

"I'll leave my cell phone on. Let me know if you need me to come out there," I said before hanging up. We didn't pick up the conversation we were having this morning, which was fine with me. Stevie being sick was more important than that. I didn't mention that I was going over to Grandma's. Michele was aggravated enough without worrying that my family would be poisoning me against her.

I packed my bag for work and grabbed my cell phone and a clean uniform out of my closet.

The sun was just starting to go down and the sky was clear with streaks of pink as I drove up Clove Road. The parking lot of my grandmother's six-floor, rent-controlled apartment building was pretty full. The property was taken over by a building management company in January, and they started charging tenants for parking spaces. My grandmother didn't drive, so she had no spot. I parked in 4A's spot. I knew 4A didn't have a car but still had a parking spot, and I wondered if the building managers were making good on their posted threats to tow cars unauthorized to park there.

I buzzed 1C from the lobby, looking up into the camera in case Grandma had her TV tuned to the lobby station.

The station lets the tenants see who's buzzing them before giving anyone access to the building. When they first installed it, we all sat around Grandma's living room watching everyone who came through the doors. Until people realized there was a camera there, they sniffed their armpits, picked their noses, and pulled at their pants that were riding up.

The door buzzed, and cooking smells hit me as I entered the lobby. My grandmother's apartment is three doors to the right off the lobby, and she was out in the hallway in her housedress and slippers when I turned the corner. I could hear her TV blasting and wished for the thousandth time that she'd get a hearing aid.

She caught me in a bear hug and her hair spray stuck to the side of my face as she pulled away, like it always does.

"You never come see me anymore," she said, making me feel guilty. "You're losing weight."

"I'm trying to." I patted my stomach.

"You're too skinny," she scolded.

"I'm a hundred and eighty-five pounds, Grandma," I reasoned.

She shook her head. "I knew you lost weight!"

Denise was setting a place for me at the table, and I didn't realize until I came all the way into the room that my father was there. I should have realized he was there by the way Denise was dressed—she does it to provoke him. She wore jeans slung low on her hips, a belly button ring, and a short white T-shirt. Her long dark hair was ironed straight, and her blue eyes were accented with black eyeliner.

"Hey, Denise." I kissed her cheek. "Hi, Dad," I said.

He was also wearing jeans, but his were with a tight black shirt and work boots. He had his arms folded over his chest, and he was watching *Everybody Loves Raymond*. He looked at me and nodded and turned back to the TV.

I looked at Denise, who smiled and arched an eyebrow. I gave her a "What's going on?" look, hoping I wasn't going to regret coming here.

"Come and eat," Grandma said, her answer to any uncomfortable situation. I looked around the apartment. The bathroom door was open, and the room was dark.

"Where's Marie?" I asked, not that I cared. It was more curiosity.

"She's in *Florida* with her sick mother." Denise accented the word *Florida* with a smile. "Isn't it sad that her mother's sick?"

My father looked at Denise, his eyes deadly. "Since when do you care where Marie is?"

Denise ignored him and said, "What a good daughter, going all the way to *Florida* to take care of her mother."

I looked back and forth between the two of them, feeling the muscles in the back of my neck bunch. I didn't care that

Marie was gone, but Denise obviously knew that Marie was somewhere she shouldn't have been.

My father took a similar trip right before he left my mother for Marie. He said he had to go to *Florida* with one of his buddies from work whose father was dying. They had to clean out the house and transfer him to a nursing home in Tampa. My mother saw my father's credit card bill a couple of weeks later and for the first time in her life opened his mail. She saw the charges for two plane tickets and a week's stay at a resort in St. Maarten.

"That's enough, Denise," Grandma warned. "Where Marie is doesn't concern you."

Denise ignored her too.

"Will she be back in time for the party?" I asked. Marie not at my engagement party would be the only gift I'd ask for.

"She'll be here; she's flying in on Friday," Grandma said as she put out a small platter of chicken over sautéed spinach and a plate of spaghetti with marinara sauce. She filled a wooden salad bowl with lettuce, tomato, and olives with oil and vinegar and gave it to me with half a loaf of Italian bread.

"I can't eat all this," I said, taking a bite of the chicken. "I want to lose some weight before the wedding."

"Whose wedding?" my father asked, still watching TV.

"My wedding."

"Your brother is getting married first, and if you had any respect you'd let him and Christie have their time. Instead, you make everyone go through the expense for another wedding a month later. I don't know what the big rush is," he said as he shook his head in aggravation.

That's what I love about my family, anything could set them off. I put my fork down and silently counted to ten.

I looked over at him. "If it's a problem for anyone, they don't have to go."

He waved his hand at me. "How are they not gonna go? Do you think your grandmother has the money for two weddings in one year? It's bad enough she's paying for the engagement party, and who knows if Denise will even have a job by the time the wedding rolls around."

"I didn't ask Grandma to pay for an engagement party, Dad. I don't even *want* an engagement party. I didn't ask anyone for anything," I said, running my hands over my face to calm down.

"Don't worry about me, Tony," Denise said. "I wouldn't miss your wedding for anything. And nobody told Grandma to throw an engagement party, she did that on her own. If she keeps wearing her red underwear when she plays the lotto, she can pay for the wedding too."

I looked at my father. He was staring at Denise with his face set in anger. Even though he was mad, I could see it was bothering him that Denise wouldn't talk to him. I could see Denise was happy about it, and I wondered for the millionth time why I couldn't have a normal family.

My father gave me a hard look and went back to watching TV. I thought about when we were here Christmas Eve and he talked for the first time in his life about being in Vietnam.

I was born on the Marine base in West Cherry Point a couple of weeks before he shipped out to Vietnam. It was during the worst part of the war, late 1969 and 1970. I wanted to believe that whatever it was about him was a result of being in Vietnam, but the atrocities of war didn't seem to bother him as much as me and my sister did.

He was in Vietnam at the time when we had the most casualties and the country here at home despised our efforts there. He didn't keep in touch with anyone from the war and never played up the fact that he was there. Everything I know about Vietnam I've seen in movies or read in books. I never associated my father with the Vietnam vets—I just couldn't conjure up a picture of my father smoking a joint and listening to Jimi Hendrix while firing away at the Vietcong.

I'd like to think it was the war that hardened him and not something in our bloodline he might have passed down to me. I prayed to God right there that I wouldn't turn out to be anything like my father. I never wanted to feel anger and resentment toward Stevie; I love him and I always want to be close to him.

"Eat, Tony," Grandma said. "I'll get one of the centerpieces and show you."

I started to eat again while Grandma went into her bedroom. Denise got her pocketbook, took out a piece of paper, and started writing something down. She pushed the paper toward me, and I read "Bobby Egan's off this week too!!!"

"Not now, Denise," I said. I ripped up the piece of paper and got up to throw it in the garbage. I'm sure this was adding to why my father was so mad. It shouldn't surprise him, Marie's just sticking with whatever worked for her before. If she did this to her last husband, why should my father be any different? Marie was making a fool out of him, and I made the decision right there that I was gonna tell him. It wouldn't be tonight; I'd go see him alone.

"Here it is!" Grandma announced, carrying a ceramic birdbath about the size of a basketball. It was red, with bluebirds and flowers on it, gaudy as anything.

"Wow," I said, nodding.

"That's not the best part." Denise's smile was devious. "Show him, Grandma."

"It's a fountain!" Grandma said, flipping the switch on the bottom. It made the sound urine does when it hits the toilet, followed by birds chirping. "It's battery operated, double A's." Like I needed to know what kind of batteries it used.

"That's something," I said for lack of anything better to say.

"And it's red, to help keep the *malokya* away," Denise added.

"What is *wrong* with you?" my father yelled at her. "You don't know when to shut your mouth!" He shook his head.

Denise ignored him again. "Tony, did you know Grandma thinks Michele put the horns on her Christmas Eve and made the new building managers raise her rent?" Denise held up her hands. "Huh? I think you should know the extremes the family is going to so your wicked fianceé doesn't blast us all into oblivion with her *malokya* superpowers."

"Is that true, Grandma?" I asked quietly.

"Yes, Tony, they raised me the day after Christmas," she said quietly.

"No," I said patiently, "is it true you think Michele had something to do with it?"

She shrugged. "Do you think it's a coincidence that she left here mad Christmas Eve and two days later my rent got raised?" She looked like she was actually waiting for an answer.

"One has nothing to do with the other," I insisted.

She didn't look convinced. "I don't know, Tony. After I started wearing red underwear and the two horns, I've been winning money from the lottery. I won another two hundred last week," she said as she pointed her finger at me, "and I know the cashier didn't like me and was putting the horns on me. Lucy Dellatore from the dry cleaners can tell when someone is putting the horns on you, and she said she never seen it so bad with me. So don't try and tell me it doesn't work!" She was slapping the back of her right hand into the palm of her left hand as she talked.

"I'm gonna go to work now," I said, getting up from the table.

"You didn't finish your dinner," Grandma said, raising her voice.

"I'm not hungry anymore." I put my napkin next to my plate, stood up, and kissed my grandmother's cheek.

"Ya see, Denise." Grandma turned on her. "You always have to start trouble."

Denise tried to look innocent.

"Grandma, did you get those red"—I gestured with my hand—"bird things because you thought they'd keep Michele from putting the horns on you?"

"Tony, I didn't mean it that way. Denise should learn to keep her mouth shut." She shot Denise a look.

Denise smiled.

"Don't blame Denise," I said as Denise's eyebrows shot up.

"Walk me out?" I asked Denise. "Go see Dr. DelGrecco, Grandma. I'm sure they have medication for this kind of thing."

"That's not funny, Tony," Grandma said, putting her hands on her hips.

"I know."

Denise grabbed her pocketbook and followed me out the door.

"What's with you?" I said once we were in the hallway.

"I'm sick of all the two-facedness in this family—smile in your face, stab you in the back," she spat.

"I'm telling Dad about Marie and Bobby Egan," I said, holding the door open for her.

"Go ahead, he won't believe you," she said.

"Why wouldn't he believe me?" I asked, annoyed.

"Because he doesn't want to believe it, but he knows. Plus he knows we hate Marie, and he'll use that," she said.

"You think he knows? How?"

"Trust me, he knows. Deep down they always know."

"I thought I told you to stop stalking Marie. Why would you call to check on Bobby Egan?" I said.

She shrugged. "Just to see if my instincts are right."

"Your instincts are right—Marie's a snake, and we've already established that she's cheating on Dad." I kissed her cheek. "Stay out of it. I'm telling Dad after the party on Sunday."

"Be careful tonight," she said.

"I will."

Traffic was backed up on the Staten Island Expressway, so I went through Jersey, taking the turnpike into the Lincoln Tunnel. I had left Grandma's at nine, and even with backtracking on the expressway and going through Jersey, it was only five to ten.

I parked on the sidewalk on 36th Street and threw my new yellow parking plaque in my windshield. I wasn't worried about getting a ticket; our precinct self-patrols 35th and 36th streets between 9th and Dyer, so the DOT can't tag me.

Rice and Beans pulled up in an RMP, and I talked to them for about twenty minutes before going into the precinct to change. I went down to the locker room and changed into my uniform and spent another twenty minutes cleaning out all the crap in the bottom of my locker. I tossed useless paperwork, old thank-you letters from the district attorney's office letting me know how a perp pled on a case or how much time they got. I threw out old Polaroids of perps, a letter from a woman I gave a ticket to asking me out, and arm patches from cops around the country who visited the city and sent me stuff from their commands. I found a birthday card from two years ago from my old girlfriend Kim, saying we'll be together forever, and a camera a perp asked me not to voucher and promised to pick up but never did. I saved pictures of myself and other cops from my drinking days, some in the bar on 9th Avenue, others around the precinct. I didn't want to throw them out—these were guys I worked with, and once in a while one of them dies and I wish I saved the picture.

I finally went upstairs to the desk at five to eleven. Vince Puletti, the old-timer who runs the radio room, was talking to Sergeant Hanrahan. I got a cup of coffee and went back outside to smoke a cigarette on the front steps.

The four-to-twelve cops were starting to come in, standing outside smoking and talking like we're not supposed to do.

"Tony, did you hear about O'Brien?" Jimmy Murphy, who works the Madison Square Garden detail, asked me. I was on the bottom step and had to tilt my head back to look up at him. He's about six feet tall, blue eyes, Irish looking.

"What about him?"

"I heard he got jammed up," he said.

"How?" Jammed up means suspended, gun and shield taken, usually IAB—or the rat squad from internal affairs, as we call them—is involved.

"I don't know," Murph said with a shrug. "I just heard he got jammed up."

When I saw O'Brien last night he didn't look like anything was wrong, then I remembered that McGovern said he left early. It could be bogus, half the stories you hear around here are lies anyway.

"How's your sister?" he asked. Murph had met Denise at a hockey game last December. He was working his detail at the Garden and moved Denise and me from a couple of nosebleed tickets she got to behind Montreal's bench. Then he showed off some more by taking Denise back to the locker room for some Ranger autographs.

"She's fine," I said.

"Tell her I said hello," he said. The last time he asked me to set him up with her, I was in no mood for anyone from work meeting my family. I insulted him by telling him I'd knock him out if he went near my sister. The truth was he was divorced and he was Irish, two strikes already against him as far as the family's concerned. Plus he was a nice guy and Denise would probably eat him alive—the type she usually goes for are yo-yos. Sal Valente, a neighbor of ours growing up, was the last guy she dated. He's a real nice guy, but then he dumped her and went back to his psychotic ex-wife.

I finished my cigarette and went back inside. Vince Puletti was in the radio room, and he gave me a "come here" signal with his hand.

"What's up, Vince?" I said, shaking his hand. Vince was big, beefy, and bald. He was also the source for gossip in the precinct. If it happened, he knew about it.

He grabbed his belt loops and looked around. "O'Brien got jammed up today," he said quietly. He was talking to me but looking around the room to make sure no one heard him.

"That's what Murph said. What happened?"

"He left early this morning," Vince said.

"I know, McGovern told me he had a lot to do today."

Vince nodded and took a deep breath. "He caught his wife in the sack with another guy." He shook his head and looked sympathetic, but I'm sure he was loving this.

"Who's the guy?"

He shrugged. "Supposedly some guy she met online."

"She told him that?" I asked, skeptical.

"I guess him holding a gun to her head made her talkative." He put his hands out in a "don't ask me" gesture. "I don't know what he was thinking," Vince added.

"He's thinking he caught his wife cheating on him—what else was he gonna do?" I said. "She's lucky he didn't shoot the both of them."

"And blow a million-dollar pension?" Vince shook his head. "Tony, it's not worth it."

Vince lives for his pension. He could have retired ten years ago, but he's still packing it away in his pension fund. I've met old-timers like him. They leave the job, have a heart attack the next day, and never collect a dime of their pension. The guys who I came on with have a saying, "not a day over twenty," meaning the day you make twenty years, you're out of here.

When Fiore came up from the locker room, I told him about O'Brien. He had already heard about it on the train in, but he didn't go into detail.

The muster room was almost full now, with a low buzz running through it about O'Brien. Heads were shaking and McGovern, his partner, was surrounded.

"What happened?" I asked him.

"I talked to him this morning, it's not what everyone is saying," he said like he'd already told it ten times.

"Did he think something was going on, is that why he went home?"

He shrugged. "Well, he'd noticed she's been on the computer a lot lately, but that's not why he went home. He's finishing his basement and wanted it done for his son's confirmation next week. He was quiet going into the bedroom, he thought everyone was sleeping—"

"She had a guy in her bed with her kids in the house?" I snapped.

McGovern called her a couple of names that I thought were on the money and said, "After that she calls the cops and says he held the gun to her head and then let off a round when the guy tried to run out."

"Did he let off a round?" It wouldn't look good discharging his gun with his kids in the house.

"No, and he gave them his gun. I'm sure they'll test it and see it wasn't fired. Once they know she lied about him letting off a round, they're not going to believe he held the gun to her head either," McGovern said.

"Did he?" I asked.

He shrugged with a smile.

"He lives in Suffolk, right?" I asked, thinking that Fiore knew a couple of Suffolk cops and maybe they could help O'Brien out.

"Yeah, he actually knew one of the cops who answered the job, so he's not really worried. I was gonna take off tonight, but he said he'd be staying with his brother. I'll talk to him in the morning," he said.

"Tell him I was asking for him, and tell him if he needs anything, a place to stay, just let me know."

"Will do, Tony."

Nick Romano and Rooney had their heads together, and when I walked over to them Romano gave me a "come here" gesture and pulled a name plate that said MASSAGE out of his pocket.

"Where'd you get that?" I asked.

"From a hotel up on 44th Street."

"What's it for?" I asked.

"Decorations for the inspector's door." He and Rooney laughed. He walked over to the inspector's door, which is behind the muster room, slid out the inspector's nameplate, and slid in the "Massage" sign. "Rooney has the rest of the stuff, it's hysterical."

Rooney got Romano in a headlock. "Good work, buddy!"

Rooney was about to show me whatever he had when Sergeant Hanrahan called, "Attention to the roll call."

"The color of the day is white," he said. He gave out the sectors and the foot posts and a description of an eighty-year-old male white who was missing.

"His name is James McGoughey," he said, but it was pronounced "Magooey."

74

He smirked and waited until the ranks got it out of their system.

"Is that Mr. Magoo?"

"Sarge, that was a male white, three feet tall, bulbous nose, wears Coke bottle glasses and a fedora hat and cane?" Rooney asked.

"Last seen driving backwards through the Lincoln Tunnel," McGovern yelled.

"He was last seen yesterday at Penn Station," Hanrahan continued. "He wandered away from his family. He has Alzheimer's and no foul play is suspected. He was last seen wearing a short-sleeved, blue button-down shirt and black pants. Keep an eye out for him. If you see him, hold on to him and give me a call on the radio."

We wrote it down in our memo books.

"Tonight's the elephant walk down 34th Street," Hanrahan said. He was talking about Ringling Bros. and Barnum & Bailey Circus. Every year they make the rounds, first out in Jersey at the Meadowlands, then to the Nassau Coliseum in Long Island. From the coliseum they take the animals by train into the Long Island Railroad yards in Queens and walk them through the Midtown Tunnel and down 34th Street to Madison Square Garden.

Hanrahan finished up with, "I just want to give you a heads-up. They should be coming into the train yards around midnight and coming down 34th Street after that. There should be a detail handling it, but there'll probably be protestors crying about how the animals are treated, so keep an eye out."

We grabbed Romano and stopped for coffee on the corner of 39th Street. Fiore went into the deli, and Romano was in the backseat looking like he'd been hitting the sauce again.

"Out with Rooney this morning, Nick?" I asked him.

"For a little while. We were working on the picture for the inspector's door," he was saying as he put his head back against the seat and closed his eyes.

"I used to drink a lot with Rooney," I said, looking at him in the rearview mirror.

"What's your point, Tony?" he mumbled.

"My point is I was someone to drink with, and so are you. If you didn't go to the bar, Rooney would find someone else to hang out with."

He still had his eyes closed. "I'll be gone soon and he'll have to find someone else." He opened one eye.

"What about you—will you find someone else to drink with?"

"I won't be drinking as much once I'm in FD; I'll be too busy," he said.

"Busy doing what? You think they don't drink in the fire-houses?"

He shrugged. "I'm sure they do." He met my eyes in the mirror. "I'm not you, Tony—I'm not an alcoholic, and I don't need to find God because I don't like the way my life turned out."

"Sure you are, you're just like me," I said calmly. "You're alone, and your personal life is in shambles. Your girlfriend left you, and you don't live with your daughter." I was counting out on my fingers for effect. "And you go to the bar with Rooney in the morning so you're too drunk to look at how much your life sucks."

"Thanks, Tony, I feel much better now," he said dryly. He rolled down the window and lit a cigarette.

"You know what, Nick? I wish someone had talked to me the way Joe and I try to talk to you. It would have saved me a lot of trouble," I said.

"Maybe I want trouble. Maybe I don't want to go to church on Sunday and suck up to someone who didn't give a crap [I'm editing] about me and let my father get shot in the face when I was ten years old." He turned his head to look at the window, his eyes staring at the ground. "And if God's so almighty, then how come he couldn't do anything about it?" He swung his eyes up to mine again in the mirror. "Huh? How come I have a daughter that I don't live with 'cause her mother's a friggin' slut? Nothing to say, Tony?"

"You better duck when you say something like that, Nick," I said. "Don't be blaming God because you got some girl pregnant or because some lowlife shot your father. People are accountable for their own actions. Anyway, I'm not God's lawyer. If you need to know about something he did or didn't do, why are you talking to me? Ask him yourself."

"I'm not talking to him," Nick said sullenly.

"Not talking to who?" Fiore said, getting in the car. He

handed Nick his coffee and put the other two in the cup holders.

"Nobody," Nick mumbled.

We were quiet on the ride up to 44th and 8th. "Can you pick me up for my meal?" Romano asked.

"Sure. You want us to sit with you while you drink your coffee?" Fiore asked.

"No thanks, I've already had my lecture for the day," he said as he slammed the door.

Joe looked amused. "You lecturing him, Tony?"

"I was trying to talk to him, he's hungover again."

He nodded.

"What?"

"Nothing," he laughed. "I think it's nice you're trying to help him."

"He don't want my help—he's mad. He reminded me of myself when my life was in the toilet. He said if God is so powerful, how come he couldn't stop his father from getting shot?" I shrugged. "It's a valid question."

"Don't feel like you need to have an answer for him, he's gotta go to God about it," Fiore said as I drove over to Broadway. We didn't have any jobs yet, so I parked near the corner of Broadway and 34th Street.

It was 11:50, and a small crowd had already gathered. There were about twenty people on the corners of both Broadway and 6th Avenue where they almost intersect at 34th Street. Nothing stood out about the crowd to make me think they were waiting for the elephants to walk by; they could just be hanging out.

"I guess the Pirates knew there'd be a crowd," Joe said, nodding his head toward the southeast corner of Broadway and 34th.

They were standing opposite the entrance to the subway station. They're not usually out this late, and they were preaching without their usual microphones.

"I've never seen them down this far. They're usually up on 7th Avenue between 42nd and 45th streets," I said.

Over the years there's been all kinds of street preachers in Times Square, some legit, some whackos. The legit ones mean well; they're down in the trenches trying to help the down-trodden. Some of the storefront types have signs that say "All Welcome." Some offer food, shelter, or prayer.

For the most part the whack jobs are harmless, just strange. Some preach on the sidewalk with something in front of them for people to toss money into. Others mumble about the devil and the end of the world or yell things out that nobody understands, but not these guys.

The Pirates, as we call them, are a group of hate preachers. I don't know what religion they are, but they use their constitutional rights to religious freedom to spew their poison at people walking by on the street. They dress all in black almost like Ali Baba, but they're not Arabic. Black parachute pants, black shirts with the sleeves cut off at the shoulders, and black leather bandannas tied around their heads. They usually have a sound system set up and stand militant style around the grand poo-bah, who stands on a small platform, dressed in white.

The lead guy, in a robe and headpiece, spouts out his anti-government/anticop/antieverything garbage. He blabs his conspiracy theories and makes threats of murder and destruction, inciting the people as they walk by.

What surprises me is that some people actually stand there and listen. Some look uncomfortable and others get angry, like this guy in a Yankee hat walking by with his kid.

"Why are you doing this?" he yelled at them. "You don't even know what you're talking about!" He was staring at the guy in white, and three of the Pirates in black took a step toward him and folded their arms to intimidate him.

The guy in the Yankee hat shook his head and started walking away. Someone yelled "Psycho!" as they passed our car, and the leader started after them. He saw Joe and me in the RMP and stopped. He stared at us, thinking we were watching him, which we were. He started walking toward us in slow, deliberate steps. His Pirate paesanos were watching this and came closer.

Joe's face was blank as he watched the guy approach his side of the car.

"What are you looking at?" he said contemptuously to Joe.

"Just making sure the peace is kept," Joe said, his voice even.

"There'll be no peace," he said ominously.

I saw red. "Are you threatening us?" I said, leaning toward Joe's side of the car.

Joe stopped me with his hand. "There'll be peace as long as I'm here," Fiore said, taking a sip of his coffee.

"We're praying you die," he said to Fiore. Then he leaned in and smiled at me, and I saw his eyes. They were green like a cat's, sinister looking. "We're praying you all die."

Joe smiled now and looked him in the eye. "He who has been born of God keeps himself, and the wicked one does not touch him. You can pray all you want—no weapon formed against me shall prosper," he said.

I guess the guy had no comeback for that. He straightened up and stared at us for a second or two before walking away. He walked a couple of steps, then turned and glanced back at us with a confused look on his face and continued on.

"What was that about?" I asked, confused.

"Just letting him know who's in charge," Fiore said.

"I know that one about no weapon shall prosper, but what was the other thing you said?" I thought it was pretty good in case I ever got into something with the Pirates again.

"It's in 1 John," Fiore said. "We know that whoever is born of God does not sin; but he who has been born of God keeps himself, and the wicked one does not touch him."

"What's with his eyes? They were freaky," I said.

"They're contacts, he does it to scare people," Joe said with a shrug, unimpressed.

"How do they call themselves preachers? They're the exact opposite of what God is. He's love, and all they talk about is hate and death," I said.

"That's why no one but the real nut jobs listen to them," Joe said.

"Yeah, but that's what makes them dangerous."

The Pirates preached for about another ten minutes, but the crowd was ignoring them now, so they packed up their stuff and went down into the subway.

About ten after twelve, the first Ringling Bros. and Barnum & Bailey truck came down 34th Street. The crowd got excited and moved up to the curb and into the street to see if the elephants were coming down. After a couple of minutes, they went back to hanging out when nothing else came down the street.

About fifteen minutes later, the truck came from Madison Square Garden and went back toward the Midtown tunnel. Then the circus trucks started coming every couple of minutes down 34th Street—the trains must have come into the railroad yard.

"We should have brought the kids," Fiore said. "They would love to see the elephants." Fiore has three kids, two boys and a baby girl.

"Stevie couldn't come anyway. He's sick, got an ear infection."

"I hate when the kids are sick, especially ear infections—the kids are miserable."

"Yeah, Stevie sounded like he was in pain."

A small truck with a white cylinder on it pulled up and started watering the planters around Herald Square. It looked like a miniature fuel truck with WATER written in black letters on the side. Normally I wouldn't have noticed it, but I was sitting there with nothing to do. The planters had small shrubs with yellow tulips around them, the only sign of spring in Midtown Manhattan. The truck had two guys, and one stood sanitation style on the back footboard, holding on to a handle. He would hop off, grab a hose, and water the plants as the truck made its way down Herald Square.

It was a great night to be outside, warm and clear. A block over to my left, the top of the Empire State Building glowed in red with a white antenna.

There were more people out now, standing along 34th Street but concentrated on the corners.

At ten to one we started to see red and blue flashing lights reflecting off the storefronts on 34th Street.

"I think they're coming now," Joe said, getting out of the car. He walked to the corner of 34th Street and Broadway and looked down toward the East Side. He waved me over, and I pulled the car up just shy of the crosswalk that cuts off Broadway. I got out and lit a cigarette, leaning against the hood of the RMP.

The crowd started to step out into 34th Street to see them coming. The street had been closed off in both directions at 7th Avenue, so they didn't have to worry about walking out into traffic.

Two unmarked police cars, one in the eastbound lane, one

in the westbound lane, were whooping their horns and had the red bubbles flashing to force the people back onto the sidewalk. People were putting their kids on their shoulders, and I could hear the rise in the crowd as the parade started.

Bello the Clown, dressed in his showduds and sporting a six-inch blond flattop haircut, was riding the lead elephant. He was their biggest elephant, wearing a red headpiece that said "The Greatest Show on Earth."

Animal activists protesting the circus were running on the sidewalks on either side of the street alongside Bello and the elephant. They had that way about them that thumbs their nose at authority. A lot of them were young updated versions of the sixties protestors. They were holding signs that said "Cruelty to Animals," and they chanted, "They hurt animals!" while chasing Bello.

Bello, to give him credit, didn't let it faze him. He smiled at the crowd, pointing at the people and saying, "Thank you, thank you for coming."

The protestors could only get the crowd's attention for a second before they dismissed them and went back to waving at Bello and the elephant. The crowd was cheering now, yelling, "Bello, Bello."

Photographers were on us now, running and trying to get a picture of Bello, their press passes hanging from their necks.

The other elephants followed a small ways back from Bello. They were cute. They walked in one line, some holding the tail of the elephant in front of them with their trunks. Some had straw on their backs, looking like there was a straw fight in the train car.

The thing that hit me was the smell, like the worst room in the zoo. Kids were making faces and holding their noses as the line of elephants, eight in all, walked past. They were followed by five brown horses being walked by a male and female in street clothes. Next were ten white horses in headdresses. Surrounded by four trainers, they marched in pairs, doing a military-type left, right, left, right thing in unison. Last came the three miniature horses scampering along, their little legs racing to keep up. There were oohs and aahs as people pointed to the little horses.

A Sanitation car with a couple of bigwigs, a task force car, a Sanitation van, and a bunch of task force vans followed the horses in line. At the end of the line was a little Sanitation sweeper truck. It was skinny, almost like our scooter trucks, and had the job of cleaning up the poop left in the middle of 34th Street.

The whole thing was over in less than ten minutes, and five minutes after that the crowd was gone.

We went out on patrol from there. I drove one block past 34th Street and up 33rd. On 33rd Street between 6th and 7th, I saw a hand-to-hand transaction outside an exit door of the Manhattan Mall. A female passed money to a male, and he dropped something into her hand.

"Did you see that?" I asked Joe.

"Yup."

They both looked up at me when I pulled in next to them and got out of the car. Their eyes widened, and he slipped his hand in his pocket while she put her hand down at her side. He seemed confused and started looking around like he was gonna run.

The guy was grubby. Ripped jeans, holey sneakers, and in spite of the heat, he was wearing a lightweight sweatshirt with a hood.

She had that Wall Street look about her, that competitive executive look all the downtown women have. She was nice looking, tall and thin, with long dark hair styled nice. She was wearing a light-colored silk blouse and a tailored skirt and jacket. She had high-heeled shoes on, classic type, not funk, with a matching small leather pocketbook. She reminded me of my old girlfriend Kim. I wouldn't have pegged her as a crackhead.

"What's going on?" I asked as we walked up on them.

"Nothing, Officer," she smiled. "Just talking to my friend." I saw she had her left hand clenched.

"Talk to him," I told Joe, pointing to the skell.

I put my hand toward her shoulder to steer her away. "What's your friend's name?" I asked her.

She was trying to look over at him for some help.

"Don't look at him, I'm asking you a question. Now what's his name?"

"Bob?" she said, but it came out like a question.

"I don't know—he's your friend. Are you sure that's his name?"

She half nodded. "His name is Bob."

"What's his last name?"

"I don't know, I just met him." She seemed high. She wasn't getting nasty, just acting innocent, almost childlike.

I looked over at the skell Joe was talking to. We didn't toss him; we usually watch someone do three hand-to-hand transactions before we search them.

"What did he hand you?"

"Nothing," she said, her eyes wide.

"I saw him put something in your hand," I said patiently.

She opened her right hand. "See, I don't have anything."

"No, the other hand."

She put her hands behind her back, switched it into her right hand, and put her now-empty left hand out in front of her. "See, nothing there either."

I gave Joe, who was hiding a smile, an "Is she for real?" look.

"Are you kidding me?" I asked.

She gave me a blank look.

"Put your other hand out."

She put it out, her fist clenched and pocketbook dangling. "There's nothing in it," she said.

I grabbed her wrist and held it so she couldn't pull it away. "There's nothing in there," she said again.

"Open your hand before I open it for you," I said.

She opened up and there were four blue-topped crack vials with a rock in each of them.

"See, nothing's in there," she said innocently. Sometimes I'm amazed at the crap we put up with.

I gave Joe another look and heard him choke on a laugh.

"Did you get these from him?" I nodded toward the skell.

"No," she said, shaking her head, "I didn't get them from him."

"I didn't give her anything," the skell insisted. He probably figured she could get out of this on her looks. He had nothing going for him and probably had a record.

I looked at Joe and shrugged. "Let him go."

The skell looked like he hit the lotto and started to take off, when Joe grabbed his sweatshirt. "Don't let me see you out here again. If I catch you out here again tonight, I'm gonna lock you up," Joe told him.

"Don't worry, Officer, you won't see me again," he said with meaning. "I'm going home." He took off down 6th Avenue, walking fast.

I was taking the vials out of her hand when she said, "My fiancé is a cop."

"Oh yeah?" I said skeptically. "Where's he work?"

"The six-two," she said, talking about the precinct in Bensonhurst, Brooklyn.

"How do I know you're telling me the truth?" I asked, figuring she was lying.

She went into her pocketbook to get something. I thought maybe she'd pull out a PBA card, the cards we get from the police union. Instead, she pulled out a small phone book and turned to his name and handed it to me. It had his name with both his home number and the number of the precinct with a Brooklyn exchange. I wrote the numbers down in my memo book and said, "Okay, turn around," as I pulled out my cuffs.

She started to cry. "Please don't lock me up."

"Listen, I'm just gonna bring you back to the precinct and give you a desk appearance ticket."

Reality set in when I snapped the cuffs on her, and she really started crying and pleading with me not to lock her up or call the fiancé.

I put her in the backseat with Fiore, who was on the radio with Central.

"South David to Central," Fiore said.

"Go ahead, South David."

"We have one under at three-three and six."

"That's 0130 hours," Central gave us the time.

When we got to the precinct, we had Terri Marks take her in the back to search her while we did the pedigree and ran her name.

I went into the back to the now-empty Anti-Crime office to call the boyfriend. I tried the house first, and after about six rings I got a sleepy "hullo."

I identified myself and asked his name to make sure I had the right guy. I asked if he knew a Renee Palmieri.

"Yeah, it's my fiancée. Is everything alright?"

"I just caught her buying crack up on 33rd Street," I said.

"No, oh no," he sighed and got quiet for a couple of seconds.

"She just got help for that; she went away." He paused again. "She was clean for a while."

"Listen, I'm really sorry to tell you this, but if you plan on marrying her, you need to know. She was with some real skell, and I don't know where it would have went if we didn't pick her up. Maybe you should rethink this," I said.

He started to cry. "Listen, I appreciate the call, you know. When she got help I thought she'd be okay, but I'm kidding myself here."

"It's up to you to decide what you want to do," I said. "I just thought you'd wanna know."

"I can't keep going through this," he said.

"I understand," I said with feeling.

"Is she going through the system?" he asked, meaning is she going downtown.

"No, I'm gonna give her a DAT and send her on her way." A DAT is a desk appearance ticket, which is basically a slap on the wrist.

I felt terrible telling him, but if it was me, I'd want to know before I made the biggest mistake of my life.

I went back to the arrest room where she was cuffed to the bench outside the cell and started the paperwork on the arrest. Even though she wasn't going through the system, I still had a couple of hours of paperwork to do.

"I called Chris," I told her, talking about her fiancé.

"Why did you call him?" She looked horrified.

"I wanted to know if this was the first time you've been locked up for this."

"What did he say?"

"He's upset."

She put her head down and started crying again.

"He said this isn't the first time. He said you just went away and got help for that."

I talked to her for a little while. I told her how much she's hurting the people around her and asked her if this is what she planned on doing with her life.

"I don't want to do it," she said, "but you have no idea what it's like."

She said it in a way that made me think she loved the high, not that she was struggling to stay away from it. Not a good sign.

She had no outstanding warrants, but she'd been locked up a couple of times for possession.

Joe went across the street to the deli for sandwiches while I did the paperwork. He got turkey and cheese for himself and pastrami with mustard on rye for me. He picked up Romano at 4:30, and we slept through our meal and went back out on patrol at 5:30.

When we were driving Romano back to post, we pulled up next to Sector Eddie, which is Rooney and Connelly. They were about thirty feet from the corner of 43rd Street on 8th Avenue. They were having coffee, their cups sitting on the dashboard of the RMP.

"Tony, take a look at this," Rooney said, handing something through Fiore's window.

Fiore looked at it and shook his head, saying, "I don't think this is a good idea, Mike."

"It's a great idea, Joe," Rooney said.

Fiore handed me the picture, and I barked out a laugh. It was the inspector's face superimposed over a picture from a porn magazine. It was from one of the raunchier magazines, and there was the inspector smiling away.

"I don't know, Mike, it's pretty nasty," I said, laughing.

"I know, this looks pretty real." He sounded proud of himself.

"Let me see it," Romano said from the backseat, and I handed it through my window into his.

A Sanitation sweeper truck came up behind us, moving slowly up 8th Avenue and cleaning the street. It was one of the bigger trucks, with an older guy driving it. It releases water while it brushes so it isn't kicking up dust all over the place.

"I'm gonna pull up," I told Rooney. I didn't want the sweeper truck to have to go around both of us, so I pulled across the street to the other side of 43rd Street.

I pulled into the second lane, thinking Rooney would pull up behind me and let the sweeper pass. After the truck passed, he could pull up beside us again, but Rooney didn't move. The sweeper truck pulled up behind Rooney and gave him a beep. Rooney didn't respond so he beeped again, but still nothing from Rooney.

The sweeper truck pulled out, and as he went to go around Rooney, the water shot out of the truck with the force of a fire hydrant.

Rooney's windows were open because he was talking to us, and we saw the water shoot into the car. I saw the coffee cups go flying off the dashboard and Rooney's and Garcia's arms go flying as the water hit them. From where we sat, it looked like chaos in the car.

Joe, Romano, and I started roaring as the truck passed them and the water trickled back down to a dribble. I was laughing so hard my side hurt, looking at Rooney trying to wipe the water off his face.

Rooney threw his lights on and went after the truck, yelling over the PA system for the driver to pull over. He ignored Rooney at first, then pulled over about twenty feet down.

Rooney got out of the car and slammed the door. We laughed even harder when we saw his hair plastered to his head and the top of his shirt soaked. He stomped over to the driver's side of the truck, and Connelly went to the passenger side.

Rooney's a big Irishman, about six foot two, 240 pounds. Usually he's a good guy, but he was furious, and we didn't want him pounding on the guy.

I pulled up next to them, and the three of us got out of the car. Joe and I went to the driver's side with Rooney, and Romano went to the other side with Connelly.

Water was dripping off Rooney's forehead, and there were streaks of dirt on the side of his face.

He screamed at the driver, "Get out of the truck!"

Up close, the guy looked about sixty years old. He was wearing his Sanitation greens, looking scared.

Rooney got up on the side of the truck and opened the door.

"Easy, Mike," Joe said before Rooney pulled him out.

"Get out of the truck," Rooney said.

The guy looked scared and confused as he got out of the truck. "What's the matter?" he asked.

"What's the matter?" Rooney bellowed. "Are you kidding me?" Rooney wiped some more water off his head and shook his hand. I saw the coffee stain on his pants from when the cups flew, and a soaked match was stuck to his neck.

"You soaked me with the truck because I didn't move!" Rooney yelled.

"Officer, people don't move all the time for me," he said patiently. "Sometimes when I go around them, the water shoots out. I'm sorry." He sounded real apologetic.

"You had no idea the water would hit me?" Rooney let off a string of curse words, some including the guy's mother. "I should lock you up." Rooney was breathing heavy and took his cuffs out.

"Officer, I'm sorry, I'm really sorry." This guy was good—not even a smirk. I guess all those years of doing sanitation, you learn to keep a straight face.

"Let it go, Mike," Connelly, who was now behind Rooney, said. "He's saying it was an accident—what are you gonna do?"

Rooney stared at the guy for a couple of seconds and said, "Get in your truck and get out of here."

"I'm sorry, Officer," he said again before getting in his truck and puttering away.

Joe, Romano, and I busted out laughing again. Connelly started laughing, and I saw Rooney smirk.

"He's full of it! He knew exactly what he was doing," Rooney said.

"Next time move your car," I said.

"Next time I'll lock him up."

"At least your car's clean," I said, laughing again. The car was filthy. Splashes of brown water covered everything but Connelly's side of the car.

"Come on, we'll get you a new coffee," Fiore said.

"Nah, I'm gonna go back to the house to change and clean up the car," Rooney said.

Rooney radioed Central. "South Eddie."

"Go ahead, South Eddie."

"Put us out 62 at the house."

"10-4."

6

About a half hour later, we were dropping Romano at his post when we heard Central come over the airwaves with, "South Eddie."

"South Eddie," we heard Connelly answer. I guess they were already back out.

"We got a possible EDP." Central gave the address of one of the big hotels on a West 44th Street address between Broadway and 6th.

"10-4," Connelly responded.

Romano had already stepped out of the car when he heard the transmission, and he walked back up and reached for the door handle.

"Come on, Nick," I said as I heard Joe tell Central that South David was on the back.

I pulled away a little as Romano tried to get in the door, just to let him know he didn't get the upper hand when he stormed out of the car.

He stopped and gave me a bored look, like I didn't bother him in the least. When he got the door open, he jumped in before I could take off again and gave me a smirk. I made a sharp right turn so he had to wrestle with the door as gravity made it hard to close.

"Cut it out, Tony!" he yelled.

"Cut what out?" I asked.

"You two sound like my kids," Joe said, shaking his head.

"He started it!" Romano whined.

"Next time don't slam my door when you get out," I snapped back.

"Next time don't lecture me—"

"Are you two done?" Joe cut him off. "Or can we back up Eddie on this job?"

"Joe, we're a block and half from the job—we'll probably get there before them," I said.

When we pulled up in front of the hotel, Sector Eddie's RMP was parked out front. I pulled in behind them, and we walked into the lobby.

Rooney and Connelly were in the lobby, talking to who I guessed was the manager. She looked about twenty years old and reminded me of a librarian. She was all business in her pressed gray uniform and yuppie glasses. As we walked up to them, we overhead her saying, "He's in Room 1025; he destroyed the room. I went up there and heard him screaming and breaking things. I saw the fire hose in the hallway—he broke the case and there's water all over the place."

"When did he check in?" Rooney asked her.

"This afternoon—he seemed fine then," she said.

"How many people are in the room?" This from Connelly.

"As far as I know, just him."

"You got keys for the room?" Rooney asked.

She held them up and nodded.

We walked over to the bank of elevators and the six of us piled in. We got off at the tenth floor, pausing to listen as we got out. The only sound was the *ding* from the elevator and the muted sounds of our footsteps on the carpet.

I was surprised there was no one in the hallway. Usually people love this kind of thing, and you find them standing around with their arms folded, shaking their heads in disgust as they point to where the trouble is.

The glass case where the emergency fire hose is usually folded up like an accordion was broken, and the hose was stretched about a quarter of the way down the hall and lying on the floor outside the last door on the left. As we walked down the hallway and got closer to the door, our feet started squishing in the wet rug. The manager put her hands over her face when she saw how much water was in the hallway. I guessed she was gonna get in trouble for it 'cause the damage was happening on her watch.

"Maybe he's a disgruntled hosehead," Rooney whispered.

We were keeping quiet as we walked toward the door, holding on to our cuffs to keep them from jangling.

As we approached the door, I noticed there was a six-by-six-inch cutout in the door where the peephole usually is. I didn't understand why it would be like that, but I didn't want to ask the manager and risk having him hear us outside the door.

I walked up to the hole in the door and stood on my tiptoes to look in.

The room was destroyed. The mirror over the desk was smashed, the beds were overturned, with the sheets and blankets strewn all over the floor. The TV was facedown on the floor, and the cable had been pulled out of the wall. The lamps were broken, and the furniture looked like it'd been tossed around the room.

To my left I saw this huge musclehead guy wearing a T-shirt and a pair of blue gym shorts. He had short black hair and he was breathing heavy, flexing and pumping his arms like the

Hulk. He was pacing while he flexed, and it looked like he was psyching himself up for his next wave of destruction.

I pulled my head back before he could see me and looked at Rooney. When Rooney saw the expression on my face, he pushed past me and said, "Let me see," as he put his face up to the hole in the door. Since Rooney's bigger than me, he didn't have to stand on his tiptoes, and I heard him mumble, "Look at this psycho."

Rooney looked back at me, and I could see we were both trying to figure out how to get this guy out of there without any of us getting hurt.

Rooney turned the knob on the door and found it unlocked. He pushed it quietly until he hit resistance, and we could see the chain lock was on. Rooney closed the door as quiet as he could while I waved Joe and Romano up to the door. Joe, Romano, and I stood to the right of the door, while Rooney, Connelly, and the manager stood to the left.

Romano's radio let out a blast, and we heard Central yelling something to South Charlie. We all turned to look at Romano, who obviously forgot to lower his radio and gave us up. He fumbled to turn the volume down while we shook our heads at him.

Then we heard the chain on the door slide. From where I stood, I could see the top of his head. I could hear his breathing and see his hair was soaked with sweat.

The door flew open and he stepped into the hallway one leg at a time, swaying his arms. His eyes were going from one side of the door to the other, sizing us up; he looked like King Kong. I half expected the manager to put her hands on her hips and stamp her feet and say, "You big ape! Who's gonna pay for this mess?"

Instead she skulked back behind Connelly and looked over his shoulder as he pulled out his mace.

Kong was breathing so heavy now it almost sounded like a growl. He was mouth breathing, with his bottom lip protruding out, wet with saliva.

Rooney stepped up to him and said, "Hey buddy, where's the fire?"

We hid our smirks as Kong looked up at Rooney from the corner of his eye. I was thinking, *How are we gonna take this guy down without him going berserk and Connelly macing us by mistake?* I pictured us holding our eyes and bumping into each other while he ran down the hall morphing into the Hulk.

He fixed his eyes on me since I was closest to him. I was aware of Joe next to me, ready to move. I pulled out my cuffs and looked straight at him. "Do you want to cuff yourself, or do you want me to do it?" I asked, jingling my handcuffs in front of him with my index finger and thumb.

He seemed to be thinking about it as he did some more deep breathing. I couldn't tell what was going through his mind, and I was watching to see if he was gonna come at me.

Then he turned around and put his hands behind his back for me to cuff him. I was thinking, *This guy's done this before.* He was still breathing heavy while I got the cuffs on him.

Rooney handed me his cuffs, shrugged, and said, "That was easy," as I stuck them in my cuff holder on my belt.

"You want your shoes?" Rooney asked him.

He nodded yes, and Rooney went into the room to look for his shoes. He found one sneaker on top of the overturned dresser and searched around until he found the second one under the mattress. Kong stuck his feet into the unlaced sneakers and didn't say a word as we all took the elevator back down to the lobby.

When we walked outside, the sun was starting to come up. Streaks of pink crossed the sky against the darker blue. It was a cloudless day with a warm breeze, the kind that would heat up later. Rooney and Connelly took the collar back to the house. Romano walked back to his post, and we told him we'd stop back with some breakfast.

We went back to our vertical patrol of our sector, driving west to east between 34th and 40th streets. We were driving westbound on 37th Street when we got a call from Central for a drug sale at west 36th and 8th. When we got there no one was around, so Fiore radioed Central for a callback number. There was none, so we sat there to see if anything happened.

We drove up to the Sunrise Deli and picked up breakfast. I got two bacon, egg, and cheese—I figured I'd be nice and get Romano a sandwich. Joe got an egg whites and turkey on a roll.

Bruno Galotti, another rookie who reminds me of an Italian Baby Huey, was waiting with Romano at his post on 44th and 8th, so we picked them both up at 7:20 and drove back to 36th and 8th to see if anything was up with the drug sale.

There was a small group of people in front of a brick building near 35th Street. It's a methadone clinic that opens up at 7:00 a.m. A couple of minutes later, the first methadonian, as we call them, came around the corner.

"Here's some entertainment," I said.

He was emaciated, his brown stingy hair was shaggy, and his ears stuck out. He was wearing black jeans with a black fanny pack around his waist, a grey button-down shirt, and white sneakers. He had hollowed-out, sunken eyes, and you could see the pronounced skeletal structure of his cheekbones and chin.

He was high as anything and doing the methadonian shuffle down the street. It's not like a drunk who takes exaggerated steps; with junkies it's all in the upper body. They barely move their feet, and their arms are weightless. As he shuffled toward us, people were looking at him as they walked by. One good

Samaritan, a heavyset woman in a floral print dress, stopped to say, "Are you okay?"

He moved in slow motion, and it looked like it took some effort for him to shift his eyes from his walking semicoma to look at her. He didn't answer, just slowly moved his head forward again. His movements looked like they were being orchestrated by a puppeteer.

He finally got to the corner. He stopped and his knees bent forward, his back arched, and he kept his weight in his middle while he rocked inch by inch toward the ground. He lowered in slow motion until his knuckles just about touched the ground.

"He's gonna fall!" Bruno said, sounding worried.

"They never fall," I said.

"Look, he's falling," he said again.

"Trust me, he won't fall," I said as Romano and I laughed.

"Good morning, Mr. Methadonian," Romano said in a radio announcer's voice. "How was your fix today?"

The clinic pumps methadone addicts full of methadone for what they call "a safe and effective way to treat drug dependence and withdrawal."

"Look at this, Bruno," I said. "Our tax dollars at work."

"Why do they give them this garbage?" Romano asked.

"So they don't kill themselves," I said. "They don't want them getting AIDS from an infected needle, and supposedly this stuff keeps their blood levels stable so they can engage in everyday activities. They say they can work and do anything the rest of us can do. What do you think, Bruno, would you go to this guy for a haircut? He looks like he could be a barber."

"Isn't *this* killing him?" Bruno asked.

We all looked at him, drooping down again in slow, jerky movements.

"Ya think?" Romano said.

99

"Only if he walks into traffic, otherwise he's fine," I said as Romano and I started laughing again.

I saw Joe bowing his head, and I knew he was praying for the guy.

"Alright, I'm sorry," I said. "Let's pray for him. Lord, please help this methadonian get home safely so he can come back tomorrow and get more drugs."

"Amen," Romano said, making the sign of the cross.

"There's something wrong with you guys," Bruno said, and just like that the fun went out of it.

"Yeah, there's nothing wrong with him, though," Romano said. That made me feel worse because I realized that instead of looking at Joe's good example, Romano was looking at me—and I wasn't acting anything like Joe.

The methadonian's knuckles scraped the ground, and he jerked back up.

"He's a walking dead, right, Tony?" Bruno asked.

"No," I said quietly. "Walking dead is a crackie looking for a vial in the gutter." So much for me being better with the skells.

I don't know what's wrong with me sometimes, it's like this stuff just flies out of my mouth before I even realize I say it. I was disgusted with myself for acting like that in front of Romano and Bruno.

We drove back to the precinct and signed out for 7:50. I changed into street clothes and was on my way home by 8:00.

Northbound traffic on the West Side Highway was bumper-to-bumper, but it was lighter on the southbound side. The sky was overcast. We were supposed to get thunderstorms today and about half an inch of rain. When I lived in Shore Acres, the streets never flooded. Where I live now, half the streets fill up every time it rains.

The Brooklyn Battery Tunnel was down to one lane to accommodate the inbound traffic. I lit a cigarette and lost my radio signal, listening to the hum of my tires as I drove through the tunnel.

When I came out on the Brooklyn side, there was a torrential downpour. It was raining so hard people were pulling over on the side of the Brooklyn Queens Expressway. I was driving pretty fast and hit a puddle on the Gowanus near 38th Street and hydroplaned, so I took it easy after that.

I got most of the way home without incident but had to go around to Lincoln Avenue because the block before mine was flooded.

I was soaked from the sprint from my car to the side of my house, and I fumbled with my keys as the rain dripped off my nose.

I changed out of my wet clothes and checked my messages. Michele was in class already, but she called to say good morning and that her mother would be taking Stevie to the doctor today.

I took out my Bible to read before I went to sleep. I wasn't sure what to read—I had read the book of John so much I could practically recite it, so I went over to Psalms. Fiore always reads Psalm 91, so I figured I'd stay on that one for a while. I don't understand a lot of it, but Fiore's been studying it a long time and I get a lot out of what he tells me.

I started at the beginning. "He who dwells in the secret place of the Most High shall abide under the shadow of the Almighty. I will say of the LORD, 'He is my refuge and my fortress; My God, in Him I will trust.'"

Fiore says when you dwell in the secret place, the hiding place of God, you have to live there. He said it can't be that you run in and out when you're in trouble. If we stay there every day, we'll remain under God's shadow. It says in the Amplified Bible that no foe or enemy can withstand God's power when we're under that shadow.

The next part is "I will say of the LORD, 'He is my refuge and my fortress; My God, in Him I will trust.'" Fiore says that when the Lord is our refuge and fortress and the one we trust, it says in the Amplified that then God will deliver us from the snare of the fowler and from the perilous pestilence.

I can understand why most people don't understand the Bible. Before I met Fiore, I had no idea what half this stuff was. Like this fowler thing—I figured it had something to do with birds, but Fiore told me it was a bird catcher. This kind of bird catcher would take young birds with a trap made with hair or something and tame them. When the young birds were big enough to make some noise, the bird catchers would hide them in cages to attract other birds. Sometimes they would sew the birds' eyelids shut so they would squawk enough to attract large numbers of birds for them to kill or catch.

So to deliver us from the snare of the fowler is to deliver us from evil plans to ruin us. "I take God at his word," Fiore always says. "He loves me, and he's not gonna be vague and tell me something that isn't true. If he says he'll deliver me, then he will."

Farther down in verse 7, it says that a thousand may fall at my side and ten thousand at my right hand, but it shall not come near me. Last week we were talking about it while Romano was pretending he wasn't interested. He does that—he snaps at us for talking about God, but I see he's soaking it up like a sponge. Joe was saying that if there are eleven thousand people dead around him, he trusts God that he will be the guy standing.

Romano was asking how eleven thousand people could be dead around us and did we think a bomb, terrorist attack, or something else was gonna happen.

"Nick, I don't worry about stuff like that," Joe told him. "Because even if something did happen, I know I'm protected. When I pray this psalm, I put myself in the prayer."

"How?" Romano asked.

"I say, 'Lord, I thank you that I dwell in your secret place, under the shadow of the Almighty. Lord, you are my refuge and fortress, you are my God, it's in you that I trust. And you will deliver me from the snare of the fowler and from the deadly pestilence. You cover me with your feathers, and under your wings I take refuge—'"

"But people get hurt and die all the time," Romano said. "What if you pray that and die anyway?"

"Then at least I died believing," Joe said. "I have faith in God's faithfulness. I believe he'll protect me."

"Why don't I understand all that?" Romano asked.

Fiore shrugged. "I guess because Jesus isn't your Lord."

"I believe in God, Joe," Romano spat.

"I know, but he's not exactly running your life, is he?"

Romano accepted that with a shrug. "I guess not."

"You know, Nick, it says in the Bible, in Joel 2:32, that everyone who calls on the name of the Lord will be saved," Fiore said. "So anytime you're ready, just call on him."

"And say what?" Romano asked.

"Whatever's on your mind, he's always listening," Fiore said, then added, "Jesus is a good guy, he'll never do you wrong."

"That's what you keep telling me," Romano said.

I fell asleep reading the psalm and forgot to set my alarm clock. I woke up at 5:30. I could hear the rain falling steadily outside my window and the sound of an ambulance going down Greely Avenue.

I showered and shaved and called Michele. She said Stevie went to the doctor and got some antibiotics, but they hadn't kicked in yet and he was still running a fever. She gave him some eardrops and Tylenol, and he had been sleeping on and off most of the day.

We made plans for the next day. I was off tomorrow night so I could do a day tour Friday, and I would head out to Long Island in the morning. Michele would be at work and Stevie would be at her mother's, so I'd let myself in and sleep there. I told her if Stevie was feeling better, we'd go out to dinner and to a movie.

I was about pick up the phone to order some pizza when it rang.

"Hullo?"

"Tony, it's Grandma," she said.

"Hey, Grandma, is everything alright?"

"I want you to come over."

"Why? I was just there last night."

"I need to talk to you, and no one is here. Did you eat yet?"

"No, I was gonna order some pizza."

"Don't order—I made soup, it's raining. And I have chicken from last night."

She always makes soup when it rains, even in the summer. I debated it for a minute and decided I might as well get it over with. I had to see everyone this weekend and if there was something going on, I want to know ahead of time.

"I'll be there in a little while," I told her.

I packed my bag for work, bringing clothes for tomorrow and Friday. I brought my cell phone charger and *Cloudy with a Chance of Meatballs*, a book I bought to read to Stevie.

The air was warm and wet, and the rain was down to a drizzle. I took the service road to Clove Road and got to Grandma's by 7:00. She buzzed me in and was waiting in the hallway when I got there. She got me in one of her choke holds and kissed my cheek. She felt frail and bony as I hugged her.

She was alone like she said, and she had the table set for two. She must have gone shopping. Her red folding cart that all the old Italian ladies take to the stores was resting against the wall in the entranceway.

"What kind of soup did you make?" I asked.

"Pasta faggioli," she said, but it sounded like "pasta fazool," which is cannollini beans and macaroni. She makes hers with proscuitto, garlic, and basil, and it's delicious.

She ladled the soup into the bowls and took a loaf of Italian bread out of the oven. She pulled out a bottle of Bell'Agio Chianti, the kind the old men drink playing checkers in the park. She poured herself a small glass and held the bottle up to me. I shook my head no, and she put it back on the counter. I sent up a silent prayer for the food and dug in.

"So what'd you want to talk to me about?" I asked between bites.

"I need help with the seating arrangements."

"Why do we have seating arrangements at an American Legion hall?"

"Because, I can't sit Aunt Rose with Little Gina. Little Gina didn't invite Aunt Rose to her engagement dinner, so Rose wants nothing to do with her. Uncle Mickey's not talking to Uncle Henny since they got in trouble with the bookies. Denise isn't talking to your father, and I can't sit Marie near your mother. Anna Morreale and—"

"Grandma, do you even hear yourself?" I cut her off.

"What?" She gave me a blank look.

"There's something wrong with this family. You can't even

105

put them all in a room together without half of them fighting about something. Why does there always have to be a problem?" I asked, exasperated.

"You know, Tony, you keep telling me that this woman isn't poisoning your mind, so how is it that since you met her you turned on your family? You never said stuff like this before. No family is perfect, but we're your family, and we don't appreciate her coming in here and turning you against us." She was pointing her finger at me.

"Grandma, this has nothing to do with Michele. Why do you blame her for everything? Maybe it's because I don't drink anymore that I'm seeing all this stuff," I said.

"Maybe it's that church you go to, teaching you to look down on everyone else!"

"That's not what they teach us," I said, wondering if that was what I was doing.

She got up and went over to the oven and pulled a towel off the handle. She took two dishes of leftover chicken out of the oven, set them on the table, then went back and turned off the oven.

"Grandma, I love you and I love my family. I'm just tired of all the fighting. How about we don't have seating arrangements and just let everyone sit where they want?" I said, trying to smooth it over. "This way no one has to sit next to someone they don't want to."

"Because they'll fight!" she snapped, proving my point whether she realized it or not.

"If they fight, they fight," I said, resigning myself to it.

We finished our dinner and had coffee. She had picked up seven-layer cookies at the bakery, the ones that have a pink, green, and yellow layer with raspberry jam in between, with a chocolate-covered top and bottom. I'm trying not to eat too many sweets, but I love these and I wound up eating six of them.

We watched the Yankee game until I left for work. The Yanks were down at Camden Yards playing Baltimore. They were tied 5-5 until the bottom of the fifth inning. I left after Soriano scored in the 6th inning. If they won, it would be their fourth win in five games.

There was an accident on the Gowanus with a fatality near 39th Street. The expressway was down to the center lane. A van collided with a smaller car that was demolished, facing traffic in the left lane. There was a body on the ground on the side of it, and I could see a pair of sneakers sticking out from under a blanket, probably waiting for EMS to come out and pronounce him dead.

I got to Midtown at 10:40 and parked on 36th Street. I went downstairs to change, and Hanrahan caught me on my way up from the locker room.

"Rooney's a schmuck," he said.

"I know. Why, what'd he do now?" I asked and then re-membered what he was planning to do to the inspector's door. It must have shown on my face that I realized what he was talking about, because he shook his head and walked into the muster room.

Cops were cracking up around the room, listening to Rooney brag about what him and Romano did to the inspector. Hanra-han gave the fall in order, and the room got quiet. He gave out the sectors, the foot posts, the color of the day (green), and the return date for C-summons before he brought up the subject of the inspector. "Uh," he stuttered a little, and I could see he was biting his lip. "It's been brought to my attention that the inspector's door was decorated with some pornographic ma-terial this morning. To say the least, he was not happy seeing his face superimposed over this kind of—" He stopped and coughed to cover his laugh. His shoulders started to shake and he snorted, then he turned around to compose himself. He held up his hands as the ranks started to roar.

"Don't laugh," he said seriously, "he's ripping."

"So what?" Rooney spat. "Who cares if he's ripping? We're ripping."

"Careful, Mike," Hanrahan said. "He might think you're the one who did it." He looked hard at Rooney. It might be funny, but the inspector could play games with Rooney.

He finished up with, "I don't want anyone off post tonight. Foot posts, pick up your jobs." He was basically telling us we have to watch our backs now that we humiliated the inspector.

Fiore and I grabbed Romano, who was acting cocky as anything for helping Rooney disgrace the inspector. We stopped for coffee on the corner of 9th Avenue and made Romano go in. We drove him up to 44th Street and sat with him till he finished his coffee.

We had no jobs, so I drove west to 9th Avenue to patrol our sector, driving east to west on the streets and south on the avenues. I was coming back westbound on 39th Street, and as we passed an empty lot on the north side of the street, Fiore said quietly, "Stop the car."

"What?" I asked.

"Shhh, did you hear that?" He turned his head to the side, listening intently.

"What?" I said. I didn't hear anything.

He held up his hand. "Pull the car over and lower your radio," he said as he was already getting out of the car.

I shut the car and lowered my radio, following him into the lot. The lights from the street lit up the front of the parking lot, but the back of it was dark. I couldn't see anything but I heard it now, a faint cry and the slap, pop sound of someone being hit. I heard a blow being delivered again, some mumbling, and then more clearly a deep voice said, "Shut up, you—" with some pretty foul adjectives.

Joe and I looked at each other and moved quickly out of the light before they could see us, holding our handcuffs so they wouldn't make noise. Once we stepped out of the streetlight, we could see the outline of a man kneeling down with his back to us and his arms moving. He was huge, I could see his massive upper body. He was wearing jeans down around his ankles and a white muscle shirt.

I heard a female crying and then a couple of more hits being given as his hands pounded her. We had our guns out and we both raised them toward him.

I went to the left and Joe went to the right. I stayed back behind a little; I didn't want the perp to get in between Joe and me, 'cause if we were standing on either side of him and had to shoot, we'd shoot each other.

As we came up on it, we saw what was going on. There were two men, the one with his back to us was holding a female down with one arm as he raped her, alternating with blows to her face with his fists. The second man was kneeling by her head, holding her down by the shoulders as he watched. Neither one of them saw us until Fiore put his gun to the big guy's head and yelled, "Police! Don't move!"

I yelled a command to the second guy, "Get down!" He let go of the female, who was lying there limp. I keyed my radio, still holding my gun at the second guy, "Central, 85 forthwith, empty lot on three-nine between eight and nine, closer to eighth," which means officer needs assistance, and put the radio in my back pocket.

The second guy, the smaller of the two, had let go of her but was still kneeling.

"Get down now," I said as I lunged at him with my gun out

in front of me. When he looked down the barrel of the gun, he complied pretty quick and lay down on the ground with his arms and legs out.

"Get down on the ground!" Fiore yelled to the first guy, still on his knees. He was massive, solid muscle, with the hint of a smile on his lips.

"Yo, yo, chill, man," he said, putting his hands out. He got up, wiping the gravel off his knees. He reached for his pants that were still down around his ankles.

"Don't move!" Fiore barked.

"You got this wrong, this is my girl—tell them." His eyes swung a warning look to the female, who was crumpled on the ground.

"I said get down on the ground!"

Neither me or Joe would look at her and take our eyes off him. We could hear her crying, saying, "Thank you, God," over and over.

Joe poked him in the back of the head with the gun and said, "Get down on the ground or I will kill you!" Fiore colored it up a little. I was surprised in a disconnected sort of way—I've never heard him curse before.

The radio was babbling, but I wasn't listening to it. I could see the big guy looking around, seeing where he could run. He looked like a psycho, shaved head, thick neck, and the tattoo work and jailhouse muscles of a recent stint in the joint.

He started talking again. "Oh, come on, dude, just let me pull my pants up. I'm telling you, she's my girl." He was looking at me, sizing me up.

Joe hit him with the gun again behind his ear, this time harder, and yelled, "This is the *last* time I'm telling you, get down on the ground or I will blow your head off!"

I could see he was thinking of taking us on. He reached down to pull up his pants, and I saw I had a clear shot at him. I kicked him in the groin as hard as I could and heard the *oomph* as I connected with his family jewels. As he bent over, I holstered my gun and grabbed his right wrist and gave him an armbar, pushing my elbow into the back of his upper arm while holding his wrist. His face slapped against the ground as he went down, and I put my knee in his back and cuffed his one wrist.

Hitting the pavement stunned him for a second, but his left arm was still free. He pushed himself up with a roar as I yelled, "Joe, grab his other arm before I lose leverage here."

The sound of the radio came into focus, and I could hear the sectors responding, "Eddie 84, Henry 84," telling Central they were on the scene. A sector car came into the lot, scraping its bumper against the entrance ramp as it pulled in. Rooney and Connelly got out and ran over to us.

Joe holstered his gun and grabbed the guy's other arm, but he had a huge upper body and his muscles made it difficult for us to cuff him. We strained to pull his arms together to cuff his wrists. He started to buck and we rode him like a bronco for a couple of seconds, till Rooney came over and closed his arms so we could cuff him.

Connelly cuffed the other guy and stepped back from him and said, "Oh man," when he saw the victim.

We had forgotten about her while getting the cuffs on the big guy. She was beaten bloody, with welts and bruises all over her face. She was petite, with dark brown hair disheveled around her shoulders. One eye was swollen shut, and the other one was just about closed. Her nose was broken and bleeding, and her mouth was swollen and split. From the amount of swelling in the face, I'm sure more than her nose was broken. She was sitting now, curled up and shaking, with her arms around her knees. Her legs were scraped and bleeding, and she was missing a shoe.

Fiore was on the radio, breathing heavy. "South David to

Central, I need a bus forthwith to north side of three-nine between eight and nine."

Central came back with, "Twenty minutes out."

It happens sometimes, EMS is backed up with multiple injuries somewhere or stuck at Bellevue finishing something up.

Connelly was talking to her in soothing tones, but she was rocking now, looking at the ground and saying, "Thank you, God," over and over. The big guy was yelling, not so tough now, with his hands cuffed and his pants down around his ankles.

"Tell them," he spit out some more curses at her. "Tell them you were hooking us up; tell them we were chilling, having beers."

Connelly gave him a shove with his foot. "Shut up, shut your mouth."

He shut his mouth.

Rooney and Connelly patted them down while I called Central.

"South David to Central," I radioed.

"Go ahead, South David," Central answered.

"Slow it down," I said so the other sectors weren't rushing to the scene. "We've got two under at the lot on three-nine between eight and nine."

"Zero zero twenty hours," Central responded, putting the time of arrest at 12:20.

The boss and most of the squad were on the scene now, and Nick Romano came whipping around into the parking lot on foot.

"What happened?" Hanrahan asked as he approached Joe and me.

I took a deep breath and let it out. "Joe heard a noise, we didn't know what it was. We came up on these two mutts holding her down and raping her."

He looked at the victim. "Do you have a bus coming?"

"Yeah, twenty minutes out," I said.

"I'm not leaving her on the ground in the parking lot or put-ting her in a sector car—take her back to the house," Hanrahan said. "Let the bus meet us there. You and Joe take the victim. Let Rooney and Connelly take the musclehead, and Noreen and I will take the smaller perp."

Rooney pulled the big one up by the cuffs and the back of his pants and said, "Come on, you piece of garbage." He and Connelly put him in the car.

I went over to the victim still sitting on the pavement, rock-ing back and forth while she stared at the ground.

"Hey," I said quietly. "How 'bout we take you back to the precinct? The ambulance is gonna meet us there and take a look at you."

She stopped rocking and tried to focus on me. Her eyes were pretty much swollen shut, so I doubt she could see me. "Are you an angel?" she asked.

I smiled and shook my head. "No, just a cop," I said.

She started to cry.

*T*hey must have taken the scenic route to the precinct, because Joe and I were the first ones back. The boss left Romano in the parking lot to watch the crime scene. I opened the back door of the RMP to get the victim, and she swung her legs around and put them on the ground. Her legs were bloody, and I could see pieces of glass and gravel imbedded in them.

She was saying, "Thank you, thank you, Officer. I was praying to God, and you guys showed up. They were gonna kill me, I know they were gonna kill me."

She was right, these guys were psychos. With the size of the big one and the force he was using, she wouldn't have lasted much longer. I was thanking God too—it's rare we get to stop something like this while it's going on. Usually we're called in afterward to pick up what's left of the victim. I wish I could say we stopped it before anything happened, but the big guy had already assaulted her. The smaller one would have taken the leftovers.

"They can't hurt you now, we got you. Come on, let's get you inside and let the EMTs take a look at you." I put out my arm for her to grab onto and lift herself up. She held my hand and carried her shoe in the other. She was a little wobbly, so I put my other hand under her shoulder.

Joe was silent as he came around to my side of the car. He took a look at her face and turned away, balling his hands into fists. I've never seen him this angry, usually it's me who goes off. He composed himself and helped me get her up the three stairs into the precinct.

She was barely walking, and by the time we got to the desk the lou, Terri Marks, and Vince Puletti were staring at us. The lou looked at her and then looked at me with anger and disgust flashing in his eyes.

"Lou, I'm gonna take her in the back to the Anti-Crime office and come back." We didn't want to bring her in the muster room where she would have to see the perps again.

"Go ahead," he said with a nod. Normally the lou just puts his head back down to whatever he's doing, but he was staring at her. He looked over at Fiore. "You okay, Joe?"

Fiore gave a quick nod and followed me. As we were walking toward the back, I heard him call Terri Marks.

"Terr, can you come in the back with us and wait with her?"

"Sure, Joe. Can I get her something to drink?"

"No. She won't be able to drink. Her face is pulverized," Fiore said with disgust.

We took her into the crime room and sat her in one of the cushioned chairs.

"What happened?" I asked her. I was glad she didn't know what she looked like—she had enough to deal with right now.

"We were at Port Authority, waiting for a bus together. They were from Queens, so they started talking to me."

"But you were in a parking lot on a deserted street with

two guys you don't know at twelve at night." I said it softly, but I'm not stupid.

She put her head down.

"Why'd you go from Port Authority to the parking lot?" This from Terri Marks.

"They said they knew where to score some weed. They were nice at Port Authority, they seemed harmless," she said.

"I don't know how you could say the big guy seemed harmless," I said. "They looked like they just got out of jail."

"They did get out of jail, but they said it was for drugs. They were helping a friend, holding some of his stuff, and the apartment got raided. They wanted to score and told me that their guy is usually in the back of that parking lot."

"You knew they just got out of jail and you walked into a dark parking lot with them?" Terri said, amazed.

"I know, I know," she sobbed. "They seemed so nice. But then right before we walked back there, I saw the big one look up and down the street." Her breath hitched as she spoke. "I thought he was looking for their guy, but I guess he was making sure no one saw us go in there. As soon as we got in the back where it's dark, the big one started whaling on me."

"It doesn't matter why she went, Terri, she wasn't looking for this," Fiore snapped at Terri.

"I'm not blaming her for what happened, but I don't understand why she'd put herself in a position like that—they could have killed her!" Terri said to Joe.

EMS came into the room, an older male who looked to be in his late forties and a younger female in her twenties. Joe and I left Terri in the room while they took a look at her.

I went out to the desk and went behind it to the green property locker to grab the Polaroid camera. There were four pictures left, so I grabbed some more film.

The vestibule door opened, and the sarge came in with

Noreen. They had the smaller of the perps with them, and Rooney was right behind them with the big one.

The perps had their heads down and their mouths shut. Rooney and Connelly searched them again at the desk, this time emptying their pockets and counting their money. They had rolling papers and forty-six bucks between them. The only ID on them was their discharge forms from Riker's.

I shook my head. They just got out of jail and already they're looking to hurt someone. It didn't shock me. It's not uncommon for us to lock up perps with nothing but their release papers from Elmira.

What a mistake to let these two out. I don't know who the moron was that paroled these two, but he definitely should find another job. They'd go back to finish their original sentence and then face charges of rape, sexual assault, and unlawful imprisonment, all in the first degree.

"Ya know," Vince Puletti said loudly, his voice sounding like he gargled with sand from all his years of smoking, "when I came on, we'd throw scum like this off a rooftop. They'd never make it to the precinct." He was walking toward them from the radio room with his hand on his gun. The big one looked up, and Vince gave him a hard look.

"Yeah, the good old days," Rooney said.

"Take them back to the cells," Lieutenant Coughlin said. "Don't take the cuffs off them in the cell, and make sure you search them good."

"Who's taking the collar?" the lou asked me.

"Let Joe take it. It's got Cop of the Month written all over it, and I got enough abuse last time," I said. I took a gun collar in March and this month I was up for the Cop of the Month award, complete with a certificate and a savings bond. My face was on the wall of the precinct, and everyone wrote cartoon balloons over my mouth with "Let me kiss your butt, inspector," "Wipe your nose, soldier," and other degrading remarks. You get abused for it, but secretly I was glad I got it. It's nice to be appreciated.

"Alright, Joe takes the collar. You go to the hospital with the victim."

The inspector would love that two of his guys picked up a rape in progress—it would make up for the geisha house thing he got nailed for.

It was before 1:00, so I was able to call the Special Victims Squad. On any first-degree sexual assault, we have to call in Special Victims. After 1:00 and until 8:00 a.m. it goes to the Detective Borough night watch dispatcher. They said they'd have someone meet us at Bellevue. The rape kit would go to the chief medical examiner's evidence unit. Any other clothes of the perps with blood on them would be taken to the property clerk's office.

I went back into the crime room with the camera. I took pictures of her face and head at each angle. The choke marks on her neck, the bloody legs, ripped clothes, and bald spots where her hair was pulled out. EMS put her in a chair to take her over to Bellevue.

I walked back to the cells to tell Joe I was leaving. He was sitting at the desk inside by the cells, doing the paperwork.

"You okay, buddy? You want me to take the collar?" I asked.

He shook his head. "No, I'm okay."

"You sure? If you want, you can go to the hospital with the victim, and I'll process this for you."

"No, I'll be alright. Thanks."

"Hey, Officer, can you take these cuffs off? They're too tight," the big mutt said, his face scrunched up in pain.

"They're new. Break 'em in for a while, maybe they'll loosen up," I said as I smiled at him.

I took the RMP and followed the ambulance across town on 34th Street and down the service road to the back of the hospital. I was starting to feel like I lived at Bellevue, I've been here so many times this week. I parked the RMP and waited for EMS to get the victim out of the bus. She looked worse now; her face was more swollen and her eyes looked like Rocky Balboa when he fought Apollo Creed.

"How you doing there?" I almost added "champ" but caught myself.

"Oh, it's you," she said, trying to focus on me. "Thank you so much. I don't know what would've happened if you didn't show up," she said as she started to cry again.

I banged down the fury starting to rise up in me and said, "It's okay now, no one's gonna hurt you."

"Let's get you inside," the female from EMS said to her.

People were staring at us as we walked her down the hall in the emergency room. A nurse brought us into the last room at the end of the hallway. I stood in the doorway as they got her onto the gurney.

"Can I get you some ice chips or something?" I asked.

"No," she said and balled herself up, wrapping the sheet around her.

I backed out into the hall, wanting to give her some privacy. I heard the nurse talking to her in soft tones, asking if she could help her into a gown.

A female doctor, looking professional in her lab coat with a stethoscope around her neck, approached me and asked me what happened. She looked around my age, with dark brown hair and big blue eyes. She had a dark red birthmark on her face that I tried not to stare at while I gave her a brief rundown of what happened.

She went into the room, and the nurse came out a minute later. She came back with the rape kit and closed the door again, leaving me to amuse myself with the various machines that were stored at the back of the hallway. There were a couple of standing blood pressure machines, a complicated-looking thing that might have been for X-rays, and two gurneys with black plastic mattresses parked next to the wall.

The Special Victims detectives came in about twenty minutes later. One was a short, stocky male with brown hair cut military style. He was wearing a gray suit with the tie loosened, and he introduced himself as Detective Macklin and his partner, a female, as Detective DePalma. She was tall and thin, late thirties, with long dark hair pulled back from her face. She was wearing a beige suit and no makeup. She gave me a nod and dismissed me.

"Is this where the victim is?" he asked.

"Yeah, the doctor's with her now," I said.

"Were you at the scene for it?" This from DePalma.

I nodded. "We got it as a pickup." I went through it again with them. I talked to both of them, but he was the only one who would look up and acknowledge anything I was saying. I was concerned that maybe she wouldn't be nice to the victim. The female detective seemed pretty cold, and I didn't want this to be any worse for the victim than it already was.

"You got them both in custody?" he asked.

"They're at the precinct; their only ID was their release papers from Elmira."

"What were they there for?" She looked at me for the first time.

"I have no idea. My partner is back at the house, processing the arrest."

They went into the room, and I moved closer to the door to hear how they handled it. The female detective surprised me by smiling at the victim while she introduced herself, and apologizing for what the victim went through. I smiled at the victim and pulled the door closed, leaving them in there with the doctor.

When the detectives came out, they said they would wait while the victim had stitches, X-rays, and some kind of scan. The doc was thinking about admitting her but would wait until after the tests were done.

I scribbled out an aided card naming the injuries that I could see on her. While they took her over to radiology, I sat on a chair in the room, bored out of my mind.

I must have dozed off. I sat up when they came back with the gurney and tried to look like I hadn't been sleeping. It was now 2:30, and we had to wait another hour for the test results.

When the doc came in, she told us they would be admitting her. Apparently she had a fractured skull and a broken nose and cheekbone, and they were concerned about damage to one of her eyes. They were calling in a plastic surgeon to deal with the stitches on her face, and several of her teeth were broken.

I was feeling guilty and thankful at the same time. I wished we'd gotten there sooner, and I was glad we didn't get there later.

I got the admission number, EMS's info, the victim's pertinent info, and talked to the detectives again before I left. They were doing the notification and would contact the victim's mother. The doctor gave me the rape kit to bring back to the precinct.

I left the hospital at 4:30. I drove across town and stopped on 34th Street to pick up coffee and a buttered roll for Joe and me. I wasn't hungry, it was just to absorb the acid in my stomach.

"How's the victim?" Vince Puletti asked as I walked in.

"A mess. Fractured skull, broken nose and cheekbone. Her teeth were busted, and they were calling in a plastic surgeon to sew her face back up," I said.

"Good collar, Tony," he said gruffly—and let go a stream of curses about the perps.

I locked up my gun behind the desk in the gun locker. We do this so in case of a scuffle with the perps, they can't get our gun and shoot us.

I went in the back to look for Joe. He was still sitting at the desk in front of the cell, looking worn out.

"How's the victim?" he asked.

"They're keeping her at Bellevue. They messed her up pretty bad." I went through her list of injuries again.

He shook his head and looked over at the cell.

The perps were in the cage, untouched by the whole thing. The big one was laying on the bench and snoring; the smaller one was sleeping sitting up with his head back against the concrete wall.

Watching them sleep enraged me, and I wanted to go in there and see how well they slept after I made them look like the poster boys for police brutality. I thought about what Vince Puletti said about a time where you could throw them off the roof for doing something like this, and to tell you the truth, I could understand it. As far as I'm concerned, for something like this, they should have no rights.

"They give you any trouble?" I asked.

"The big one complained until I loosened his cuffs. After that they went to sleep," he said as he rubbed his hands over his face.

"I need the complaint report to take the evidence kit up to the evidence unit on 1st Avenue."

He looked around on the desk and pulled it out for me. "Here, it's finished. You just need the complaint number."

I walked past the desk to go to the complaint room for the number and saw the two Special Victims detectives come in.

"Tony, can you tell Joe to come out—the detectives are here," Terri Marks said.

"I have the complaint report. I have to get the number and I'll give you copies." I filled in the complaint number and made four copies before I went back to get Joe.

I gave Joe the original three copies and kept one for the kit.

"I'm gonna drop off the kit. The detectives are here to see you," I said. "You want anything while I'm out?"

"No, I'm good, thanks."

The medical examiner's office was across the street from Bellevue, so I took 34th Street across town again, but took 2nd Avenue over to 30th Street instead of the service road. I parked outside the white brick building and was met by an old-timer at the door. He looked like a cop, and it turned out he worked at my precinct twenty years ago. I dropped the evidence off on the third floor, came back down, and threw the guard a wave on my way out.

I got back to the precinct at 6:20. The lou had gotten someone to take the perps downtown, and Joe was asleep downstairs in the lounge. I didn't want to wake him, so I tried not to make any noise as I took off my shoes, belt, and vest.

Joe's watch beeped at 7:15, but he didn't move. "Hey, buddy." I gave him a shake.

"I'm up," he said, still sleeping.

I went into the locker room to change. Joe was awake when I went back into the lounge. He was talking on his cell phone. I threw him a wave, telling him I'd talk to him later, and went upstairs to sign out.

I drove crosstown and took the Queens Midtown Tunnel to the Long Island Expressway. Michele lives way out in Manorville at exit 70 off the LIE. The LIE was congested through Nassau County but eased off once I got out to Suffolk. The drive took me an hour and fifteen minutes, and I was in Manorville by five after nine.

I was gonna stop at the Starbucks on 111, but I didn't want any more coffee. I stopped at a deli in the King Kullen shopping plaza for a bacon, egg, and cheese on a roll.

I had a key to let myself in the house, and I wondered how Michele manages to keep it clean in the middle of construction. I ate my sandwich, then used the ladder they threw together from two-by-fours to go upstairs and see how the work was going. They didn't put the stairs in yet, which is fine with me. I'd rather wait until the upstairs is done before Stevie could get upstairs alone and, God forbid, get hurt on something.

When I was here on Sunday, the rooms were framed and they had put plywood floors down. The electrician must have run the initial wiring, because they were starting to Sheetrock. Michele and I are going this weekend to look at paint, the new front door, and carpet for the bedrooms. It's pretty exciting watching it come together, and I couldn't wait for it to be done.

There was no crew here. I knew the contractor had a couple of jobs going, and sometimes he didn't get here until the afternoon. I heard the phone ring downstairs and went down to get it, figuring it was Michele.

"Tony?" I heard my mother's voice.

"Yeah, hey Mom." I guess I sounded surprised.

"Oh, I didn't expect you to be there—I was leaving a message for Michele."

"She's at school," I said.

"I know, that's why I was leaving a message," she said logically.

"Well, what's the message? I'll give it to her."

"Um, no, that's okay. I'll call her later."

"Why can't you tell me?" I asked, suspicious.

"Because it's about her wedding dress and I'm not telling you," she chuckled.

"What do you have to do with her wedding dress?"

"Tony! I don't want to tell you. What are you doing there? I thought you were working."

"I'm off tonight. I'm doing a day tour tomorrow," I said.

"Are you ready for Sunday?" she asked.

"I guess. I just hope it doesn't end up in a brawl."

"Well, neither of us will be drinking, so that should help," she said good-naturedly.

We've gotten better at this, my mother and me. She's surprisingly honest about herself and her drinking, so it makes it easier for us to talk.

"We won't be drinking, but everyone else will," I said.

"Who else will be there? I thought this was something small," she said, sounding uneasy.

"Everyone. Grandma invited the whole family."

"Aunt Rose, Uncle Mickey? That whole family?" Now she sounded panicked.

"Even the cousins," I said.

"Why? They weren't at Vinny's party."

"Christie's parents threw Vinny's party, and it was only the immediate family on both sides."

"I don't know if I'm up for all of them and Marie," she said quietly.

"Suck it up, Mom. If I can do this, so can you. Besides, we'll get to see what everyone's like when we're not drinking."

"Tony, it's things like this that are triggers, things that make us vulnerable to drink again."

"We're not gonna drink again," I said, meaning it. Although last time I fell off the wagon, it was after a family brawl.

A thought popped into my head and before I realized it, I was asking her, "Mom, was Dad always like this?"

"Like what?" she hesitantly asked.

"You know, like he is. Difficult. I mean, was it Vietnam or was he always this way?"

"Tony, I really don't want to talk about your father. Why don't you ask him?"

I barked out a laugh. "Yeah, like he'd tell me anything. Come on, was he always this difficult, or did the war make him mean?"

"Well," she paused. "He was always headstrong." Her tone was guarded.

"Mom, how about an answer here? I'm trying to find out what his problem is with me."

"Well, he was from South Beach and a lot of his—"

I cut her off. "Don't give me the recap of his childhood. I know all about the gang he hung with in South Beach. I know he says the Marine Corps was the best thing that ever happened to him, that it straightened him out. Tell me about *him*. What about when he came back from Vietnam?"

She sighed. "He was quiet. He'd been through a lot over there, but he wasn't bitter about it like a lot of guys that went over there. He felt he served his country and was proud of it."

"He said he didn't have any of that post-traumatic stress stuff or battle fatigue—is that true?" I asked.

"No, he didn't. He was happy to be home, happy to be with you and me. As much as Marie would like to say he married me when he didn't want to, that was a lie. We were engaged before he went in the service. I'm not saying I wasn't pregnant when we got married, but he wanted to get married. It was after Denise was born that we started having problems, and even that had nothing to do with our home life. It was something that happened at work," she said.

"What happened?"

"Tony, I don't think it's my place to tell you. It's something very personal to him, and if he wanted you to know, he would have told you. But it was after that happened that he changed. He became angry and distant, and we started having problems."

"What was it?"

"Tony, I really don't—"

"Come on, Mom, I have a right to know." I raised my voice. "If something happened that affected all of us, I'd like to know so at least I could understand."

She sighed again and was quiet for a couple of seconds. "He killed a kid."

"*What?* When?"

"He was a rookie, working a four-to-twelve. The kid was ten years old and came out between two parked cars about ten o'clock at night. It was dark . . ." Her voice trailed off.

"Where was this?"

"The lower East Side, down by Knickerbocker," she said, meaning Knickerbocker Village.

"Did he get in trouble?"

"No, it was an accident. This was a long time ago, Tony, back in the days when an accident was an accident and didn't wind up in riots and cops going to jail. But it changed him. I couldn't get him to talk about it, and back then the department wouldn't force him to go for counseling."

"Wow," I said, trying to absorb it. "I don't know what to say. He's my father and I feel like I don't know anything about him."

"I know. I think that was a lot of my problem. I kept waiting for the person I married to come back, but he's gone, Tony. He's been gone for a long time," she said sadly. "But," she tried to sound cheerful, "that's all water under the bridge. This is a new start for you, so enjoy it and don't let anyone ruin it for you."

"Any more skeletons in the closet that I should know about?" I asked, wondering if I really wanted to know.

"Sure, we've got graveyards in this family. But today's not the day for it. Go get some sleep, I love you," she said.

"I love you too, Mom. Thanks for telling me about Dad. I'll see you Sunday."

I went outside and sat on the front steps to smoke a cigarette. It was so quiet compared to the city. I could hear the wind rustling through the pine trees and actually saw some rabbits out on Michele's lawn. This area of Long Island was in the Pine Barrens, thousands of acres of protected pine forest. The cul de sac across from us had three houses whose property touched the Pine Barrens. It was pretty rural out here. Directly across from our house was a horse farm.

No cars passed by, no sirens or horns honking, just peace and quiet. I could live here. I think the only things that bother me are the skunks and the commute. The commute is only for another nine years, but the skunks are a different story. We don't have skunks in Manhattan or Staten Island. It's a disgusting smell—maybe it's me, but I'll take rats and garbage over skunks any day.

I went inside and changed into sweats. I didn't set the alarm—the minute Stevie saw my truck, he'd come barreling in and jump on me. I slept in Michele's room. The bedroom set we picked out wouldn't be delivered until September, and like me she had a full-size bed with no headboard. Granted, hers had flowered sheets and it smelled good, but pretty much the same bed I had at home.

I lay awake for a while; I don't know if it was too quiet or too bright in the room. I found myself thinking about my father. I also must have been thinking about the female who was assaulted last night, because I saw her face being smashed and my body jerked me awake. The last time I looked at the clock, it was five to eleven.

I heard Stevie's squeal and rolled over to look at the clock—4:30. I groaned and rolled back over on my stomach so at least when he jumped on me, he wasn't hitting anything important.

"Tony! I didn't know you were coming!" He jumped on my back and was trying to tickle me.

"Hey buddy!" I rubbed my hand over my face. "How's your ear feeling?" I asked, turning to look at him.

"Good, but I still have to take the medicine."

He looked fine to me. "Do you know how to make coffee?" I asked him.

"Nooooo," he giggled. "But Mom does. Mom, make us some coffee," he called to Michele.

"Come on, get up," he said trying to pull my arm.

"Okay, do me a favor, let me talk to Mom a second, then I'll get up."

"You always say that and it's more than a second!" he argued.

"I mean it, give me five minutes."

"You promise?" He had his hands on his hips.

"I promise."

"O-kay," he said as he walked out, dragging his feet.

Michele was leaning against the door frame, dressed in a blue suit with a white silk shirt. She was tall and thin, with big brown eyes and shoulder-length light brown hair with some blond threaded through it—the best-looking teacher I've ever seen.

"Come here, legs," I said and smiled at her.

"Not on your life, Tony, I'm staying here."

"Afraid to be alone with me?"

129

"Absolutely. Especially when you look all rumpled and sexy in my bed."

"Rumpled and sexy, I like that." We stared at each other for a couple of minutes until she asked, "What do you want for dinner?"

"Let's go out. I thought we'd have dinner and take Stevie to a movie."

"Out to dinner with Stevie is a happy meal," she said.

"I know, but it's nice out. We can pick up food for you and me, get him the happy meal, and eat it outside at the McDonald's on Main Street where they have that play thing. There's tables there."

"I don't know if we can bring food in."

"They're not gonna say anything. We can stop at that fish place, the one with the shark jaws, and take it to go." I was talking about a seafood place on Montauk Highway. It was a fish store with a restaurant in it. You can buy the fish fresh and take it home and cook it, or you can eat it there or take it out.

"Sounds good." She smiled. "It's nice to see you."

"Nice to see you too."

"Are we going to finish our discussion from the other night?" she asked, still smiling.

"Is there any way I can convince you to marry me in the biblical sense before November?"

"No."

"Then I guess there's nothing to discuss," I said, a little disappointed. "It's not worth fighting over."

"No more alone in the bedroom," she said seriously. "Even if it's under construction."

"We're alone in the bedroom now," I pointed out.

"No, you're in the bedroom and I'm in the hallway, heading for the kitchen." She turned and walked toward it. "I'll make some coffee."

"Coward!" I yelled after her. I go back and forth between being frustrated out of my mind and wanting to do the right thing. Right here proves the basic differences between men and women—Michele counts the days until we get married, I count the days till we can have sex.

I got in the shower and couldn't find shampoo that didn't smell like flowers or come in a Winnie the Pooh bottle. I took the Winnie the Pooh over the girlie one, and my hair felt like straw, so I had to use the pink crème rinse anyway.

I ran my electric razor over my face and changed into a T-shirt, jeans, and sneakers. Michele had changed into jeans and a black shirt and was packing a couple of juice boxes and some fruit snacks to take with us. She added some hand wipes and an apple and zipped the thing closed. Stevie was jumping up on me, his blond hair was spiked up, and he was wearing a Bob the Builder shirt.

We took my truck, stopping first at the fish store for two dinners. Michele got crab-stuffed shrimp with Newburg sauce, and I got sole stuffed with crab, spinach, and artichokes. Both dinners came with herb risotto and grilled asparagus.

Since the weather was nice, the playground at McDonald's was packed. We got Stevie a chicken nuggets happy meal, but he was too interested in climbing in the playground. He'd go through the tubes and take a bite, then go down the slide and take a bite. It was only four chicken pieces and a small fries, and Michele gave him the juice box instead of the soda. The toy with the meal was from *Shrek*, the movie we were taking him to. It was a statue of the princess in a green dress, but when you turned her head around, she turned into an ogre. I hoped the movie wasn't scary, because the toy was.

We sat at one of the tables and ate while Stevie played. We stayed at the playground until 6:45 and drove down Montauk Highway to the movie theater in Shirley. I got a bucket of pop-corn, a box of DOTS, and two sodas. Michele didn't like to give Stevie soda to begin with, never mind this close to bedtime.

I always think these kids' movies are gonna be boring, then I wind up liking them more than Stevie does. This one was really good. There were a lot of adult innuendos, but they went right over Stevie's head. I thought at the end that the princess was going to stay a princess, but she turned into a girl ogre. It was cute, but what do I know?

Stevie fell asleep in the car on the way home. We woke him up to give him his medicine, and he went right back to sleep. Michele made coffee for me and tea for her, and we sat talking in the kitchen. I told her about being at Grandma's and what my mother told me about my dad killing that kid.

"Wow," she said. "That's tragic. For everyone—your family, the child's family." She shook her head sadly.

"My mother said he changed after that," I said with a shrug. "I'd think the war would have more of an effect on him, but that doesn't seem to bother him."

"Doesn't bother him? He can't even talk about Vietnam without getting enraged—remember how he was Christmas Eve when he was talking about the protestors from the war?" She shook her head. "Tony, he has issues from that war."

"That's what I think."

"But I could see how killing the child would be the thing to get him. Vietnam was war. This was an innocent child, and I'm sure the fact that it was an accident doesn't make him feel any less responsible." We were quiet for a couple of minutes, and she looked up and smiled at me. "So how's work?"

A few months ago I started doing something I'd never done with anyone else, telling her about my job. I don't like to tell her a lot of stuff because it's depressing. She says it doesn't bother her, she'd rather know what's going on while I'm at work. I told her about the guy that got stabbed and the woman that was assaulted last night. She usually asks me their names so she can pray for them. A lot of times I don't know the names, but she prays anyway. She says God knows who they are.

I stayed until 11:00. Michele watched me walk out to my car, and I started the long drive back to Staten Island. There was no traffic on the road and it only took me about an hour and a half, putting me at my door by 12:20. I was tired by then—I'd only gotten about five and a half hours' sleep. I set my alarm for 6:15 and was showered, shaved, and on the road by 6:45.

The sun was bright, and a warm breeze blew as I cruised along Father Cappodanno Boulevard. Because I grew up along the Narrows of New York Bay, seeing the water was part of my everyday life. I miss it, so I found myself staring at it as I drove along this stretch of road that lets me see the ocean.

I watched the sun dance on the calm waters, thinking that it would be low tide now. I couldn't see the shoreline, but I knew the dirt-colored sand would be clear of footprints. I snapped out of my daydreaming when I almost slammed into the back of a silver BMW that slowed down around the turn at Lily Pond Avenue.

Rush-hour traffic was horrendous. It bottlenecked at the tolls on the Verrazzano Bridge, it eased up somewhat through Bay Ridge, but it was stop-and-go along the Gowanus. As I came around where it meets the Prospect Expressway, I could see the line for the Brooklyn Bridge. I took the Brooklyn Battery Tunnel—I'd rather pay the three bucks than spend half my life trying to cross the bridge for free.

The West Side was congested until Chambers Street, then backed up again in the meatpacking district. I got off and took 10th Avenue. I threw my parking plaque that showed my license plate and precinct name in the windshield and parked on the sidewalk on 36th Street.

The daytime skells were hanging out on the corner of 36th and 9th. I threw them a couple of bucks to watch my truck. They'd stay until they got bored or someone chased them.

The day tour is a lot noisier and a lot more crowded than the midnights. Horns blared, parking lots were backed up, and there was so much pedestrian and vehicular traffic. The streets were full of cabs, city buses, express buses, private express buses, school buses. Trucks making deliveries were double-parked. Businesses were open now, so people were going in and out.

I stopped on the corner of 9th Avenue for a cup of coffee. Geri was gone and a Korean guy waited on me. He wasn't as friendly as Geri, but at least I didn't have to bend over to get my change.

The precinct was busy. The day tour has a lot more cops, plus the bosses were in. People were coming in filing complaints and were sitting on the benches outside the desk. I signed the court sheet, seeing that Romano and Fiore had already signed in. We sign the sheet so whoever is behind the desk can keep track of who's working a day tour and make sure you're on the roll call.

I went downstairs to change. We were testifying in uniform, so I put on a short-sleeved shirt so I didn't swelter later on. I met Romano and Fiore at the desk, and we walked over to 34th Street to catch the train. We bought the *Daily News* and the *Post* and went down into the subway. The temperature in the subway had risen 10 degrees, intensifying the smell of urine and homeless. We were taking the A, C, E line, and we only had to wait a couple of minutes for the train.

People tend to stay in the center of the subway platform.

New York is famous for psychos pushing people who get too close to the edge of the platform into the path of an oncoming train.

We caught the C train. A lot of people had gotten off at 34th Street, but it was still crowded. Joe and I stood on opposite sides of the train in front of the doors, while Romano held on to the overhead bar. There was a mix of students, suits, and blue-collar workers on the train, all keeping to themselves and not making eye contact with anyone. Aside from a couple of kids talking to each other, no one interacted.

"I hate testifying," Romano said, shaking his head. "The last time I testified, the guy's lawyer reamed me. He was such a snake."

"They're all snakes," I said. "I was reading something in the paper that said these defense attorneys actually take acting lessons so they can showboat for the jury."

"Acting lessons?" Fiore laughed. "They need acting lessons—lessons how to act right."

"This guy kept twisting my words," Romano continued. "Firing off questions to me, one after the other. Then he starts asking me these bogus questions, like did I know the defendant had diabetes. How was I supposed to know that? And the ADA was no help. Every time I looked over at him for help, he had his head down, writing on a legal pad."

"The ADA can't look at you—the defense attorney will say you're looking at him for the answer," I said. "All the lawyers do that stuff, Nick. When they do that to me, I mess with them. I watched an old-timer do it once. I was in the courtroom on an unrelated case, and this homicide cop was testifying in front of one of the meanest defense attorneys I've ever seen. The detective knew what he was doing, and the lawyer couldn't rattle him. I studied what he did, and I've used it ever since."

"What do you do?" Romano asked.

"I take a sip of water and ask them to repeat the question slower. Then I take another sip of water and tell them I didn't understand the question. I usually answer the third time, but I say Ummm and talk real slow," I said.

"Don't mess with the lawyers, Nick," Fiore said. "Tony does that stuff 'cause he enjoys it. You're too nervous. You can slow it down to your pace. If you don't know the answer to a question, say you don't know. If you don't remember, say you don't remember."

Romano nodded, looking like he was trying to remember all of it.

We got off at Canal Street, which is actually a block off Canal, and walked two blocks over to Lafayette Street.

Traffic was bumper-to-bumper on Lafayette Street as the cars fought with the trucks that were loading and unloading merchandise.

The Chinese were in Columbus Park doing their morning routine, like they are every time I come here. I watched as they did these slow, fluid movements in unison as they faced the morning sun. They were older; some looked at least eighty years old as they stretched and turned. They looked like something out of an old *Kung Fu* movie, and I wondered if there was a three-second pause from the time they talked until the words came out.

The coffee vendor was packed in front of the courthouse, so we went down the ramp to 60 Centre Street to punch in with our ID cards, figuring the line would be shorter when we got back.

When we came back up, the line was doubled, but we only waited ten minutes for coffee and blueberry muffins. The vendor had bagels, but they were disgusting. The muffins were pretty good.

We brought our coffee and muffins into the Criminal Court building and took the elevator to the seventh floor.

There was a receptionist there when we got off the elevator, a pleasant middle-aged woman with blond hair who's been here as long as I have. She never lets anything get to her; she handles a waiting room full of people, twelve phone calls, and an office full of ADAs without breaking a sweat.

"Good morning, Officers," she said.

"Good morning, Yvette," Joe said, remembering her name. "We're here to see ADA Flannigan."

"Let me see if he's in yet," she said as she dialed a number. "He's not in his office," she reported. "Have a seat, and I'll see if I can find him."

We'd sat in the waiting room for about fifteen minutes when Flannigan walked in with a cup of coffee and a briefcase. "Be right with you," he said as he walked past us and down the hall to his office.

He called me in first, and I followed him down a hallway with sets of offices on both sides. The offices were small at first and got larger as they reached the end of the hallway. The four corner offices belonged to the bureau chiefs who worked right under the district attorney.

Flannigan was the second to last, and he shared it with one ADA instead of two like the newer ones.

"I'm only putting you and Romano on," he said.

We were there on an evidentiary hearing or some other crap the attorneys come up with to slow down the trial if their perps are out on bail. The case was something that Romano, Fiore, and I all wound up on together.

It happened this past winter on 8th Avenue between 42nd and 43rd streets at one of the porn places. This place had peep shows, videos, booths, and live dancers, more like a porn department store. Joe and I had just dropped Romano off at his post and were heading out on patrol. A cab was about thirty feet in front of us, with two guys sitting in the backseat. A guy came running out of the porn place and grabbed Romano, telling him the two guys robbed him before they jumped in the cab.

Romano yelled to Joe and me to stop the cab, so I threw the lights on and whooped him with the siren. We pulled up behind him before he even got a chance to merge into traffic, and Joe and I stepped out of the RMP. As we walked over to approach the cab, Romano and the complainant came running up behind us saying the guys in the cab had a gun.

Fiore went back to the RMP and told them over the PA system to put their hands on the back of their heads. They didn't comply the first time, but the second time I saw three sets of hands go up behind their heads, the two perps' and the cabbie's.

We took them out of the car at gunpoint, me on the left, Joe on the right. Romano and I tossed and cuffed our guy while Joe got the other one. The gun was on the floor of the cab's backseat. The complainant pointed out who had the gun, the guy Romano and I had tossed. We also found the peep show coins and the fifty-five bucks he took off the complainant.

It was a pickup, a good collar, but Romano didn't want it. I think he was intimidated by the whole thing, but he told us he was picking up his daughter in the morning and couldn't take it. Joe and I took the collar, but because Romano talked to the complainant and initiated the stop, he was called in.

I went over what happened with the ADA again. Apparently the perp was saying that the gun was already in the cab when he got in.

"What else is he gonna say?" I said. He wasn't gonna admit it. He knew the ins and outs of the judicial system and how fickle juries can be.

Romano went in next, and then we all went up to the twelfth floor to the courtroom. The ADA went through the dark wood double doors, and Romano, Fiore, and I went down the hallway to the witness room.

It was a small room with a table and chairs and no AC, but the window was open to let in a warm breeze.

We sat there until 11:00, when the ADA came in to say we wouldn't be going in until after lunch. He had us wait until 11:30 just in case the judge called us, and then told us to be back by 12:45.

"You mind if we stop and see my father first?" I asked Joe and Romano. I'd been thinking about what my mother told me, and for some reason I wanted to see him.

"Where is he?" Romano asked.

"Over at the Federal Courthouse," which is only a couple of blocks away.

My father started working security for the Federal Courthouse with a bunch of retired cops he knows. Frank Bruno, his partner from the job, started working there first and got about six other cops, including my father, in with him.

We crossed Baxter Street and walked through a courtyard to the next block. We crossed again and went in the side entrance to the Federal Court Building.

Frank Bruno was at the entrance with another old-timer. They were dressed in pants and a blue jacket—not a suit or a uniform, but they all wore basically the same thing.

"Tony!" Frank Bruno smiled. "Good to see you! Ready for the big party Sunday?" he asked as he waved us around the metal detector. I guess he was invited too.

I smiled. "Oh yeah, can't wait. Is my dad here?"

"Yeah, he's down in the break room. You remember how to get there?" I'd been there once before and knew the way.

Frank pressed the code for the door lock to let us in. We

took the stairs right inside the door and walked a long hallway to the break room.

It was a conference room with white walls and had a big round table with chairs around it. There was a couch and love seat at the far end of the room, where my father was sitting with two other guys.

"Hey, Dad," I said. He looked surprised and happy all at once and got right up. It's funny, at Grandma's he barely gave me a nod.

"Hey, Tony, what are you doing here?" he asked as he hugged me.

"We got court today and had some time on our hands."

"Pete, you know my kid, right?" my father said to one of the other guys that I'd met before.

"Yeah, sure. How you doing, Tony?" He shook my hand. "Congratulations! I heard you got engaged, and your father told me you made Cop of the Month last month." He was smiling, still shaking my hand.

"Yeah, we're down here on that case."

What I don't get is that my father's so nasty in front of the family and so nice when his friends are around. Actually I do get it, I just don't understand why an outsider's opinion of him, someone who's not even blood, should be more important than mine.

"Dad, this is my partner, Joe." I pointed to Fiore. My father never met Joe, but I know he feels Joe is partially responsible for me not drinking and meeting Michele.

My father shook Joe's hand while he eyed him up and down. "I heard a lot about you," my father said, smiling a cynical smile.

"Same here." Joe gave a genuine smile.

"Dad, this is Nick Romano." I pointed to Nick.

"How you doing, Mr. Cavalucci?" Nick said, putting out his hand.

"Hey, kid," my father said, dismissing him.

Normally retired cops don't mind talking to rookies. They miss the job and like talking about it. My father still works with a bunch of cops, so I guess he hasn't had to lower himself to talk to a rookie yet.

"Come on, take your stuff off. Put it on the chair, relax," he said, pointing to one of the chairs at the conference table.

We took our gun belts off and opened our shirts. There was no air-conditioning in this room either, and we were getting warm from the weight of all our gear.

"Can I get you some coffee?" Pete asked.

"No thanks, we're taking our meal soon," I said.

"So how's work?" Pete asked, looking at my collar brass that says the name of my command. "Hey, you work at the South. Is Richie Ingrassia still a sergeant up there?" he asked.

"No, he retired last year," I said.

"How about Brian Gallagher?"

"He's out at the end of the month. In fact, tonight we're going to his retirement party," Joe said.

"Where is it? Maybe I'll stop by," Pete said.

We named the pub up on 45th Street and gave him the time.

"If I don't make it up there, tell him Pete Catalano wishes him the best. And tell him if he's looking for an easy gig once he's out of there, to give me a call."

We stayed a little while and talked about the job. Apparently all the old-timers who worked here were on a health kick. They had a gym there that they worked out at every day. The conversation moved on to the yogurt and flaxseed they've been eating for breakfast and some herb they were taking for their enlarged prostates. Something to look forward to.

Pete said the marshals had been testing them and tried to

sneak weapons past them by having people act like lawyers and putting dismantled weapons in their briefcases.

"Your dad got 'em," Pete said affectionately. "Nailed 'em right at the door."

"Good for you, Dad," I said.

Obviously my father talked a lot about me. I could tell by what Pete was saying that my father was proud of me, but I'd never know it by the way he acted. We got up to leave and my dad said, "I'll walk you up, I gotta relieve Vito anyway."

He walked us upstairs to the side entrance, hugged me, and shook Joe's hand. He threw Romano a nod and said, "I'll talk to you later, Tony."

We walked over to Little Italy to a deli that we have lunch at while we're at court. They're expensive, but the lunch specials are a good buy, usually eight bucks. Today's specials were roast chicken or an eggplant hero.

Romano got a dish of roast chicken and risotto with mushrooms and peas. Joe and I got fried eggplant with mozzarella and roasted peppers on Italian bread. They each came with a soda and a small salad or potatoes and escarole. Romano and Joe got the salad; I got the escarole and potatoes.

We took our food back over to the courthouse and ate it in the witness room. If we weren't in uniform, we would have eaten in Columbus Park.

We finished our lunch and started reading. Romano and I had the newspapers; Joe had his Bible and devotional books. Once he was done, we'd switch off and I'd read one of those daily devotional books.

I read an article about how the city got rid of the last of the coal-burning furnaces in the public schools, then moved on to an article about how the last garbage barge arrived at the Fresh Kills dump on Staten Island. According to the article, the city's been dumping its garbage on Staten Island since 1948, for fifty-three years, to be exact. It went on to talk about the high cancer rate in the people who live around the dump and the poor air quality and number of asthma cases. It only took them fifty-three years to figure out that surrounding people with toxic garbage is gonna make them sick—that's a record.

"Joe, did you know they were having problems last year with the lobsters on the Long Island Sound?" I asked him as I scanned the paper.

He looked up from his reading. "Yeah, the lobstermen were saying it's pesticide runoff. They lost a lot of lobster."

"Yeah, well the paper says it's a parasite." The article said hundreds of thousands of lobster died off and that up until 1999, the Long Island Sound brought in 11 million pounds of lobster a year. The only two other places in the country that had more lobster than us were Maine and Massachusetts.

"I didn't know we had an earthquake here in January," Romano said as he read the paper.

This is the kind of mindless thing we do to pass the time. I bet if they ever made a game show out of worthless trivia, cops would be winning money left and right.

"Yeah, it was in the city," Joe said. "It happened like five miles under the Upper East Side, but it was a small one."

"It was 2.5 on the Richter scale. But it says that people felt it all the way out to Queens. I don't remember anything about it," Romano said.

"You were probably in the bar with Rooney and thought you just had too much to drink," I said.

"Did you feel it?" Romano asked me sarcastically.

"Nope, but I heard about it."

"My stomach feels funny," Romano said, getting up. "I'll be right back."

He came back ten minutes later, sweating and chalky looking.

"That food ran right through me," he said.

"Is testifying making you this nervous?" I asked him.

"No. But I hate judges and I hate lawyers and I hate this job. Once I'm at FD, I'll never have to testify again."

"It's funny, Nick, I was just reading about the Supreme Court of heaven," Joe said.

"Yeah, I'll bet there's no defense attorneys in heaven—they all went the other way," Romano said. "What's it say?" he added.

"It's talking about that in the High Court of heaven, God is the righteous Judge, and we will have to stand before him and give an account of our lives. He isn't influenced by politics or bribes, and he doesn't base his decisions on public approval or votes. His decisions are based on his Word alone."

"What does that mean, the Ten Commandments? Like if we steal and lie and stuff?"

"Yeah," Fiore said, "but we're only judged if we don't judge ourselves and repent."

"How do you judge yourself?"

"Confess your sins to God. It says in 1 John 1:9 that if we confess our sins—"

"I know, God is faithful to forgive us and not give us unrighteousness," Romano said from memory, even though it was wrong.

"Close." Fiore smiled. "'He is faithful and just to forgive our sins and to cleanse us from all unrighteousness.' If we're cleansed of our sins, then we're not guilty of them anymore. Just say you're in heaven, God is the Judge, and there's no jury there—he's the boss. There's a prosecutor, a mean-looking guy, evil as anything."

"Okay," Romano said.

"You get a lawyer, Jesus, your brother, God's Son. Hopefully, before you get before the throne room, you'll be familiar with him and know him when you see him."

Romano nodded.

"The prosecutor is presenting his case before God, showing all your sins and saying he's got the evidence to back it up. He tells how you lied and cheated, slept around, anything deep and dark you didn't want anyone to know about. He'll bring up stuff you forgot you did, every vile, filthy thing you ever did or thought of doing. Once he's done presenting his case, he'll say that you are guilty of these sins and the wages of sin are death, and you should be condemned to hell."

Romano and I were both staring at Fiore.

"Then your lawyer gets up and approaches the bench. He smiles at the Judge, who smiles back at him just the way you smile, Nick, when you see your daughter. He tells the Judge that his client is innocent and asks to see the evidence in question. The court officer brings up a videotape and puts it in a machine. He presses play, but there's nothing but static. Next is an audiotape that is silent. Books with empty pages are submitted. The Judge looks at you and asks how you plead. What do you say?"

"There's no evidence?" Romano asked.

"Nope. If you believe that Jesus is the Son of God and that he died on the cross for your sins, and you acknowledge him as Savior and Lord, then your sins are forgiven. He'll remember them no more," Fiore said.

"Then I walk," Romano said.

"Yup, you walk."

He looked at Fiore for a couple of seconds. "I'm not ready. I'm still too mad about my father."

Fiore nodded. "Don't wait too long."

"You always find a way to get this stuff in there, don't you, Joe?" Romano asked.

Fiore smiled. "I thought it would take your mind off having to testify."

As if on cue, the court officer came in and said, "Romano?"

Romano threw him a wave.

"You're up, buddy."

"So did those two mutts say anything after I left?" I asked Fiore, talking about the assault from the other night.

"No. Rooney and Connelly must have humbled them before they got back."

"You were pretty upset the other night—not that I blame you," I said.

"I'm sorry about my language," he said, and I almost laughed.

"We catch these two almost killing this girl, and you're gonna apologize for cursing? Don't worry about it." I did laugh now. "You're funny."

"Nothing about that was funny."

No, it wasn't.

Romano was in there for about fifteen minutes and came out looking frazzled. He put his head down and said, "Good luck, Tony," as the court officer called me in.

I wondered what I was in for as the court officer walked me up to the witness stand. He swore me in and poured me a glass of water from a pitcher and handed it to me.

The perps looked a little cleaned up, but you could dip these guys in bleach and they'd still look like perps. There were two sheister-looking public defenders with them. One had greasy hair and a cheap suit; the other looked like he should be working for Save the Whales or something.

The ADA went through it with me first. "State your name, shield, and command." I repeated it back to him in that order, spelling out my last name. I told the story, how the gun was retrieved, who the complainant pointed to. Then he asked if I could point out the perp in the courtroom. I played it a little, scanning the room to look at the judge, stenographer, and court officer before pointing to the perp sitting right in front of me. "The gentleman with the black shirt sitting at the table," I said.

He showed me my voucher from when I vouchered the gun, then he was finished.

The greasy public defender strutted over and said, "Officer Cavalucky."

"It's Cavalucci," I countered.

"Right. Did you have a conversation with the DA, Flannigan, before this hearing?"

"That's ADA Flannigan," I said, because his next thing would be "Are you telling me you spoke to the district attorney of Manhattan before you came in here?" Then I said, "Yes, we had a conversation before I came in here."

They do that to make you feel like you were doing something wrong by discussing it with the ADA. If you say no, they'll say, "Do you expect us to believe you didn't say a word to each other?" and we'd dance from there. When he saw I wasn't falling for his crap, he switched to, "Isn't it true that you didn't find the gun on my client?"

I took a sip of water and looked innocent. "On his person?"

"Yes."

"No," I said.

"So where did you find the gun?"

I took another sip. "On the floor of the cab." I looked at the judge as I talked to include him in the conversation.

"On the floor of the cab that he stepped out of?"

"That's correct."

"What color was the gun?"

Sip. "A silver-colored 9 millimeter Beretta."

"So you found a silver gun in the cab and not on my client?"

There's the bait again. If I said silver, he'd say how did I know it was silver and was I an expert in metals that I could make that kind of statement.

Sip. "No, I found a silver-*colored* gun in the cab and not on your client."

"Did you see my client put the gun there?"

I sipped and cleared my throat. "Your client was moving around in the back of the cab. We had to give him two commands to put his hands on top of his head."

He went on, firing away at me with the questions. "Isn't it true that anybody could have put it there? How do you know the gun came from my client? Isn't it possible the person who was in the cab before him left the gun?"

I answered and sipped until he finally ran out of steam when he realized he couldn't get me and wound it down with, "What's the complainant's name?"

"Jon Orlostanzki," I said, remembering how the complainant pronounced it.

"Nothing further," he said.

The second lawyer came up now. "Did the complainant ever point out my client as having the gun?"

"No."

"Nothing further."

I walked back out to the waiting room, and the ADA came out a couple of minutes later.

"I'm sorry I kept messing up the complainant's name," Romano said.

"Don't worry about it, you got the point across. Good job, guys." We shook hands all around. "I'll be in touch."

We went down and punched out at 2:00. We walked back up to Chambers Street and caught the train uptown. When we got back to the precinct, we took our meal, but since we'd already eaten, we went down to the lounge to sleep.

We woke up at 4:30 and went upstairs to sign out. Brian Gallagher's retirement party wasn't until 7:00, so we had some time to kill. We changed into clothes, and all three of us were wearing short-sleeved black shirts. Joe wore jeans, but Romano and I both had beige pants on. We didn't notice it until Terri Marks pointed it out, asking if we shopped at the same place.

We walked up 8th Avenue to 42nd and over to Times Square, to the new Toys R Us store on Broadway between 44th and 45th streets. It was Fiore's son Josh's birthday next week, and he wanted to look around.

The store is a kid's dream. It's got a sixty-foot working Ferris wheel in the middle of the store. For the girls it has a two-story Barbie dollhouse with about a million Barbie accessories. They have a pretty big copy of the Empire State Building done in LEGOs, and a twenty-foot-high, thirty-four-foot-long T-Rex dinosaur. The T-Rex was pretty real looking, and a lot of the littler kids looked scared as they walked by.

We spent about an hour in the store. Joe didn't buy anything, and we wound up staying in the video room playing games on plasma screens.

The streets were packed as we made our way up to 45th Street around a quarter to seven. It's the heart of the theater district, and the shows would be starting soon. The pub was off Broadway, and I've been to it a few times since I've worked here, although tonight would be the first time I was there without drinking.

The downstairs was done up in a lot of mahogany wood, stained glass windows, and tiffany lamps. It was a long brass and wood bar with tables and booths in the back. The place was packed, and we wove our way through the after work crowd to take the staircase to the second floor, which was rented out for the party.

The second floor had a smaller bar with a line of bar stools and a bunch of tables. There were a lot of signs for Harp and Guinness on the walls. There were pictures and maps and signs for Ireland, and if it wasn't for the smoked glass New York skyline that separated the bar from the dining area, you'd think you were in a pub in Dublin.

There were about thirty people there already, most of them cops. Terri Marks had changed into a black sleeveless dress and high-heeled shoes and sported a face full of war paint. Even without the haze of booze, I had to admit she looked good in the soft lights of the bar.

There weren't a lot of cops from our squad there. I think Rooney and Terri Marks were the only ones who were taking off tonight to come in. We had court today so we were off tonight, and we were already in the city anyway.

"Hi, Joe," Terry said as she sized up Fiore.

"Hey, Terr, how you doing?" Joe asked.

"Good."

"Hi, Terr," I said.

"Tony, Nick." She nodded to the both of us.

I looked around the place. Just about everyone had a drink in their hand, and some looked like they'd been at it for a while.

We moved along the bar, saying hello to the cops we knew as we walked by.

"Tony! Joe!" They'd shake our hands and slap our backs as they gave Romano a nod.

"I hate this job—it's like I'm friggin' invisible," Nick mumbled.

We made our way over to Brian Gallagher to congratulate him on his retirement. He was feeling no pain already, holding a glass of Guinness that was half full. He was happy to see us and thanked us for coming, showing us his police ID card that was now stamped RETIRED under his picture.

"So what's next?" I asked him. He was a big drinker, and I'm not sure how ambitious he'd be once he was getting his pension.

"I'm gonna chill out for a while," he said. "I got a couple of offers."

"Oh, you know who I saw today? Pete Catalano," I said, remembering Pete's message.

"Really? Where'd you see him?"

"He's doing security with my father for the marshals down at the Federal Courthouse. He said to put your application in before the pile gets too big. He might stop by tonight," I told him.

Someone slapped him on the back and sloshed his Guinness all over his pants leg. A group of people surrounded him, so we moved on to the bar. Joe and I ordered ice water, and Romano got vodka on the rocks.

"Whoa, slow down there, soldier," I said. "Work your way up to it."

He smiled. "You want one, Tony?"

"Nah, I'll stick to water," I said, thinking that I would have started out with beers and switched to vodka later on. This was gonna be an interesting night.

The first hour was strictly booze, and I found myself kind of disconnected from the whole thing. I was glad Fiore was there with me—the last time I was in a bar, I fell off the wagon. The thing about being in a bar when you're drinking is that you fit right in. Drinking water I felt like an outcast.

The room was filling up now. Mike Rooney came in for the party; his wife is a stewardess and was out of town. He went up to the bar and ordered a scotch on the rocks, I guess to make up for the forty-five minutes he missed.

Eileen Toomey came in with two other detectives from the squad. Freddie Puro, who's also a detective, came in with four females. He's been married twice already, and since none of them were his wife, I guess he was working on number three.

They started bringing out hot trays of food and placing them on sternos in the dining area. Since Romano hadn't eaten since lunch and was on his third vodka on the rocks, I figured he needed something to absorb the alcohol.

"You ready to eat?" I asked him and Joe. Romano finished his drink, I downed my ice water, and we walked over to the food.

It was a nice spread, mostly finger food, but it was good. I grabbed a plate and filled it with shrimp cocktail, buffalo wings, stuffed mushrooms, mozzy sticks, beef on skewers with some kind of teriyaki glaze, chicken fingers with honey mustard sauce, and fried artichoke hearts and cauliflower with a horseradish sauce.

The music went on, and the sound of a sad ballad filled

the room. They'd be singing later—they just weren't drunk enough yet.

I could tell who was hammered by the way they were eating. Brian Gallagher had sauce from the wings on his chin and cocktail sauce in his mustache. Freddie Puro had finished one of the beef sticks and was using the skewer to tickle one of the women with him. Romano dropped a mushroom in his lap twice before getting it into his mouth—the way he was drinking, he'd be enjoying his food on its way up too.

The crowd made their way back over to the bar when Terri Marks came out with a camera for a group picture. It took ten minutes to get everyone in the picture. Some sat on chairs, stood on chairs, kneeled on the floor, or held their hand in the horns over somebody's head.

"Okay, everybody smile and say this job sucks," Terri said.

"This job sucks!" we all said in unison, laughing and smiling.

A couple of big shot brass came in to see Brian. Both the captain and lieutenant from the Times Square detail at the South stopped by in their white shirts. They both ate, but neither one of them were drinking. There was a time cops could drink in uniform, but that was a long time ago.

Lenny Tobin, a cop from the midnights, was hammered out of his mind. Maybe he forgot he was getting married this summer, because he was sucking face with an overweight female from the day tour. It looked like they were wrestling—she had pushed him up against the bar, and I could see hands fumbling with her bra strap.

"Get a room!" someone yelled. Everyone laughed, but neither one of them heard it.

It was funny to overhear the conversations without the sway of alcohol. For the most part, cops in bars talk about the job.

Even if they start out talking about other things, it always comes back to it.

Mike Rooney was yapping about a car bombing in Jerusalem and talking about all the ways a suicide bomber could get explosives into the city.

"Think about it," he said. "Trunk of a car, a briefcase, backpack, even underclothes. It would be so easy to do it here."

Lenny Tobin was talking about the pictures of the inspector. "Hey, where's the naughty inspector?" he yelled out.

"Down the Village, looking for some action," someone yelled back.

The music changed, and the crowd broke out singing "When Irish Eyes Are Smiling." They were all off-key, and half of them had the words wrong.

I found myself going back and forth between wanting a drink and talking to someone and forgetting about it for a little while. As the night wore on, I was glad I wasn't wasted, but I noticed I could relate to the falling-down drunks more than the social drinkers.

I caught Terri Marks watching Fiore from across the room. She belted back her drink and sauntered over toward us, smiling, with her eyes on Fiore. He groaned and rubbed his forehead as she approached. She didn't bother with small talk, just walked up and leaned into his chest. He took a step back, but she leaned in closer.

"Easy, Terr," he said. "You've had a little too much to drink."

She smiled a cat's smile. "I know exactly what I'm doing, Joe."

"I know exactly what you're doing too," Joe said, not smiling.

"Good, as long as we're on the same page here," she said as she moved in for a kiss. He put his hands out on her shoulders, keeping her at arm's length. "Listen, Terr, this isn't a good idea."

"Why not?" she asked, trying to lean in again.

"Number one, I'm married and I love my wife—"

"Are you saying you never cheated on your wife?" she cut him off.

"No, I never did."

"Come on, Joe, everybody cheats," she said cynically.

"No, they don't," he said. "And number two, we have to work together and this isn't a good idea."

"Are you turning me down?" she asked, sounding surprised and insulted.

"Yeah, I am." He nodded seriously.

I was starting to get uncomfortable here, so I said, "Terri, can I get you a drink?"

"Forget these two, they're not even drinking. Come on, I'll get you a drink," Romano said, already half in the bag.

"Sure," she said, still looking at Joe. "Why not?"

"I think you hurt her feelings," I told Joe as they walked over to the bar.

"I wasn't trying to hurt her feelings, Tony, but my wife's feelings are more important than hers." He shook his head. "This is why I don't like coming to these things—there's too much drinking, and people get out of hand."

"Terri's right, though," I said. "Most people cheat—in fact, a lot of people here are cheating."

"A lot of people here are drinking," Joe pointed out.

"Drinking isn't the only reason," I said, thinking of my father and Marie.

"No, it isn't. It's also not loving God. He's faithful, and the only way we're ever gonna learn how to be faithful to our wives is by being faithful to him first. People get married all the time without having a clue about what marriage is all about," Joe said.

"Meaning?"

"Meaning that marriage is a covenant, not just with you and your wife, but with God too. When you break covenant by cheating, it's not just on your wife. You took a vow that included God, and it shouldn't be taken lightly."

I was learning a lot of this stuff anyway. Michele and I have to go to counseling for six months before Pastor John will marry us, and it's pretty serious stuff. Divorce statistics are high both in and outside the church, and Pastor John is teaching us how to avoid it.

He asked Michele and me what was the number one reason for divorce, and we both got it wrong. I said sex, or lack of it, and Michele said communication. And while I guess both of them had something to do with it, Pastor said it was selfishness. He said that he counsels people all the time who are having marriage problems, and while both partners complained about sex, money, communication, the kids, and all that other stuff, what they were really being was selfish. "He doesn't talk to me," "She won't sleep with me," "He doesn't make enough money," or "She spends too much money." Everyone is pointing the finger at the other person because they're not getting what they want out of the marriage, instead of each one thinking about the other person.

Even tonight with Joe, his loyalty was to Donna—where it should have been—instead of worrying about hurting Terri's feelings. He doesn't owe Terri anything—she knows he's married, she's the one who's wrong.

I looked over at Romano, who looked like he was arguing with Rooney. "Let's go check on Romano," I told Joe and nodded toward the bar. Joe looked over to see Rooney getting up in Romano's face.

"Nick's drinking way too much," Joe said as we walked over to them.

"She's like a serial killer," Rooney was saying to Romano.

"Who?" Joe asked.

"Terri Marks. She collects an article of clothing from every guy she sleeps with and saves it. She's got ties, underwear, shirts, pants, you name it. She took my 'one tequila, two tequila, three tequila, floor' T-shirt and wouldn't give it back. It's freaky, Joe. That's something a serial would do, and now she's giving Romano her 'come to mama' spiel, trying to get him to go home with her." He looked at Romano. "I'm telling you, Nick, don't go home with her. She's older—how old is she?" He looked at me.

I shrugged. "I have no idea, maybe forty. Where is she?" I looked around the bar.

"In the john," Rooney said.

"Since when are you so concerned about me, Mike?" Romano asked, slurring his words a little. It was taking him a couple of minutes to process the conversation. "I'm just a rookie to you. You only talk to me when no one else is around, so why should I listen to you? I'm leaving soon anyway, and I'll never have to see her *or* you again."

"Yeah, and you'll be a big shot fireman, right?" Rooney said like he didn't believe it.

"That's right, and I'll get some respect, not like this job."

"Keep telling yourself that, kid. You'll be nothing at FD. What do you think you're gonna do over there?" Rooney shook his head.

"I'm gonna cook—I like to cook. And I'm gonna sleep and work out and watch porn and block the fire lanes in front of Shop Rite while I buy food," Romano said, sucking down the rest of his drink and slamming it on top of the bar for effect.

"And I'm gonna party and get a lot of women. Women love

firemen, and not the skelly women we meet—these are hot-looking women. Bartender!" Romano yelled. "Another vodka on the rocks, please."

The bartender looked at Joe and me to see if we wanted a drink, but we shook our heads no.

"You think you'll be a big shot over there?" Rooney laughed. "You won't be cooking, that's for the real firemen. You think they'll give you a 'kiss the cook' apron? They'll give you a 'kiss the toilet' apron, 'cause that's what you'll be doing, cleaning the toilets. And your helmet will say PROBEE 'cause that's what you'll be, so don't get a big head here, kid. You'll still be a bottom-feeder."

"Shut up, Mike," Romano slurred, "or I'll shut your mouth for you."

"You getting beer muscles, kid?" Rooney moved in closer to intimidate him, but Romano was too wasted to notice.

"I'm not drinking beer, they're vodka muscles."

"Mike, leave him alone," Joe said. "He has no idea what he's saying."

"He's got a big mouth," Rooney said loudly. He was drunk too, and he likes to fight when he's drunk.

"Mike." I looked him in the eye. "That's enough."

"We're taking him out of here, the party's just about over anyway," Joe said.

There were a couple of hundred dollars left over from what they collected for the party, so they were taking it and putting it on the bar downstairs for anyone who wanted to keep drinking. It was ten to eleven and we still had to stop at the precinct and get Joe on the 11:30 train.

Romano was having a hard time walking, so Joe and I got on either side of him as we took him down the stairs. We walked outside the bar, and I made Joe keep Romano by the entranceway while I got us a cab. The cabbies don't like drunks in their cars and might have passed us by if they saw us holding up Romano.

The cabbie looked at Romano as Joe walked him over. "No, uh-uh, he's not getting in my cab if he's drinking."

"He's not feeling good—we're only going a couple of blocks," I said, which was true.

"He's not going to vomit in my cab, is he?" The cabbie was sizing me up.

"No, definitely not." Hoping I meant it.

"Don't you vomit in my cab!" the cabbie told Romano once he was in the car.

"Go shell a rug, you friggin' camel jockey," Nick slurred, but I doubt the guy understood what he said.

"Shut up, Nick," I said.

We got out of the cab on 36th and 9th and got in my truck. I drove over to the precinct and parked out front. I tried to get Romano's locker combination out of him, but he was nodding off and wouldn't answer me. He would look up at me and smile, then lob his head down on his chest. I locked the truck and took my keys before going in just in case Romano woke up and decided to drive.

Joe and I ran down to our lockers and got our bags. I grabbed two dirty uniforms and threw them in my bag so I could wash them tomorrow. I drove over to Penn Station and stopped at the 34th Street entrance.

"Will you be okay with him?" Fiore asked me.

"We'll be fine. I just hope we make it home before he pukes."

"What time will I see you tomorrow?" Joe asked.

"I'm going out to Michele's in the morning. We're going shopping, and we'll be by later in the afternoon."

"Are we fishing tomorrow night?" he asked.

"Yeah, as long as it doesn't rain. My poles and stuff are out at Michele's; we can pick them up there."

"Take it easy there, Nick," Joe said to Romano, who threw him a delayed wave.

I put the AC on full blast and opened Romano's window as I drove downtown. We got through the tunnel okay, but Romano started groaning once I hit the Gowanus Expressway.

"You okay, Nick?"

"I'm gonna puke," he slurred, reaching for the door handle. I hit the lock button and got over into the right lane. I slowed down to about thirty-five and turned my flashers on.

"Put your head out the window and puke, not in the truck," I said as I grabbed his shoulder. He was too drunk to get out of the car, and I didn't want to chance him getting whacked by a car.

He stuck his head out the window and threw up. I kept my hand on his shoulder while my eyes went back and forth between him and the road. He went at it for a couple of minutes and finally got himself down to dry heaves before he pulled his head back in.

I pulled some napkins out of my console and handed them to him. He wiped his face and looked over at me, trying to focus.

"Where do you live, Nick?"

"I don't know," he slurred. I laughed at him, hoping I never looked that pathetic but thinking I'd been there a time or two.

"Is anyone expecting you home tonight?" I thought he lived alone, but I've never been to his house.

"No, nobody loves me," he said sadly.

"Terri Marks loves you," I said.

"No, Terri loves Joe. It's my birthday soon," he said.

"When?"

"July 21."

"Okay," I said, wondering what that meant since it was April.

"I'll be twenty-five," he said as if I asked him.

"Good, where do you live?"

He shrugged.

I tried a couple more times to find out where he lived. I knew his mother lived on the South Shore, in Annadale, but I wasn't taking him there in this condition.

"Why don't you sleep it off at my house?" I said, but he was nodding off again.

I parked my car and came around and opened his door. I got him out of the car and took his gun off him, sticking it in my gym bag. I didn't think he'd shoot himself on purpose, but he was wasted and it wouldn't be the first time a gun went off in a drunk cop's hand.

I held on to him as we walked down my steps. I sat him on the bottom step and he fell over, clonking his head against the cement foundation. He put his hands up and held his head. I picked him back up and steered him toward my couch, where he proceeded to fall over face-first onto the cushions.

I went into my bedroom and locked both our guns up in a safe that I bought for when Stevie's around. I grabbed a pillow and blanket out of the closet and brought them out to Romano. I pulled his shoes off and went into the bathroom for my fail-proof hangover remedy, two aspirin and a multivitamin. I got a glass of water and put them on the coffee table while I sat him up.

"Here, take these," I said.

"Whash thisht?" he asked.

"Aspirin to bypass the hangover."

He nodded and swallowed the aspirin. I gave him the vitamin, and he choked a little on it.

162

"Drink the water and get it down," I said.

"Big ashprin."

I set my clock for nine and fell asleep with my Bible in my hands, in spite of Romano's snoring. He was still blasting away when the alarm went off, and I was glad he didn't wake up and wander anywhere.

I showered and shaved and dressed in jeans and a T-shirt. My living room stunk of stale booze. It's different being on the other side of this and seeing someone else after a night of drinking. There were a couple of times last night when I wanted a drink, just to feel normal and not like an alcoholic. In the light of day I was glad I didn't.

I drove to the bagel store on Father Cappodanno Boulevard and got bagels and coffee.

"Hey, Nick," I said, shaking him. "I'm going to Long Island and you gotta get up."

He sat up and looked at me. His hair was sticking straight up, his eyes were bloodshot, and he had crease marks on his face.

"Hey, Tony." He looked around. "We at your house?"

"Yeah, I thought it'd be better if you slept it off here. Plus I don't know where you live, so I couldn't drop you off there."

"Oh. Where's my car?"

"At the precinct."

He nodded and paused. "Where's my gun?"

"In my safe." I've gone out drinking with my gun on me more times than I could count. In the condition he was in last night, it was pretty dangerous, and I was feeling thankful that I never killed myself or anyone else in that state.

He sat thinking a minute. "Did anything happen with Terri Marks?" That seemed to scare him more than losing his gun or car.

"No, and you can thank Rooney for that," I said. "You were pounding 'em down last night. How are you feeling?"

He shrugged. "Not as bad as I thought I would."

"I got you a bagel and coffee. Get something in your stomach, you reek," I said, handing him his bagel.

He went to use the bathroom, so I sat down at the kitchen table. I was halfway through my everything with butter when Romano came out of the bathroom and was staring at me, looking scared.

"Tony, I think something's wrong with me."

"What?"

"I think I damaged my kidneys—my urine's a funny color," he said.

I thought for a second what it could be from and busted out laughing. "I gave you a vitamin last night. It helps with the hangover."

"Oh. Thanks." He still looked out of it and was just standing there.

"Come on, eat your bagel. It'll make you feel better. I'll drop you off at the precinct and you can pick up your car."

Romano finished his breakfast and jumped in my shower. He put the same clothes back on and must have finger-brushed his teeth, because he had toothpaste smeared on the side of his mouth and on his index finger.

We finally left by 10:30. If I'd left earlier, I could have beat most of the Saturday traffic. Leaving now would probably put me in gridlock for the rest of the day.

It was one of those rare Saturdays when the weather is perfect. The sky was cloudless and clear, the sun was bright, and the air was warm enough to make it T-shirt weather.

The parks were full along the boardwalk on Father Cappodanno Boulevard. The paddleball courts at the end of Greely Avenue were in use, and I could hear the pop as the ball was whacked against the cement wall as I drove past. There are four playgrounds, three baseball fields, a hockey rink, and bocci ball courts along the three-mile stretch of beach and boardwalk where the kids play during the day and the dealers sell drugs at night.

There was a softball game at the Midland Avenue fields and a street hockey game in the parking lot past Seaview Avenue. Girls were jumping rope; double Dutch it looked like, by the concession stands in South Beach. The old ginzos were out playing bocci ball near Lily Pond Avenue, like they do every Saturday.

"You ever play that?" Romano asked, nodding toward where they were playing.

165

"When I was a kid, we played at my grandfather's house," I said. "You?"

"Yeah, I used to play. When I was little, before my father was killed, our family used to go to this resort upstate. An Italian place, I forget the name. We used to go there on vacation every summer, and we always played bocci ball. They had tournaments my mother and father used to play in."

"It sounds nice," I said. "You still go there?"

"We went back there once or twice after he died, but it wasn't the same." He sounded sad.

I felt sorry for him. I mean, I know I don't see my father a lot and we have our problems, but I don't know how I'd feel if anybody ever put a bullet in him. Especially when I was ten years old and he was the person I wanted to be like when I grew up—long before I found out he was as screwed up as everyone else.

I found myself questioning God, not about why it happened, but about how he could help Romano get past it. I know it happened a long time ago, but I think it has a lot to do with why Romano was drinking now. Since I'm nobody's shrink, I concentrated on getting through the traffic on the Verrazzano Bridge.

"I hope I wasn't too much trouble last night," he said.

"Nah, I was glad to help. You were pretty hammered, though. Just be careful—don't let the drinking get a hold of you," I said.

"I went a little overboard. I just hate this job. I'll be out of here in a couple of weeks, and I bet no one at that party will even notice that I'm gone," he said quietly.

"Joe and I will notice."

"Besides you two," he said like we didn't count.

He was right, no one else will notice once he's gone. I see it all the time. Aside from your partner, it doesn't matter to anyone else. Someone else will take your place, and everything keeps on going. If you run into anyone from the job, they're happy to see you, but that's about it.

Romano closed his eyes as traffic was stop-and-go along the Gowanus Expressway. I doubt if he was sleeping—some moron pulled up next to us in a black Nissan and had the bass up so high our doors were rattling. I figured he just didn't want to talk, so I left him alone.

I lit a cigarette and was driving slow enough to look at the garbage along the side of the road. Pieces of tires, brake lights, and hubcaps were littered along the elevated section above 3rd Avenue in Brooklyn. I saw broken glass, a wrapped-up diaper, a brick, and pieces of wood and cardboard. Underneath this particular stretch of the expressway, the area is hopping with skells, prostitutes, and crackheads. They hang out near the strip joints and porn shops, buying, selling, or using, depending on what it is.

Traffic cleared once we reached the tunnel, and we got to Midtown in fifteen minutes.

"So what're you doing today?" I asked when I pulled up in front of the precinct.

He shrugged. "Not much. I don't have my daughter this weekend. I'll probably just relax." Which meant he'd go home, sleep it off, and be out in some bar by 10:00 tonight.

"What about you? You going to see Michele?"

"Yeah, then we're going to Fiore's later for a barbeque. If the weather keeps, maybe we'll go fishing tonight," I said.

"Sounds good. Have a good time and I'll see you tomorrow." He shook my hand then asked, "Two o'clock, American Legion hall on Clove Road, right?"

"That's it. See you then, buddy." He waved me off.

I took 34th Street across town to the Queens Midtown Tunnel. The Mets must've had an afternoon game, because traffic was bumper-to-bumper on the Grand Central Parkway. The LIE was the same as it is every day, bumper-to-bumper through Queens, stop-and-go through Nassau, and moving in Suffolk. I finally got to Michele's at 12:30, two hours later than I planned on. Michele was out front planting flowers along the walkway, and Stevie was playing with his little yellow bulldozer. He screeched when I pulled up and ran out to meet me with a flying jump.

"You're late!" he said, hugging me. He was dressed in an NYPD T-shirt that I got him and jeans and sneakers. Michele was wearing jeans too, but hers were dressier, and she had on a red short-sleeved shirt.

"Sorry, there was traffic," I said, kissing Stevie's cheek.

I kissed Michele, who had walked over to my truck. "Traffic?" she asked.

"Ah, Nick Romano stayed with me after the party, and I had to drop him off at the precinct."

"Why?"

"He left his car there. I didn't want him driving home last night."

She nodded. "How is he?" She knew a little of what was going on with Nick. She had met him at Fiore's on New Year's Day when he talked to Fiore's dad about his father getting shot.

"He's drinking a lot. He goes over to FD in a couple of weeks," I said with a shrug. "He thinks he'll feel better about things once he's there."

"What's FD?" Stevie asked.

"Fire department," I said.

"He'll be a fireman?" Little kids always like firemen.

"Yup."

"Oh. Are we going to get our new door?"

"Whenever you're ready," I said, putting him down.

"Did you eat? I have cold cuts and salads," Michele said.

"We could eat now or we could go out, it's up to you."

"It'll be faster if we eat here," she said.

We left the flowers and went inside. Stevie and I went upstairs so he could show me the progress on the second floor of the house. The unfinished staircase was in, and the rooms were starting to take shape. Most of them were Sheetrocked, and I could see the BX cable from the electricians. The second floor looked smaller now that the rooms were closed off, but still nice-sized. Stevie chattered away, telling me he wanted a red room. I thought of my grandmother's couch and told him no, a red room would give him a headache.

Michele put out a platter of cold cuts, roasted peppers, and tomatoes. There was Boars Head baloney, turkey, roast beef, Muenster, and American cheese. She had a couple of tubs of macaroni and potato salad, store-bought but not bad.

We finished lunch and were on our way into Riverhead by 1:30. We went to Home Depot first to look at doors. We needed a new front door and doors for the bedrooms, bathrooms, and closets.

As soon as we got to the store, Stevie had to do "pee pee." I took him to the bathroom and then held him up in the air while he went, because the toilet was disgusting. Then he saw the display of power tools and got his hands on three of them before I could grab him. We tried to look at paint, but Stevie started collecting the sample cards, so I went out and got one of the orange carts to put him in. He sat for about three minutes while we looked at interior doors. We picked primed six-paneled doors with pewter press-down handles for the bedrooms and closets. For the front door Michele picked out a Victorian-style double door with molding so we could paint it with a couple of different colors for contrast. I liked the mahogany door with frosted glass on the front and matching glass panels on the side. But I didn't like the glass. I pictured someone smashing their fist through the glass and unlocking the door while I wasn't there, but at least you could see who was out there. With the wood door, you couldn't see who was on the other side, and I didn't like that either.

Stevie was climbing out of the cart now, bored out of his mind, trying to open the display doors. Michele didn't seem to notice. She just put him back in the cart and took out a fruit snack. I couldn't take my eyes off him, worried he'd fall out of the cart onto his head. We went over to the flooring section and checked the prices of the wood floors. There wasn't much of a selection with the tile, and I wanted something more than just plain tile.

We decided to order the inside doors and come back without Stevie to pick out the paint for the front door.

We stopped at a tile place on Main Street in Riverhead and let Stevie amuse himself flipping through carpet samples while we looked at the tile. There was a light-colored, weathered terra cotta that we both liked for the floor. We were gonna do plain off-white tile on the walls around the tub, but we saw accent tile in the same color as the floor. It was three sizes of tile, one with glass, one with metal, and the other with stone in it. It should have been gaudy as anything, but it was sharp and went great with the floor. I looked at the price and almost said forget it, then I looked at Michele and figured out how much overtime I would need to buy it.

We put a deposit on the floor and the wall tiles, even though Michele was concerned about the price. "It's so expensive, Tony, and I don't know if it's a good idea. We have to pay for the wedding—"

"The wedding's almost paid for—don't worry about it," I said, nuzzling her neck. "I'd rather work the OT now and have a beautiful bathroom so after we get married, I can stay home and enjoy it."

She looked skeptical for a second, then said, "Are you sure?"

"Yes."

"It's beautiful." She hugged me and whispered, "I can't wait to get married to you."

"Let's hope you feel that way tomorrow when you meet the rest of the family."

We got to Fiore's house by 4:30. He lives in Holbrook, closer to Ronkonkoma, where he catches the Long Island Railroad. It's real suburbia here and a lot more crowded than where Michele lives.

Fiore lives in a white split-level home with green shutters on a cul de sac with about ten houses. Some of the houses are done up in brick or stone with professional landscaping, and others like Fiore's are average but nice.

He has three kids, Josh, Joey, and Grace. Josh and Joey are dark haired like Fiore, and Grace, who's a little over a year old, has a head of dark peach fuzz. She's adorable, and for some reason she took a liking to me. I guess because I'm over there a lot and always play with her. She dropped the ball she was trying to pick up and squealed when she saw me. She ran toward me with unsteady steps. Her arms were out, and she had a big smile on her face. She laid her head on my shoulder when I picked her up and started chomping on my shirt.

"She loves you, Tony," Michele said, holding her hands out to Grace, trying to see if she would come to her. Grace turned her face away and stayed on my shoulder.

"I have that effect on women," I said, then added, "She's so light."

"She'll get heavy after a while, Tony," Donna said, kissing my cheek.

"Where's Joe?" I asked.

171

"The tank was empty on the barbeque, so he went to the store. You want me to take her?" She nodded toward Grace.

"No, I got her."

Josh, Joey, and Stevie went over to play with the Little Tykes basketball hoop in the driveway.

"So Joe was telling me about the party," Donna said, smiling.

I nodded. I didn't know what he told her, and I didn't want to say anything I shouldn't.

"How was Nick this morning?" she asked.

"Pretty hungover. I gave him some aspirin and a vitamin before he went to sleep and got something in his stomach this morning, so he should be alright."

She was looking at me like she was expecting me to say more.

"What?" I asked.

"Tony, are you hiding something from me?"

Now Michele was looking at me too.

"Why would I hide something from you?"

Donna laughed out loud, a full belly laugh that made Grace smile at her. "I'm sorry, Tony. That was mean." Her eyes were tearing from laughing.

"What are you hiding, Tony?" Michele squinted at me.

"Nothing, ah come on. I don't even know what she's talking about," I said, wishing Fiore would get back here.

"Nothing. Last night one of the cops from the precinct was drunk and came on to Joe. Or should I say came on to Joe stronger than she usually does?" It came out like a question and Donna raised her eyebrows at me.

"Don't ask me—I was too busy making sure Romano didn't fight with Rooney," I said.

Joe pulled up then in his white Plymouth Voyager and parked it at the curb, I guess so the kids wouldn't hit the van with the ball. I walked toward the curb, thankful to be away from the women.

"Hey, Tony," he said as he shook my hand. Grace might like me, but she loves him, and she threw me over the minute she saw him. He was kissing her cheek and saying "yum-yum" as he pretended to bite her neck while she giggled like crazy. Sometimes he acts like an idiot with the baby.

"Your wife is grilling me about last night," I said. "What'd you tell her?"

"She's playing with you. I told her about Terri Marks."

"Why?" I asked.

"Why not?" he shrugged. "She's my wife."

That would've been a good enough reason for me not to tell her.

"Did she get mad?" I asked. I didn't understand why he mentioned it.

"Mad about what? Come on, help me carry this stuff in," he said, dismissing it.

He had food and ice and the tank for the barbeque. Donna took the baby while we carried the stuff inside.

Michele and Donna got the food together, and we set up the grill. Joe hooked up the propane tank while I used a wire brush to clean off the racks of the barbeque. Once we got the grill going, we threw on some burgers and hot dogs.

Fiore's pool was still covered from the winter, and Stevie, Josh, and Joey were amusing themselves with the bulldozers in the sandbox.

We had burgers and hot dogs and a London broil that Donna marinates for two days before it hits the grill. It was so tender you could cut it with a fork and tasted delicious. They also grilled zucchini and portabella mushrooms and corn on the cob and had homemade macaroni salad and coleslaw.

Once we sat down at the table and Fiore said grace, the talk turned to the engagement party tomorrow.

"Is anyone from your job coming?" Donna asked.

"Just Rooney, Romano, McGovern, and O'Brien are supposed to, and Connelly," I said.

"What about the boss and Garcia?" Fiore asked.

"Garcia's working his second job, and the boss has a wedding," I said, which was fine with me. I didn't want anyone from work coming to begin with, so I limited it to just my squad. I didn't want to insult them by not inviting them.

"Are you nervous?" Donna asked Michele.

Michele looked at me and smiled. "A little. After Christmas Eve, I don't know what to expect—or maybe I do."

"If things get out of hand, we'll just leave," I said.

"We can't leave, Tony, it's our party," she said, exasperated.

"It's Grandma's party. Let her deal with it."

"Who's gonna be there?" Fiore asked.

"I think all my cousins, aunts, uncles—how many from your family?" I asked Michele.

"My parents and grandparents, Aunt Mary and Uncle Dennis, Aunt Ginny and Uncle Dave. Your grandmother told me I could only invite ten people—" Michele cut off, embarrassed.

"You never told me that," I said, getting angry.

"Tony, it doesn't matter. We weren't planning on an engagement party anyway."

"So Tony," Fiore said, changing the subject, "how do you like the stuff on fatherhood that Pastor's been teaching?"

I was still looking at Michele, thinking I was going to call my grandmother to tell her I wasn't going. She invites almost a hundred people from my side and tells Michele she can invite ten—who does she think she is?

"Tony?" Fiore said a little louder.

"Yeah, it's good. I like the stuff on fatherhood," I said sharply.

"Don't get upset," Michele said. "It'll only make things worse tomorrow."

I nodded.

Fiore had set up a volleyball net, and we spent the rest of the time playing with the kids.

Michele, Stevie, and I piled in Fiore's minivan at 8:00 and drove the twenty-five minutes out to Manorville. It was just about dark now, with a clear sky and a hint of chill in the air. I left my truck at Fiore's. I was sleeping at his house tonight and would head home after church in the morning. Stevie fell asleep in the car, and I carried him inside and put him to bed.

Fiore wanted to see how the addition on the house was going, so I let Michele show him around while I got my fishing pole and tackle box out of the garage. They were still up there when I came back in, so I went upstairs to hurry Fiore along.

"This is nice and big," Fiore said. They were standing in the bathroom, which is almost the size of my old bedroom in my parents' house.

"It looked bigger before the walls went up. It's coming along good; so far he's on schedule," I said. I had gotten the name of the contractor from Jimmy Murphy. He did work on Jimmy's ex-wife's house, and Murph said he was reliable.

"You ready to go?" I asked him.

"Yeah, I don't want to be out too late," Fiore said.

I kissed Michele good night. "I'll see you in the morning," I whispered in her ear.

"You okay about tomorrow?" she asked, searching my eyes. "I don't want you to be upset about who was invited and who wasn't—it'll just get us off track. Let's look at it as an opportunity to show our families God's love. Jesus never got upset when people didn't treat him right, and we shouldn't either."

"Jesus got to drink wine," I said. "When I drank wine, I didn't get upset either."

"Jesus didn't drink like that," she chuckled and kissed me again. "Have fun fishing."

Fiore took 111 to Sunrise Highway and drove east toward Hampton Bay. One of the things I love about New York is you can drive an hour and a half in any direction from Manhattan and be in the country. It's beautiful out here, wide open, with farms along the road and little country towns. There's no streetlights out here. The only reflection of the headlights was the yellow line on the road.

We drove out past the town of Hampton Bay over an arched bridge and looped around to a parking lot. We grabbed our gear and walked out onto a cement bridge with metal railings. It was chilly out here, and the wind was blowing in off the water.

It was early in the season to be fishing, and there were only about four other people out there with Fiore and me. We used jigs for bait, but we could only see their sparkly green bodies when we reeled them in close. There were no lights out here, and it looked like there were a million stars over our heads. You don't get stars like this in the city, but you don't get the Manhattan skyline out here either. I think both are beautiful and powerful in their own way.

The dark water was pretty turbulent as it swirled around us and through the cement pillars under the arched bridge. I didn't talk at first, just enjoyed being out by the water. The smell of the salty air and the soft *ping* of the buoy out on the water reminded me of home. It was quiet out here, and aside from the clicking of the reels and the sound of the line going out, it was all nature.

We caught a couple of small stripers, but nothing big enough to keep.

"I called to check on Janice Ladeas," Joe said.

Janice Ladeas, the name sounded familiar. "Who's Janice Ladeas?"

Fiore chuckled. "You're so bad with names. She's the assault victim from the other night."

"Oh, right. You talked to her?" That surprised me.

"Yeah, I wanted to make sure she was okay."

"You're a nice guy, Joe," I said, meaning it. I'd been thinking about her too, I just wouldn't have called her. I'm careful with stuff like that. I wouldn't want to give her the wrong idea and the next thing you know, you got a stalker on your hands. "How's she doing?"

"She was doing better. I didn't talk to her long—she was pretty medicated. Her mother was there with her. She got on the phone to say thank you, telling me how the New York City Police Department is the greatest in the world and she was writing a letter to the mayor. She was nice."

Once in a while people do stuff like that, but it's rare.

I was quiet for a couple of minutes, and then said, "Janice'll probably be traumatized by it for the rest of her life. I mean, it's good we caught the guys and she'll live, but the truth of the matter is we stepped in after the fact. She'll be busy with the trial if they don't plead, and they'll go back to jail, but something like this stays with you."

"But she had a good attitude," Joe said. "She was grateful to be alive, and she said she was praying and God helped her—sent us to help her."

A part of me wished his timing could have been a little better. We finished up around midnight, packed up our gear, and headed back to Fiore's.

I woke up at 7:30, thankful that I was downstairs in Fiore's house and didn't have to compete with the rest of his family for the bathroom. The battery was dead on my electric razor, so I'd have to go to church looking like an outlaw. I changed into gray dress pants and a black silk shirt and followed the smell of bacon and coffee upstairs to the kitchen.

Josh and Joey were eating pancakes at the table, and little Grace was in her high chair, playing with her Cheerios.

"Good morning, Tony." Donna smiled and grabbed me a cup of coffee.

"Thanks, Donna," I said, going in the refrigerator for the milk.

"How about some pancakes?" she asked. I saw she had her makeup on and her hair done but was still in sweatpants and a T-shirt.

"No, I'm good. Go finish getting ready. I'll watch the rug rats," I said, pulling up a chair next to Grace.

Donna opened the oven and pulled out a dish piled high with pancakes and a second plate of bacon. "Thanks, Tony, but please eat something. There's enough for an army."

178

"Where's your husband? Why is he lounging around while you're running around like a chicken?" She laughed, knowing I was kidding. In fact, Fiore probably made the pancakes.

"He's in the shower. Be a good friend and put more coffee on," she called as she walked toward her bedroom.

"There's coffee in here," I yelled back.

"It's old—make some fresh."

I rinsed out the pot and basket and scooped in some more coffee and hit the *on* button. I walked back over to the table and Grace had her face down on the tray of the high chair. I panicked for a minute, thinking she might have choked, and went to grab her out. Of course she was buckled in and I took the high chair with me, scaring her awake in the process.

She let out an ear-piercing scream and Joey said, "What's wrong, Tony?" looking scared.

"I thought she was choking," I half yelled. I unbuckled her and picked her up, but she was still crying, looking at me with big, teary, scared eyes.

"I'm sorry, Gracie," I said. "I thought you were choking."

"She was sleeping," Joey said, logically.

"She was awake a minute ago—what is she, narcoleptic?" I asked him.

"No."

"Do you even know what narcoleptic is?" He was like eight years old.

"No."

"What's the matter, Gracie?" Fiore asked as he breezed in, getting a big smile from the baby, who was still doing pathetic little hiccup sounds. "Is Tony's face scaring you?"

She went to Fiore, then turned around and smiled at me; she never stays mad.

"Joe, one minute she's eating her Cheerios and I turn around

179

to make the coffee, and the next minute she's out cold. I thought she choked or something."

"No, she won't choke," he cooed. "Daddy's girl has lotsa teeth—show Daddy your teeth." She smiled and drooled; she really was adorable.

I ate some pancakes and bacon while Josh and Joey cleaned off the table. Fiore and I had coffee and left in separate cars for church by 8:30.

From Fiore's house it's only one exit on the LIE and another mile to the church. Michele was waiting for me by the door, holding Stevie's hand. We brought him downstairs to the Sunday school and went upstairs to get a seat.

Pastor had been teaching for a couple of weeks on being a godly father. Personally it couldn't have come at a better time, since I was about to step up to the plate with Stevie. And to be honest, I didn't know the first thing about being a father. I think if you start when they're infants, you can screw up a little and they're too young to remember, but Stevie was old enough to remember everything I did.

Pastor was saying that what we do as fathers will affect our children for the rest of their lives. Even when they're adults and long after we're dead and gone, whatever we do, good and bad, is gonna stay with them.

"Fathers have a powerful role," he said, "and the thing is, we can never go back and change what we've done. Like the hard drive on your computer, every memory is stored. One of the strongest influences in a child's life is their father."

He talked about some book he read where the guy said if we didn't stop being selfish parents, we could end up with a fatherless society. He went on to talk about daughters. I almost tuned it out, thinking that growing up a daughter wasn't as important as growing up a son and then sat up, wondering where that came from.

"I think one of the biggest reasons young girls are having sex is because they're not getting the love and attention they need from their fathers, and they're looking elsewhere for it," he said.

It reminded me of my sister, Denise. She went out looking for love when she was way too young. If she was a boy, it would have been applauded, but I remember my father calling her a *putana* when she came home with a hickey when she was about thirteen.

This was some of the truest stuff I'd ever heard, and I felt the weight of the responsibility of being a father. As Pastor talked about being parents and the consequence of taking it lightly, I thought of my own parents. I factored in the effects Vietnam, the police department, my mother's alcoholism, and my father's cheating had on them as parents, but to tell the truth, they still sucked at it. Then a little voice inside me told me not to spit in the wind, that I had no idea what it was like to be a parent and I shouldn't be so sure of myself.

Service ended at 10:30, and I wanted to get on the road before traffic got too bad. Michele was leaving by 12:00 with her parents and would meet me at the hall. I had less than three hours to drive to Staten Island, change, shave, and pick up the cake.

I took the Southern State Parkway into the Belt Parkway and over the Verrazzano Bridge. Except for a stalled car in the right lane in Coney Island, I sailed right through and was home by 12:00.

I was running late to the party because I butchered my face while shaving and I couldn't get a couple of spots to stop bleeding. I kept little pieces of tissue on the cuts while I wrestled with my tie. It took me three times to get the lip straight in the middle, and then I had to change my shirt because my chin bled onto the collar.

I stopped at the bakery on Hylan Boulevard in Grasmere to pick up the cake. My grandmother had ordered a full sheet cake with two fillings, half chocolate cannoli cream and half fresh strawberries. "Congratulations Tony and Michelle" was written in red gel, and blue and pink icing flowers decorated the four corners. Michele's name was spelled wrong, and I wondered if Grandma spelled it wrong on purpose. There were also two trays of Italian cookies and fresh Italian bread.

The American Legion hall was about two miles from the bakery, on Clove Road. It was a red brick building with the post number on it and a flagpole out front with the American flag and the black POW-MIA flag under it. There was a parking lot to the side, already half full.

I spotted my cousin Paulie Two Toes outside, smoking a cigarette and talking on his cell phone. We call him Paulie Two Toes because he had a run-in with some fireworks on the Fourth of July when he was fourteen. He put an M-80 under his mother's macaroni pot and stepped on the pot to hold it down, and he blew off all but two toes, hence the name. Actually, he's my second cousin. His mother, Aunt Rose, is my father's cousin and the side of the family Dad always tried to keep us away from. Paulie's the oldest of three sons, a schmuck wannabe who got arrested last year for running numbers out of his city job. I guess he's following in the footsteps of his uncle Henny, Aunt Rose's brother, who's also a bookie. He was dressed in a black silk turtleneck and gray pants. His black hair looked styled with cement, and I could see his pinky ring glinting in the sun while he moved his free hand around so he could talk.

"How ya doing, Paulie?" I asked. He put the phone between his chin and shoulder and shook my hand. He held up his hand for me to wait. He finished his conversation, cursing out whoever was on the other end of the phone and telling them he couldn't do anything about it, he had to be with his family today.

"Women," he shook his head. "I should just kill myself and get it over with."

"Who was that?" I asked, wondering if he was here alone.

"My girlfriend," he said and spit on the sidewalk.

I wondered if his wife was already inside.

"Here, gimme some of that, you're gonna drop the cake," he said, taking the cookies and the bread from me.

"Thanks, Paulie," I said, feeling the acid rise in my throat at the thought of Michele's family and the guys from work seeing my relatives in action.

"Hey Tony, I hear the wedding's in November," Paulie said as we walked up the front steps.

"Yeah, the Saturday before Thanksgiving."

"That's kinda soon." He lowered his voice. "She in trouble?"

"Paulie, it's seven months from now. If she was pregnant, she'd be having the baby by then," I said, wondering why everyone said that. It was so stupid—if I had to get married, why would I wait seven months to do it?

The post had two floors. Upstairs was used for catering and I guess their meetings, and the downstairs was a full-service bar.

Grandma was already there putting the tablecloths on the tables. She had eight tables set up, four on each side of the room, with room to dance in between. She was a scary sight in a red velour jumpsuit that showed off her potbelly, gold shoes, and tangerine hair.

"Tony, put the cake in the fridge," she said, pointing me toward the kitchen. She took the bread and cookies from Paulie, kissed his cheek, and set them up on the dais where the sternos were set up for the food.

Denise was in the kitchen, putting foil trays into one of the ovens. She was wearing a sleeveless dark red dress and had her hair up in one of those complicated dos lacquered with hair spray. She looked nice, and I told her so.

"Thanks." She kissed my cheek. "I just hope everyone on our side doesn't show up wearing red. Grandma told me she wore red so no one in Michele's family could put the horns on her."

"Why does she think that?" I said, exasperated. "Half of them aren't even Italian! She's getting nuts in her old age."

"She was always nuts, but you—being the first grandchild and the apple of her eye—were never on the receiving end of it." Denise smiled when she said it, but there was a bite there.

"Are you sure she was always nuts?" I asked.

"Absolutely. You're only seeing it now because you're marrying someone her and Dad don't approve of, and that takes you out of the favorite slot and puts you on the 'we barely tolerate you' slot." She smiled and said, "Welcome to my world."

"I'm gonna go help set up," I said.

Grandma had most of the work done. The room was decorated with white and silver streamers draped from the four ceiling fans to the corners. There were white tablecloths on each table with the birdbath centerpieces in the middle. Silver and white balloons were tied to the backs of the chairs, and the tables were scattered with silver matchbooks with silver wedding bells on them that said, "Tony and Michelle April 29, 2001."

A bartender behind the bar on the back wall was talking to one of the waitresses.

Vinny was in the back of the room with Christie and my cousin Gino, who everyone calls Brother because he's Paulie's brother. They were setting up what I thought was the deejay equipment.

"Hey, Brother," I said, shaking his hand. "You playing deejay tonight?"

"Yeah, and I brought my karaoke machine." He had the screen so people could read the words and a fat binder full of songs.

"Smile, bro," Vinny said, pointing his video camera in my face.

Great, an open bar, a karaoke machine, my family, and a video camera to capture it all on film.

My mother came in carrying a tray and a shopping bag. The hostility she used to bring with her to family parties was gone, and instead she looked like she wanted to run out of there. She looked good, her hair was styled and tucked behind her ears. She was thinner now and dressed in a knee-length, dark blue dress that was tailored but wasn't showy. Denise went over and kissed her, took the tray, and they disappeared into the kitchen together.

Mike Ellis, who I've been best friends with since I went to St. Michael's, came in with his girlfriend, Laura. I've only seen him a couple times since I quit drinking, and we haven't had much to say to each other. I'm guessing my grandmother invited him. She's probably hoping I'll get nostalgic by seeing him, get smashed out of my mind, and dump Michele.

"Hey, buddy!" He gave me a big smile as he walked over. "How come I have to hear from your grandmother you're getting married? How you been?" He hugged me, and Laura kissed my cheek. She looked the same as she did last time I saw her, anorexic, streaked blond hair, long acrylic nails, and dressed in black. Mike looked bloated, and I noticed the lines around his eyes and mouth seemed more pronounced.

"So where is she? I hear she's got a kid," he said, looking around. His eyes stalled on Denise as she came out of the kitchen. She stopped when she saw him, and I saw a look of disgust pass on her face before she looked away.

"She's not here yet, and his name is Stevie," I said.

"Who? Oh, the kid, yeah, can't wait to meet him." He smiled, and it looked like his lips were sticking to his teeth. "I guess this means you won't be coming down the Shore anymore."

"I guess not. We're getting too old for that, Mike. We're those old people we always thought were losers ten years ago when we first started going down there," I said.

That's the thing about the Jersey Shore. You go there with your parents as a kid and you're scared of the older kids, who act like psychos. Then you go down after senior prom and become one of those psychos and make fun of the over-thirty crowd that never got married and still hangs out down the Shore.

My father came in with Marie, looking like Robert DeNiro with arm candy. He was dressed in a black suit and crisp white shirt, his hair was slicked back, and either he got himself a suntan or his blood pressure was up.

Marie was wearing half a dress, a black tacky thing with no back to it and enough cleavage showing to make it look like a baby's bottom was sitting on her chest. She had her hair longer now, ironed straight. She was heavy on the makeup, and someone who didn't know her might say she was beautiful. I watched her eyes narrow when she spotted my mother coming out of the kitchen with Denise, then she plastered on a smile and looked adoringly up at my father. I walked over to say hello to my mother first, then said hello to my father and Marie.

People were coming in all at once now. Fiore and Donna, Rooney and his wife, Connelly and his girlfriend, O'Brien, and McGovern and his wife all walked in at the same time. Michele, Stevie, her parents, and her grandparents were behind the guys from work, and I saw Aunt Rose wearing a flowered muumuu and a red rose in her hair.

Michele was wearing a light pink suit with matching shoes and a pair of legs that made my mouth water.

Stevie looked adorable. He was wearing a little suit and tie, and he had his hair spiked up.

"Hey, buddy! Wow, you look sharp," I said.

"Yes, he does," my mother said, smiling and walking toward us.

"Grandma Mariryn, I have a surprise!" he singsonged.

Grandma Mariryn?

"What is it?" she played along.

"Look!" He pushed his sleeve up and showed us a Bob the Builder watch.

We all made a big deal over it, saying, "What a big boy" and "What time is it?" He was smiling like anything but couldn't tell us what time it was.

"And I have a surprise for you," my mother said, holding a shopping bag behind her back.

"What is it?" He sounded almost hysterical.

"Let's see," she said as she handed him the bag.

"Bob the Builder construction site!" He ripped it out of the bag. "Mom, look at it! Thank you, Grandma Mariryn." He hugged her around the waist.

"You're welcome, honey." She looked happy, and I felt guilty for thinking what rotten parents her and my father were. They were, but at least she was trying with Stevie.

"Can I play with it?" Stevie asked, looking at Michele.

"How about we play with it later if you get bored. We don't want to lose any of the pieces," my mother said. "I hope this is okay," my mother said to Michele. "Maybe I should have asked you first."

"No, it's fine. It was very thoughtful, thank you," Michele said.

My uncle Mickey, Gino and Paulie's father, came in with his wife, Elena. I never understood what she saw in Uncle Mickey besides his ill-gotten money. When I was little I thought she was gorgeous, and even now she was nice looking. She had straight black hair and exotic-looking brown eyes, and she always smelled sexy. Her eyes lit up when she saw me, and she walked over, leaving Uncle Mickey talking to Aunt Rose.

"Congratulations, handsome," she said and kissed my cheek. "I hear you're taking the plunge."

"Yeah, it's about time," I said.

"Is this her?" She smiled at Michele.

"This is her," I said proudly.

"Hi, I'm Michele," Michele said to Elena, shaking her hand.

"Michele, this is my aunt Elena."

"Nice to meet you, Michele. Congratulations, you snagged the best of the bunch."

"Yes I did," Michele said, looking at me.

Michele and I went to each table, shaking hands and kissing cheeks while I kept my eye on the crowd. The bar was busy and Gino was playing music, but so far no one was singing karaoke.

I went over to Denise, who was standing near the kitchen by herself, staring at Marie and my father.

"You okay there?" I asked.

She nodded. "I tried to put Michele's parents at the table—" she cut off as her eyes focused on something behind me. "Hi." She smiled and tilted her head to the side.

I turned around to see Romano staring at Denise. She was staring back and said, "Don't I know you from somewhere?"

Said the spider to the fly.

"Denise, right?" Romano asked, looking way too happy.

"How do you know my sister?" I scowled at him.

"She's your sister?" He looked at me and then back at Denise and said, "No way."

"Yes, I really am his sister," Denise said.

"I never would have thought that, you're so nice," Romano said to her.

"How do you know my sister, Nick?" I asked again.

"Wednesday nights at the bowling alley." He was still staring at Denise.

New York might have millions of people, but in Staten Island, everybody knows everybody.

"Nick! Your name is Nick. I'm sorry, I couldn't remember it—I'm busy helping set up for the party," Denise said, beaming. "The suit threw me. How've you been? Carla and I were wondering why you don't come out anymore. I see your friends there, but we haven't seen you."

"You have friends?" I asked Romano.

"I've been working a lot," Romano said while they both ignored me.

"You're a fireman, right?" she asked.

"He's a cop," I snarled. "And he works with me."

"I'm going over to the fire department in two weeks," Romano told her.

"He has a kid, Denise," I warned, hoping she'd remember that her last boyfriend had kids and dumped her to go back to their mother.

"I know, she's adorable. He showed us pictures. Oh! Your friend John got in a fight the other night—those guys from Sunnyside showed up again." She rambled on while Romano looked starstruck. Great.

"You're sweet," Michele said, kissing me. "Stop scowling at him. It's not working, he knows you too well."

"This is not a good idea," I said.

"This is none of your business," she said softly. "And you don't know whether or not it's a good idea." She was smiling as she watched them.

"Why are you smiling?"

"Your father's gonna hate him." She shrugged when I looked at her. "Takes the pressure off us."

I made my way over to the table where Michele's family was sitting. They looked out of place here, quiet, no talking with their hands. They had polite smiles on as they looked around the room at some of the bizarre outfits some of my family was dressed in.

I saw Michele's mother's eyes lock on my uncle Mickey's hairpiece, and I barked out a laugh.

"Is that a toupee?" Vinny asked from behind me.

I turned around to him. "Oh Vin, I didn't see you there. This is Michele's mother, Phyllis." Vinny reached over to shake her hand. "This is my brother, Vinny. Vin, this is Lee, Michele's father." I went through the table with him and told him there'd be a quiz later.

"Is Uncle Mickey's hair real?" Vinny was asking, talking low so no one could hear.

"You're kidding, right Vin?" Uncle Mickey had the worst hairpiece I'd ever seen. It looked like a helmet, and a couple of times I wanted to ask him if it came with a chin strap.

"It is, right?" Sometimes Vinny could be so naïve.

"Yes, Vin, the hair that sticks out from under it is gray. I bet if you pulled it off his head and look under it, it says STARTER on it."

"Starter? Oh I get it, the sports equipment."

"Nothing gets past you, Vin," I said and slapped him on the back.

Little Gina, Uncle Mickey's daughter, was making her way to

the middle of the dance floor. "Come on, Brother," she yelled to Gino. "I wanna dance." There was a round of whoops from the crowd as Gino put on "Mambo Italiano." Little Gina was bopping, shaking her ample hips along with the music. They called her Little Gina because she was the baby of the family, not because of her size. She had squeezed herself into a tight black dress that showed off the rose tattoo on her chest and the butterfly on her calf. Her hair was black but she had blond streaks in it, giving her a gothic look.

Most of the tables emptied when they heard the song, and the dance floor got crowded all at once.

I walked over to the table where the guys from work were sitting. I had never met Rooney's wife before and was curious to see what she was like. I was surprised at how she looked, considering he met and married her on a drinking binge at Hedonism in Jamaica. She was tall, with brown hair and blue eyes, pretty in a low-key kind of way. She was nursing a glass of white wine while Rooney drank beer.

"Hi, I'm Jodi," she said, reaching across to shake my hand. "I heard a lot about you."

"Really? I hope you didn't believe any of it," I said, smiling.

"Michael likes you, he never says anything bad about you." I wondered who Michael was and realized she was talking about Rooney.

"It's nice to finally meet you, Jodi. I heard a lot of nice things about you too," I said.

"What I think is amazing," she continued, looking around the table, "is that for the first time since I've known Michael, I'm hearing about his job." She seemed a little upset about it.

"I'm sure he just doesn't want to upset you with what goes on," Donna said cautiously. "It took me a few years to get Joe to talk to me about it without having to pull teeth."

A lot of cops don't talk about the job to their wives. Like

I said, before I met Michele I never did either. I think out of our whole squad Fiore and I are the only ones who bring any of it home. We're also the only ones in the squad who don't drink—might be something to that.

The food was coming out now in long silver trays. Denise and Romano were carrying the bread, rolls, and salad, and I went over to give them a hand and ask Romano what he thought he was doing.

The waitresses were putting out pitchers of soda and water on the tables while trays of hot food were brought out of the kitchen. There was eggplant rollatini, chicken marsala with parslied potatoes, penne alla vodka, baked ziti, broccoli with garlic and oil, and Grandma's meatballs.

For the cold food there were trays of cold cuts, potato salad, grilled vegetables, and a cold antipasta.

"I'd like everyone's attention," Gino said over the microphone. "Before we sit down to eat, my cousin Vinny here would like to make a toast for Tony and Michele."

Hoots and shouts of "Here! Here!" could be heard around the room.

"Great," I mumbled as Michele stood next to me.

"Tony and Michele," Vinny started, looking like he was gonna cry. "I'd like to wish the both of you a very happy marriage. May you have many more children and nothing but good times all of your life. Salute!"

"Salute!" the crowd cheered. Vinny handed the microphone back to Gino, who added, "And may all your ups and downs be between the sheets!" Some numbskull always has to say it.

The crowd cheered for that too, and I looked over at Michele, who colored a little but smiled anyway.

"Okay everybody, enjoy the food," Gino said, and the tables emptied as people made their way to the buffet. The room got quieter as everyone sat down to eat.

*O*nce dinner was over, all of the males in my family from about twelve years old on went over to the bar for shots of sambuca. The bartender lined them up while the room chanted, "Tony! Tony! Tony!"

The guys from my precinct went over to the bar for a shot, leaving Fiore and all the wives sitting there. I was standing in the middle of the dance floor, on my way down to the bathroom, when they started. I looked over at Michele, who was talking to Donna. I guess I looked panic-stricken, and I felt like everyone in the room was looking at me, which they were. My mother seemed disgusted as she watched them, especially my father, but gave a small smile and a wink when she saw me looking at her.

My cousin Paulie brought a shot over to me, then put his arm around my shoulder while holding his own shot in the other hand.

"Salute!" He held up his glass.

"Salute!" everyone cheered.

Michele gave me what looked to be a "Go ahead" nod, and I threw back the shot but didn't drink all of it. It burned my throat and my eyes teared, but I held up the glass to everybody so they could clap.

Yeah, clap, you morons, I thought. *The alcoholic just had a drink, highlights at eleven.*

I walked over to Fiore's table and set the shot glass down. I guess I wanted them to see that I didn't drink it all.

"Don't worry about it, honey," Michele said as she forced a smile. "There was nothing else you could do without making a scene."

"There's no booze at the wedding, right?" I asked.

"There's those little complimentary bottles of wine from the vineyard at each table as the favors, and a champagne toast, but that's it," she said.

Our wedding is an afternoon thing at one of the wineries on the North Fork of Long Island. Since it's an afternoon and in the off-season, it was pretty reasonable. The place is beautiful, and the people who go there drink wine and listen to classical music. My family leans toward shots of sambuca and Frank Sinatra. If there's no booze there, I'll probably find most of them in some local dive halfway through the wedding, like they do at the funerals.

Gino started playing "YMCA," and Grandma was out on the dance floor lifting her arms up and down trying to make the letters. The next song was a slow one, and Gino called Michele and me out to the dance floor.

Since the last time I danced I was in my underwear doing a bar slide, I felt a little self-conscious. "You alright there?" I asked Michele, keeping my voice low while we danced.

"So far, so good," she said.

"No way, babe—the alcohol hasn't started taking effect yet. They'll really get going in about an hour."

"You did your shot, you could get out of the next one." She smiled at everyone while she talked.

"That's it for me. My future son is here—don't want to set a bad example," I said, smiling back.

"He didn't even see it. When Paulie walked over to you, your mother brought him over to show him the cake," she said.

We clapped when the song ended and got off the dance floor, heading for Fiore's table, when "The Twist" came on. Denise was still talking to Romano, but she grabbed Stevie and pulled him out on the dance floor.

"You okay, buddy?" Fiore asked.

"A little more relaxed now that I have a little sambuca in me," I laughed.

"There was nothing you could do without drawing more attention to it. You didn't even finish it." He nodded to the glass, still about a third of the way full.

"Yeah, but I still drank it."

A couple of my cousin's kids were there; they were gathered around the karaoke machine, picking out songs. Paulie's daughter, who was probably thirteen but looked nineteen, took the microphone and started singing a Britney Spears song. She was moving her hips and pointing at one of the other kids as she sang, "Oops! I Did It Again." She sang off-key and looked ridiculous. I'm not saying I've never sung karaoke, I've just never done it without a few hours of drinking behind me.

My uncle Henny was next to grab the mic. He was wearing a blue suit and was holding a drink against his stomach. He had dyed black hair and a jowly face with broken blood vessels from years of whiskey sours. He was singing "Hound Dog" while he swayed his hips, rheumatoid style, doing a bad impression of Elvis.

Stevie was still dancing with Denise, only now Romano had

joined them and put Stevie on his shoulders. They clapped while Uncle Henny sang.

Gino called my father into the middle of the dance floor and played the song everyone in the family always says is about him, "Macho Man." The crowd on the dance floor circled my father while he hammed it up, sticking his fists in the air, egging them on.

"I'll be right back," I told Michele.

"Where are you going?" she asked, and I hoped she wasn't worried about me having a drink.

"Gonna use the bathroom." I wanted to say a quick "I'm sorry" to God about the drinking. I still have some of that old "God's gonna get me" mentality and I had to shake it off.

I went downstairs and saw there was a line outside the bathroom.

It was smaller down here, with dark-paneled walls adorned with the American Legion crest, Sons of the American Legion, and the American Legion Auxiliary.

The old-timers were sitting around the bar, their eyes glued to a baseball game on the TV perched over the bar.

There was one guy waiting in line for the bathroom; since he wasn't from my party, we weren't talking to each other. I concentrated on reading the notices on the wall. Monday is hot wing night, twenty cents a wing. I folded my arms and read about an upcoming spaghetti dinner, complete with bread and salad for five bucks. The budget meeting was Wednesday, Bingo was Friday. I heard Marie's voice and looked over to see her on the pay phone with her back to me.

"I can't get away, Bobby," she said impatiently. "It's an engagement party for Vince's son—I have to be here."

She played with the metal wire to the phone while she listened, then said, "Yeah, well, Vince isn't as stupid as Ellen. No one could be as stupid as Ellen, and he didn't buy the trip to

Florida thing—he called my mother." More listening and an impatient huff. "Bobby, she didn't tell him anything except that I went to the beach for the day. She understands what I'm going through."

I wanted to take the phone out of her hand and rip it out of the wall. I couldn't believe she had the nerve to call her boyfriend while her husband was upstairs at her stepson's engagement party. I took a step toward her and heard her say, "I'm not going to empty the account until I'm ready to leave."

My head snapped up at that.

"Vince checks it all the time, and he wants to invest it with Pete Catalano's son-in-law, supposedly he's some financial wiz. No, I won't get half his pension. We haven't been married for ten years."

Whatever he said seemed to aggravate her more, and she said, "No, I can't stick it out for a few more years!"

I thought about all the damage Marie had done to my family because she supposedly loved my father so much. Just last Christmas she was telling me and Denise that he had to leave our family because he was so miserable with us and she made him happy. She reminded me of the tornados I see on the weather channel. They blast through, oblivious to the damage they do, and move on looking for something else to destroy.

The bathroom door opened, and the guy in front of me walked in. As I moved up, Marie looked over her shoulder and saw me standing there.

"Are you spying on me?" she asked indignantly.

"I'm waiting to use the bathroom," I said angrily.

"You're a snake, Tony," she spat.

"I'm a snake? You're really something, lady." I shook my head.

"I have to go," she said into the phone and hung up.

"Don't you have anything better to do than snoop in my business, like make sure your mother isn't at the bar sneaking a drink?" She folded her arms to enhance her already augmented chest.

She smiled when she caught me looking, but the smile dropped when she realized it was with disgust.

"Get out of my way," she said as she pushed past me and headed for the stairs.

"I like your apartment," I called after her.

She stopped and turned. "What apartment?"

"The one in Brooklyn."

"I don't have an apartment in Brooklyn."

She said it nasty, but I knew I had her.

"I'm telling my father, and don't even try to empty the bank accounts," I said, dead serious.

She smiled. "He won't believe you."

"I know," I said. "But I have pictures, and a copy of the lease to your apartment with Bobby Egan."

"You had me followed?" She had the chutzpah to look appalled.

"No, but someone else did. I just wound up with the information. You'd think you'd be more careful—didn't your last husband catch you the same way?"

"Don't mess with me, Tony, you'll only get hurt."

"Oh yeah, tough girl, what are you gonna do? Marry my father and make my life miserable?" I laughed cynically.

She threw out something more suitable for a dockworker and turned to walk upstairs.

I went into the bathroom and splashed cold water on my face. I looked at myself in the mirror and tried to feel right about what I said to her. The truth was I was mad at myself for stooping to her level, and for drinking the shot of booze. I told God I was sorry and asked for some help. I looked at my watch—4:00. Two more hours of this and I could leave.

The party was rocking when I got back upstairs, and the train passed me as it made its way around the room.

Grandma's next-door neighbor Margie was leading the train. She was grayhaired, stoopshouldered, and doublewide, wearing blue polyester pants, a white turtleneck, and orthopedic shoes. She kept pulling an imaginary horn, yelling, "Toot! Toot!"

"Come on, Tony," Grandma said as she passed. She pulled me in behind her, and I tried to follow as my hands slipped on the material of her pantsuit.

I choo-chooed around the room, grabbing Stevie from Denise. He was sweating and his cheeks were flushed, so I took his jacket off him and tossed it on a chair.

Gino pulled out a box of party favors, blow-up guitars, big plastic hammers, sunglasses, glow necklaces, and those Hawaiian things you put around your neck. Being a deejay he gets them cheap, but he probably charged my grandmother an arm and a leg for them.

He put on the song "Hammer Time," and everyone started bashing each other with the hammers. Denise saw Marie standing at the edge of the dance floor, scowling at me. I saw Denise smile, and she walked over to Marie and hit her with the hammer, hard enough to knock her head to the side.

"It's hammer time, Marie!" Denise yelled, laughing.

"Oh no," I said, walking toward them.

Marie's hair was messed where Denise hit her, and she was spitting mad. She looked like she was gonna go after Denise, but she saw me coming over. She told Denise where she could stick the hammer and stomped over to the bar.

"Sorry," Denise said, laughing and not looking sorry at all.

"I just want to get through this without a brawl, okay?" I said calmly, holding up my hands.

"Okay, no more. I promise," she said seriously.

"Good shot," I said, wishing I was the one wielding the hammer.

The guys from work were having a good time. Cops are funny like that—no matter how raunchy and obnoxious they are, when your family's around they act right.

Everyone was getting wild now, and with the exception of the table with Michele's family, everyone was on the dance floor or at the bar. Michele was dancing with Donna, and when the song ended and some line dance that everyone else seemed to know started, she walked over to me.

"Your mother looks like she's gonna have a stroke," I said as I nodded toward her mother, who was watching the dance floor and playing with her necklace.

"No, finding out I was pregnant with Stevie and not getting married almost gave her a stroke. She'll put up with anything as long as there's a ring on my finger."

"Let's elope," I said. "Now, this week."

"No way, Cavalucci, I want to see you wear the monkey suit," she said, kissing me.

"I don't know, legs, I'm picturing a beach, maybe in Maui at sunset. Flowers in your hair, no family." I put my arm around her.

"You're just picturing no family," she chuckled.

"A beautiful hotel," I continued. "Breakfast in bed, white sand beaches, no family."

"Forget it," she said. "I want a wedding."

Uncle Charlie, my mother's brother, was singing Sinatra now. "Is he for real?" I asked as he started singing "My Way." He was drunk and dramatic, and when he sang, "I did it my way," everyone else sang, "I did it sideways."

They brought out the trays of cookies and the cake and acted like it was a wedding. They had Michele and me cut it and feed each other a piece. They whooped it up when we were feeding each other, hoping one of us would go off and smash the other in the face, stuffing canolli cream up in our nostrils.

My cousin Michael, Uncle Charlie's son who's two years older than me, showed up late. As usual, he was dressed like a psycho. Black T-shirt, jeans, black stomper boots, a spike dog collar, and his hair cut in a Mohawk. There's always been something wrong with him. When we were kids, his favorite pastime was torturing cats and scaring girls. Denise still twitches when she sees him.

Gino played the "Electric Slide," and the tables emptied again as everyone hit the dance floor. Stevie was in a sugar rush now, and his face was flushed as he rolled around on the floor. He alternated between playing his blow-up guitar and bashing whoever was next to him with it. He looked up and saw my cousin Michael's Mohawk and stared at him for a minute before running away.

The younger kids were on the dance floor now. All the girls looked the same in low-waisted jeans, belly shirts, clodhopper shoes, and long straight hair. I was surprised at the amount of tattoos and belly rings I saw on the girls. I couldn't believe that their parents let them do that at sixteen years old.

The guys were more or less dressed the same, in beige pants and black button-down shirts. One of them stuck out by wearing an orange shirt with a grey bulldog on it.

I was standing by the dance floor, making sure Marie didn't come after Denise, when Michele came over, fanning herself from the heat.

"Having fun?" I asked.

She smiled at me. "Yeah, come and dance."

"Give me a minute."

"What's the matter? You look upset."

"I'm fine," I said. We stood, not talking, watching everyone on the dance floor.

Little Gina was really going now, gyrating in sync to some disco song. She danced around my father seductively, and if he was sitting down, it would have been a lap dance. I was half expecting him to stick a dollar bill down her shirt.

Michael had pulled Grandma out on the dance floor, and she wiped out in the middle of "Cotton-Eyed Joe," a complicated-looking country line jig. She fell into Little Gina, who fell into my father, and they all wound up on the floor. Aunt Rose had half a load on and wound up in the middle of the dance floor, doing the worm in her muumuu.

"Just think," I said, "pretty soon you'll be related to all these people."

Michele gave an unladylike snort.

The dance floor cleared as Gino changed the music back over to the Italian songs "That's Amore," "Buono Sera," and "Shaddup-a You Face." I danced with my mother to "Mama" and called it a day.

I made nice, collected envelopes at each table, kissed cheeks, and schmoozed with everyone. I walked Michele and Stevie out to the car. He was tired and cranky and would probably pass out before they got out of the parking lot.

"Are you coming out to the house tomorrow?" she asked.

"No, I have something to take care of," I said.

"What?"

"I'll talk to you about it tomorrow." She looked concerned and I said, "It's nothing. I love you—go home and dream about me."

I had given Michele the envelopes from the party to go

through so she could put the money in the safe I keep out on Long Island. We'd have to go through them and sign the checks and put the money in the account we opened out there.

I breathed a sigh of relief when the only people left were Denise and Romano, who was sticking to her like glue, me, Fiore, and Donna. We were standing outside on the front steps where me, Romano, and Denise were smoking cigarettes.

"Tony, are you coming out to the island tonight?" Donna asked.

"No, you two need a night without me," I said.

"We don't mind, Tony, you know that," Fiore said.

"I know, Joe, I appreciate it. I have some stuff to do tomorrow." Like go see my father.

When I first met Joe, I had been flirting with the idea of eating my gun. When he realized how depressed I was, he wouldn't leave me alone. We went back and forth from me staying with him and him staying with me, until I was out of the woods. It seems like a long time ago, when in reality it's been less than a year. I get hit with waves of gratitude toward him sometimes, but I didn't want to get too emotional about it. Instead, I threw a dig to Romano.

"So Nick," I said. "You feeling better after the other night?" I noticed he wasn't drinking too much tonight, and I wanted Denise to know he was a boozer at heart.

He didn't try to hide it, he just said, "Yeah, I appreciate you looking out for me, Tony. You too, Joe." He nodded at Fiore.

"Joe's a good guy." Denise smiled. "Still praying for me, Joe?"

"Always, Denise." Joe smiled back.

"What about Nick—do you pray for him too?" she asked, half kidding. Denise is like Romano in that sense, they always bring up God. While Romano throws in some comment when Joe and I are talking, Denise says stuff like "Did you pray for me?" or "Is it true you go to hell for having sex before you get married?"

"Yes, I always pray for Nick too," Fiore said, amused.

"He prays for God to protect me and tries to teach me how to pray about thousands of people dying around me and I'm the only one that lives. You know, real upbeat stuff." Romano laughed.

"Joe, what are you teaching him?" Donna asked.

"I'm trying to teach him Psalm 91 for when he goes over to FD and Tony and I can't watch his back anymore."

"What was that Scripture you were reading the other night?" Donna asked. "You said you wanted to give it to Nick."

"What Scripture? Oh yeah, about the fire. It's in the Old Testament in Isaiah, I think chapter 43. God was talking to the nation of Israel. It said something like 'When you pass through the water, I'll be with you; when you pass through the river, it won't sweep over you; and when you walk through the fire, you will not be burned.' It says the flames will not set you ablaze," Joe said.

"Yeah, but I'm not Jewish," Romano said.

"No, but you're still God's child. The Bible says that if we are Christ's, then we are Abraham's seed and heirs according to the promise. That means that if you belong to Christ, you're the seed of Abraham and his heir, so all the blessings God had for Abraham can belong to you."

"Are you Christ's?" Donna asked Romano seriously.

He shrugged. "I don't know, I used to be. What about you, Denise?" Romano turned it on her.

Denise blinked at him. "I don't know, I guess I used to be too, until I grew up and stopped believing in him. When I worked at Macy's, there was this lady, Nancy, who reminds me of Joe and Donna," she said, nodding her head toward them. "She was nice, she really cared about me. I went to church with her a few times, and I remember one time going up to the altar and saying a prayer, but I never followed through."

Story of her life.

"It's never an accident when God puts someone in your life that leads you toward him," Donna said. "He's reaching out to you because he loves you and wants to draw you to him."

"That just doesn't seem real to me," Denise said. "The only reason I put any stock in what you're saying is the way Tony has changed. He's different now—I mean, he's still Tony, but better. I wish he still drank though. Hey, you had a shot today!" she turned on me.

"It was half a shot and it was under pressure," I said.

"Are you okay? Do you feel like you want a drink?" She looked worried and happy at the same time.

"I'm fine, I'm not gonna drink."

"Denise, you and Nick should come out some Sunday and go to church with us," Donna said, changing the subject. "Then you can see for yourself what we're talking about."

They looked at each other and Denise shrugged. "Maybe we will," Romano said.

"What's this 'we'?" I snapped at Romano. "There's no 'we.'"

"What are you doing tonight, Tony?" Denise cut me off.

"I'm still on the 'we,' Denise," I said. "You don't know anything about this guy."

Romano said, "What do you mean, 'this guy'?"

At the same time Denise huffed, "Yes I do, Tony, and stay out of my business. Answer the question, what are you doing tonight?"

"I'm going home and getting some sleep." I was dead tired now that the whole thing was over.

"It's not even seven o'clock!" she said. "Nick and I might go up to Dave's," she said, talking about the neighborhood bar we practically grew up in. I hadn't been there since I quit drinking, but Denise still goes there. "Why don't you come with us? We'll play some pool."

I thought about it. I could talk her into giving me the envelope from the private investigator about Marie and keep an eye on Romano at the same time. When she showed me the stuff about Marie, she said she didn't want me to tell my father and took the envelope home with her. I wanted it with me when I talked to him so I had something to back up what I told him. At the same time I didn't want to be in a bar, especially one that I spent a lot of nights drinking in.

"Come on, Tony." Denise read my thoughts. "I'll make sure you don't drink. You can keep an eye on Nick, and I can beat you both at pool."

"Okay," I said with a nod. "Let me go home and change first. What about you, Joe, feel like playing some pool?"

He looked like he was considering it. "We better not. The boys have school tomorrow, and we still have to go out to my parents' house and get them."

We said good-bye to Fiore and Donna, and we each got in our cars and left. I stopped home, changed into an old pair of washed-down Levi's and a black T-shirt, and drove over to Bay Street where Dave's Bar is.

Denise and Romano were still in their clothes from the party and were chalking up their pool cues when I walked in. They each had a drink. Romano was drinking beer, and Denise's looked like a Sea Breeze. It was early and a Sunday and the place was empty, which was fine with me. I didn't feel like meeting up with any of my old buddies. Dave was there though and grabbed his chest when he saw me.

"Hey, Dave, look who the cat dragged in," Denise said.

"More like look what the sewer backed up. Tony Cavalucci, how you been, man?"

He came out from around the bar to get me in a bear hug.

I've known Dave a long time, since I was a kid really. His dad ran the bar up until a couple of years ago, when he had a heart attack. I used to come in with my father when I was a kid, and Dave and I would play shuffleboard and eat barbequed potato chips and drink black cherry sodas.

"I heard you quit drinking," he said.

"Yeah, it was getting out of hand."

"You quit being my friend too?" he asked, looking hurt.

"Not at all, Dave," I said, meaning it. "I just wanted to stay away from the booze for a while. I'm okay now."

"Good." He smiled and shook my hand. "Go shoot some pool. You hungry? I got turkey club tonight."

"Nah, I'm good, I just came from my engagement party. I'm getting married in November."

"So soon? She pregnant?" Dave tilted his head to the side like a dog that doesn't understand what you're saying. He reminded me of a golden retriever, friendly, with scruffy blond hair and big innocent eyes. He was dressed in his usual duds, black Harley shirt, threadbare jeans, and black boots.

"No, she's not pregnant," I said tiredly. I wanted to scream that I probably wouldn't be getting married so soon if I was having sex, but I didn't want anyone to know I wasn't actually getting any. They just wouldn't understand. Where I come from, sex comes first, marriage comes way later.

I played two games of pool. I won the first, Denise won the second. Denise's friend Carla showed up, dressed in a short flowered dress with a jeans jacket thrown over it and high-heeled sandals.

"Tony!" she screamed. That's what everyone knows her as, Carla the screamer. "Hey, Carla," I kissed her cheeks and tried not to wipe my mouth. Carla's made the rounds in the neighborhood, and I think I'm the only person she hasn't slept with.

A couple of guys came in who were friends of Nick's. They

were all Italian except for one, all heavy on the attitude, wearing gold jewelry and lots of cologne.

I pulled Denise to the side. "I want the stuff you have on Marie," I said quietly.

"Why?"

"Because I want to show it to Dad."

"No, Tony. If you want to tell him, that's your business, but you're not getting the stuff."

"Why not? I'm already telling him." I didn't understand her logic.

She waved her hand dismissively. "He won't believe you."

"When I was at the party I went down to use the bathroom, and I heard Marie on the phone with Bobby Egan. She was talking about emptying the bank accounts before she left Dad," I said.

"Good. Then everything's going according to plan," she said, smiling.

"Why do you want to hurt him so much?" I asked.

"Why did he want to hurt us so much?" she countered.

"He didn't want to hurt us—he just didn't give us that much thought," I said honestly. "It still doesn't make it right for us to let her take his money. And remember, the money she's looking to take is from our house. Technically, it should have gone to Mom."

She put her head down and closed her eyes. "I'll think about it," she said.

"Well, think quick. I'm going into the city tomorrow to talk to him while he's at work so he has to act right."

"You're telling him in front of his friends?" She looked appalled, which is ridiculous considering she wanted his viper wife to rip his heart out and empty his bank accounts on top of it.

"What time do you go to work?" I asked.

"I have to be in by ten."

"Where do you work now?" She changed jobs so often I couldn't keep track.

"The same place I've been at for eight months!"

"The motorcycle place on Bay Street? That's a record." I was impressed.

"No, it's not my record. I worked at Macy's for two years," she said dryly.

I kissed her cheek. "Stay away from Romano, he's too young for you."

"No he's not. He'll be twenty-five, I'm twenty-eight," she said.

"You'll be twenty-nine," I reminded her. "And he drinks too much."

"Don't worry about me, Tony, I know what I'm doing."

Famous last words.

I said good night to Nick and Dave and walked out to my truck. It was a warm night and there wasn't a cloud in the sky. I drove down my old block toward the water and parked the truck. My old house was surrounded with a plywood fence to hide the construction that they were doing on it. I didn't look at it as I passed. I just wanted to see the water.

It was such an awesome view from here. The Verrazzano Bridge stood to my right, the lights on it twinkling against the night sky. I looked across the water to the Brooklyn side and watched the fast-moving current head toward the Atlantic. To my left were the ferry terminal and the city. I could see the skyline and the Twin Towers spearing toward the sky, and I thought how much I loved it.

I didn't want to get sentimental about it—I was afraid I'd start toying with the idea of going back to the bar. I shook it off and got in my truck and drove home. I watched *Law and Order* and read my Bible and was asleep by 11:30.

I woke up to the sound of someone banging on my door. I looked over at the clock—8:45. I threw a pair of sweats on, thinking it was Denise bringing the pictures of Marie, then I heard my father yelling.

"Open this door," he yelled. He used a few choice words that I won't repeat to describe the door.

"Hold on," I said.

He banged louder now, and I found myself shrinking back a little at hearing him, like I did when I was a kid. My heart was pounding and that aggravated me, so I unlocked the door and yelled, "Cut it out—there's people upstairs!"

He pushed past me into the apartment, and I looked to see if Marie was with him.

"What's the problem, Dad? Why aren't you at work?" I asked.

"*You're* the problem," he yelled. "And don't worry about why I'm not at work. You stay away from my wife! You hear me?"

"Tell your wife to stay away from Bobby Egan," I said. I didn't plan on blurting it out like that, but I was still half asleep.

He got deadly quiet. "You two don't give up, do you?"

"Who?" I wished I knew what he was talking about, but I was pretty sure Marie came up with a doozy to cover her tail.

"You and your sister, that's who. Do you think I'm so stupid to believe a copy of an apartment lease that anyone could have signed? Marie told me she saw the lease and she could tell the signature was forged." He was breathing heavy, shaking his head in anger.

"Where did she see the lease?"

"You showed it to her!"

"No I didn't."

"And you had pictures of her and Bobby walking out of the precinct together after work. They work together, Tony—they aren't doing anything wrong. Forget it," he spat. "It's over with your mother. I wouldn't go back to her if she was the last woman on earth!"

I ran my hands over my face and walked back to the door and opened it.

"Go home, Dad," I said quietly and nodded my head toward the door.

"What?"

"You heard me. There's no sense talking if you're gonna be like this."

"You're throwing me out of here?"

This seemed to enrage him more.

"You come barging into my apartment, yelling loud enough for the neighbors to hear you, without even asking me what happened. If you made up your mind about what happened yesterday, then why'd you come here?" I put my hands out in front of me.

"I came to tell you to stay away from my wife," he said through gritted teeth. "You and your sister have tormented her since the day you met her."

"Yeah, poor Marie. I'll tell you what, you can either listen to what I have to tell you or you can leave. And in case it means anything to you, I heard Marie telling Bobby Egan on the phone that she was gonna empty your bank accounts," I said.

He waved me away. "She told me what you said! How you and Denise think since your mother's sober that I'd go back to her. You think I don't know these things?"

I wondered how all this ended up being my fault. His wife is a lying cheat and makes me and Denise look mean and conniving.

"Dad, you're kidding yourself if you think Mom would ever go back to you," I said quietly. "And if you think Denise wants you back with Mom, you're kidding yourself even more."

"You and your sister hate Marie." He got up in my face again.

"I don't hate her anymore," I said. "But I don't want anything to do with her either. Denise may hate her, but she hates you more. She doesn't want to give me the pictures and the lease to show you. She wants to wait until Marie cleans you out and leaves you, and then she wants to let you know she knew all along."

He waved me away again and walked toward the door. "Stay away from my wife. I'm not gonna tell you again," he said as he went to leave.

"Hey Dad," I called, and he looked at me. "Is Pete Catalano's son-in-law the guy you were looking to invest your money with?"

"Why?"

"Because I heard Marie telling Bobby Egan about it."

"You could have heard that from anyone," he said.

"Maybe, but you and I both know I didn't."

He left then, but he didn't seem as sure of himself as when he stormed in.

I took a shower, feeling myself getting enraged. He caught

me off guard, half asleep, and now I was thinking of all the stuff I should have said.

I didn't shave, but I charged up my electric razor so I could run it over my face before I went to work tonight. Michele was at work already and I couldn't call her, so I thought about what to do today. I drove around the corner for coffee, a bagel, and the paper and ate breakfast in my kitchen.

I packed up my laundry and put it by the front door. Now that I already saw my father, I might as well catch up with it.

My apartment didn't look too dirty to me, so I did the basics. I took the sheets off the bed and added them to my laundry pile, sprayed the bathroom sink and shower with scrubbing bubbles, and swished my toilet.

I threw on jeans and a Yankee T-shirt and brought my laundry out to my truck. It was sunny out, probably around 75 degrees, a good day to be outside.

I drove to the Laundromat on Sand Lane and loaded up two machines. The place was empty, so I felt okay to leave my laundry there. One time I left stuff in the dryers and somebody stole my sheets.

While the clothes were washing, I drove up to Hylan Boulevard and went through the car wash. I had hosed it off the other day at Michele's, but the remains of Romano's puke were still stuck along the passenger side of the truck.

I went back to the Laundromat and threw my stuff in the dryer. These were good commercial dryers and I had it down to a science—four quarters, twenty-eight minutes, and the clothes were perfect.

My cell phone rang while I was folding, but I didn't recognize the number.

"Hello," I said.

"It's me," Denise said.

"Where are you?"

"I'm at work."

"Dad came to see me this morning," I said.

"I guess Marie beat you to the punch," she chuckled.

"How did you know?"

"Because that's Marie. She lies through her teeth and gets her side of the story in first. Then she cries and does what she does best, leaving Dad dazed and feeling like a man and voilà!—he falls for it again."

"Well, I tried to tell him. Whatever happens now, he can't say I didn't warn him."

"What are you doing today?" she asked.

"Nothing, I'm at the Laundromat folding my clothes, then I don't know what I'm doing."

"Wanna go for lunch?"

"Sure," I said. I had nothing else to do. I might as well get the scoop on her and Romano. "What time?"

"One o'clock, meet me at the diner on Clove and Hylan."

"No, I don't want diner food. How about the bakery on Old Town Road?" It was more a trattoria than a bakery, fresh bread, good Italian food, and outside tables.

"Ooh, I love that place. Okay, one o'clock, and you're buying," she laughed.

When I drove home to drop off my clothes, I found my landlord outside arguing with the guy across the street. Everyone calls the guy the mayor 'cause he thinks he owns the place. Alfonse was up in his face, and it looked like it was getting heated.

"Hey, Alfonse," I said when I got out of the car. "Everything okay?"

"No it's not, Tony. I saw him take my recycle pail and I want it back."

My landlord was talking to me but looking at him. I don't know the guy's name, but he's a problem. He puts cones out in the street so no one can park in front of his house. He takes his dog out and lets him crap on everyone's lawn and never cleans it up. He's always fighting with his wife, and you hear them screaming all the time. Last week he was fighting with someone for driving over his cones and parking in front of his house. It got to the point where he went inside and grabbed a bat and broke two of the windows in the car. The guy took off and no one called the cops, so no charges were pressed against him. It was escalating with him, and eventually he was gonna be a real problem.

"I didn't take your pail," he dismissed Alfonse. "How can you tell it's your pail anyway? They all look the same." He was short and round and shaved his head to deter from his baldness. He weighed about two hundred pounds, and he was wearing a muscle T-shirt (we call them guinea Ts) and nylon shorts. He was about thirty-five and worked nights like me. I think he was a corrections officer.

Part of me wanted to walk away and leave it, but to tell the truth, the guy was shady enough to bat Alfonse in the head and leave him lying in the street.

"I put my name on the bottom of the pail," Alfonse said. Recycle pails are stolen regularly around here. People put their names on them in permanent marker, and then someone steals them and slaps a bumper sticker over the name. It's ridiculous, but you need the recycle pail to get rid of the cans and bottles. If you put the cans and bottles in the regular garbage, you get a summons and have to pay a fine. They actually have Sanitation police now who look through your garbage.

"How you doing, guy," I said to him and put out my hand to shake. "I'm Tony."

"Ralph," he said. "I don't know why he thinks I got his pail." He shrugged and put his hands out.

"I saw you take it!" Alfonse was raising his voice again.

215

"Do me a favor, get the pail and let him see it just to humor him," I said, staring at him with a smile that never reached my eyes.

He matched my stare and said, "Anything to shut him up."

He stomped into his yard, walked into the house, and slammed the front door.

"I guess he's not showing you the pail," I said.

Alfonse went to walk onto his property and I grabbed him. "Whoa, hold on there. It's only a pail, Alfonse, and this guy's half a nut. Leave it alone and we'll steal it back next week on recycle day," I said.

"I can't stand him, Tony, he's always making trouble."

"I know, but when he loses it you don't want to be around."

I stayed in the yard, talking to him a while to calm him down. He was a nice old man, and he was good to me. He brings me food when his wife is making something special, and on Easter she made me a grain pie.

I put the clothes away and puttered around until 12:30, when I left to meet Denise.

The parking lot for the bakery was full, and I wound up parking across the street in the lot for the bank.

The place was packed with the lunch crowd. All the tables were full outside, and I found an empty table in the back corner. I could see why this was the only empty table—every time I leaned on it, it went up on one side and down on the other. I guess a piece was missing off one of the legs.

There must have been about ten women working behind the counter, most of them pretty and young. It looked like the owner preferred thin blondes, because that's all that worked there.

I waved to Denise when she walked in and half the heads

in the place turned, females included. She squeezed through to the table and sat across from me.

"Did you order?" she asked. She was dressed in black pants and a button-down, light pink shirt, or unbuttoned-down shirt was more like it.

"They let you dress that way at work?" I asked.

"Are you kidding, Tony? I've led the shop in sales four months in a row." She was reading the menu on the wall as the waitress approached. "I'll have the grilled chicken salad, a cappuccino, and one of those stuffed breads with the broccoli rabe," she told the waitress.

"No more broccoli rabe, just spinach or the potato, eggplant, and red pepper," the waitress said, rattling it off like she'd said it ten times already.

"The eggplant one," Denise said. "Will you split it with me, Tony?"

"I'll have a piece. You can take the rest home."

The waitress was looking annoyed as I read the menu on the wall, so I told her, "I'll have two Sicilian slices."

"So," Denise said when we were alone. "Marie already got to Dad, huh?"

"Looks that way. She told him that you and I said we were gonna tell Dad she was cheating so him and Mom could get back together now that Mom's sober." I shook my head. "What a piece of work she is. I got him thinking, though—I told him that Marie said Pete Catalano's son-in-law wanted to invest his money for him. There was no way I could have known that, since he didn't tell me. I just hope he invests it before she can take it."

"I don't care either way, I just hope she leaves him soon."

"So what's the deal with Romano?" I asked.

"I've known him for a while, Tony. I'm surprised it never

came up that he worked with you. He never talked about being a cop, just that he was going to the fire department."

"He leaves soon, in a couple of weeks. He hangs out with Joe and me a lot at work." I couldn't tell how interested she was in him, so I added, "He drinks a lot, Denise, and he has a lot of trouble with his ex-girlfriend over his daughter."

"I've met her—the ex-girlfriend, I mean. When I first met him, he brought her to the bowling alley a couple of times. She's full of herself, looked at the rest of us like we were beneath her. Nick's so down-to-earth, he seems sad a lot though, kind of reminds me of Eeyore."

"Who's Eeyore?" I asked, then remembered the donkey from Winnie the Pooh. "The donkey from the cartoon, right?"

"Yeah, you know, cute, kind of sad." Denise smiled.

"He's all wrong for you, Denise," I warned.

"We're just friends, Tony," she countered, but I didn't believe her.

We finished lunch and left by a quarter to two. I went home and flipped the channels on my TV until 3:30, when Michele called.

"Hey babe," I said. "How was school?"

"It was good. What about you, what'd you do today?"

"Laundry, cleaned up a little, had lunch with Denise," I said, going through it with her about what happened with Marie and my father.

"You told him, honey. If he chooses not to believe it, there's nothing you can do. Oh, Tony, you're not going to believe this. I went through the envelopes last night from the party—guess how much money everyone gave us?"

"How much?"

"Over twelve thousand dollars!" she squealed.

"Really?" I hadn't even thought about it. "Wow."

"I know, that's the rest of the money for the wedding." I could hear the excitement in her voice. "We got over seven thousand between both our parents—it was so generous of them."

"How much did my father give us?" I was curious.

"Your mother and father gave us twenty-five hundred each, and my parents gave us another twenty-five hundred."

"Wow," I said again. That really took a lot of pressure off us for all the crap we had to pay for. The money for a wedding really adds up. The hall was a small fortune, then you add the flowers, music, favors, and invitations—everything costs so much.

We talked for a couple of minutes more. She was going with Donna to pick out some bridesmaid thing while Fiore watched all the kids.

I fell asleep surfing the channels and woke up at 7:00. I shaved and packed my bag and ordered out a meatball hero. I ate my sandwich, watching *Who Framed Roger Rabbit*, and washed it down with a soda. I was bored out of my mind. There's no one I hang out with anymore, so I couldn't call anyone. I picked up my Bible and thumbed through it. I read through Mark 4 about the sower and the seed. I keep reading through it because it's the one where Jesus says if you don't get that parable, then you won't get any of the other ones.

Pastor John at our church uses this one a lot, about the Word being sowed in our hearts and that we have to be good ground for it to grow. He said if your heart is hard, it's like the ground being hard and the seed won't grow good in it. I took it to mean that if you're what Italians call "thickheaded" and won't listen to what anybody tells you, you're not gonna learn anything. I read through it again and asked God to keep me from being thick about it and help me be able to hear what he says.

I left by 10:15, looking forward to getting back to work. Since it was a Monday night, traffic was nil all the way in. I parked on the sidewalk on 36th Street between 9th and Dyer and walked over to the precinct.

I went down to the locker room to change and found a Xerox picture of the inspector in a Speedo bathing suit taped to the door. His face was superimposed over some buff guy in a bikini bathing suit. I thought someone was being a little generous with the physique, but it was still pretty funny. I went upstairs and found Joe talking to Vince Puletti in the radio room.

"Hey, Tony." Vince shook my hand.

"How's it goin', Vince?" I asked.

"No sense complaining," he said.

"Anything on O'Brien?" I asked. If anyone knew, it would be Vince.

"They got him over in the pension section until the investigation is over. His wife got a temporary order of protection against him, and he's been staying with his brother. Friggin' women, it's not enough she's cheating on him—she's gotta grind him into the ground by ruining his career." He grabbed onto his gun belt and heaved it up over his stomach, only to have it slide back down.

Hanrahan's attention to the roll call announcement stopped me from having to comment, and Joe and I went over to the muster room. I noticed Terri Marks was missing from the desk and wondered if she was embarrassed to face Joe.

There were more pictures of the inspector in the Speedo taped around the room. Hanrahan pulled them off as he walked toward the podium. He pulled another one off the front of the podium and tossed them in the garbage.

He walked behind the podium and looked down, shook his head, and pulled another picture off the podium and crumpled it as the ranks laughed.

"You're opening up a can of worms here, guys," he said,

trying not to smile. He didn't agree with what the inspector was doing, but this wasn't helping things.

"The color of the day is yellow," he said. He gave out the sectors and foot posts and meals and finished up with, "Oh, we had a stabbing the other night up on 9th Avenue. The perp's name is Daniel Browning, he goes by the street name Easy. He was seen earlier by the Port Authority cops, but they lost him in the subway at four-o and eight," which is right by Port Authority.

He was talking about the stabbing Fiore and I handled. He gave a description of the perp and the clothes he was wearing, which sounded like what he was wearing the night of the stabbing. "A copy of his picture is over by the desk," he finished.

We filed out, and Joe and I grabbed Romano outside on the steps and went out to the RMP. We threw our hats in the back with Romano, our memo books on the dashboard, and jammed our nightsticks in the console before driving thirty feet to the corner to get coffee.

"I'll go in," Romano said, getting out of the car. "You guys want anything with your coffee?"

"Just coffee for me," Joe said.

"Being nice to me isn't gonna work, Eeyore," I said.

"Huh?"

"Just coffee," I sighed.

"Eeyore?" Fiore chuckled when Romano went in the deli.

"Yeah, Denise says he's cute and sad like Eeyore from Winnie the Pooh." I made a disgusted sound.

Fiore barked out a laugh.

Romano got back in the car, and we drove him up to 42nd and 8th and let him sit in the car while we drank our coffee. He was trying to be nice to me, telling me what a great party it was yesterday. I'm usually suspicious of anyone that's nice to me but Fiore, and Romano's no exception.

I tossed him out of the car and drove eastbound on 42nd Street to take a look at the Deuce before patrolling our sector. We drove on 39th Street over to 9th Avenue, when we heard Central come over the radio with, "In the South a 10-10 disorderly at four-two and eight." She gave the address of Midtown's favorite porn store.

Technically the job was in Henry's sector, but Henry had an aided when we left the house. Someone inside Port Authority had a breathing problem that they were handling, so Central threw it over the air.

We heard Bruno Galotti on the radio answer, "Robbery post 5 to Central, I'll take that job."

Central went into the job—apparently a customer in the porn shop was knocking over tapes and arguing with the manager. Romano came over the radio with "Robbery 4 on the back."

I turned on 8th and drove toward 42nd Street. The last time I got called to a disorderly at that store, it was an EDP.

"Let's give them a hand," Joe said. "We don't want Nick getting jammed up before he goes to FD."

Fiore radioed Central with "South David on the back."

"10-4, South David."

As I passed Port Authority, I looked over to see if Easy was around. Romano was on the radio now, yelling, "He's running north on 8th Avenue."

I looked at Joe and hit the gas a little. As I got toward the front of the porn place, I saw a trail of white smoke going north on 8th Avenue and Romano running in the street, trying to stay away from it.

As we approached Romano, I heard Central say, "Who is in pursuit?"

Romano put his radio to his mouth and said, "Robbery

4, black shirt, blue jeans, running north on 8th Avenue past 43rd Street."

We could hear him breathing heavy over the transmission. When I passed Romano I could see the guy, a male white with a black muscle shirt, faded jeans, and work boots. He was muscular and looked like he worked construction. He was holding his right arm up and was spraying a handheld can that was letting out a stream of fog. He was looking behind him and running at the same time.

I passed him and stopped at 44th Street and 8th so he had to run into us. Joe and I got out of the car, holding our nightsticks in our hands. We surprised him, and he stumbled down to a walk as he turned his head around to look where he was going.

I hit the back of his hand with my nightstick and heard the crack as I connected. The can went flying out of his hand, and I grabbed his right wrist and chest and Joe grabbed his left wrist and chest simultaneously. We half lifted him as we threw him against the wall of the building in front of us. I heard the hollow sound of the can hitting the sidewalk and the *oomph* as his chest hit the wall.

I smelled booze and the acrid smell of a chemical on him. We put him down on the ground as I cuffed the right arm, and Joe cuffed the left as Romano ran up.

"Get off me!" he roared and bucked. "I didn't do nuthin'!"

Perps always say that.

Romano picked the can up off the sidewalk and said, "Pepper fog." The can had a little foghorn for a nozzle, nothing like I'd ever seen before.

Romano put the can up in the perp's face and yelled, "If you didn't do nothing, then what are you running for and spraying this stuff?"

The perp turned away from the can and said, "Get out of my face!"

"Where's Bruno?" Joe asked Romano.

"He's still back at the store—he got hit with the mace."

Joe and I hoisted up the perp and tossed him in the back of the car with Romano and drove down to 42nd and 8th. Bruno was in front of the porn place with another guy, both bent over on the sidewalk. We got out of the car, locked the doors, and trotted over to him. We could hear him coughing, spitting, and gagging.

"Bruno, you okay?" Joe asked.

"Ahhh, he hit me with the mace." His eyes were swollen and tearing.

"You want a bus?" Joe asked.

He threw us a wave that looked like a yes, so Joe got on the radio.

"South David to Central, we have an officer having trouble breathing. We need a bus at four-two and eight; have South Sergeant respond."

"10-4."

Then Fiore added, "Robbery 4's got one under at this location."

"Robbery 4, that's 0015 hours," Central said, giving the time of the arrest.

"Who's this?" I asked Romano, nodding toward the guy with Bruno. His face was red and his eyes were tearing, but he didn't look like he was hit as bad.

"He's the manager," Romano said.

He looked like he managed a porn store—tall, dark, and greasy, wearing a black silk shirt and four gold chains around his neck.

Bruno was groaning, "Oh man, this hurts," and then he

cursed in Italian. Joe went into the deli next to the porn shop to get him a bottle of water.

"How did this guy get away from you?" I asked Romano.

"When we walked up, he was arguing out front with the manager. Just as I walked up on them, he sprayed the manager, and when he turned around to run, it sprayed Bruno. He kept spraying it as he ran. I chased him, but I stayed in the street so I didn't get hit with it," he said, then added, "Good thing it wasn't windy."

Joe came out with a big bottle of water and brought it over to Bruno. "Cup your hands," he said.

Bruno was trying to open his eyes, but they were tearing too much. He stood up and put his hands out in front of him.

Joe poured some water in his hands, getting most of it on the sidewalk. "Don't drink it," Joe told him. "Just flush your face and eyes with it."

"Did you get him?" he asked Joe, his eyes red and swollen. He burped and grimaced, then he gagged and puked.

"Yeah, we got him," Joe said.

"Ahhh, I swallowed it!" Bruno wailed. "It's disgusting!" He spit again. "What does this stuff do to you?"

"I hear it causes impotence," I told him.

"What's that?" he asked. No wonder people think cops are stupid.

Joe brought the bottle of water over to the greasy manager and had him flush his eyes with it.

Hanrahan got to the scene, and the bus pulled up a minute later. It was a couple of veterans, two males. One was short with blond hair and glasses, the other dark haired and heavyset. They split up; one went over to Bruno and the other went to the manager.

"How you doing, Bruno?" Hanrahan asked.

"I'll be alright," he said.

"What happened?"

Romano held up the can of mace like he caught it in the end zone. "He got shot with this."

"Let me see that," Hanrahan said, taking the can. "You're gonna have to get an exposure number."

"For what?" Bruno looked startled.

"You ingested this stuff. You don't know what kind of reaction you could have down the road. What if six months from now you have a problem breathing 'cause of this?"

The boss was giving him some good advice here. A good cop looks ahead in case he can get out on three-quarters later on.

The manager of the porn place wouldn't go to the hospital and went back into the store.

We decided that Romano would get the information from the manager. He would take the collar and ride back to the house with the boss. Joe and I would follow Galotti in the ambulance to Bellevue.

When we got to Bellevue, the emergency room was packed. They put Bruno in a room, but that was about it. An Asian nurse came in to take his vital signs. She wasn't very talkative and left as soon as she was done. I'd like to think we'd get preferential treatment if it was serious, but this wasn't an emergency.

We sat there for a while listening to Bruno burp, groan, and cough, when the doctor came in.

He was young, maybe about thirty, looking wet behind the ears. He was tall and thin with black hair and glasses, and he had that *Revenge of the Nerds* look about him.

He said the effects of the mace could last from forty-five minutes to several hours, but Bruno'd be fine. He said they'd flush out his eyes and give him something for the burping.

"Don't call my mother," Bruno said with feeling. "She'll freak."

I passed up a great opportunity to goof on him here, like we'd call her over him getting a little mace in his eyes.

Joe fell asleep on one of the chairs in the room, and I went outside to smoke a cigarette. The night was clear, but you couldn't see any stars with the lights from the city. I could hear the traffic from FDR Drive as I stood there, and I heard the screech of tires locking up and the thump that followed, telling me someone got rear-ended.

It was 1:30 and I was starting to get tired, so I went up to the cafeteria on the second floor and got three coffees. I got a package of chocolate chip cookies so Bruno could put something in his stomach to absorb the mace. They had other food there, but nothing we would eat. I wondered what it is that makes hospital cafeterias and school lunchrooms smell the same.

Joe woke up when he smelled the coffee, but Bruno wouldn't drink the coffee or eat the cookies until the doc said it was okay. I went out to the desk to ask if he could have it. It took them twenty minutes to get us an answer, so the coffee was cold by the time Bruno drank it anyway.

Bruno started going off again about how upset his mother was gonna be that he got hurt.

Joe surprised me by asking Bruno, "Is your mother that overbearing?"

He thought about it and shrugged. "She gets nervous. She's not young, Joe, she didn't have me until she was forty. I'm her only child, so she's overprotective."

"You're not a kid anymore, Bruno," Joe said. "She doesn't need to be protecting you. You can handle yourself."

"Kiss Momma good-bye," I said, and Joe smiled.

"Huh?" Bruno looked confused.

"The pastor of our church tells this story about some preacher who was counseling a couple that were having marriage problems," I started. "The wife was complaining about the mother-in-law always butting in to their business."

"How did she butt in?" Bruno asked, I guess to see if it was any of the stuff his mother did.

"The husband would say his mother was a great cook and why couldn't the wife be more like her. Telling the wife to bring up the kids the way his mother did. You know, stuff like that," I said.

"Yeah, but shouldn't she help them? I mean, she knows stuff they don't, so why not let her be involved?" Bruno asked.

"Well," Joe said, "if she was there to help, she'd be teaching her daughter-in-law how to cook. As far as raising the kids and stuff, unless they ask her, she should mind her business."

"Anyway," I continued, "the pastor tells the married couple to come in and bring the mother-in-law. She was all excited, thinking they were asking her there to show all the stuff the daughter-in-law was doing wrong. The mother tells the pastor how the daughter–in–law doesn't cook good, she don't clean right, really nailed the daughter-in-law. So the pastor says, 'You're here today so you can say good-bye to your son.' She pretended not to understand what he was saying, then the pastor tells the son, 'Kiss Momma good-bye,' and after the son kissed her, the pastor tossed her out of the room."

"That's terrible," Bruno said, coughing.

Joe and I looked at each other.

"You have a girlfriend, Bruno?" Joe asked.

"Yeah."

"Is she a nice girl?"

"Yeah, she's a nurse, takes care of kids with cancer."

"How long you seeing her?"

"About three years."

"Does your mother like her?" Joe smiled.

Bruno shrugged and said, "Not really."

"Kiss Momma good-bye, Bruno," I said, "or you're gonna have problems later on."

"Come on, Tony, she's my mother. What kind of son tells her good-bye? Did you say that to your mother?" he asked me.

"No, but my mother's not like that. My grandmother was, and it caused a lot of problems with my parents," I said.

"What about you, Joe?"

"No," he said as he shook his head. "But like Tony, my grandmother was like that. My mother remembers what it was like, and she minds her business. She gets along good with my wife, and everybody's happy. I see my parents a lot, Bruno. If they didn't get along with my wife, we wouldn't see them as much."

"I see what you mean," Bruno said. "But I wouldn't want to hurt my mother."

"Better your mother than your wife," Joe said. "You gotta live with *her*."

They finally discharged Bruno at 4:30, and we drove him back across town to the precinct. His eyes were still a little red and he was still burping occasionally, but otherwise he was okay.

We notified Central that we were headed back to the house, and Sergeant Hanrahan met us there.

"I think I'm gonna head home, Boss," Bruno said.

"Can you drive home, or you want me to get someone to take you?"

I could see he was thinking about it, but he said, "No thanks, I can drive." He went down to the locker room to change and left about ten minutes later.

We took our meal for five o'clock. Romano had finished up the paperwork on the arrest and offered to go across the street to the deli to get us sandwiches. This was the second time tonight he went into the deli without complaining, a record for him.

He got roast beef with Muenster and tomato for me and turkey with lettuce and tomato for Joe and Boar's Head baloney and cheese for himself. We ate in the lounge, took off our vests, shoes, and gun belts, and passed out on the benches.

Fiore's watch beeped at five to six, and I sat up and got dressed. Romano was sound asleep, so I nudged him with my foot.

"Come on, Nick, time to make the donuts."

"I'm up." He sat up and ran his hands over his face.

Fiore was still asleep, so I shook him a little and said, "Come on, Joe, get up."

They were both sitting up now, looking groggy and disoriented.

"Today!" I called as I went out and heard something hit the door as I closed it.

Hanrahan was talking to Lieutenant Coughlin at the desk and stopped me as I went to walk outside for a cigarette.

"Tony, do me a favor," he said. "One of Diane Winston's kids is sick, and she's gonna be late. Take Romano over to the abortion clinic around 6:30. It opens at seven, and we don't want any trouble over there. Stick around and make sure everything's okay. If you get a job, pick it up, otherwise stay with him until you get a call."

"Sure, Boss," I said.

The abortion clinic is over by Park Avenue. I've worked it a couple of times, and I don't like it. Diane, the female who usually works it, knows the deal over there. I don't think Romano's ever worked it, so I could see why the boss wanted us with him.

The boss went over it with Joe and Romano when they came upstairs, and they met me outside on the front steps of the precinct.

The sun was up, but the day was still pretty cool. The city was getting moving, and southbound traffic on 9th Avenue was steady.

I stopped at the corner, and Joe went inside for the coffee.

"You ever work this detail?" Romano asked from the backseat.

"Yeah," I said.

"Is there trouble?"

"Not really. You're just there to make sure nothing gets out of hand," I said.

Joe got back in the car with the coffee. I took 34th Street to 5th Avenue and turned at the Empire State Building. The clinic was between Madison and Park, and I made a left on 31st and parked the RMP just past the front entrance.

The job was a fixer, which means you sit there until someone relieves you. Diane Winston usually works it, and unless there's some kind of rally, we're there without barricades.

The clinic doesn't open until 7:00 and there were already four protestors, two pro-life and two pro-choice.

I wondered, like I do whenever I come here, why these people don't have jobs and have nothing better to do than come down here and yell at complete strangers.

The pro-choice people stood on the left side of the entrance, the pro-lifers took the right. The pro-life ones were both men, one dressed up like Friar Tuck from Robin Hood, the other in jeans and a T-shirt that said, "Smile, your mom chose life." They had signs set up along the curb and on the sidewalk, but we couldn't see them until we were up on the sidewalk.

The pro-choice were two women, one young in her twenties, the other looked like she was pushing forty. The forty-year-old had a T-shirt that said, "My Body, My Choice." The younger one had a T-shirt that said, "I had an abortion."

Both sides were radical, and they each seemed to have an agenda that had nothing to do with why they were there. It was like a contest to them, and I had a hard time believing either one of them was there for the right reason.

At ten to seven, the first customers, a scared-looking girl and what looked like her boyfriend, came walking up.

"Let the games begin," I mumbled.

"You have other options," the pro-lifer in the robe called. "This baby can be raised in a loving home."

It sounded right until the second guy whipped out the pictures of the aborted fetuses and shoved them in front of her face and said, "Look at what you'll be doing to your baby!"

"Don't listen to them," the older of the pro-choice women yelled. "Your body, your choice."

"Don't kill your baby!" He held up more horrific pictures of dead fetuses.

"Don't listen to them, come with me," the younger woman said and walked over and opened the door and held it until the couple walked inside.

The pro-choice girl looked smug once they walked in, and I thought she was gonna high-five her partner.

"That's disgusting," Romano said, nodding toward the abortion pictures.

"Is it me, Joe, or is that wrong?" I asked.

"Which part?" he asked, looking troubled.

When I was in high school, I thought I knocked up Marie Elena Carlino. At the time I didn't think there was anything wrong with taking care of it in a place like this. Knowing God the way I know him now, I could never do it, but back then I was more concerned with myself and how to get out of trouble.

I thought about Michele and the turmoil she must have had when she got pregnant with Stevie, or Romano with his little girl. You can say what you want, but in the end it's a life, a son or daughter. As each of them rallied around us on both sides of the coin, I couldn't help but think that this wasn't the way Jesus would have handled it.

A girl of about seventeen walked up with what looked to be her mother. The pro-lifers rushed her with the pictures, and the kid started crying. The older pro-choice woman looked angry and stomped over toward them. The girl's mother held up her hand and stopped her.

The daughter was crying hard now, holding on to the mother. I could hear the mother say, "You don't have to do this. You don't need to make this decision today."

The pro-choice lady came closer and said to the mother, "Come with me, we'll get her inside."

The mother's face got hard and she snapped, "You're pro-choice? Well, it's her choice—don't try to influence her!"

"Okay, sorry," the woman said and held up her hands.

The pro-life side had a new sign, "Abortion leaves one dead and one wounded."

"This is messed up," Romano said. "It's sick, all of it."

The next to walk up were two women, both in their twenties. Since neither one of them looked particularly upset, neither side knew whom to rush.

Pro-life came out first with the blood-and-guts, and one of the women stalled. The older pro-choice lady got fed up and went over to take the arm of the undecided and lead her toward the entrance.

The friar started yelling, "You can't touch her! Officer, she is *not* supposed to put her hands on anyone! What is she going to do, drag them in there to kill their babies?"

He was right, and Joe and I looked at Romano, who was clueless what to do. I went over to the pro-choice side and said, "Ladies, you know you're not supposed to touch anyone. If you want to open the door, that's fine—otherwise it's influencing."

Like I said, it seemed like a game to them. They had no compassion for the people, just fire for the agenda. Maybe it's me, but I'd be more likely to listen to someone I thought actually cared about me rather than this radical stuff.

We wouldn't be here by the time they walked out of the clinic, but I knew how it'd go. Both sides would be quiet as the woman walked out. The pro-choice would be smug, the pro-life defeated, and neither one of them would realize their attitudes had more to do with winning or losing, and they seemed to forget that there are people involved.

I couldn't wait for someone from the day tour to relieve us; I hated this fixer.

I left the precinct at 8:15 and took the West Side Highway downtown. I stopped at Montey's Deli on Bay Street for a peppers, eggs, and potato sandwich. I hadn't been here in a while, not since I moved into my apartment, in fact. Montey's face lit up when he saw me, and he wiped his hands on his apron and reached over the counter to shake my hand.

"Tony! How are you, buddy?"

"Can't complain, Montey. How you been?"

"Good. I hear you're getting married, congratulations," he said, smiling.

"Who told you?"

"Denise, she comes in a lot for lunch." That made sense since the showroom she worked in was less than a mile away and Montey probably gave her food for free half the time.

"What can I get ya?"

"Ah, two potato and egg sandwiches. You still use the peppers left over from the sausage and peppers?"

"Of course, but don't be giving away my secrets." He cut two rolls and stuffed them, wrapping them both in wax paper.

"Anything else? Coffee?"

"Nah, I'm good. Thanks, Montey," I said as I paid him and shook his hand again.

"Don't be a stranger," he said.

I drove home and parked in front of my house. I grabbed my gym bag with my gun in it and the bag with the sandwiches and noticed someone watching me in a car across the street. I realized it was Ralph, the recycle-pail-stealing psycho. He was staring at me with a hard look meant to intimidate.

I wasn't about to skulk into the house, so I crossed the street and walked up to the driver's side of his car.

"Is there a problem?" I asked, probably a little hard.

"Nope, just waiting for my wife," he said, nodding toward where a woman in red plaid pajama pants and a black T-shirt was walking back from the corner. I've seen her before; she always wears pajamas to bring her kids to the bus stop.

My mother says that's a Brooklyn thing, going outside in your pajamas. I think she just likes to believe that people from Staten Island are more civilized than people from Brooklyn. Donna, Fiore's wife, is from Long Island, and I've seen her drive little Joey to the bus stop in her bathrobe, so maybe it's a New York thing.

"Have a good one," I said to him, but he didn't answer. He was still staring at me. I had a bad feeling about him and thought about calling my friend Louie Coco who works at Riker's to see if he knew this clown.

I went inside and checked my messages. There was one from my brother, Vinny, who said, "Call my cell, I'm at work" in a clipped voice.

I plugged in my cell phone and took my address book out of the drawer next to the sink. I never bothered to fill it out right, so I went to the *V*s for Vinny and dialed his cell phone.

He picked up on the third ring and said, "Hey."

"Hey Vin, what's up buddy?"

"Tony, what is going on with you and Marie?" he said, sounding upset. I was surprised he called about it—he never gets involved.

"What do you mean?"

"She's flipping out, Tony. Her and Dad are fighting. She said you attacked her outside the bathroom at your engagement party, and she's threatening to leave Dad over it."

I'll bet.

"Vin, I went downstairs to use the bathroom and she was talking on the pay phone outside the door to her boyfriend. Let me finish," I said when he started to interrupt me. "It had nothing to do with me. Denise had her followed. I heard her telling this guy, Bobby Egan, that she was gonna empty the bank accounts and leave Dad."

"You think she would do that?" he said, sounding skeptical.

"No, not Marie," I said sarcastically. "If you don't believe me, go see Denise. She'll show you the stuff the investigator got on them."

"Why can't we have a normal family?" he sighed.

"Don't ask me."

We talked for a couple of minutes before he had to get back to work. I missed living with Vinny. I didn't see him a lot when we lived together, but I missed having the connection with him. I brought my sandwiches over to the living room and turned on the TV so I wouldn't have to think about it.

I put the morning news on in case I missed anything while I was at work last night. A developer leased the World Trade Center for ninety-nine years in the biggest real estate transaction in New York history. The guy that leased it agreed to pay 3.22 billion dollars for the 10.6-million-foot complex. He signed a thousand pages of contracts, leases, and agreements. Makes my three rooms for seven hundred bucks seem so insignificant.

Next the blonde talked about how the city pays over forty thousand dollars for a mentally ill person to be homeless in

New York City. "If they're homeless, why are we paying for them?" I asked the TV.

She answered me by saying that the cost to city agencies such as hospitals, jails, shelters, and medical offices averages out to $40,449 a year for each mentally ill homeless person. The skells cost more than most cops make in a year.

I shut it off when she started talking about the genetically modified salmon that would be making its way soon into American markets. She said that we were already eating genetically engineered corn and potatoes, and I vowed that next summer I'd be growing my own stuff like Alfonse.

I switched to ESPN and was starting to doze off when I heard yelling. I sat up to listen, and I could hear a man yelling and a woman crying. I heard Alfonse outside my window yell, "Hey! Get your hands off her! I'm calling the cops."

I knew without seeing it was Ralph across the street. I sighed and grabbed my gun out of my bag and stuck it in the waistband of my jeans. I walked upstairs. Alfonse was on the phone, telling 911 that the guy was in the street hitting his wife.

When I got to the front gate I saw he had her on the ground, still in her pajamas. He was kicking away at her as she screamed. I walked toward them and Romano's father flashed through my head, shot in the face in a domestic dispute. I would have hesitated, but I was raised that you never hit a woman and you never let anyone else hit a woman.

"Ralph!" I yelled. "Get away from her."

He cursed me out, telling me to mind my business. He talked big, but when I walked toward him, he backed away from her.

He was screaming, telling me what a lying whore she was. He was past the point of rage, and all I could think was, *This guy works corrections and he's got a gun.* I was thinking, *If he pulls his piece and starts shooting, I'm gonna take him out.*

When the wife realized he backed away, she looked up and tried to move away from him without him seeing her. Out of the corner of my eye, I could see she had her eyes on him the whole time as she moved.

She was beat up pretty bad. From where I was standing, I could see choke marks on her neck. Her face was swollen and bruised, and she was holding her ribs.

"Let her go, Ralph, it's not worth it. Why would you risk your job for her?" I said. Guys like him think everyone thinks like they do, so I humored him.

He seemed to deflate somewhat and let off a stream of curses about women in general and how we give them everything and they spit in our face.

"Then get rid of her," I said. "Why are you with her?"

"She's crazy—how am I gonna leave my kids with her?"

The sad part is he was serious.

An RMP pulled up from the precinct in New Dorp, and two cops got out of the car.

"You happy, Sandy? You're going to jail," Ralph yelled at her.

"I didn't call," she told me, looking terrified. "Tell them to leave."

I walked over toward the RMP, out of earshot of Ralph. I knew one of them, Eddie DiTommasso, who I ran track with in high school. He was big and built, with light frizzy hair. His partner looked more Italian than Eddie. He was big too, but not as bulky, with dark hair and eyes.

Eddie's partner walked over to Ralph with his nightstick tucked under his arm.

"Listen," Ralph told Eddie's partner. "The last cop told her if you guys have to come out here again, he's locking her up too."

"Really? And who was that?" he asked.

"His name was Lambert." I could tell by Eddie's partner's face that he knew the guy, and what he thought of him.

"What happened?" Eddie's partner asked Ralph, stone-faced.

Ralph was breathing heavy. "I'm at work, trying to call my house, and she's nowhere to be found."

"I was sleeping," she said. She was crying and having a hard time getting the words out. "Where would I be at three o'clock in the morning?" She sounded beaten down, like there was no sense in her answering anyway.

"You won't be happy till I'm dead," he screamed at her. Eddie's partner was standing in front of him now, blocking his view of her.

"Hey, Tony," Eddie said, shaking my hand. "What's going on with these two?" he asked as he gave a slight nod toward them. He didn't want them to see us talking about them.

"He was beating the crap out of her, and she wasn't saying a word to him."

Alfonse walked toward us, and I noticed he was wearing his gardening gear, a faded Yankee hat, a cotton sleeveless shirt, old blue work pants, and stained construction boots.

"Officer, I'm the one who called," Alfonse said, looking more upset than I've ever seen. "He's no good, this guy. He beats his wife. Someone parked in front of his house, and he took a bat and broke the windows in the car." Alfonse shook his head. "And he stole my recycle pail."

"This guy's a nut," I said.

"Yeah, we've dealt with him before," Eddie said.

"Listen, the guy's with corrections and I'm sure he's got a piece," I said, keeping my voice low.

"Thanks for the heads-up," Eddie said.

The wife was sitting on the ground with her head down on her knees, trying not to draw attention to herself. The neighbors were out on their front stoops, looking to see what was going on but not surprised by any of it.

Eddie's partner was trying to keep Ralph under control. I heard him say, "Stop looking at her—you're talking to me. She's not going anywhere," as Ralph tried to look around him at the wife.

I stayed with Alfonse while Eddie walked over to the wife. She stood up as he approached, wincing and holding her side. I heard Eddie talking to her quietly and then heard her answer when Ralph started yelling.

"What are you telling him? You're a liar, a lying whore!"

In New York, when people say *whore* it sounds like *who-uh*.

Eddie's partner warned him, "I'm not gonna tell you again, shut your mouth and talk to me."

I saw Eddie get on the radio, then walk over to his partner and Ralph. As Eddie approached, Ralph held up his hands and said, "I'm on the job—can I show you my ID?"

"You're on the job?" Eddie asked. "What job?"

"Corrections."

"So you're a corrections officer. You have a gun on you?"

"Yeah," Ralph said, looking wary.

"Well, we need to have your gun," Eddie said diplomatically, but he was looking to lock him up now and he wanted to get the gun first.

"Why do you need my gun?" He was catching on now. He was expecting some professional courtesy so he could tell his wife he could do whatever he wanted to her and no one would stop him. It was obvious that's happened a time or two for him to be as bold as he's been, but no one was gonna cover for him here.

"Because you're in the middle of a dispute and I don't feel like getting shot," Eddie said impatiently.

"I'm not gonna shoot you," Ralph said, then looked over toward his wife and yelled, "but I might shoot her!"

She was sitting on the ground again with her head down, trying to be invisible.

He unbuckled his belt and went to slide his gun off. It looked like a snub-nose .38 five-shot and me, Eddie, and his partner all had our eyes on it. He saw us looking and he snapped, "You female dog! [I'm editing here.] This is your fault, you don't know when to stop! You just keep pushing and pushing," he said as he accented each word with a stomp of his foot, with his hand on his belt.

Eddie saw Ralph was losing it, and he looked at his partner. A second later they both moved in as Eddie grabbed his right arm and the partner grabbed the left. I ran toward them as they put him on the ground. Eddie got Ralph's right arm behind his back and pulled the gun off the belt.

"Tony, take this," he said as he handed me the gun, and they cuffed him.

"You can't lock me up!" he screamed and started to buck.

"Listen, calm down," Eddie said. When he didn't, Eddie got in his face and said, "I said calm down!"

"You happy now?" Ralph screamed toward his wife. "Get off of me!" He tried to push Eddie away and move toward her. "You're dead, you hear me? You're dead!"

She put her arms around her legs and buried her head and started rocking back and forth.

The sergeant pulled up and was out of the car before his driver could stop. He ran over to Eddie and his partner to help them, and I saw the bus pull up behind the sergeant's RMP.

EMS got out of the bus, and I pointed toward the wife. One of them, an overweight middle-aged woman, shot the wife a dirty look and shook her head. Her partner was younger, bald and skinny, and mumbled something under his breath. He looked at the holstered gun in my hand but didn't say anything.

Once they got Ralph in the RMP, I heard bits and pieces of Eddie and his partner talking to the sarge, saying, "The guy's a nut job; he works for corrections."

Eddie and the sarge came over to me.

"Did you call?" the sergeant asked.

"No, Boss, my landlord did," I said as I pointed to Alfonse standing by the curb. I handed the holstered gun to Eddie. Alfonse took that as a cue and walked over to us.

"Eddie, be careful," I said. "This guy's a nut, and I don't doubt he's coming back after her."

"Would you be willing to be a witness?" Eddie asked with a smirk.

"Only if I have to," I said and smirked back. If it wasn't my collar, I'd rather not be involved. Then I looked over at her all beat-up and said, "Okay, if you need me to, I'll do it."

"I'll definitely be a witness," Alfonse said.

I was more concerned with Alfonse testifying against this guy—I didn't want Ralph coming after him.

The sergeant walked over to where EMS was checking out the wife and asked her if there were any more guns in the house.

She nodded and said, "I think there's two more."

"Where are they?"

"In the safe."

"Do you have the key?"

"No, it's on his key ring."

"Joe, get the keys off this guy so I can get into the safe," the sergeant said.

Once he had the keys, she took him in the house. They came out a couple of minutes later, and the sarge had a brown paper bag tucked under his arm.

"You need to go down to Family Court today and get a temporary order of protection," the sergeant told her.

"What good will that do me?" she said with a strangled laugh. "You see how he is—you think that's gonna stop him? He'll be back tomorrow."

"Not if you get the order of protection," he said. "He's going through the system, that should help. Is there anywhere you can go?"

"If I had somewhere to go, do you think I'd be here? It doesn't matter where I go, he'll find me." She put her hands over her face, and her shoulders were shaking as she cried.

"Put him in my car," the sarge said, talking about Ralph. "You two go with her to the hospital," he said to Eddie and his partner, "and we'll start the paperwork back at the house."

EMS put her in the ambulance. My next-door neighbor was gonna follow her to the hospital and give her a ride home.

Eddie took the information from me and Alfonse, and I told him to call if he needed anything.

I said good-bye to Alfonse and went back down to my apartment. The message light was blinking on my answering machine.

"Hi, it's me," Michele said. "I'm sorry I missed you. Are you working? Did you collar?" I heard her laugh. "I love you. Call me tonight."

I smoked a cigarette and went to bed, trying not to think about whether or not Ralph would be back for his wife tomorrow.

*I*woke up at 7:30 to the sound of my phone ringing. I purposely don't have one in my bedroom so I don't have to answer it, but I left the volume turned up on my answering machine and heard Michele talking.

I ran out to the kitchen to pick up my cordless and got a blast of feedback as I fumbled to shut it off.

"Hey," I said.

"Did I wake you?" She sounded surprised.

"Yeah, I got to bed late."

"Did you collar up?" She was getting the lingo down pretty good.

"No, the psycho across the street was beating on his wife, and there was a whole big thing going on outside."

"Is she okay?"

"They took her to the hospital. She was beat up pretty bad, but she seemed okay."

"That's horrible," she said.

"Yeah, it is," I said, then changed the subject. "So how are you? How's Stevie?"

"Good, we're both good. I was wondering when we're going to see you this week."

"I don't know, maybe Thursday night." I don't usually go on Wednesday unless I'm off because she goes to church and I have to leave for work before the service is over. "I'm off this weekend, Saturday, Sunday, and Monday, so maybe we'll do something."

"They started taping today," she said, excited. "If they get some of the rooms finished by the weekend, maybe we'll be priming the walls on Saturday."

"Sounds good," I said. I was a little antsy to get off the phone, I felt like my bladder was going to explode. "Listen, let me jump in the shower and get something to eat and I'll call you back about 9:30."

"Okay, I'll talk to you later."

I showered and shaved and drove over to the Chinese dump on Midland Avenue for some chicken and broccoli that looked like cat and broccoli but tasted delicious.

I called Michele back at 9:30 and talked to her until 10:00, then left my house by 10:15.

It was cooler tonight, and I drove with my windows rolled down to catch the breeze coming in off the water along Father Cappodanno Boulevard. The roads were clear until 39th Street on the Gowanus, where an accident was blocking the left and center lanes and traffic was slow from the rubbernecking.

I parked on the sidewalk on 36th Street next to Romano's white Blazer. He was sitting in the car, talking on the cell phone, and held up his hand for me to wait. I lit a cigarette and leaned up against my truck and watched the traffic going into the Lincoln Tunnel. I wondered if he was talking to Denise. I could see him smiling as he was talking. I was glad he was out of his funk, I just hoped it wasn't because of her.

"Hey, Tony," Romano said, shaking my hand.

"Hey, Nick, still counting the days till you're out of here?"

"Yeah," he said, not sounding as sure now.

"What's the deal? I thought this was what you wanted."

"It is, but I'll miss the guys."

"I know, but you won't miss the job," I said.

"No, this job sucks." He shrugged like that was a given.

We went down to the locker room to change and admired Rooney's newest artwork on the inspector. Today he had the inspector's face superimposed over Wolverine from *X-Men* with his arms crossed over his chest and his metal claws showing.

"He's a character," I said.

"You can't even tell where he altered it," Romano said, staring at the picture. "He's pretty good at this."

Terri Marks was back behind the desk tonight. I thought maybe she'd be embarrassed to see Joe after the party the other night, but she acted like nothing happened. She winked at him and said, "How you doing, Joe?"

"Fine, Terr, and you?" Fiore asked just as easy.

"Better now that you're here," she said with a smile. The lou looked up at her from the corner of his eye and smirked.

I guess everything was back to normal.

Bruno Galotti was back in tonight, which surprised me. He looked okay, no bulging eyes or skin rash. He said he still had a little aftertaste of the mace, but otherwise he was fine.

We mustered up at Hanrahan's attention to the roll call order. He didn't have as much patience today for Rooney's antics and pulled the picture of Wolverine off the podium and tossed it in the garbage without comment.

He gave out the color of the day (red), the sectors, and

foot posts, and ended with, "Be careful out tonight. As Bruno learned last night, there's all kinds of weapons out there."

"What is wrong with you, Galotti? What are you doing here?" Rooney barked. "You could have been out for at least a week."

"But I feel okay," he said with a shrug.

Rooney shook his head. "What a dope."

We stopped to get our radios and threw the bull with Vince for a couple of minutes before we went out to the car.

I drove to the corner, and Romano went in for the coffee and the paper again without complaining. This time he went the extra mile and got blueberry muffins all around.

We ate the muffins on the way up to 44th Street. Romano and I got out to have a cigarette with our coffee and talked to Joe through the window as he thumbed through the *Daily News*.

"Ah, again with this stuff," he said.

"What is it?" I asked.

"The West Nile stuff. Did you know the country spent fifty million dollars getting rid of the mosquitoes?" He shook his head as he read on. "Listen to this: the battle plan is less pesticide spraying and stiffer fines for anybody who has standing water on their property."

"Are you kidding me? Anything for the city to make money," I said, disgusted. "Now we get fined if there's a puddle in our backyard. I love how they throw everything back on us."

Joe laughed. "You gotta hear this. The city put together 'rapid response teams' that move in when infected dead birds are found and spread larvicide and remove standing water."

"What are they gonna use, a straw? I wish I could have that job," I said sarcastically. "It probably pays eighty grand a year and the only qualification is being related to someone at City Hall." I flicked my cigarette and got back in the car.

"Pick me up for my meal?" Romano asked.

"Nick, have we ever forgotten to pick you up for your meal?" I asked.

He was still thinking about it when we drove away.

"There was a dispute across the street from me," I said.

"Domestic?" he asked.

"Yeah, this psycho across the street was knocking his wife around," I said, telling him the story.

"She should leave," he said.

"I think she's afraid of him."

"Smart girl, she should be," he said.

I was driving westbound on 42nd Street when we got a call for an alarm.

"South David, we got a 10-11 at 330 West 40th Street, fifth floor."

Before Fiore could answer, I heard Romano on the air.

"Robbery post 4 to Central, I'll take that job. Have David disregard."

"The little brownnose," I said. "He's definitely sleeping with my sister."

Joe busted out laughing, and we heard Galotti come over the radio.

"Robbery post 5 on the back."

Central came back over with, "Robbery 4, the firm name is Extravagant Fabrics, Suite 510."

"10-4."

"We might as well go up there," I said. "There's a magnetic lock on the door to the building, and those two won't be able to get in." I'd responded there before and had to wrestle with the door.

330 West 40th is between 8th and 9th, and when we pulled

up in front of the building, Romano and Galotti were already there wrestling with the door.

The street was deserted. Gates were down over storefronts, and I could see litter strewn along the curb. The building was old, seven stories high, with an intricate design carved into the stone. Over the door was colored tile work set to look like a garden.

Galotti was shining his flashlight into the vestibule when we got out of the car. I put my radio in my pocket and stuck my nightstick through the loop in my gun belt.

"Listen," Romano said. "You guys didn't have to come here—we can handle this."

"You can't even get in the door," I said. "How are you gonna handle it?"

"It looks secure," Galotti said, still shining his flashlight inside.

"It's on the fifth floor, Bruno—how can you say it looks secure?"

It was a glass door with a metal recess cut into it where the handle is. I grabbed the handle with both hands on top of each other, one-potato two-potato style. I braced my body and yanked with enough force that the magnets holding the door in place separated. The wobble sound reverberated in the air around us. The perps know how to do this too, which is how they get in the buildings half the time.

"How did you do that?" Bruno asked, sounding impressed.

"You like that, huh?"

"Close it again, let me try," he said.

"So you can break the door? Get inside. Are you handling this job or not?" I said.

The lighting in the lobby was dim. The elevators were to our left, and on our right, above the stairwell door, was a camera. It was set so you could see who walked out of both the stairway and the elevators.

"Smile, you're being watched on camera," I said, and we all looked up at it.

The elevator was open, and I checked the key panel next to the elevator. The fifth floor wasn't keyed off, so I told Joe to press 5.

"Five lights up, we're in business," Fiore said.

Joe pressed the "close door" button. The door closed, and the elevator kicked up.

When the elevator stopped and the door opened, we heard the *ping* echo in the hallway, letting whoever was in here know we were there.

It was a long hallway with every other light lit, but we could see where we were going. We listened for sounds of movement, but there was silence.

There was a big metal door in front of us that said "Cosmic Enterprises" in red letters on the door.

"That's not it," Romano whispered. It was an *L*-shaped hallway, and Romano walked around the corner to the right. He went about ten feet down the hallway and stopped in front of a metal door. He put his ear next to the door and tried the knob, pulling on the door. We could hear it was locked, and he started walking back toward us.

I looked to the left of the elevator and saw a door a little farther down the hallway that looked partly open. I walked from the elevator to get a better look, and I heard Romano say, "Everything looks secure."

"Is it?" I asked. I put my finger to my mouth and the four of us started to walk toward the open door. As the elevator door closed, I heard someone's shoes squeaking and I turned toward them.

"It's not me," Joe said.

Romano took a couple of steps. "Not me either."

We all looked at Galotti.

"They're new," he said.

We started to walk down the hall again, *squeak, squeak, squeak.* I unlocked my gun as I approached the door and took out my flashlight.

The door had no handle, just a push bar from the inside that someone had accessed. I entered the premise and moved to my right, letting my eyes adjust to the dark room.

I smelled something, and water too, like the smell after it rains.

Joe and I had our flashlights off, but Romano and Galotti turned theirs on. They were holding them up and away from their body with the beam pointing straight ahead. They teach you this in the Academy. The theory is if you hold the flashlight away from you and someone shoots at you, they'll miss, aiming for the light.

Joe and I have been around long enough to know to look for a light switch instead of fumbling around in the dark, hoping you don't get shot.

One of them crashed into something that sounded like a metal wastepaper basket, and then I heard the thud of someone hitting something solid.

"Joe, get the light before they kill themselves," I said.

I heard the click of the switch, and the light above us came on.

I saw the overturned basket and the table they walked into. There was a black curtain next to me running the entire length of the premise. Next to the light switch was an electric panel box.

I moved the curtain with my flashlight, but it was pitch-black in the room beyond us. Once I moved the curtain, I felt the humidity, and a strange smell hit me. It smelled like an herb, but not the basil or oregano that Grandma grows on her windowsill. Then I realized what the smell was.

"Joe, see if one of the circuit breakers will turn on the lights in there," I said.

Joe started clicking the switches, and we squinted and heard the buzz of the lights as they flicked on in different parts of the room.

I pulled the curtain all the way across and turned to look at Joe. He blinked, and the four of us leaned in past the curtains to get a better look.

The first thought that went through my head was, *This room is worth a lot of money.*

"What is it?" Galotti asked.

"It's pot," Romano said.

The room was an open loft that looked about seventy-five feet long by thirty feet wide. There were long tables throughout the room with hundreds and hundreds of pot plants in different stages of growth from small to several feet high.

They had some operation going here. We walked deeper into the room to look at the setup. We saw heat lamps, rotating grow lights, and humidifiers.

Fiore was on the radio. "South David to South Sergeant."

"Go ahead, South David."

"Can you 85 us, 330 West 40th Street, fifth floor, no emergency?"

"10-4."

"Let's search the premise," I said quietly. "Be very quiet, 'cause whoever's stuff this is, they're not gonna be happy that we found it."

If you calculated the street value of one mature pot plant, which I think is about a thousand dollars, you were talking some big money here.

We walked down through the rows of tables, looking under them. We got to the main door of the premise and tried the light switch next to the door. Florescent lights went on overhead, but nothing like the grow lights they had for the plants.

There was a bathroom with just a sink and a toilet, with the roll of toilet paper sitting on top of the tank.

Next to the bathroom was a closet with gardening tools, soil, thermometers, and containers for the plants. There was also a pile of black plastic bags and duct tape that they used to cover the windows, which was why it was so dark in here.

There was an irrigation system set up using PVC pipe above the pots on each table. It looked to be set on a timer, kind of like the sprays of mist you see in the produce aisle of the grocery store.

"South David on the air." Hanrahan came over the radio.

"South David," Fiore responded.

"Can you come down and open the door?"

"10-4, someone will be right down."

"I'll go," Bruno said.

"Take Romano with you. And be careful—whoever left that door open might be coming back."

Fiore and I went back to our search and found a small office next to the bathroom. It held a desk, a phone, no computer, and nothing on the walls. A TV with a VCR built into it sat across from the desk on a small wooden table. The TV was on, and we could see the lobby downstairs. We watched Galotti and Romano get off the elevator and disappear out of sight when they reached the front door.

"Look at this," I said, scanning the room. "Farming in Midtown."

Joe sighed. "This is gonna be an all-night thing."

Hanrahan came in with Noreen, his driver, followed by Romano and Galotti.

He whistled as he looked around the place. "How'd you get in here?" he asked.

"Someone left the door open. Welcome to Cosmic Industries," I said.

We walked him through the place. He was trying to get an estimate on how many plants were there, but there were too many to count.

"Oh," Noreen said out of nowhere. "You know who died?"

"Who?" We all turned to look at her.

"Remember the rubber band man from up on 43rd Street?"

"Did he die? He's been here forever," Hanrahan said.

"He's been here as long as I've been here," I said.

"Why'd they call him the rubber band man?" Fiore asked.

"He used to play music in his mouth with rubber bands," I said. He was a skell. He was harmless enough and played those stupid rubber bands so people would throw him a buck as they walked by. When I first came on, I had Romano's post. We worked six-to-twos then, actually it was 5:00 in the afternoon until 1:30 in the morning.

"Every night like clockwork he would come stumbling up 8th Avenue at 11:30, drunk out of his mind. As soon as he crossed 43rd Street, about twenty feet off the corner he would collapse on the grating in the sidewalk," I said.

In the winter the subway would keep him warm. I laughed out loud and said, "The tourists would say, 'Officer, look at that guy, he's wasted! He can't even walk.' I'd tell them, 'He'll be all right—watch, he'll go right up to that grating and collapse.' Sure enough he did. The tourists would look amazed and ask, 'How did you know that?' 'It's a gift,' I'd tell them.

"Now, who told you he died?" I asked.

"They found him dead on his grating this morning on the day tour. The detectives had to notify someone, and they were asking around to see if anybody knew his real name."

I was getting a little nostalgic about it. The rubber band man's been here all these years, someone who was part of the scenery. It was a shame he died alone on the sidewalk, and I hoped he was drunk enough that he just fell asleep.

"Nick, he's on your post. Did you know him?"

"Who?"

"The rubber band man, what do you think we're talking about here?" Noreen said. "The skell that sits on the grating on 43rd Street right off 8th Avenue."

Romano seemed to be thinking about it. "John Harris," he nodded. "Yeah, he played the rubber bands. What about him?"

"That's his name?" Noreen asked.

Romano nodded, and she looked at Hanrahan. "Did the detectives ever find out his name?"

"I'll call them," Hanrahan said, and I saw him write John Harris in his memo book.

"What about him?" Romano repeated.

"He's dead," Noreen snapped. "Are you even listening?"

"What do you mean he's dead? I was just talking to him last night right before Bruno got shot with the mace." Romano looked upset. "He seemed fine to me."

"Nick, he was sick," I said. "You see how he looked, his stomach all bloated, his arms and hands all swollen. He had that sore on his leg—it was disgusting."

"He was a good guy," Romano said. "He was in Vietnam. He's not as old as he looks. We used to talk a lot when things were slow."

"Do you know anything about him?" Hanrahan asked, looking curiously at Romano.

"He was married, well, divorced I think. He said his wife still lived in Brooklyn, Flatbush I think. He was a truck driver for an outfit out in Red Hook before the booze got him."

"Well, now we know he was a veteran," Hanrahan said. "They can track down the next of kin through the VA."

We actually had a moment of silence for the guy. I felt a little ashamed that Romano knew so much about him, that he bothered to find out the guy's name. I never did. I'd just say, "Hey, rubber band man," and he'd smile his drunken smile and say, "Evenin', Officer." I didn't know anything about him except he drank Thunderbird and wet his pants.

Hanrahan got on his cell phone and called the desk. We listened to his half of the conversation.

"Lou, we got a loft here filled with marijuana plants . . . Maybe a couple hundred . . . They were answering a job, an alarm on the fifth floor . . . Tony, was this the alarm?"

"No," I said, "the premise is around the corner."

"Extravagant Fabrics," Romano threw in.

"No, it wasn't the premise for the alarm. They saw the door open and investigated." He listened again. "Hold on a second. Tony, is this your job?"

"No, it's Romano and Galotti's."

He got back on the cell. "It's robbery posts 4 and 5's job. David was just backing them . . . I don't know, might be possible . . . All right, give them a call."

He hit the *end* button on his cell and asked, "Did you search the premise?"

"There's an office over there." I pointed to it. "It's got a camera taping the lobby downstairs." I filled him in with the rest of the details, that the premise was unoccupied. "It's possible whoever came in to check on it went out the back door and didn't realize he left it open." Him being high was a definite possibility. "There's no alarm system set up here," I added.

"Yeah, they don't want us responding," Hanrahan said.

Hanrahan's cell phone rang to the theme from *Friends*. We all looked at him, and he said, "My daughter did it, and now I can't get the friggin' thing off it."

He hit the *send* button and said, "Yeah . . . I'll feel more comfortable with all four of them doing it . . . Uh huh."

I love listening to one side of a conversation.

"I'll take Hennessy and Pizzolo off of foot posts and put them in, David. Okay, good," he said and disconnected.

"Okay," he started, "OCCB said they'll send somebody down in the morning with a warrant and a tractor trailer. They asked if we can have someone sit on it for the night in case whoever's growing this comes back here. If you four want to do it, the lou said get the keys to the Anti-Crime car and you can watch the front door from up the block."

We looked at each other. "Sure," we said with a shrug. Better than working patrol.

"You can go back to the house and get changed out of the bag and pick up the car. Noreen and I will sit on the block until you get back," Hanrahan said.

As we went to leave, Hanrahan added, "You're sure nobody saw you, right?"

"Not unless they're seeing all the cars out front now," I said. "Oh, we're gonna have to take the tape out of the VCR and put another one in."

I went into the office and opened the metal cabinet where they kept the tapes. I hit eject and popped out the tape that was in there and added it to the pile they had with tapes labeled with dates and times. We'd wind up taking the tapes and vouchering them once we got the warrant. I put a new tape in the machine but didn't hit record, hoping they'd think they forgot to do it.

I also grabbed a roll of duct tape out of the closet to use on the stairwell door.

As we exited the premise, I checked to see if the fifth floor had stairwell access. The sign said "5th floor access," so I took the stairs down and used the push bar to release the door in the lobby. I put the tape over the lock so it wouldn't engage, and we left the building.

We went back to the precinct and changed into street clothes—or got out of the bag, as we call it—and met up at the front desk.

Terri Marks was asking Joe about the loft.

"How many plants were there?"

"Hundreds of them," Joe said.

"What was the firm's name?"

"Cosmic Enterprises," Romano cut in.

"Figures," Terri said.

They were talking about the grow lights and the irrigation system, and Terri said, "You ever smoke pot, Joe?" as she smiled at Fiore.

The lou's eyebrows went up.

"No, Terr," Fiore said. "Never did."

"Don't feel bad, Joe," Galotti said to Joe. "I didn't know what it was either." He was quiet for a second and said, "But Nick and Tony did."

"Bruno, I knew what it was. I just never smoked it," Fiore said.

"You're a cop, you knucklehead—you're supposed to know what it looks like," I said to Galotti.

"I've seen pictures of it, I just never saw a live plant," Bruno said.

"Here you go, you Boy Scout," the lou joked as he threw a set of keys to Fiore. "It's the black Lumina parked on 9th Avenue."

"Bruno," I said, "why don't you pull your shirt out of your pants and put it over your gun so nobody sees it." He had his shirt tucked in, with his gun on the gun belt. We're not allowed to show our weapons out of uniform. He pulled his shirt out as we walked out the front doors of the precinct.

We walked down 35th Street toward 9th. Since we were gonna be sitting in the car for a while, we stopped to get more coffee in the deli on the corner.

Geri's eyes lit up when she saw us, and she smiled. "What can I do for you guys?"

I don't think she was talking about coffee.

"Just getting some coffee," Fiore said.

It was a self-serve counter, and we each fixed our coffee, with Geri flirting with us.

"Why aren't you guys in uniform? Not that you don't look good this way."

"Ah, we got tired of wearing the uniform," I said.

"I feel so safe with all of you in here."

"I don't feel safe," Romano mumbled, picking up a bag of potato chips, some peanut M&Ms, and both the *Daily News* and the *Post* since we forgot to take the paper out of the RMP.

We paid for our stuff, each of us except Bruno tossing a couple of bills on the counter, and said good night.

"You want your change?" she called after us. We laughed as Bruno bent over when she dropped his.

We picked up the Lumina and drove back over to the premise. The car had tinted windows so anyone walking by wouldn't see us. We pulled up next to the sarge's RMP on 40th Street, next to the Port Authority wall that runs the length of 40th Street.

I rolled down the window. "Hey, Boss."

"Make sure if you see anyone go into the building, that you call me," he said.

"You got it."

"Just be careful."

"We'll be fine, Boss. What time is OCCB coming?"

"Probably around eight o'clock."

I pulled into his spot when he drove away and parked next to the curb.

"Where's the cardboard condos?" Romano asked.

"Port cops probably did a sweep after the stabbing last week," Joe said.

I figured we could keep an eye out for Easy while we waited.

I picked up the paper and started reading the sports section. "Tickets went on sale for the Brooklyn Cyclones," I told Joe, talking about the Mets' farm team they built the stadium for in the old Steeplechase park on Coney Island. This was their first season, and the paper said over a thousand people waited in line to get tickets.

"Yeah, I saw that. I think you had to buy them at King's Plaza," Joe said, which was the mall in Brooklyn. "I have to call them. I want to get tickets for my father—he loves the Mets, and he'd love to see them play baseball in Brooklyn again."

There was an article about the Jets' owner, Woody Johnson, moving the team to LA if they couldn't get a stadium in New York. There's a lot of talk about a stadium on the West Side of Manhattan that the mayor's in favor of. After New York lost the Brooklyn Dodgers, we won't be so quick to lose another team to Los Angeles.

"It says here that murder is down 18 percent," Galotti said from the backseat.

"In what country?" I asked.

"Here in the city," he said. "It says in the paper that in fourteen of the city's seventy-six precincts there were no murders."

"That's a lie," I said.

"Really, it says the five-o in the Bronx is a murderless precinct, and murders were on the rise for the past two years. There were no murders in six Manhattan precincts, four Brooklyn, and three Queens precincts."

"Let me see that," I said, taking the paper from him. "Do they really expect me to believe that there were more murders in Staten Island than up in Riverdale?"

That was impossible. Staten Island had 1,229 crimes, as opposed to the Bronx, which had 8,111 crimes when they broke it down into borough commands. If they ever told the truth about their stats, I bet murder would be up 18 percent instead of down like they said.

We were bored out of our minds. We passed the papers back and forth while we watched the building. Romano and I would get out of the car every so often to smoke a cigarette. Galotti passed out around three, and Romano not long after him. Bruno was snoring lightly, and at one point Nick jerked awake. He looked around and realized where he was and went back to sleep.

"You really think he's seeing Denise?" Fiore asked quietly.

"I don't know, maybe."

"Why is that a bad thing?"

"Come on, Joe, they're both screwed up. He's got a kid." I

lowered my voice. "His girlfriend is always causing trouble," I said. "Plus, Denise's too old for him."

"A couple of years isn't gonna make a difference, and they're talking about going to church together. Isn't that what you want? You tell Nick he needs to get with God, and you tell Denise the same thing. Why would it be so bad?"

"Joe, do you really think anyone in my family is ever gonna go to church?"

"Yeah, I do," he said, meaning it. "Remember the story of Paul and Silas when they were locked in the jail in Acts 16?"

"I think so." Something about an earthquake.

"They were in prison, their feet were in the stocks, and at midnight they were praying and singing to God." He looked at me like he was waiting for an answer.

"Yeah, so. What's your point?"

"So an earthquake opened the doors to the prison and the stocks came off, and the jailer was gonna kill himself 'cause he thought they escaped. Paul and Silas told him not to harm himself, that they were still there—" He held up his hand. "Just let me finish the story before you start rolling your eyes," he said.

"I don't see how this has anything to do with this, but you always manage to bring it around, so I'll listen," I said.

"Then the jailer asked Paul and Silas what must he do to be saved. And Paul told him, 'Believe on the Lord Jesus Christ, and you will be saved, you and your household.'"

"What does this have to do with my sister and Romano?"

"You, Tony. Paul said if you believe on the Lord Jesus Christ, you *and* your household will be saved. That includes Denise, your parents, Vinny, even Granny with the red underwear. I don't know if things will work out between them, but I think both of them are searching for God. Actually, most people are searching for God, they just don't realize it."

Maybe he was right. The truth was I liked Romano, and while he may not have had his life in order, underneath it all he was a good guy. The same went for Denise. I just wanted her to be happy. I guess it didn't matter if it was with Romano. It was probably too soon to be thinking that way anyway.

The air was getting cool and a film of condensation settled on the car. I had to use the wipers every so often to keep the windshield clear.

Galotti woke up around five and woke Romano up when he left the car to use the bathroom, the side of the building actually.

I must have been dozing, because I jumped when I heard Fiore say, "Tony."

I looked at the clock, ten to six. He was looking at a guy walking eastbound on 40th Street from 9th Avenue on the opposite side of the street, which is the same side as the premise.

"I like this guy," Joe said.

"Yeah, he's got pothead written all over him." He was a male white, midtwenties, with long brown hair pulled back in a ponytail.

We watched him as he walked down the street, unlocked the front doors, and entered the building.

"Bingo," I said, putting the car in drive.

We gave him a couple of minutes to get into the elevator and drove the car down. I parked right before the entrance to the building.

I turned to Galotti and Romano. "We're gonna be quiet when we go in there. You changed your shoes, right?" I asked Galotti.

"I got sneakers on now."

"We're gonna check the elevator," I continued. "Once we make sure it went up to the fifth floor, we'll go up the stairs. And whatever you do, don't look at the camera."

We were careful not to slam the car doors when we got out. As we approached the glass doors in the front, we stopped. I walked past the building nonchalantly and looked to see if he was still in the lobby. The lobby was empty, so I waved them over.

I pulled the door open and grabbed the glass to dull the noise, not that he'd hear me. Joe went in first and looked in the elevator. He turned his back to the camera and held up five fingers to show where the elevator stopped, and we walked toward the stairs.

I could feel my heart start to pound on the way up. I was straining my ears to hear if the elevator was moving.

We took our guns out as we approached the stairwell door on the fifth floor. We tiptoed down the hallway and entered the premise through the back door that we left open.

It was pretty dark in there. I peeked through the black curtain and saw florescent lights on overhead and saw someone moving around in the office.

I waved the others into the room, and we each walked down through a row of the wooden tables. The guy was in the office and had no idea we were coming toward him. I saw him in the metal closet. He had his back to me and he was going through the VCR tapes. He was probably wondering why the VCR wasn't on. When we got about ten feet from the door, I pointed my gun at him and yelled, "*Police!* Don't move!"

He dropped the tape and grabbed his chest. "Dude, why'd you have to scare me like that?"

"Don't move!" I said again.

He put his hands up. "Dude, I don't know nothing," he said as he took a deep breath. "Wow, you scared me."

"Put your hands on your head and turn around," I said.

"Dude, this is wrong," he said as he turned.

I holstered my gun, and Joe covered me as I cuffed his right hand and then his left.

He kept blubbering the dude stuff. "Dude, don't do this. Dude, it's all a misunderstanding."

I hate being called dude.

He was wearing old jeans, brown leather shoes, and a South Park T-shirt that said, "That sucks, dude." I guess that's why he talked that way.

Fiore called the sarge. "South Sergeant on the air? Roll over to 9."

"South Sergeant on the air."

"Boss, this is Joe. Listen, we got a guy up here."

"Inside the premise?"

"Yeah."

"I'll be right there."

Joe turned to Galotti.

"Yeah, I know, go let him in. C'mon, Nick," Bruno said.

"Dude, what are you locking me up for? Dude, I just work here. I make sure the lights are on and check the tapes, then I go to my job."

I let him ramble. I didn't answer him and didn't ask him anything. Romano would take the collar, and the detectives would handle it after that.

"Dude!" He was getting loud now. "If I get locked up, I can't go to my work, and I'll lose my job!"

Romano and Galotti came in with the sarge and Noreen.

"Is anyone else gonna be coming here today?" the boss asked the dude.

"No, dude." He seemed relieved that someone was finally talking to him. "I just come here to turn the lights on, change the tape, and make sure everything is working right. Then I stop back on my way home from work."

"Where do you work?" Hanrahan asked him.

"Up on 53rd Street. I'm a graphic artist."

"So what are you doing here?"

"Helps pay the bills, dude. Do you know how much rent is in this city?"

"I'm a cop," Hanrahan said. "I can't afford to live in the city."

Hanrahan and Noreen took Romano and the dude back to the precinct and left me, Joe, and Bruno to watch the premise. Hanrahan wanted one of us to stay and help OCCB and two cops from the day tour handle the loft.

Carl Beers and a Spanish female cop that I never met showed up right before 8:00 to relieve us. Galotti wanted the OT, so Joe and I went back to the precinct in the crime car.

"I wonder if you'll still make Cop of the Month for the assault collar now," I said as I parked on 35th Street near the corner of 9th.

"Why?"

"That's a nice collar for Romano."

"I hope he gets it before he leaves," Joe said.

I went down to the locker room to grab my bag, and I signed out at 8:10.

The morning was cloudy, and a fine mist was spraying the air as I drove downtown. I cleared the tunnel and the Gowanus, but the fog was so thick around the Verrazzano that you couldn't even see there was a bridge there. I took the lower level and exited to the right at South Beach.

I saw Ralph's wife at the corner with a group of mothers and kids waiting for the bus. She was dressed today in black pants and a beige silk blouse, and her hair was pulled back away from her face.

Alfonse's car was gone. He was probably down at the fruit

stand down on Hylan Boulevard buying his vegetables for the day.

I saw the school bus pull up in my rearview mirror as I parked, so I stood outside my car and waited for Ralph's wife to walk down the street.

She walked on her side of the street, slowly, keeping her head down. I think she wanted to avoid talking to me, but manners won out and she crossed the street.

"Hi," she said, looking embarrassed. "I'm really sorry about yesterday."

"Not a problem," I said. "Did you go to court for that order of protection?"

"I was in the hospital most of the day, and I had to get home for my kids. I'm going now," she said. "I don't know how this is gonna work—it's Ralph's house."

"How is it his house? Aren't you married?"

"Yeah, but the house is in his name. When we got married, the deed somehow wound up in his name only." She gave me a look that said it was no accident. "If I can get on my feet and get a job, I can get another place—if he doesn't come back and kill me first."

"Have you left him before?"

"I've tried. He always comes back, though."

"Is he sorry?" I asked. Who knows, maybe he cries to her that he'll change and she believes him.

She gave a cynical laugh. "He's never sorry."

"Then why do you take him back? You know this isn't gonna change with him, right?" I asked.

"I know, it's getting worse. It's been building all week. Yesterday he broke two ribs and my nose," she said as she touched her nose and winced. Her eyes filled, and she said, "I don't know what to do. He keeps saying if I leave he'll take my kids away from me because I'm taking antidepressants."

Living with him, she probably needed antidepressants. "You have any family you can go to?" I asked.

"I do, but no one I'd ask for help." Probably why she was in this situation to begin with.

"When you go to court today, talk to someone there. There's help out there if you know where to look for it," I said. "You'll definitely get an order of protection, find out where to go from there."

She nodded. "Thanks."

"Yeah, good luck today," I called after her for lack of anything better to say.

I jumped in the shower. I felt like the dampness and grime from the pot greenhouse was sticking to me. I left my hair damp, pulled a pair of sweats on, and picked up my Bible to read before I fell asleep. I think I opened it, but I was asleep before I read anything.

I woke up with a jump, aware that someone was yelling my name. My heart was pounding, and I heard banging on my door and Alfonse's voice. "Tony, please! Open the door, Tony."

I jumped up and went toward the door, hearing him louder now. "Tony, oh no!" He rattled off a couple of things in Italian that sounded like Ave Maria or something as I opened the door.

"Tony, thank God." He held his hands together like he was praying. "Ralph's back—he's got her in the house."

"Did you call the cops?" I asked behind me as I went back into my bedroom for a shirt and my gun.

"Yeah, about two minutes ago."

I put sneakers on without socks and tried to maneuver my feet into them while I trotted out the door. As soon as I hit the top of the steps, I could hear yelling from across the street.

"Didn't they give her an order of protection?" I asked Alfonse. "I saw her this morning—she was on her way to court." I was hoping that no one did him a favor and let him off, though I couldn't see that happening.

"I have no idea," Alfonse said.

I tried not to think of Romano's father again as I crossed into the street. Instead I started praying Psalm 91 like Fiore's been pounding into my head. *I ask you, Lord, to give your angels charge over me, to keep me in all my ways.*

"Stay here," I said to Alfonse. The last thing I needed was him getting hurt.

I heard something smash as I approached the front of the house and I heard her scream, then sob. The front door opened and the wife tried to get out, clawing her hands against the latch to make it open. Ralph grabbed her by the hair and smashed her head into the wooden door with such force that I winced.

"Ralph," I yelled. "Let her go!"

He yelled something raunchy and dragged her back in. "Help me," she choked. "He stabbed me—please help me," she cried, her voice sounding like it was at a distance. I had no idea what time it was or if her kids were in the house.

I felt my hands start to shake and heard the sirens, sounding like they were coming from Father Cappodanno Boulevard.

"Alfonse," I called as I turned back to him. "I told you to stay across the street," I snapped when I realized he was about ten feet behind me. "Get back on the phone, make sure they send an ambulance—she said he stabbed her." He had a cordless in his hand and dialed, walking back toward his house where the signal was better.

I wrestled with it for a second. This guy was too far gone to hear anything now, and I couldn't see this ending good. I was torn. I didn't want to deal with this, but I couldn't walk away and let him kill her. Nobody should have to live like this.

I took my gun out of the holster and dropped the holster on the ground. I took a deep breath and climbed the stairs.

I was quiet when I opened the door, and thankfully it didn't squeak and give me away.

It was a basic ranch house, small entranceway, living room to my right, kitchen straight ahead, and the dining room off the kitchen.

There was blood on the wall in front of me, and a line of it was smeared into the rug.

I looked to my right into the living room. He had her on the floor about ten feet away. She was lying on her back, with blood saturating the front of the silk blouse I saw her wearing this morning. On her left arm the shirt was cut, and I could see a bloody gash. Her eyes were vacant as she stared at nothing.

His back was to me, which gave me the advantage. He was still wearing the clothes they locked him up in yesterday, leaning over her as he amused himself terrifying her.

"This is *my* house. These are *my* kids," he said slowly, methodically. "*You* are nothing but a *crazy, washed-out whore,* and you don't dictate how *I* run *my* life. You think you got me today? No judge is gonna tell me that I can't come in my own house. Where's your order of protection?" He laughed in her face. "You can't keep me out of here."

I came up behind him and smashed into him with a body shot. He lost his balance and went forward, crashing into a wooden coffee table that pushed out when he hit it.

"Get out!" I yelled to her. She seemed to stall, and I yelled again, "Get out of here!" She sobbed then and crawled on her hands and knees toward the front door.

I heard the sirens outside as I aimed my gun at his chest. "Get out of my house!" he yelled.

I saw him looking around, and I took a couple of steps

back toward the door to let him know he wasn't getting out that way.

"You don't know who you're dealing with," he said, standing up. "Or you'd go out that door and mind your own business."

"I'll take you out right here," I said. I wasn't gonna play word games with him.

He looked out the window and saw the RMP. He looked at me and ran to his right into the dining room.

At that point I couldn't shoot him as he was running from me and I knew the wife was safe. The cavalry was here—let them handle it.

I went to the front door, keeping my hand with the gun behind me. I didn't feel like getting shot in case someone thought I was Ralph.

Eddie DiTommasso was coming up the steps, so I yelled, "He's going out the side door."

"Side door," Eddie yelled to his partner. We heard the side door fly open, and Eddie and his partner took off after him. I stepped outside, holding my gun inside the waistband of my sweatpants. I heard a lot of yelling in the backyard, and I saw them grab him as he was trying to get over the back fence.

The wife was lying facedown on the front lawn. Alfonse was leaning over her, looking like he was crying. The woman who lives in the house next to me, I think her name is Joanne, came running across the street. She was the one who took her home from the hospital yesterday.

"Oh dear God," she said, crying. "Sandy, look at me."

Sandy was half conscious, looking chalky. The bruises on her face stood stark against her white skin. Some were new ones from today, others from yesterday, and some yellow in color, even older.

EMS was finally here, this time two males. They were both

young but seemed to know what they were doing. One hustled over to us; the other went to the back of the bus for the stretcher.

Eddie was walking Ralph out of the backyard by his cuffs. "This isn't over," Ralph said.

"Shut up," Eddie said.

"I was defending myself. She attacked me—she's friggin' nuts," Ralph kept going.

"I said shut your mouth."

"She was gonna kill me!" Ralph yelled.

"There's not a mark on you. And she has an order of protection. You're not allowed near her," Eddie said, losing his patience.

"This is my house! No piece of paper is gonna change that!"

Eddie pulled him up by the cuffs, a favorite maneuver of mine to shut someone up.

"Tony, you okay?" Eddie asked as he walked him past me.

"Yeah, did you get the knife?" I didn't see it when I was in there, but Ralph didn't have time to get rid of it.

"We'll get it," Eddie said. Ralph spit in my direction, and Eddie slapped him in the head. "Cut it out," he said. "You don't learn, do you?"

The sergeant was here now, along with three other sector cars and ESU. The Emergency Service Unit on Staten Island is about a mile from here, so they got here quick.

I walked over to the RMP. "Ed, do you have a cigarette?" I asked. Alfonse smoked but not cigarettes, only those stinky little cigars.

He tossed me a pack of Marlboro Lights and I lit one, taking a deep drag. I noticed my hands were shaking as I held the cigarette, and I balled them into fists to stop it.

Half the block was out now, gawking at the spectacle. EMS

had wrapped and twisted a bandage around her arm to slow the bleeding. I saw the bandage on her stomach as they got her on the stretcher.

"We gotta get her to the hospital," they told the sergeant. She looked worse now, completely unconscious. I hoped it was more from the trauma than the stab wounds, but I had no way of knowing.

"I'll follow in my car once I get the kids," Joanne the neighbor was saying.

"Where are her kids?" I asked.

"They're still at school."

"What time is it?"

"Ten to three. Chris will watch them after I get them off the bus," she said, while nodding toward her husband, who was talking to the sergeant. I didn't know him that well. He was a fireman and worked all the time. They had five daughters, little blond girls who all looked alike to me.

EMS left with their sirens blaring and drove the wrong way up Greely Avenue. Eddie had Ralph in the RMP, and him and his partner were talking to EMS and their sergeant.

I stood there talking to Joanne and Alfonse. Joanne was crying, saying, "What am I gonna tell these kids?"

"I have no idea," I said. "But at least he won't be coming back here."

"You're a good man, Tony," Alfonse said with feeling. "But you should have shot him."

"Ah, let him go to jail," I said. "He won't get out now. They'll keep him in until trial."

Eddie walked over and shook my hand. "What is this? I don't see you for ten years, now it's two days in a row."

"I know, Ralph's keeping you guys busy," I said.

"He's keeping you busy too," he laughed.

We stood there for a couple of minutes talking. He was telling me he got married, had two kids. He took out the pictures and showed me his family. He said his father died and him and his wife bought the house from his mother, who moved to Florida.

They took Ralph out of there before the kids got home. The neighbor, Joanne, told her husband not to tell the kids anything until she could find out how serious the mother was.

The neighbors were out now, talking about Ralph now that he was gone.

"He's half a nut."

"He took my son's football because it went over his fence."

"He's out of his mind. I hear him hitting her all the time."

"Steals my paper all the time, 'cause he didn't pay the paperboy and they canceled him."

"He killed my cat—I found it dead on my front steps."

I shook my head. This guy was terrorizing the neighborhood.

I was still outside talking to Alfonse when Joanne went up to get the kids off the bus. The kids looked scared as she walked them into the house. I could hear them saying, "Where's Mommy?"

"I'm going to see her as soon as I bring you inside," Joanne said.

"I want to come too," the little boy said, starting to cry. "I want Mommy."

I went inside after that and took a shower. I was gonna make some coffee but decided to go back to sleep for an hour or two so I wasn't exhausted tonight. The initial adrenaline rush had worn off, but I was tired and wired at the same time.

I set my clock for 6:00 and crawled back into bed. I didn't think I'd be able to sleep, but the next thing I knew, my alarm was beeping. I hit snooze three times and finally got up at 6:27.

I brushed my teeth and shaved and was about to order some pizza when Alfonse came to the door. He was carrying a plate wrapped in foil and what looked like Italian bread.

"Here, Tony," he said as he held it out to me. "Julia made this for you. She said you were a hero today and shouldn't be eating pizza."

I laughed. "How did she know I'd be eating pizza?"

"Because you always eat pizza."

"Sometimes I get a hero, or Chinese," I said.

"Same thing," Alfonse said. "Still not homemade."

"Any word on—" I tried to think of Ralph's wife's name.

"Sandy? Last I heard she was in surgery."

"Is she gonna be alright?"

He shrugged. We were both quiet, and then he said, "How about that girl you're engaged to, can she cook?"

"Yeah," I said. "But not as good as Julia. Tell her I said thanks."

Michele is a great cook, but so was Alfonse's wife.

The dish was still warm, so I grabbed a fork, a soda, and a napkin and sat down to eat. I said thanks to God for the food and added a big thank you for everyone making it out alive today. I asked him to help Sandy make it through surgery so she can get home to her kids.

I took the foil off, and my mouth watered. It was rigatoni with sausage in a tomato cream sauce, and lots of basil. I ate the bread, dunking it in the sauce and wiping the plate clean with it.

I called Michele when I was done eating. Stevie answered and spent ten minutes telling me about our new upstairs house. He said the workers were letting him help them spackle. He rambled on about everything. Can we get a dog when we get married? Can he go on vacation with us when we get married, but he said it "baycation." I said we'll wait and see about the dog and said probably not to the honeymoon, but I promised him we'd go away together, just the three of us, another time.

I talked to Michele for a couple of minutes. I told her I'd be coming out tomorrow after work, but she forgot she wouldn't be there. There was a spring concert at her school that she was going to, and I'd wind up seeing her for only about an hour. I didn't go into anything heavy; she was getting Stevie ready for bed and ironing clothes for the morning. She told me that Denise offered to come out Monday to help us paint. Denise works Tuesday through Saturday, so she's off anyway.

I showered again and started going through one of the boxes in my bedroom that I still hadn't unpacked. I had some time on my hands, so I might as well get it done. It was old stuff, my high school yearbook, photo albums, concert tickets, playbills, magazines, and things like that.

I went through the pictures that included old girlfriends and summers down the shore that I didn't want Michele to see and threw them in an envelope. I kept the yearbook and the pictures that wouldn't get me in trouble down the road and tossed the stuff from the concerts and the magazines. I was surprised to see it was after 10:00 already, so I put the rest of the stuff on the floor and left for work.

Traffic was backed up down Lily Pond Avenue, so I turned on 1010 WINS to see what was up. An accident had closed down the upper level of the bridge, so I swung around onto the Staten Island Expressway toward the Goethals Bridge so I could go through Jersey.

The Goethals Bridge is so narrow that you have about two feet of space between you and the car next to you. The road is always being worked on, and I slammed my shocks every six feet when I hit the metal plates in the road.

I was clear once I was on the turnpike, but the detour cost me some time and I heard the attention to the roll call order as I came upstairs from the locker room.

I waited for Hanrahan to go through his regular spiel, and I approached him after roll call.

"Hey, Boss," I said while I shook his hand. "I just wanted to give you a heads-up. I had an off-duty incident today. Yesterday too, actually, but today was more involved."

I went into it with him. I told him I had to pull my gun but that it never went in the report. I told him I knew one of the cops, that I'd gone to school with him.

I could see the wheels turning. "Did you fire your weapon?" he asked.

I shook my head emphatically. "No."

"He was cuffed by uniformed officers?"

"Yeah. He ran out the back door, and they caught him as he was going over the back fence," I said.

"Alright." He nodded. "You got nothing to worry about. I'll let the ICO know. He may wanna be kept informed on how the case is going."

The ICO or Integrity Commanding Officer is actually a lieutenant.

"Oh," he said as I was leaving, "if anyone comes to try and talk to you about this, get representation from the PBA. Don't say anything without someone there."

"No problem, Boss," I said. I knew the drill.

I didn't think anything would happen. I didn't do anything wrong, but it wouldn't be the first time a cop tried to help someone off duty and wound up getting screwed for it. The other side of this is it makes the inspector look good that his cop rescues someone off duty, as long as he's sure it won't turn around and bite him.

"Hey, Tony," Romano said when I got in the car. "How's the house coming along?"

"Good. Michele told me today that a couple of the rooms might be ready to be painted by the weekend," I said.

"Yeah? Maybe I could come out and help you. I have my daughter Saturday and Sunday, but we're off Monday and I'm not doing anything," he said.

"You're gonna help me paint," I said dryly. I could see Fiore biting the inside of his cheek.

"Sure, what are friends for?" He smiled as he got into the RMP.

"Is this because Denise is off on Mondays and she'll be going too?"

"Is she gonna be there?" He asked like he was clueless.

"Have you talked to Denise, Nick?"

"Uh, not lately," he said.

I looked at him in the mirror to see which way he looked. They say if someone looks to the right, they're telling the truth and if they look left, they're lying. Since I was looking backwards at him in the mirror, I couldn't tell, so I just took it that he was lying through his teeth.

"Nick, if you want to come and help me paint on your day off, that's fine with me," I said. I could use the help anyway, and I didn't want to bother Joe when he was off.

"Great. Give me directions before the weekend, and I'll be out Monday morning," he said.

I almost told him to get them from Denise but decided against it.

Romano went in the deli for coffee and a paper. As we were driving up 8th Avenue to drop him off at his post, I saw a line of cabbies double-parked outside the Pakistani Restaurant between 39th and 40th streets. Through the window I could see all the cabbies sitting inside, looking like the Mideast summit.

Every night they do this, so they're easy targets to summons to get my numbers in for the month. Not that the city gives us a quota. The police department would never make us write tags to make money for the city. I'm sure the city doesn't need the tens of millions of dollars they rake in every year from summonses. (Yes, I'm being sarcastic.)

I pulled up behind the last cab and gave a whoop with the siren to let them know I'm here and to move their cabs.

Three of them came out, jumped in their cabs, and drove up the block to park them. There was one cab left sitting there.

I pulled out my memo book to look for a summons for the last one. The cabbie registrations are all the same, so I don't have to get out of the car to look at the windshield. All the registrations expire on December 31, and since I can get the information off the plate, banging out summonses is pretty quick. The cab was new, a yellow 2001 Chevy Caprice.

I sat and wrote him out the summons, and just as I finished writing the tag, he ran out of the restaurant and jumped in the cab. I drove up alongside the cab and stuck it on the windshield.

He rolled down the passenger side window and yelled, "Officer, I'm just getting something to eat!"

"You should have come out sooner—that's gonna be a pretty expensive meal," I said.

"Officer, please!" he yelled.

I didn't feel sorry for him. He heard me whoop and had a chance to move the cab. If he was that worried, he should have come out and moved it. You're in the middle of New York City, and a cab blocking the lane can slow down an ambulance or tie up traffic and cause accidents. Sometimes they have someone standing at the door of the restaurant to let them know a cop was there, but I guess they didn't think of it tonight.

There was no reason for him to double park there. After 7 p.m. he could park a block up on 8th between 38th and 39th streets.

He was yelling and cursing in a mix of English and his own language. I was hoping he didn't get hot with me. I didn't feel like locking him up.

"Next time, don't park here," I said—the last thing I was gonna say to him.

He turned the cab off and yanked the keys out of the ignition and grabbed his food. I guess he figured he got the ticket, he might as well stay and eat his food in the restaurant.

He slammed the door to let me know he wasn't happy, and we heard the sound of glass breaking as the driver's side window shattered into a million pieces. We were all quiet for a couple of seconds, then the driver stared at the pieces of glass twinkling on the street and let out a howl. "Aaahhhh!" He started pacing around the cab, still holding his Styrofoam tray.

"Alright," Romano said from the backseat. "I think our work is done here."

I choked on a laugh, and Fiore said, "They just don't make 'em like they used to."

I left the cabbie pacing and yelling and drove Romano up to his post.

We sat in the car, drinking our coffee, when we got a call from Central. "South David," Central radioed.

"South David," Fiore responded.

"We got an EDP at three-four and seven, walking in traffic."

"10-4."

"See you later, Nick," Fiore said.

"Don't slam that door, Nick," I said. "And watch those cabbies in the crosswalk."

"Yes, we'll pick you up for your meal," I said before he could ask me.

I drove up to 44th Street and headed east toward 7th Avenue, when Central came back over.

"South David, I'm getting numerous calls on this incident. It's a female EDP, running naked on 34th Street." I heard a choked laugh, and the transmission ended.

"10-4." Fiore looked at me and said, "Great."

Central came back again, composed this time, and said, "Let me know when you're 84, David."

I threw the turret lights on, and as we passed 35th Street I could see someone in the intersection and cars slowing down as they passed.

As we got closer, we could see that she was naked.

"Whoa," Fiore said.

"That's a big momma," I said, not looking forward to wrestling with her.

I whooped a little as I entered the intersection at 34th and 7th. She had run to the southwest corner and was standing next to the telephone pole. Her knees were moving up and down, and she was frantically brushing her hands on her body like she was trying to get something off her.

I parked the RMP in the intersection and hit the yellow button to pop the trunk. I wanted to make sure the cars going south on 7th Avenue would see the flashing lights in the trunk and slow down coming into the intersection. I didn't want any of us getting hit by a car.

Fiore radioed Central with a "David 84," and we both grabbed a pair of latex gloves out of our memo books and threw the books on the dashboard.

As we approached her at the corner, she threw her hands in the air and started running into the street toward the southeast corner, screaming, "Get 'em off me! Get 'em off me!"

"Hey, get over here!" I called to her. She looked at Joe and me and ran toward us, screaming "Eewww!" and "Aaahhhh! Get 'em off me—there's snakes on me!"

"Listen, there's nothing on you," Joe said. "It's okay, calm down."

She stopped as if to see if he was right and started jumping up and down, throwing the imaginary snakes off her.

Maybe it's me, but seeing an EDP running naked head-on into traffic, trying to get snakes off her because she got high and it freaked her out, is enough to keep me from doing drugs. Forget the egg "this is your brain on drugs" commercials. They should film this stuff and use it as a public service announcement, let the kids know what they're in for.

Cars were stopping to look at her do her dance. Even the

cabbies were slowing down with their faces pressed against the driver's side windows of the cabs.

She took off again, past us to the back of the RMP.

"We better grab her before she gets hit by a car," I said, not looking forward to it.

Fiore got on the radio. "South David to Central, we're gonna need a bus at three-four and seven."

We followed her to the back of the RMP, and I grabbed one wrist and Fiore grabbed the other.

She was heavy, with wild, gnarled, brown curly hair. She looked maybe late thirties, early forties. She was sweating profusely, and her hair was matted to her head and sticking to her neck and face. The smell of sweat was strong on her, a sour mix of sweat and unwashed body.

She was hysterical now, scared, not violent, and we were talking to her to calm her down. I had no idea what she was on—if it was crack, it wasn't affecting her weight. Whatever it was, it wasn't worth it.

Our gloves were slipping as we leaned her forward toward the trunk and tried to cuff her. I wanted to get a blanket or something around her to cover her, but we had to get the cuffs on her or she was gonna take off again.

As we cuffed her, she fell forward. We could feel the weight of the car go down, and she bucked up to move herself out. Joe held her down so she wouldn't run away, and I started going through the trunk to look for a blanket. I saw a box of gloves, some flares, but no blanket. The sergeants' cars have the blankets to put over the dead bodies, but the RMPs don't have them.

I could hear the clicking of the lights in the trunk as they alternated left to right. I felt the car move forward and Joe yelled, "Hey!"

I turned around and saw she had fallen into the trunk. On

her way down, she wrapped her legs around Fiore in a scissors hold and locked her ankles. She was frantic, crying and screaming, while Fiore tried to wiggle himself out of it.

"Hey! Stop!" he yelled, looking down at himself. "No—what are you doing?"

I didn't know why he was yelling until I saw the wet stain on his pants and the urine dribbling onto the bumper of the car, his shoes, and then finally the street.

I grabbed her ankles and started wrestling to unlock her legs from around him.

"Get 'em off! Get 'em off!" she screamed.

"Oh, come on," Joe said.

"What a friggin' fiasco," I said, watching a small crowd gather around us to watch the whole thing.

I got her legs unlocked, and Joe stepped out from behind her, keeping one arm on her back. He held himself away from her and put his other hand out, looking down at his pants.

"Not a word!" he snapped as he pointed at me, dead serious.

I started to smirk.

"I *mean* it!" he said, but then he smirked.

"I'm not saying anything," I choked.

I heard laughter from the crowd that was watching us.

"Let's go," I ordered as I stomped toward them, waving them along. "Show's over." I half laughed, saying, "Nothing to see here," then couldn't hold it anymore. I cracked up.

The ambulance pulled up. It was the male and female who handled the stabbing by Port Authority with us. When the female saw the EDP was naked, she went back to get a blanket.

The female was good with her, saying, "We'll get the snakes off you. Come with us, honey, we'll take care of it." I liked her; she was always sweet to the drunks and EDPs.

Her partner grabbed the stretcher, and they lowered it down to get the EDP on it. The female smelled the urine on the EDP and saw it on the street and on Fiore. Even though our pants are dark blue, you could still see the stain. The female EMS looked up at Joe, and he held up his hand. "Don't say anything."

She pressed her lips together and went back to helping the EDP.

I threw Joe the keys to the RMP. "Why don't you go back to the house and change? I'll ride with her to Bellevue."

He nodded as he closed the trunk. "I'll meet you over there."

I sat on the bench in the ambulance across from the EDP on the ride to Bellevue. I held on to a metal handle as we bumped and swayed, watching the EDP cower from the snakes.

"Get 'em off me," she whimpered, pleading.

The EMT was pretending to pick them up and toss them off her. "Okay, I got 'em," she'd say. The EDP was strapped in now so she couldn't flail all over. She was still trying to move; her eyes were wide and scared.

Neither me or the EMT were bothered by her blubbering. After a while you accept the fact that that's how they are, and they don't scare you anymore. EDPs are different than skells—not that they aren't skells, but they're a whole other dimension.

My first job as a rookie was an EDP. I was working my field training unit right out of the Academy. It was a multistory apartment building in Coney Island. I was on a foot post, and I was excited about handling my first job as a cop.

Central had put over that there was an aided case at an address that was two buildings over from where I was. She also said that the person might be cut, so I pictured someone stabbed or cut in some kind of accident. I was excited, picturing myself going in there, applying direct pressure to the wound, and saving a life.

I told Central I would take the job. I didn't even have all the cop talk down back then. I wasn't used to the radio, but I wanted to practice. I also wanted to tell the other rookies I worked with that I handled an aided by myself, hopefully doing something to come out the hero.

My father had never told me what to expect with the job. Other guys who came on with brothers or fathers on the job knew what to expect, but I didn't even know what a complaint report was. I was the son of a cop and knew nothing about it.

The building that I went into wasn't bad, not like the projects in the area. As I got off the elevator, I heard someone screaming rhythmically, "Ah! Ah! Ah! Ah! Ah!" over and over.

It was a female under a gray blanket down at the end of the hallway. I never saw her face, and when I got within ten feet of her, I saw the blanket was covered in something that looked like blood.

I was frozen to the spot where I was standing, and everything seemed to fade around me. I didn't know what to do, so I stood there and stared at her. I didn't want to see what was under that blanket. I was vaguely aware that the people out in the hallway were talking about me.

"Look at him—he's not doing anything."

"Is he just gonna stand there?"

"He looks scared."

"White as a ghost."

I stood there for what felt like an eternity. I thought if I picked up the blanket, she might be stabbing herself, might stab me.

EMS got off the elevator, and a female came over to me and said, "What's going on?"

I didn't answer her. I guess she realized I froze, and she seemed aggravated as she pushed past me. She walked over and pulled the blanket off.

"It's nail polish," I heard her tell her partner.

The female under the blanket was curled up in a ball, hands clenched, knees to chest, shaking.

I stood there while EMS worked on her and was still rooted to the spot when a sergeant and three cops got off the elevator.

"What's going on?" the sergeant asked me. When I didn't answer, he said, "Are you okay?"

I heard someone say, "Tony! Boss, I know this guy. I went to school with him. He's a great guy."

To this day I still don't know who it was.

The sergeant was looking at me. "He looks like he's gonna get sick," he said, then said to me, "Officer, why don't you go outside and get some air?" He might have said, "We'll take care of this," but I'm not sure.

"You'll be okay, Tony," the guy who knew me said. "Just get some fresh air."

My skin was clammy, and there was a roaring in my head. I felt like I was gonna throw up as I went in the elevator, and I felt claustrophobic on the way down.

It wasn't what I expected—nothing about this job was. I was mortified; I didn't even call Central back. I lit a cigarette and left, feeling like a moron.

After that I became hard toward the EDPs. I no longer answered jobs expecting them to be hurt, just nuts or high.

As time went on, I got cynical. Looking back, I was probably scared of them, at whatever madness was in their heads. I overcompensated by provoking them, and I'm sure I made things worse for some of them.

This one time I had to take an EDP over to Roosevelt Hos-

289

pital. They put her in a room, and I waited there with her for the doctor. They hadn't shot her up with anything, and she was still wrapped up in the mesh blanket to keep her from hurting herself or anyone else.

She was loony, yelling and screaming that I was doing all these things to her mother. I stood right outside the door so I didn't have to hear her anymore, and she started screaming, "Get off me! Don't touch me!" People in the hallway were looking at me. They could see I wasn't doing anything to her, but they were still looking.

I'd had enough of hearing her, so I leaned into the room and flipped the light switch on and off. I started singing la-la-la-la-la-la to the tune of "Ring around the Rosy," clicking the lights in sync.

Since she was wrapped in the mesh blanket and was big to begin with, she couldn't see over the top of herself. She looked like she was in a cocoon with only her head sticking out. She was trying to pick her head up to see what was going on.

"Who's doing that? Hey! Hey! Stop it!"

"La-la-la-la-la-la," I sang and flicked.

Okay, I bugged her out. I know it was mean, but she was getting on my nerves. I finally said, "If you don't shut up, I'm gonna keep doing this." When she didn't answer, I said, "Are you gonna shut your mouth?"

"Okay," she said, sounding like a scared little kid. "I'll stop."

She was quiet up until the doc came in. She asked him if he was singing to her and turning the lights on and off, but I was whistling in the hallway by then.

I was still thinking about this when we got to Bellevue and got the EDP in a room.

After some time on, I got to the point where I accepted

the fact that EDPs were a part of the job and I'd have to deal with them. Ironically, I could see Romano was about there now—the place where you don't care about them and they don't bother you anymore.

Now I'm starting to see it different altogether. Joe says these EDPs are tormented. Whether it's drugs or mental illness, they have no peace. When Fiore deals with them he always prays for them, even this one who urinated all over him. If he had a chance, he would have prayed for her right there. I was reminded of that, and I prayed right there and asked Jesus, the Prince of Peace, to soothe her mind and get the snakes off her.

Surprisingly, she seemed calmer after that. I realized I shouldn't be surprised that God answered me. He wants her at peace more than I do.

I was sitting in a chair in one of the cubicles in the emergency room when Fiore came in. I had taken the cuffs off her, one arm at a time, while they tied her to the bed. She was quiet now, peaceful in her drug-induced sleep.

"How you doing, Joe?" I held back a smirk.

"I'm fine. How's she doing?" he said, nodding toward the EDP.

"They shot her up with something. She's in the zone."

"What are they doing with her?" Fiore asked.

"They said they were gonna have the doc see her, then decide if they were gonna hold on to her."

"Did you get any of her information?"

"Some," I said. "She lives in Brooklyn. She's been getting high up in Times Square, living on the street. I got her name." I looked at my memo book. "Patricia Gannon."

We sat there for about an hour before they brought her up to the tenth-floor psych unit. Fiore and I went with her and had to check in with the hospital police and unload our weapons.

The guard was an out-of-shape male black around forty years old, in a blue uniform. He nodded toward the firearm station, a metal box that reminds me of a laundry chute. It has a square opening that elbows down, stationed to the floor. We use it so in case the gun goes off, the bullet is contained.

Joe stayed with the EDP as I placed my gun inside the shaft and popped the clip, putting it in my pocket. I put my hand over the top of my Glock to catch the bullet as I ejected it from the pipe. I kept it cocked back to show it was empty and put it back in my holster.

I stayed with the EDP while Joe unloaded his gun, and the guard buzzed us in. We signed the psych log and took her into the waiting room.

It was a small room with two rows of connected chairs that were bolted to the floor, I guess so no one could throw them around in the midst of a psychotic episode. Off the waiting room was a hallway with a couple of examining rooms where the doc can talk to the patients.

The EDP was waking up a little now, lifting her head up to look around and going out again. There were people in the waiting room with us. A man and a woman with a female in her twenties. The female was crying and looking despondent. I'm guessing depression here.

They weren't talking to each other, just staring into space. The doc came out to call them in, and I almost laughed out loud. He looked insane, like Albert Einstein on acid. He had white hair sticking straight up, a thick crooked mustache, and black bushy eyebrows. His white lab coat was full of stains, and I could see his shirt was half tucked in.

Our EDP opened her eyes and looked at him, then looked

at us. If I didn't know better, I'd think he was one of them and the real doc was tied and gagged in a closet somewhere.

He sounded sane enough when he talked to the family in the waiting room. He called the female in and brought her into a room.

About twenty minutes later, as he was taking the EDP into a room and leaving Joe and me in the waiting room, I told him we had to make a notification. He held up his finger, saying he'd be right back. He returned with a folder and opened it, pointing to a phone number. "She's been here before," he said. "That's her mother's number."

"Thanks, doc," I said, writing the mother's number in my memo book, along with her name.

I called the mother from the phone inside the office the guards use. She didn't seem scared that someone was calling so late and didn't react to the news that her daughter was in Bellevue. She sounded old and weary, like she'd gotten this call a lot of times before. She didn't ask if the daughter was okay, just thanked me and hung up the phone.

The doctor came out about a half hour later, saying he was going to admit her. Joe wrote down the admission number on the aided card with the doctor's name, and we left the waiting room.

We reloaded our guns, waved to the guard, and took the elevator back down to the main floor.

It was 2:00 when we drove back across town and started patrolling our sector. The radio was quiet, and we parked in the lot on 37th Street, reading the paper while we waited for a job.

I was reading an article about police officers avoiding misconduct penalties. It looked like the ACLU was at it again, complaining that the police department only disciplined 24 percent of the officers charged with brutality and other misconduct substantiated by CCRB, the Civilian Complaint Review Board.

"Look at this." I handed Joe the article. "CCRB does more harm than good. Before Dinkins, at least it was cops running it. They knew how to weed out the real complaints from baloney ones."

The cops used to run CCRB, but it was changed to civilians under the Dinkins Administration.

"We can thank Teddy Roosevelt for CCRB," Joe said. "He initiated it when he was police commissioner at the turn of the last century, when the cops were really out of control."

"Yeah, but Joe, it's nothing like that now," I said, but he

was reading the article. The ACLU was complaining that the police department was being too lenient in disciplining the cops and the punishment wasn't harsh enough for them. They questioned the effectiveness of the review board, and federal prosecutors were looking to see if the department had failed to aggressively punish officers implicated in brutality cases.

"They want to be tougher on the cops," I said, "but think we should feel sorry for the skells and let them get away with anything they do."

"I know," Joe said. "They're so concerned about the criminal's rights, but not the victims that they brutalize. They love to manipulate the Constitution, and in doing so, they've made our judicial system so twisted that it baffles logic."

The article aggravated me. I'm not saying that cops shouldn't be punished for brutality, but so many of the complaints against us are a sham. The ACLU loves to put the screws to cops.

"Let the department discipline us more and let's see what the city's gonna do when they can't get any more cops to work here," I said.

"This is true," Joe said. "They can cover it up all they want, but we know how many cops are leaving and what the caliber is of the new cops that they're getting."

Cops can now have a misdemeanor conviction and still get on the job. You can fail the physical in the Academy forty times as long as you pass it once. FD gives you one shot—if you fail, you're out. When I came on, fifty thousand people took the cop test, and now they can't get eight thousand people to take it.

A lot of it comes down to pay. If they paid us more, they'd get a better caliber of cop to choose from. It's like the old saying, "You get what you pay for."

"Remember that Russian cop that came on in January?" Joe asked.

"The female?"

"Yeah, the one who couldn't speak English. What's gonna happen when you get a department full of second-rate cops?" he asked.

"Maybe the city will wake up and give us a raise," I said.

Sometimes when I hear the guys talking, I picture us cops being overrun by the perps because there's no new cops and all the old-timers are leaving.

We sat there and talked about the sad state of the new recruits. We talked about Romano, another good cop leaving. He didn't realize it yet, but he would have eventually been okay with the job. Once you got past his rookie insecurity, he was actually pretty good at this.

We had no jobs, but we'd been so busy lately, I wasn't complaining. I smoked and read the paper, then drove over to the Sunrise for more coffee. We picked up Romano at a quarter to five and went back to the precinct.

We passed out on the benches in the lounge and went back out at six.

The sun was up, and there was a small breeze blowing. It was cool, probably in the sixties.

We stopped on 34th Street for coffee and bagels fresh out of the oven. I got an everything with butter, Romano got poppy with butter, and Joe got a pumpernickel with cream cheese.

We drove Romano back up to his post and sat with him while we ate. At 6:40 Central put a call over the air for a 52, which is a dispute, at a deli on 35th Street. Then she came back and gave it to us.

"South David," Central radioed.

"South David," Fiore responded.

"I have a customer-owner dispute." She gave a 35th Street address.

"10-4," Fiore said.

I knew the deli. It was more like a luncheonette that got a pretty good breakfast and lunch crowd. We tossed Romano out of the car and took 7th Avenue down.

We parked outside the deli and walked inside, past the now empty display bins that would later hold fruit, flowers, and ice-filled cold water and beer. When the stuff is outside, there's a guy out there making sure no one steals anything.

I smelled bacon when we walked in, and I could see a couple of the tables were filled with people eating breakfast. The register and deli counter were on our right, with the cigarettes overhead, and to our left was the buffet island they used for the hot food at lunch. Past the deli counter was an old staircase leading down to the basement, and in the back about twelve tables were set up. The tables were in an *L* shape, with the last few of them behind the staircase.

A Korean guy, who I guessed was the owner, came through the doorway in the back of the deli. I could see he was aggravated as he walked quickly toward us.

"This guy," he said and pointed toward the back of the store. "He do this every morning when he come in here! I tired of it!" He was waving his hands now. "I no want him in store no more!"

"What's he doing?" Joe asked.

"He make a mess in the bathroom and no clean it up! Every time!"

We walked into the back and saw a Mexican kid, maybe eighteen years old, holding on to the doorknob of the bathroom. His left foot was planted against the wall, and the other was on the floor to keep him balanced. I saw the door moving in and out where someone was pulling from the inside and yelling, "Let me out!"

When the kid saw us, he let go of the door and it flew open. An older guy, I didn't know if he was Spanish or light-skinned black, went to lunge at the kid. The kid got in a fighting stance, and the older one picked up his right arm and drew it back like he was gonna hit him.

"Hold on there, slugger," I said.

"He can't lock me in the bathroom!" The guy was a skell, wearing green cutoff work pants, sneakers with no socks, and a threadbare black tank top. He was grubby, with gray matted hair and a beard.

The kid backed away, and the owner, who was right behind Joe and me, told him, "Okay, okay, you go back to work."

The skell grabbed two white plastic bags filled with his stuff and came out of the bathroom.

"Buddy, are you making a mess in the bathroom?" Joe asked him.

He mumbled, "I didn't make no mess."

I stepped past him and pushed the door open to look inside. The floor was soaked, and there was white powder in the sink, on the toilet, and soaking into the water on the floor. Paper towels were strewn everywhere, and the water in the sink was running. I guess he was washing up. There was toothpaste in the sink, and he didn't have the rank smell the homeless usually do. He smelled, but not enough to clear the store.

"He lock door when he go in there," the owner was saying. "He stay there long time."

"Who made the mess?" I asked the skell.

"That was in there before I went in!" he yelled, sounding strange.

I thought a second and said, "This is what we're gonna do. You're gonna go back in there and clean up the mess."

"No!" He stamped his foot.

"Clean it up," I said.

He put his bags down and started to go in the bathroom,

when he stopped and said, "No! I won't clean it! I won't, I won't, I won't. It's someone else's mess!"

I didn't want to cuff this guy; he was pathetic. I looked at Joe, who was looking at him and not doing me any good. I pulled out my cuffs and said, "Okay, turn around," as I grabbed his arm. He started doing a sort of dance, bouncing from one foot to the other, saying, "Okay, I'll do it. I'll do it. I'll do it."

We were all quiet for a second, and it hit me that he was acting like a child would. For some reason, I got the feeling this guy was abused as a child.

Normally I would have been harder on him, but I felt bad for him. He was like a child trapped in a man's body. A wave of compassion for him hit me, and I said, "Just clean it up, then you can go."

He went back into the bathroom and cleaned it up, mumbling, "I didn't do it! You can't make me clean it!" the whole time.

"I don't want him here no more," the owner said.

"How about once he cleans the mess, we'll let him know if he comes back again we'll lock him up?" I asked.

"Okay," he said as he gave a clipped nod.

When he came out, I looked in to see how he did. He had cleaned the powder but left a couple of bundles of paper towels on the floor.

"Pick up the papers," I told him.

"No! I won't do it!" he chimed and stamped his feet.

Instead of yelling, I said, coaxing him, "Come on, pick up the paper and you're all done."

He picked up the paper and threw it in the garbage.

"Listen," I told him. "The owner doesn't want you here anymore. If we have to come back here for you, I'll have to lock you up." I held up the cuffs to him.

"Okay," he said, nudging his toe against his plastic bag like a five-year-old. "I won't come back."

He left the store, and Joe and I went back out to the RMP. I was writing the job in my memo book when a bug-eyed, hippie-looking lady walked over to the RMP. She had long salt-and-pepper hair and was wearing a brown jacket over a wrinkled skirt and sandals. She had a newspaper tucked under her arm, and she pulled it out and wrote down the number of the RMP. Then she came over to the driver's side, and I could see her looking at my name and shield number out of the corner of her eye.

"How you doing?" I asked her.

She started writing again on the paper. "I'm okay." She nodded and stared at me with her bug eyes and walked away.

"I guess I'll be hearing from the ACLU," I told Fiore.

"Second time this week," he said.

"Second time?"

"Yeah, well, first time this week. Last week it was the ten-million-dollar lawsuit," he chuckled. "You've been busy."

"Yeah."

I started to feel uncomfortable, but I guess that was what she wanted. I wondered why she did that. She didn't come out of the deli, so she couldn't have seen what went on there. The funny thing is even if she was in there, she would have only seen the cops toss a homeless man out of the deli when all he was trying to do was wash himself. On the other hand, we can't let this guy go into someone's place of business and trash the place.

I don't know why *we* never get to put complaints in against all the people who harass us. She was probably just one of those people who hate cops, but I wrote the whole thing down in my memo book, including a description of her, the date, the time, the location of the deli, and our conversation verbatim—even if it was only five words between us.

"You writing this down?" Joe asked.

"Yeah, with the date and time and the fact that you heard the whole thing," I said.

"I wrote it down too," he said.

We picked up Romano at his post and headed back to the precinct. I went down to the locker room to change and signed out by 7:50.

I stopped in Brooklyn on my way home. I got off the Fort Hamilton Parkway exit and drove to 73rd Street. I parked my truck across the street from the address where Denise had said Marie and Bobby Egan have their rendezvous and watched the apartment.

The block was full of brownstones, probably worth close to a million bucks apiece the way real estate is in New York. Actually these were light, made out of limestone, but still considered brownstone. They're not railroad rooms, I've been in those. There's no hallways in them and there's no windows in the inside room, but they're not the kind that you stand at one end of the house and can see through to the other. They used to be one-family houses, and over the years they've been broken down to accommodate three or four families. Marie and Egan's was the front basement, probably a studio. I sat there for about a half hour. I don't know why I was doing it; I guess I just wanted to see for myself. If my father didn't want to believe me, that's his business—at least that's what I told myself.

I took 4th Avenue and got back on the ramp to cross the bridge at 92nd Street. There was no traffic, so it only took me about ten minutes to get home.

There was a black Acura parked in front of my house in my

usual spot, so I swung around and parked across the street. There was someone sitting in the Acura, and I thought for a second it might be Ralph. I took my gun out of my bag and stuck it in the waistband of my pants before I got out of my truck.

My old girlfriend Kim got out of the Acura and watched me cross the street.

"Hey, Tony," she said. Her blond hair was longer than I'd ever seen it, sleek and straight hanging down her back. She was dressed in tight black pants, high-heeled black shoes, and a light-colored button-down shirt. She was heavy on the jewelry. She had diamond studs in her ears, a diamond the size of a dime around her neck, and a gold watch with a diamond-encrusted face on it.

"What are you doing here?" I was in no mood for games. No one ever came here, and every day that week someone had been knocking on my door with some kind of drama.

"Aren't you happy to see me?" she asked. As I got closer, I saw that the arrogance she had last time I saw her was missing. She looked unsure for once, and maybe a little sad.

"Not really," I said honestly. "Why aren't you at work? You don't want to make the boss unhappy." I didn't want to be sarcastic, but she did leave me for him.

"I'm sleeping with the boss," she said, just as honestly. "I can come in whatever time I want."

"Did he buy you the car?" I said as I nodded toward the Acura.

"Yes."

"How much did it cost you?"

"More than you'd think," she said.

This was probably the only honest conversation we'd ever had.

"I heard you're getting married," she said sadly.

"Yeah, I am."

"The Long Island one you were telling me about at Mike Ellis's dad's wake?"

"Yeah, same one."

"I saw Mike's girlfriend, Laura, on the boat yesterday," she said, meaning the Staten Island Ferry. "She told me her and Mike went to your engagement party."

"I still don't get why you're here, Kim." I didn't know where she was headed with this.

"My mother has breast cancer," she said, trying not to cry. "She's dying."

"I'm sorry to hear that," I said. I liked her mother, and she liked me. It was Kim who thought I was beneath her. I didn't know what else to say.

"I'm sorry to show up like this. I wanted to talk to you." She shrugged and gave me a sad smile. "I don't know, maybe I'm rethinking things. Like with you, I think I made a mistake."

"It's a little late for that," I said.

"Maybe it is. But if things don't work out with—"

"Michele," I said.

"With Michele, maybe you could give me a call," she said with a shrug.

"You made your choice."

"It was wrong, Tony, okay? I made a mistake. I just wanted . . ." She seemed to be looking for the right word. "More."

"Well, you got it."

"We were good together," she said.

"No, we weren't, not really. If we were any good, you wouldn't have taken off like that," I said, surprised that there was still a bite to it.

"Can we go inside and talk?" she asked.

"No," I said.

"Why not?"

303

The truth was I was tempted. Not because I still cared about her, but because once she went inside, it wouldn't be three minutes before I got her into bed. In fact, forget the bed, the lawn would be okay with Kim. She's the adventurous type. All of a sudden I was tired of waiting, tired of being good. I thought of Fiore and how he'd tell me to pray, but I didn't feel like praying. I felt like feeling like a man again, and I didn't want to wait until November. That was what I wanted.

What I said was, "Because I'm tired, and I don't think Michele would appreciate you being here."

Fiore would have said turning her down made me more of a man. But that was easy for him to say—he didn't have to wait till November to sleep with his wife.

"I'm sorry about your mother," I said.

"Thanks," she said, looking a little embarrassed.

"I'm gonna go," I said.

"I'll see you around," she said.

"Yeah, you take care," I said.

"Be happy, Tony," she said as she got in the car and started it. She made a U-turn and threw me a wave before she drove away.

Fiore would go inside and call Donna and tell her exactly what happened. But I'm not Fiore, and I'm not saying a word.

I went inside and checked my machine. The steady red light told me that Michele hadn't called while I was tempted to romp with my old girlfriend. I knew Michele well enough to know that this would bother her. She'd think that every time she called when I was supposed to be home, that Kim was here and something was going on. I didn't do anything wrong, and I'll leave it at that.

I sat on the couch and turned on the TV. I flipped through the morning talk shows and finally settled on a rerun of *ER*.

I was restless and couldn't concentrate, so I went inside and pulled on a pair of sweats and went up to the boardwalk to go for a run.

The way my schedule is I don't run consistently, so I was sucking wind after the first half mile. I got off the boardwalk and crossed Father Cappodanno Boulevard to a deli near the corner of Seaview Avenue for a bottle of water. I crossed back over to the boardwalk and walked the rest of the way home.

I was hungry now. The only thing I ate was a bagel at 6:00 and it was now 11:00. My refrigerator was empty except for a couple of egg rolls wrapped in a waxed bag and an unopened quart of orange juice. I didn't want to risk the egg rolls, since I didn't remember when I'd bought them, so I drank a glass of juice and went to bed by 12:30.

I woke up disoriented in my dark room. I looked at the clock, squinting to see the time—9:30. Great, I forgot to set my alarm. I showered and shaved in a half hour. Michele called, but I figured I'd call her from my cell phone on the way into the city.

I grabbed my bag, got in my truck, and headed toward the bridge. I called Michele but got her answering machine and remembered she had the spring music thing at her school tonight and wouldn't be home. I was starving; that bagel at 6:00 this morning was getting to be a long time ago.

Traffic was slow on the West Side, and by the time I parked on 36th Street it was 10:30. I stopped in the deli on the corner for a sandwich. I was rushing now. If I got to the precinct by 10:45, I could eat my sandwich and still have time to change before roll call.

Geri was off, so at least I didn't have to hear her innuendos. I ordered a chicken cutlet hero with tomato and spicy mustard from an older woman I'd seen there before. I grabbed my sandwich and crossed 35th Street, zigzagging around the cars coming down the block.

I started up the stairs of the precinct with my eye on the doors, when I heard someone say "Officer" behind me.

I turned to see three people staring at me. A male black, early twenties, hip-hop looking. He had a small, skinny female black with him and a cute little girl about four years old holding a black doll and holding his hand. They weren't skells but weren't rich either. They were coming up from 8th Avenue, walking toward 9th.

"Yeah," I said.

"Do you know if there's a fortune-teller around here?" he asked.

I went into my direction-giving mode. "Yeah. Go up to the corner," I said, pointing toward 9th Avenue. "Make a right. It's about three or four stores down. You can't miss it. There's a big palm on the door, and I think it's a purple curtain across the window."

I turned to go in, but turned back around. I told myself I didn't care, this guy going to a fortune-teller was none of my business.

"Why do you want to see the fortune-teller?" I heard myself say.

He seemed surprised that I asked him, but not as surprised as me. I thought he was gonna keep walking, but he said, "I got some stuff going on tomorrow, and I want to see what I should do."

"Why don't you just go to the source?" I asked without thinking.

"What do you mean?"

I walked back down the stairs toward him. The female and the little girl were watching me, not looking scared, just curious.

"Do you believe in God?" I couldn't believe I was asking him—usually Fiore does this kind of thing.

His eyes widened in surprise, but he didn't answer.

"Why don't you go to him and ask him? He cares more about you than some fortune-teller, and what he tells you is free," I said, wondering where the words were coming from.

I could see he was thinking about it, so I kept going. "You're gonna pay someone money to tell you some baloney story about the future, and make a major decision based on that?"

He put his head down, and it hit me that this guy knew God and was running from him.

"He loves you," I said. "He wants to help you."

He looked up at me with his lip quivering and nodded. I could see he was fighting back tears.

I forgot about my sandwich and being on time and started to talk to him.

"Listen, God loves you," I said again. "He's got his arms open to you, and you're running away." I didn't know where this was coming from, just that I needed to tell him. "He's not looking to hurt you," I continued. "He doesn't want to hammer you for all the bad things you've done." I thought about all the times I thought that. "Are you running from God?"

He nodded.

"I got locked up," he said. "For drugs. I go to court tomorrow, and I wanted to know if I'd be going to jail." He shrugged. "If I was, then maybe I wouldn't show up."

I put my hand on his shoulder. I don't know why—I'm never like this. "Whatever God's got planned for you, he's gonna take care of you."

I guess he thought I was gonna hug him, because he leaned into my chest and started sobbing. I didn't know what to do, so I hugged him, hoping no one from the roll call saw me.

I knew he was terrified of going to jail, and I couldn't blame him. I asked God to show me what to say to him, and I looked at the little girl holding her doll.

"Is this your daughter?" I asked.

He nodded.

"Look at this beautiful little girl," I said. "Do you want to go on the run with her and live that kind of life? Or are you looking to leave her and her mother alone and go on the run without them?"

He looked at them. The female was crying now too.

He shook his head. "No, but I don't want to go to jail either."

I was thinking, *Do I know the prayer of salvation? Where's Joe? He's so much better at this than me; he always knows the right thing to say.* I looked around, no Joe, and I felt like God was letting me know I was on my own here. Well, me and him. I guess he wanted me to do this. I swallowed whatever it was that was making me feel embarrassed.

"Is Jesus your Lord and Savior?" I asked him.

"Yeah," he said with a nod.

"Do you believe he died for your sins? Yours alone? That if it was just you and him, he would have died just for you?"

I saw him hesitate, and I said, "Stop feeling unworthy. None of us are worth it. He made us worth it. You're so important to him. Do you believe he died for you?"

He hesitated and nodded. "Yeah, I do."

"Are you sorry for your sins?"

"I really am," he said, and I could see he meant it.

I almost made the sign of the cross over him and said, "Go and sin no more, my child." Instead I told him 1 John 1:9.

"It says in the Bible that if we confess our sins to God, he is faithful and just to forgive us and cleanse us from all unrighteousness," I said. "You're standing before him now washed clean."

He nodded and looked scared again.

"Listen, I don't know what's gonna happen tomorrow. But I do know a couple of things. God is full of grace and mercy—that means he gives us things we don't deserve. Ask him for grace, ask him for mercy. He's faithful. He'll never leave you or forsake you."

"Can I ask him to have mercy on me with this court thing?"

"I would. In fact, I will, along with you. But I want you to ask him yourself. Like I said, I don't know what will happen, but you have to face this. Who's the person that's been talking to you about God?" I asked.

"My aunt," he said with a smile. "She told me I can't run from God."

"Go see her," I said. "Now, tonight. I know it's late, but I doubt she'll mind."

He looked at me with a hint of a smile on his lips.

"White cop," he said. "Who'd a thought?"

"God always knows who to send you to for directions," I said with a smile.

He put his arms up and hugged me again.

"God loves you, buddy," I said. "I'll be praying for you."

I watched them walk back up the way they came. The little girl kept looking back at me, and I waved to her. She was holding his hand, so she used her doll to wave back as she smiled.

I remembered I was late and ran up the steps to the precinct. I opened the door and heard Hanrahan's "Attention to the roll call."

Epilogue

My neighbor Sandy came to see me about a week after the incident with Ralph. I had seen her at the bus stop on the corner on my way home from work, still pretty banged up from the beating she took. I had thrown her a wave and thought that was the end of it, but she knocked on my door a couple of minutes later.

"Hi," she said with a smile. She had lost weight and looked pale and gaunt.

"How are you?" I asked.

"Better than I've been in a long time. I want to thank you," she said, holding up her hand when she teared up and I tried to interrupt her. "No, let me say it. He would have killed me, and I know you're a cop, but you really put yourself out. You could have got caught in the middle of it and gotten hurt."

"I'm just glad you and the kids are okay. But I gotta tell you, after all this I hope you don't go back to him," I said. You wouldn't believe how often that happens.

"No way," she said with feeling. "I've already seen a lawyer, and I'm divorcing him while he's in jail. I'll be long gone by the time he gets out."

"How are you gonna take care of yourself?"

"I'll get a job. I'm also going back to school. My lawyer said even though the house isn't in my name, we bought the house while we were married and I'm entitled to half of it. I'm sure Ralph will fight me on it, but he'll be in jail for stabbing me, and I'm hoping that the judge will take that into consideration."

"I'm sure he will," I said.

She hugged me then, and I patted her back, feeling awkward. "You take care of yourself," she said.

"You too."

I never heard anything back about the lawsuit I was named in. I checked with Eileen Toomey to see if she'd heard anything, but so far she hadn't. I also never heard anything from the bug-eyed woman who wrote my shield number down outside the deli on 35th Street, so I guess she was just a nut job.

The detectives arrested Easy for the stabbing over at the cardboard condos. They got a call saying he was up at the Port, and they grabbed him there. The detectives let Fiore and me know, and I wondered if Shorty's girl knew about it or if she was the one who called them in the first place.

Fiore told me that the Bible says a dog always returns to his vomit. I'm not sure what that means, but it had to do with Easy going back to where he stabbed Shorty.

O'Brien was transferred to administrative duty while the rat squad did their investigation of his off-duty incident. They took his gun, and now he sits at a desk all day, shuffling papers around in the pension section. His wife has a temporary restraining order. From what I understand, once they find out if his wife was lying about him letting off a round in the house, they'll decide what to do from there. McGovern told me O'Brien's pretty depressed, and I plan to go and see him next time I'm out in Long Island.

I stopped at my grandmother's about a week after the engagement party. I wanted to thank her for the party and give her some flowers. She made me dinner, chicken cacciatore, and I stayed with her until I had to leave for work.

She told me Marie got a second job. Apparently she sells some kind of cookware on the side now and has to go to people's houses and host parties. Grandma told me my father's been over a lot now because Marie is working at night and he's home by himself.

"Why does Marie have to work a second job?" I asked.

"I guess she needs money," Grandma said.

"Grandma, Dad has a pension and a full-time job. He told me he made eighty-five grand last year. Marie works full-time for the city, and they have half a million dollars in the bank. Why does she need to work?" I half yelled.

"I don't know, Tony, but you and your sister better stop saying she's fooling around on your father. She told me you and Denise were causing trouble between them," she scolded, pointing her finger at me.

"You know, it's funny, Grandma, I don't remember you being this upset when Marie was causing trouble between my mother and dad," I said. In fact, I remember her telling me how difficult my mother was. At the time all I could see was my mother's drinking, and I thought that's what the whole problem was. But now I know more about it.

"Tony, you know how your mother was with the drinking," she said. "It was very difficult for your father to live that way. Marie loves him—she wouldn't do anything to hurt him."

She said it like she believed it, so I wasn't gonna argue with her. I told my father about Marie, and he can do what he wants with it from here.

The construction on my house is really getting there. The bathroom tile is in, and instead of painting the room in white or beige, Michele wanted to paint the room a dark gold. It should have screamed at us, all the glass and tile with such a bold color, but it worked. We used a flat paint on the walls, then she went over it with a leaf-shaped sponge, using a shiny gold that gave the wall a two-dimensional look. When we were done, it looked like something out of a magazine.

I put in the frosted glass-paneled door and try not to have nightmares of a hand smashing the window and unlocking the deadbolt.

Romano had come out with Denise like he promised to help with the painting. Fiore and Donna surprised us by coming out, and we spent the weekend painting and barbequing. I asked Denise straight out about Romano and told her not to lie to me. She said they were seeing each other, but she didn't want to jump into anything like she did with Sal Valente, her last boyfriend.

I never did tell Michele about Kim coming out to my house. I told Fiore and he was happy with the way I handled it, but he thought I should tell her. If she had come back, I would have mentioned it, but she didn't.

Denise called me a couple of weeks after Kim came to see me to tell me that she read in the paper that Kim's mother had died. She asked if I was going to the wake, and I said I didn't know. I thought about going and decided against it. My being there wasn't gonna change anything, and I didn't want to see Kim again.

Nick Romano went into the Fire Department Academy on May 15. Our squad surprised him with a party over at the bar on 9th Avenue after his last tour. It was nothing like the party for Brian Gallagher, but we ordered food and had an open bar for about twenty people.

Terri Marks was there and was trying to get Romano to go home with her. She had given it another shot with Fiore, but he nicely blew her off.

"I may never see you again," she slurred, thinking she was whispering in Romano's ear, but I could hear her from ten feet away.

He was pretty hammered, not like the last time, but he was close.

"I got a girlfriend," he said. "And it's Tony's sister. He'll kill me."

"He won't know," she said.

"He knows everything," Romano said. "It's freaky."

He got emotional at one point, when he was toasting us with his drink. "You guys are out there, getting it done," he said. "I know from experience—" His voice cracked and he had to compose himself. "I know from experience just how dangerous this job can be, but you do it anyway, and you do it good."

"Here, here!" Fiore said.

"This job sucks," Rooney bellowed.

"You hosehead," McGovern yelled.

When everyone was pretty hammered, Romano included, he asked Joe and me, "Was I a good cop?"

"Sure," I said.

"Yeah, you were," Joe chimed in.

"No, really, guys, this is important. Was I a good cop?"

"Nick, you are a good cop. You're still a little wet behind the ears, but you were getting there," I said.

"Joe?" He looked at Fiore.

"Nick, it always impressed me how hard it must have been for you to do the job that killed your father. Even when you were scared, you didn't hide or try to be a house mouse—you were out there," Joe said. A house mouse is a cop that hides in the precinct. "And I agree with Tony, you were getting there. Eventually you wouldn't have struggled with it anymore."

"Do you think I should have stayed?" he asked Joe. I almost laughed at his confused face, but he was serious.

"I can't tell you that, Nick. I don't know what your reasons were for coming here in the first place," Joe said honestly.

Nick was quiet for a couple of minutes, then he started to talk. "When my father died, he had some time on. It wasn't like he was a rookie, ya know. He knew the job. And when he died, people acted like he was a hero."

"He was a hero," I said, meaning it.

"He still is," Joe threw in.

"No, I mean yes, he was a hero because he was killed in the line of duty. But he died for nothing. He was answering a job where some psycho was looking to kill his wife and shot my father instead. It was a waste; it shouldn't have happened," he said, getting a little loud now. "And back then," he continued, "everyone was so good to my family. The department, the cops, everyone. They made me feel like what my father did was important, and I became a cop so I could stay connected to him."

"I can understand that," I said.

"Did it work? Do you feel connected to him?" Joe asked.

"No. The funny thing was when I came here, it was nothing like I thought it would be." He laughed cynically. "I thought people would like me, you know, appreciate that I was out there protecting the streets, like my father before me. But no one cared about me—they hated me. I think I could have taken that if the cops accepted me, but until you guys," he looked at Joe and me, "nobody did."

"Everyone goes through that, Nick. That's how the old-timers are. You have to prove yourself. I'm not saying it's right, but that's just the way it is," I said. "Do you think that'll change at FD? It's like Rooney told you—you'll still be the new guy."

"I know that, but I'll have the time on the job behind me that the other probees won't have. And the way I look at it, with FD you can only be a hero. If I go down, it'll be saving someone's life in a fire, and it'll mean something. The only people it mattered to when my father died was my family, and it destroyed them."

"Don't kid yourself, Nick. If your father had died in a fire, it wouldn't have made it any easier on you and your family. And your father dying mattered to other people too, Nick. It mattered to the cops he worked with, his partner, and to all the cops that came after him," Joe said.

"I feel like I'm letting him down by not staying," he said.

"You can't do that to yourself. A lot of cops go over to FD. Let's be honest, it's a better gig," I said.

"But I feel like I didn't finish, like maybe he wouldn't be proud of me for leaving."

"Nick, I'm sure he would just want you to be happy," Joe said. "And he wouldn't want you to spend twenty years in a job you hate because of him."

"The funny thing is I was starting to get used to it, and at times I liked it," he said with a half smile. "The other half of the time I hated it, but I'm starting to figure it out. Now I won't be a cop, I'll be a fireman."

"Nick, no matter what you do with your life, you were a New York City cop. And you'll remember it, and you'll be proud of it," Joe said.

He thought about that for a second and said, "Yeah, I will."

Two nights later, when Joe and I went back on patrol for

the first time without Romano, I felt sad. There was no one to toss out of the car for coffee when we stopped at the deli on 9th Avenue. I was surprised at the empty feeling I had that he was gone and wouldn't be back. I drove over to 34th and went up 8th Avenue. I rolled down my window and pulled over at the corner of 37th Street, where I saw Bruno Galotti walking up toward 42nd Street.

"Hey, Bruno," I called to him. "You need a ride to post?"

Acknowledgments

The authors would like to thank the following people:

Mike Valentino for taking us on in the first place and for his continued wisdom and support, but we still think Schilling's bloody sock was a sham.

Lonnie Hull Dupont for understanding Tony and always laughing right before she says, "Take it out." Bada bing, baby.

Kelley Meyne for her great editing and for letting us know what *willy* means.

Cheryl VanAndel for her great covers.

Sheila Ingram, Twila Bennett, Karen Steele, Aaron Carriere, and everyone else at Baker Publishing Group for this awesome opportunity and for putting up with all our questions.

Tom Wilgus for his friendship and expertise in police work.

Joe Amendola, Scott Hennessy, and Vinny Benevenuto, New York's Finest, hands down. Thank you for your memories, insight, and friendship.

Sal Ventimiglia for all his help on FDNY. You're a great friend.

Al O'Leary, who knows everybody and introduces us to them. Thanks, Al, you're the best.

Ben Lauro and Pure Publicity for all their hard work.

Kathy Lione for her nursing experience and advice.

Georgie and Frankie, our amazing sons. We're so thankful that God blessed us with you. Thanks for sharing this with us.

Rob Sauerman, Alicia Lancola-Hicks, Maureen Eggly, and all of us who fought for justice that November day. Salute, and well done. Score one for the good guys.

F. P. Lione is actually two people—a married couple by the name of Frank and Pam Lione. They are both Italian-American and the offspring of NYPD detectives. Frank Lione is a veteran of the NYPD, and Pam recently left her job as a medical sonographer in vascular ultrasound to stay home with their two sons. They divide their time between New York City and Pennsylvania, in the Poconos. To learn more about the Midtown Blue series or to contact the authors, log on to their website at www.midtownblue.com